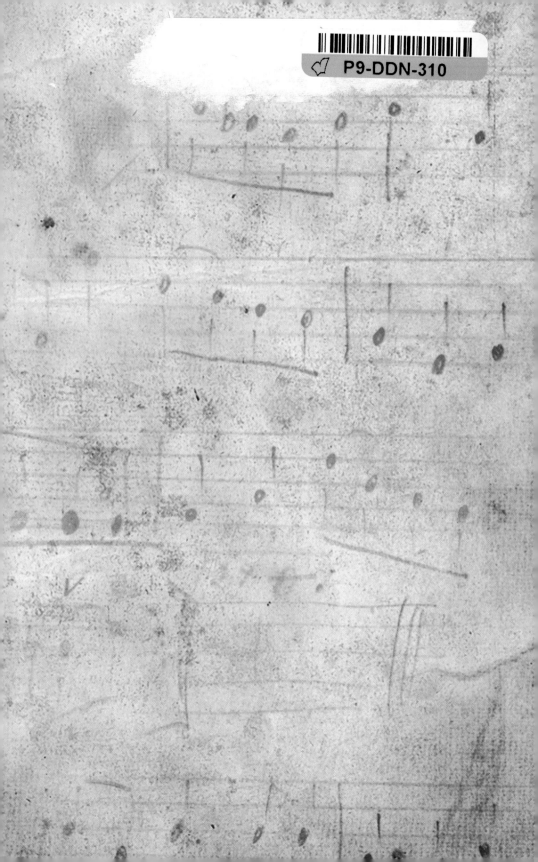

P9-DDN-310

A WHITE WIND BLEW

PRAISE FOR
A WHITE WIND BLEW

"In *A White Wind Blew*, James Markert skillfully weaves together medicine and history, a tragic love story, and a spiritual investigation into the relationship between faith and music. The result is a compelling and thought-provoking novel that will move and inspire readers of all kinds."

—John Burnham Schwartz, author of
Reservation Road and *Northwest Corner*

"James Markert tells a story of the triumph of music and faith in a dead-end place of despair and loneliness called Waverly Hills. Beautifully told, *A White Wind Blew* is set in a time when the klan and racism openly thrived. With a historian's eye for detail, Markert spins his story of a world where men and women were healed and made whole."

—Robert Hicks, author of
The Widow of the South and *A Separate Country*

A WHITE WIND BLEW

a novel

JAMES MARKERT

sourcebooks
landmark

Copyright © 2013 by James Markert
Cover and internal design © 2013 by Sourcebooks, Inc.
Cover design by Laywan Kwan
Cover illustration by Alan Ayers

Sourcebooks and the colophon are registered trademarks of Sourcebooks, Inc.

All rights reserved. No part of this book may be reproduced in any form or by any electronic or mechanical means, including information storage and retrieval systems—except in the case of brief quotations embodied in critical articles or reviews—without permission in writing from its publisher, Sourcebooks, Inc.

The characters and events portrayed in this book are fictitious and used fictitiously. Apart from well-known historical figures, any similarity to real persons, living or dead, is purely coincidental and not intended by the author.

Published by Sourcebooks Landmark, an imprint of Sourcebooks, Inc.
P.O. Box 4410, Naperville, Illinois 60567-4410
(630) 961-3900
Fax: (630) 961-2168
www.sourcebooks.com

Library of Congress Cataloging-in-Publication Data

Markert, James
  A white wind blew : a novel of Waverly Hills / James Markert.
      p. cm.
  (hardcover : alk. paper) 1. Sanatoriums—Fiction. 2. Music therapy—Fiction.
3. Physician and patient—Fiction. 4. Race relations—Fiction. I. Title.
  PS3613.A75379W48 2013
  813'.6—dc23
                          2012037249

        Printed and bound in the United States of America.
              BG 10 9 8 7 6 5 4 3 2 1

In memory of Bill Butler
A talented publisher of books…and an even better person.

To Tracy,
My wife and best friend, thank you for never letting me give up on a dream.
You've given me the best gifts imaginable in our two beautiful children. I
want for nothing, because I believe I already have it all.

BT 3/13 25.99

Requiem aeternam dona eis, Domine, et lux perpetua luceat eis.
"Grant them eternal rest, O Lord, and may everlasting light shine upon them."

—*Cantate Domino*

A person who gives this some thought and yet does not regard music as a marvelous creation of God must be a clodhopper indeed and does not deserve to be called a human being; he should be permitted to hear nothing but the braying of asses and the grunting of hogs.

—Martin Luther

Sketch by Robert Markert

PROLOGUE

Wolfgang fought the wind. It was typical Waverly, a wind that lashed around brick corners and whistled through porch screens, always lurking and unpredictable. It came in cold bursts from the hillside and surrounding woods, pulsing one minute and barely beating the next—both friend and foe, cure and killer.

He kept his eyes fixed downward as he limped across the solarium porch, well aware that many of the beds were empty because of him. He arrived outside to a mixture of chatter and coughing, which died down the moment he reached the wooden podium. This was a crowd he had illegally assembled. Well, maybe it wasn't illegal, perhaps, but forbidden, for sure. He took his trademark stance, unbalanced, his weight slightly shifted on his left leg. His breath crystallized in the frigid air. He attempted to straighten the stack of music he'd prepared hours before, but the breeze struck again and his hands were too unsteady.

Wolfgang looked up. More than thirty pairs of eyes stared back at him, waiting, tiny clusters of breath exhaled from frozen noses and chapped lips. His musicians were ready and the choir awaited his guidance, everyone trembling in the cold. They watched him in silence, these men, women, and children, and he could see the trust in their eyes: a tiny sparkle like fireflies against shadowed sockets and glossy pupils. So thin, all of them.

The surrounding woods would accompany them. Their voices would travel down the hillside, over the buffering treetops, and xiv ❀ James Markert

toward the rest of the city—a city that lived in constant fear of the Waverly wind. *Ignorance*, he thought.

He returned his attention to the choir.

He closed his eyes briefly and thought of Rose...and the last words from her lips.

Then a sole cough from a young boy in the front row stole him from the past.

Wolfgang cleared his throat. Taking a deep breath, he raised his arms, bringing forth the lyrical, soothing sound from his orchestra. He could feel it in his heart and in his bones, and he could see it making its way through the rest of them, a warmth where once there was only cold.

First Movement

Allegro tranquillo

January 23rd, 1926

Dear Wolfgang,

I apologize for not responding sooner. I've been away from the abbey for several weeks. It is with great sadness that I write to you. I am so sorry to hear about Rose's death. I know how much she meant to you. God has His reasons for those He calls early, so you must remain strong in your faith, Wolfgang. All the monks here are praying for you, and together we will get through this.

I was so proud when I heard you had become a doctor after leaving the abbey (I'm sure our Latin came in handy), but it makes me even prouder now to hear of your intentions to return and join the priesthood. Youth is on your side. Nothing can replace your love for Rose, but I'm certain God will give it His best. You are already doing His work at Waverly Hills, so I understand, with your shortage of doctors, that you must remain for the time being. Per your request (and permission granted by the abbot due to the unusual circumstances of the tuberculosis epidemic), I'm enclosing your theology books, cassocks, and studies so that you will be well on your way to completing your training when you do arrive here.

Yours in Christ,
Friar Christian
Saint Meinrad, Abbey

CHAPTER 1

Waverly Hills Tuberculosis Sanatorium
January 1929

D r. Wolfgang Pike could always tell when the rain was near. He felt the stiffness in the morning first, soon after the roosters had begun to wake the hillside, and by afternoon it had become a constant ache in the bottom of his right calf. His ankle had all but locked up, and no amount of massaging could loosen the muscles and bones of his withered right foot—his heel had been raised in a permanent tiptoe since age eight, when polio rendered the foot nearly useless and transformed it into a weather vane. On the morning of Tad McVain's arrival at Waverly Hills, the ache was nearly crippling.

Not a drop of rain had fallen at Waverly for twenty days. The woods were full of gnarled, naked tree limbs, and the dry air carried with it a crispness that led to watery eyes, bloody noses, and a tickling in the back of the throat. But these blue skies would not endure. Already the cumulus clouds skittered above the bell tower, blotting out the sun, and when the first drop plopped against the rooftop, it set loose like hail all over the grounds, pinging off the gutters and walkways like machine-gun fire. Torrential rain pelted the trees, the rooftop, and the grassy knoll that led down to the woods.

The sanatorium's buildings were under attack, it seemed, the rain coming down in sheets past the screened-porch windows, the entrances turned to mud within minutes. Nearly five hundred patients watched from their beds on the porches, and many cheered the sudden change in weather. Men and women in the cafeteria stopped eating and stared out the first-floor windows. At the children's pavilion, all the kids clamored to play in the storm. The teenagers hiding out in Lover's Lane quickly hurried back to their rooms, laughing and drenched and plotting how to sneak back to their beds. The pumpkin patch flooded. The pigs snorted and rolled in the deepening mud.

Later Wolfgang might have called it a warning. But even aspiring priests are mortal and cannot tell the future. It was already a busy day; he had just witnessed the second death of the morning, and he'd only just begun his rounds. He watched the downpour from inside the nurses' station, a small bricked structure on the rooftop that contained a handful of rooms for housing Waverly's mental patients. To get down to the fourth-floor stairwell he needed to cross the open area of the rooftop, and his skeletal umbrella provided little protection. But he didn't have time to wait, so he stepped out into the hard rain.

Normally the rooftop of the five-story sanatorium would be crowded with heliotherapy patients and children, and one could see the city of Louisville miles away, even the Ohio River and the spires of Churchill Downs on a clear day. Today visibility was a mere fifty yards, at best, and he was alone up there. He hurried away from the mental ward into the deluge, no longer protected by the length of the looming bell tower, his footfalls barely steady on the tiles. Careful to avoid the slick leaves, he braced his left hand on the brick-and-stone wall that bordered the rooftop and squinted into the wind, dragging his right foot. He passed an empty seesaw and the three rocking swings behind it—rooftop playground equipment so that the children could get closer exposure to the sun. It saddened him to see them unused.

A door slammed behind him. Wolfgang looked back toward the nurses' station. The wind had blown the door open, sending it crashing into the brick wall. Nurse Rita appeared in the doorway, holding on to her white cap as she reeled the door back in. Above her the bell tower touched the low-lying clouds and a rumble of thunder enveloped the property. Thunderstorms in January were not the norm in the River City, but neither were twenty deaths in a single day, which had occurred on three different occasions since Christmas, when the temperatures lingered in the single digits and the patients, no matter how thickly they were bundled, could not find warmth on the solarium porches.

One of the mental patients screamed—the sound cut through the noise of the storm—and Wolfgang moved away from the shrill voice. It was not deep enough to be Herman's voice. He could tell it was Maverly Simms, the fifty-year-old woman with schizophrenia and with TB in every part of her body except her tortured brain. She'd most assuredly just noticed that her roommate, Jill, had died. Jill was a mute, prone to violence against others and to herself, but for whatever reason, Maverly's bouts of hysteria and rants of sense-less drivel had calmed Jill. So they'd been placed together, and the situation worked well for three weeks. But Jill had passed away during the night.

About thirty minutes earlier, Nurse Rita had called Wolfgang up to the rooftop to help prepare Jill's body. Maverly had been awake but far from lucid when Wolfgang arrived with his black bag. She'd been in her rocking chair, staring out at the rain and approaching storm clouds, whispering softly, "Maverly at Waverly. Maverly at Waverly…"

"Maverly." Wolfgang's voice had drawn no reaction from her.

Nurse Rita stood next to Maverly's rocking chair and then turned at the sound of Wolfgang's voice. "It's like she's catatonic, Doctor." Rita had a pretty face and innocent dark eyes. She was young and, in Wolfgang's opinion, not seasoned enough for her current duty. Wolfgang had questioned Dr. Barker's decision to put her on the rooftop. Unfortunately for Rita, Dr. Barker liked to throw his staff right into things. "Baptize them by fire," he always said. And indeed, when Wolfgang had arrived this morning, Rita had been crying. Her jaw trembled. Her hands were clinched into tight balls, her finger-nails pressing hard into the meat of her palms. Wolfgang approached her but kept his eyes on Maverly.

"Has she said anything yet?"

"No." Rita glanced at Maverly. "She's just been sitting there, staring out her window. Talking to herself."

"Come on, then." Wolfgang shifted Jill's body on the bed and started the cleaning process. "Lincoln's on his way to remove the body."

Wolfgang knew that tuberculosis didn't discriminate. It invaded the bodies of the young and elderly, black and white, men and women, sane and not so sane. From a sneeze, or a cough, by speaking or a kiss, airborne particles containing tubercle bacilli floated unseen in search of another host to infect. They became established in the alveoli of the lungs and spread throughout the body, sometimes quickly. The entire process with Jill had lasted only a few months—just long enough for her to be missed.

After a moment of silence, Rita wet a rag and dabbed Jill's lips before cleaning her fingernails and combing her silver hair. Wolfgang propped her head up on pillows, closed her eyes, and put in her false teeth. It was important to get the newly deceased in the best possible condition before another patient noticed her.

"I want my cakes," a man screamed from Room 502 next door. The voice was loud and booming, as if in competition with the thunder and rain.

Wolfgang sighed, scratched his head. "Herman?"

Rita nodded, fingertips to her forehead. It was not the first time Herman had ranted about wanting cake, just the first time of the morning.

"Ignore him." Wolfgang placed a hand on Rita's shoulder on his way out. "He'll stop eventually."

Rita took a deep breath. "I'll be okay."

Wolfgang trusted that she would be.

Wolfgang reached the stairwell and lowered his tangled umbrella. He smoothed his hands over his dark wavy hair and black beard—a beard he'd trimmed regularly ever since he'd started it as a teen, never allowing it to become too thick in the fifteen years he'd had it, yet full enough to keep his face warm during the cold Waverly winters. According to some of the patients, he had a baby face, so at least the beard helped him look closer to his age of thirty-one.

By the time he reached the fourth-floor solarium porch, where dozens of beds faced the long screened windows, he couldn't hear Maverly or Herman screaming anymore. Either they'd stopped or their voices were drowned out by the sanatorium's other noises—noises that chased him down the solarium as he quickly passed the beds and sidestepped an orderly pushing a squeaky library cart of books.

Wolfgang disagreed with Barker on how the sanatorium was structured: Men on the second and fourth floors. Women on the first and third floors. Children ushered off to the children's pavilion. Lunatics sent to the rooftop. They all were able to mix and mingle in the cafeteria, workshops, in the theater, and during special events like Christmas and Easter, but for Wolfgang it wasn't enough. In fact, he thought they shouldn't separate the patients at all, telling Susannah on many occasions, "We're not a prison!"

There was a conglomeration of laughter and moaning as mist from the heavy rainfall found its way into the screened porch and onto their bed covers. Some patients smiled and talked, read, or played checkers or chess; some shaved and listened to music; some cried out in pain and spat blood into their bedside pails. Some still slept; others drank milk and watched the weather with blank faces.

Halfway down the solarium, Wolfgang spotted Nurse Susannah Figgins heading his way. Her dress was the nurse's standard white, with a matching cap atop her curly blond hair. Her skin was pale, a stark contrast to her pretty brown eyes and rosebud lips. She reached into her dress pocket, pulled out a folded piece of paper, and held it out toward Wolfgang as she approached.

Wolfgang's heart skipped a beat just before the exchange. At just under six feet, he was three inches taller than Susannah and two years older. Unlike Rita, Susannah had very little trouble dealing with the mental patients on the rooftop, and Wolfgang attributed it to her confidence. She lifted her chin slightly as she spoke. "Today's request list."

Wolfgang checked over his shoulder in both directions before unfolding the paper. He glanced at the list, slid it into the pocket of his wet lab coat, and smiled at Susannah. "Thank you, Nurse Figgins."

Susannah rolled her eyes.

Wolfgang started to walk away when Susannah grabbed his arm and gently tugged him closer. "Wolf…" She lowered her voice and handed him a tiny flask. "For Dr. Waters. Courtesy of Lincoln. See him first. Dr. Barker's on the third floor."

Wolfgang discreetly pocketed the flask next to the folded paper, nodded toward Susannah, and moved on.

Wolfgang stopped in the open doorway of Room 207, where Dr. Henry Waters, his fellow doctor, mentor, and friend, wasted away on a bed only ten feet away—eyes sunken and surrounded by pockets of shadow, a shell of the vibrant man he had once been. He'd lost so much weight it was difficult to tell he was the same man in the picture on the bedside table, where he stood on the front lawn at his riverside home with his wife and three daughters, two of whom had already lost their lives to tuberculosis.

Wolfgang gave Dr. Waters another two days to live, at the most. At forty-five years of age, Dr. Waters was the second oldest doctor at Waverly Hills—five years younger than the chief doctor, Evan Barker—and had been second in command until the disease they were trying to cure had suddenly left him confined to a bed. He'd grown thinner and weaker the past twelve months.

Dr. Waters's tuberculosis had started in his left lung, quickly spread to the right, and within months it had begun to invade his bones and skin. No amount of fresh air, sunlight, or healthy food had been able to slow the "white death." His flesh was pale, his skin tight against a defined, hairless skull. Dr. Waters had been bald since his thirtieth birthday. Wolfgang had never even seen a picture of him with hair, so the idea of it was quite foreign to him, but now the lack of hair made him seem that much closer to becoming a corpse like the rest of the bodies that Lincoln sent down the chute.

"Someone there?" Dr. Waters called out.

Wolfgang stepped into the room. "It's me, Henry."

"Wolfgang." The hint of a smile etched across Dr. Waters's chapped lips. His voice was raspy, strained. His eyes remained closed. "Have a seat."

Wolfgang sat in a folding chair next to Dr. Waters's bed and beside a second bed that was vacant for the moment, the sheets tucked against the outline of a pillow, prepped and ready for a patient they had checked in just after sunrise. Wolfgang placed his black bag on the floor between his feet and leaned toward the bed. "How are you feeling, Henry?"

"Like death…taking a shit."

Wolfgang chuckled. "Of course."

"Any questions…that aren't stupid…Wolfgang?"

Wolfgang grinned as he pulled out the request list that Susannah had given him. "Your name is on the list today, Henry. Didn't know if that was a mistake."

"No, not a mistake."

Wolfgang read the request next to Dr. Waters's name. "Niccolo Paganini." He laughed. "Caprice Number Twenty-four in A minor."

"Yes."

"You are aware that I am not an Italian virtuoso on the violin?"

"Yes. Very aware."

Wolfgang bent down, unzipped his black bag, and removed the violin that had been jammed inside next to his flute, harmonica, and piccolo. "You know Paganini bested tuberculosis?"

"But not syphilis."

Wolfgang brought the violin up to his neck and paused as he stared at his friend, whose eyeballs danced beneath closed lids. Three months before Dr. Waters's diagnosis, Waverly's only colored doctor moved his family south to Alabama to open his own practice and get away from the Ohio Valley. Dr. Waters had taken over the patients at the colored hospital before he started getting sick. But his illness had left them with only three doctors and six nurses for nearly five hundred patients and a disease with no cure, a disease so contagious that the city treated Waverly's hillside like a leper colony. Many feared even a glance up toward the trees surrounding the Gothic building, and all lived in fear of what they called the white wind that often swept down the hillside like lava from Mount Vesuvius. Citizens held their breath whenever the white wind blew, and passing cars quickly rolled up their windows.

Their third doctor, a young man named Jefferson Blunt, had left the hillside weeks after Henry was diagnosed, unable to face the pressure. He'd been married for less than a year. His wife was pregnant with their first child, and they couldn't take the risks of living and working on Waverly's hillside any longer—neither the patients nor the staff were allowed to leave. Now, until more help arrived, it was just Wolfgang and Dr. Barker covering both hospitals.

Dr. Waters coughed horribly, as if something had rattled loose inside his chest. "Wolfgang... Before I die, please."

"Oh. Sorry." Wolfgang sat straight in the chair, craned the violin against his neck, and attempted to do Paganini's composition justice. Within seconds of the bow gliding across the strings, Henry's eyes stopped moving, the tension on his face eased, and the chapped smile brightened—a common response to Wolfgang's musical medicine. Despite the pain of the past months, a look of peace overcame his friend's face. But as much as Wolfgang loved and admired Dr. Waters, he didn't have time to play for very long. He had more patients to check on, more charts to go over, three surgeries on which he would assist Dr. Barker, and many more requests on the list.

After four minutes of, in his opinion, stumbling through Paganini, Wolfgang lowered the violin and placed it on his lap.

Dr. Waters breathed in and out through his nose, a cleansing push of air. "Believe in what you're...doing here...Wolfgang."

Wolfgang reached out and patted Henry's arm.

Dr. Waters coughed. "Don't let Barker—" He coughed again. Blood appeared on the right corner of his lips. Wolfgang wiped the blood with a small towel. Dr. Waters moved on the pillow, turned his head toward Wolfgang, and opened his eyes to mere slits. "Might not have a...cure...for the disease. But you...have a cure...for the soul." He closed his eyes again.

Wolfgang stood, placed his hand on Henry's forehead, which was burning with fever, and whispered a quick prayer, remembering how Dr. Henry Waters had touched so many patients over the years with his sense of humor, convinced that laughter, although not scientifically proven, was quite often the best form of medicine they could give. He had a dry wit that charmed the adults and an infectious childlike personality that won over the kids, telling jokes, pulling quarters from behind their ears and handkerchiefs from his nostrils. He would be missed by all. Wolfgang finished his prayer and removed his hand from the older man's forehead.

"Too bad I won't be around"—Dr. Waters shifted on the bed, wincing—"to be able to call you…Father. Or to see where this… music takes you."

Wolfgang smiled. He remembered the flask Susannah had given him. He pulled it from his pocket, placed it in Henry's right hand, and closed his fingers around it. "Whiskey. From Susannah."

Dr. Waters sighed. "A beauty. Give her…a kiss for me…will ya?"

"It was Lincoln's doing," said Wolfgang. "He's Prohibition's worst nightmare. Or maybe Barker's."

They shared a laugh, but it wasn't long-lived.

"Go on, Wolf." Dr. Waters raised his arm, flask in hand. "Leave me…to my drink. And to the memories…of that…crappy rendition of Paganini."

Wolfgang placed the violin inside his black bag of instruments, zipped it up, and tapped the lid of the flask. "Try to make that last until tomorrow."

"Not a chance."

Wolfgang stepped out to the second-floor solarium and spotted an ambulance coming up the wooded hillside. Electric cones of light propped in front of a dark Buick, flickering between the trees as the car noisily climbed the serpentine road.

The choking throttle of the ambulance engine drew closer.

Another patient was coming.

Wolfgang waited in the Grand Lobby, at the corner of the sanatorium where the east and west wings joined on the first floor. Roman-style columns stood like centurions throughout the space, crowned with carved swirls and geometric shapes that matched the deep, reddish-brown woodwork, warming its grandeur with a feeling of home. He watched out the glass doors as the ambulance puttered up the hillside.

"Dr. Pike."

Wolfgang turned to find Mary Sue Helman parked in her wheelchair. She'd been a patient at Waverly for fifteen months, arriving just a week after her twentieth birthday and four weeks after her wedding to Mr. Frederick Helman.

Wolfgang smiled. "Has someone abandoned you, Mary Sue?"

Mary Sue laughed and tucked strands of her shoulder-length brown hair behind her ears, at ease in her chair. "Abandoned momentarily. Lincoln has run off to the bathroom. I saw you standing here, so I escaped down the hallway." She appeared healthier every week, gaining weight at a faster rate than most of the ambulatory patients. Of course, she was eating for two now. Her cheeks were filling out, her brown eyes and dimples prominent in a face that was now soft instead of fragile. She rubbed her belly, nearly eight months with child. "I'm strong enough to make my own trip to the bathrooms now."

"Marvelous." Wolfgang extended his hand and she gripped it. "Bedpans be gone."

Mary Sue rubbed her bulging stomach. "He just kicked."

"He, huh?"

She nodded. "Feels like a boy."

Wolfgang looked over his shoulder toward the front doors as the ambulance came to a stop on the rutted road before the sanatorium's main entrance. He faced Mary Sue again. "I'll come check on you soon and we'll talk."

"I would like that."

"Until then." He popped his umbrella open and the skeletal spokes jutted out, the cloth ripped. Water splashed down onto his shoulder.

Mary Sue giggled. Just as Wolfgang was turning away she touched his lab coat, stopping him. "Dr. Pike, could you give this letter to Frederick?"

Wolfgang took the letter from her and tucked it inside his coat.

"He hasn't responded to my last two letters."

"I'll see that he gets it, Mary Sue."

Lincoln Calponi, an orderly dressed in white pants and a white shirt, hurried into the lobby toward Mary Sue. "There you are. You trying to give me the shake?"

"I couldn't make it out the door in time." She pointed at Wolfgang. "He got in my way."

Lincoln moved behind her wheelchair and eyed Wolfgang suspiciously but playfully. Lincoln and Mary Sue were about the same age, and they got along pretty well, as well as anyone could get along with Lincoln, who was as obnoxious as anyone on staff. He had fair skin with freckles, and sandy hair that was parted but always a tad disheveled, which blended well with his tendencies of hyperactivity. He knew of Mary Sue's situation, but it didn't stop him from harmless flirtations with her. Lincoln flirted with all the Waverly women, no matter their age or appearance. He was also one of Wolfgang's closest friends on the hillside.

"Oh, Lincoln," said Wolfgang. "Dr. Waters thanks you."

Lincoln winked and then rolled Mary Sue out of the lobby.

Wolfgang opened the front doors and stepped out into the rain. With his free hand he grabbed a wheelchair next to the doorway and navigated it downhill. The concrete walkway soon gave way to mud, and pushing the empty wheelchair proved difficult with his aching foot, especially while holding on to a torn umbrella.

The ambulance was coated with wet leaves and twigs from the low-hanging boughs that canopied the roadway all the way up the hillside. The driver appeared none too pleased to be out in the rain. He rolled down his window and beckoned Wolfgang with a chubby hand. He produced a clipboard that Wolfgang quickly signed.

"Just one?" Wolfgang asked.

The driver nodded, gazing wide-eyed up at the massive sanatorium. As soon as Wolfgang let go of the pen, the window rapidly squeaked upward. Wolfgang stood ankle-deep in the muck. He grabbed the wheelchair, half kicking it toward the back of the ambulance, where the double doors burst open. A young male attendant stood with one hand propping open the closest door, holding a cloth over his nose and mouth.

Inside the shadows of the Buick was a stern-looking man with red hair sprouting out beneath a bowler hat. Later forties or fifties, Wolfgang guessed, and dressed as if he'd come from an opera. Brown trousers and a frock coat, a white cotton shirt with a club collar. Even through the rain, Wolfgang saw a gold pocket watch tucked inside the pocket of his vest, with a paisley cravat to match.

The man coughed into his right hand. The attendant flinched.

But the man's eyes looked mischievous, as if he'd summoned up the cough on purpose to put a scare into the young attendant.

Wolfgang stepped closer and shouted over the rain. "Mr. McVain?"

The man nodded.

"Welcome to Waverly Hills."

McVain didn't reply. He stood on his own and lowered himself down into the wheelchair as the ambulance attendant quickly slammed the doors. The vehicle kicked into gear with a metallic grunt and pulled away.

Wolfgang held what was left of the umbrella over McVain's head and put all his weight behind the wheelchair, rolling through the mud.

"I'm sorry for the weather, Mr. McVain. You would think at this time of year it would be snow. Is it Tad? Is that right?"

No response from Tad McVain. He sat with his hands on his thighs, his fingers spread. Wolfgang stared. The man had five fingers on his right hand, but two on his left; only the pinkie and thumb remained.

Then the wind grabbed the umbrella from Wolfgang's grip and sailed it about ten yards away. The rain tapped against McVain's hard felt hat, dripping from the crown. Still he said nothing. He just looked upward at the massive Gothic building before them.

"Don't worry. You'll receive top-notch care here, Mr. McVain. I assure you." Wolfgang tilted the chair back slightly and bent to

McVain's right shoulder. "By the way, my name is Wolfgang Pike. I'm a doctor here. I'm also in training to be a Catholic priest. You can call me Doctor, or some here already call me—"

McVain reached up, gripped the lapels of Wolfgang's lab coat, and pushed him back so forcefully that Wolfgang lost his balance and fell into the mud.

Maverly must have been watching from her rooftop window, because Wolfgang heard her screams begin again. "Maverly at Waverly," she shouted from above. "Maverly at Waverly. Maverly says welcome to Waverly."

Dr. Wolfgang Pike sat in the mud, rain pounding his head and shoulders, watching as the newest patient at Waverly Hills rolled himself into the sanatorium.

CHAPTER 2

Nestled among the trees, forty yards down the hillside from the main sanatorium, Wolfgang's cottage crackled with the cold, for the January air stubbornly refused to stay outside. It was two in the morning, and despite the fire he'd started across the room hours ago, he still felt chilled. Of course he also blamed the rain from two days ago—working that entire day in wet, muddy clothes after the new patient McVain had pushed him down. A cold front had followed behind the rainstorm. Wolfgang hadn't felt true warmth since, even in dry clothes.

A cold draft hovered around his ankles as his feet pressed the piano's pedals. He wanted to play faster to keep warm, but faster always turned sloppy. By the number of crumpled pages on the floor beside his bed, it could be concluded that he'd been playing too fast for some time now.

He blew into his hands, rubbed them together, then touched his fingertips to the keys again. He continued warming up with Mozart's piano sonata in C minor. After a few minutes he stopped. The candle flame atop his piano flickered and settled. A fresh red rose stood inside a white vase next to the candle. He looked to it for inspiration, closed his eyes, and imagined the low humming of a trio of violins. The harmony brought a smile to his face. And then, ever so softly, the clarinet eased in, rising above…

He opened his eyes at the sound of muffled laughter. Footsteps on dead leaves. Someone coughed. His fingers eased from the piano keys as a male voice called out.

"Nigger lover. The devil pisses on your pope!"

A brick crashed through the window, sending shards of glass to the wood floor. The attack sent him reeling back from the bench as cold air whistled through the broken window.

Someone coughed again, and then another shout: "Catholic heathen!"

Wolfgang curled up and covered his head with his hands, expecting another brick to come flying through the broken window, or something worse. When he finally stood up, he saw two dark silhouettes disappear into the woods, their footsteps fading with their laughter.

"Fools."

He leaned with both hands on the windowsill for a moment, staring out, daring them to come back. Glass covered the sill. He looked down—his right hand was bleeding.

A slip of paper protruded from one of the three holes in the brick lying on the floor. His fingers shook as he unfolded it. GO TO HELL, PRIEST, it read in dark block letters. *Fools.* He crumpled it and tossed it toward the wastebasket, which was already overflowing with pages. *Not yet even a priest.*

Of course it was easy to mistake him for one, especially with as many confessions as he'd been hearing. In years past, Waverly had had preachers from other denominations. There were options. But not now. Father Butler had left five years ago during the construction of the new building. And the last Baptist minister had become ill with tuberculosis after only five months at Waverly and died of the disease ten months later. So there was no other choice: if the patients couldn't spill their guts to Dr. Pike, they would take them to the grave.

Which is where the Klan apparently wanted him. Wolfgang knew that the first wave of the Ku Klux Klan flourished in the South in the late 1860s, focusing on the suppression of blacks, but the group pretty much died out in the 1870s. Then, in 1915, William J. Simmons founded the second Klan in Stone Mountain, Georgia, and in the 1920s, it surged behind its new Imperial Wizard, the dentist Hiram Wesley Evans. Only WASPs could belong. White Anglo-Saxon Protestants. The Klan hated blacks, Jews, liberals, Catholics, and anyone foreign born. They dug their claws deep into the national debate over Prohibition, and sometimes their opposition to bootleggers and saloons turned violent, a tactic that colored much of their work. They burned churches and crosses, murdered, raped, and castrated, all in the name of keeping America safe. And to the new Klan, there was nothing more un-American than the foreign influence of the Roman Catholics, who, they claimed, held allegiance to the pope and Rome over the United States and its president.

It was nonsense, and nothing roiled Wolfgang more than such intolerance. Nearly seventy-five years ago, it had been the "Natives," the Know-Nothing Party, who had caused the election riots in Louisville in 1855 that targeted the Irish Catholics. Rumors of Catholics interfering with the voting process boiled over into Bloody Monday, one of the country's worst acts of anti-immigrant violence. Homes were vandalized, businesses looted, and tenements burned, including the block-long row of houses known as Quinn's Row. Bodies were dragged out into the streets and beaten. Entire families were killed in the fires. Wolfgang's grandfather, his father's father, had been a member of the Know-Nothings involved in the riots. Wolfgang had spent his lifetime distancing himself from that hatred.

And now, with the KKK, another force of hatred was trying to force its grimy hands into politics across the south.

Wolfgang threw the brick out the window. How dare they enter his home. He surveyed the four walls of his cottage. Next to the stone fireplace was a bat, a Louisville Slugger with Babe Ruth's signature. He often held it while composing in his head, swinging it slowly as he paced his creaking, slanted floor. He hurried across the room—which contained a bed, a couch, a piano, a stack of books from the seminary, and little else—grabbed the baseball bat, and opened the front door.

His breath was visible in front of him, steaming in long plumes. Like a dragon. That's what he felt like. *Come back*, he dared them. Beating the barrel against his palm, Babe Ruth's signature smeared with blood. He stepped down from his porch, touching his right hand to his forehead, chest, left shoulder, and then right, motioning the sign of the cross.

"Come on!" he shouted. "Show yourselves."

Wind shook the treetops. In the distance, the sanatorium's rooftop was visible, the bell tower highlighted by the glow of a crescent moon. Up the hill he heard leaves crunching. He gripped the bat taut now in both hands.

A pig came running out of the shadows. Wolfgang let down his guard and watched it disappear into the trees. Lately, the pigs had been getting loose on a daily basis, and they liked to rummage through the woods. He'd seen one scurry as far as the train tracks at the bottom of the hill. Wolfgang lowered his bat and returned inside. He locked the door behind him and exhaled slowly.

Beside his bed was an empty glass, stained red from the remnants of the evening's wine, his stash untouched by nine years of Prohibition. The walls were utterly absent of any decoration except for a clock and the cross, very much like the room he'd had at the abbey at Saint Meinrad as a seminary student. The left side of his bed was currently in disarray. The other side was neat as always, the sheets pulled tight, the covers tucked around the outline of a pillow he was still accustomed to smelling before bed every night. He eyed the closet next to the piano. There was a portrait inside that he badly wanted to take out, but he remained strong to temptation. Instead he lifted the necklace from his shirt and kissed the cross.

Wolfgang grabbed the bottle of red wine from the kitchen and took a heavy swig. The rest he poured into a clean glass and took with him to the piano. *To hell with the Klan's new agenda.* It was a quarter past two in the morning and he needed a drink. Plenty of time to lose himself in his work. The ink on the yellow pages had long dried. He read now what he'd composed just before midnight, then crumpled the page into a ball and tossed it into the wastebasket. There were simply not enough notes.

He dipped the tip of the quill into the inkwell above the piano keys and stared at the blank page. He realized how much he must look like his father, sitting in that position; he used to watch his father writing like this at night, always by candlelight and always with a quill pen. "Fountain pens dampen creativity," his father had once said.

Wolfgang shook his head. Focus on the music.

He dipped his quill and found the page, searching back for his train of thought: Oh, yes, violins and the clarinet.

CHAPTER 3

Wolfgang heard footsteps in the dark, her careful tiptoes creaking over wooden floorboards, and seconds later he couldn't breathe. He inhaled, but the air just froze deep down until he thought his chest would implode. Patches of light and dark flashed across his vision. He fought with his arms, but couldn't push her away. He pleaded for his legs to come alive so that he could run from the bed, from her, but he felt nothing down there. Screams sounded from deep inside his head, vibrations that dampened with every frantic beat of his heart.

Car tires screeched.

He pulled his knees up to his chest, and finally the whistling of a chorus of birds woke him.

"Rose…"

Wolfgang opened his eyes, panting. It was only a dream. Another nightmare.

He sat up straight and yawned, staring out the broken window, spotting three of the noisy birds perched on a low branch of an oak tree that still carried brown leaves throughout the winter. It was freezing inside; no surprise, given the state of the window that he'd neglected to board up before he'd fallen asleep. He rubbed his arms and stood, accidentally knocking over an empty wineglass.

His right knee ached. He massaged the muscles, eyeing the stack of theology books next to the piano as he stretched. It had been his ritual to study them every morning before work, but with as late as he'd been staying at the sanatorium and as many hours as he'd been putting in on his writing, it had been several days since he'd opened them. But those were excuses and he knew it. With the special privileges the monks at Saint Meinrad had given him, the books deserved his full attention. And they would get it. *But not this morning.*

Dozens of his papers had blown from the piano and were now scattered all over the floor. His head throbbed as he bent over to collect them, his cold fingers clumsy against the hardwood. He gathered the papers into a stack, put them into a black lacquered box atop the piano, and slid it under the bed.

It was six thirty. His patients would be waiting.

Wolfgang dressed in a black Roman cassock that buttoned down the front from neck to toe and covered it with a white lab coat. He heard a gentle tapping on his front door. And then a female voice.

"Wolfgang."

Susannah was here.

"I'm coming." Stopping by the kitchen, Wolfgang knelt down to see his distorted reflection in the glass of the coffee percolator. He stood back up, somewhat satisfied.

She knocked again. "Wolfgang."

He smiled. Truly she harassed him on purpose. So went the morning ritual. He grabbed his black bag of musical instruments, straightened his lab coat, and opened the door. It was cool outside, sun-drenched.

Susannah waited at the bottom of his steps, gripping a small black purse. She smiled. "Morning, Wolf."

"Morning, Susannah." Together they walked up toward the trees. Under the sunlight, Wolfgang finally felt that warmth he'd been craving. "You sleep well?"

"I did. You?"

"I don't sleep, Susannah. You know that."

They walked silently through the woods for a few minutes as the wind rustled the dead leaves and naked tree limbs. The sunlight penetrated the tree branches above, highlighting the forest floor in a pattern of striped shadows. Mostly Wolfgang kept his eyes ahead, but he could feel her occasional stare. Susannah lived in the nurses' dormitory near the back of the Waverly Hills property, roughly fifty yards from Wolfgang's cottage. They walked to work every morning. Silence was sometimes their best communication.

"Do you have enemies I should know about?"

He looked at her, confused.

Susannah glanced at him. "Your broken window."

"A brick came flying through about two in the morning."

"What? Were you hurt?"

He showed her the cut on his right palm but then quickly dropped his hand back to his side. "It's nothing. Probably a few hoodlums from the KKK."

"Why would they bother us here on the hillside?"

"I fear they live here now."

"What do you mean?"

"They were patients. They must have sneaked out."

"You saw them?"

"No."

"Then how do you know they were our patients?"

"One of them coughed. I know a tuberculosis cough when I hear one."

They continued walking. The woods were full of deer, squirrels and rabbits, raccoons and chipmunks, stray cats and dogs, and at night the occasional possum would waddle across Wolfgang's porch. But the pig that darted across their path just before they reached the top of the hill was a new wrinkle to the morning ritual. This one was extremely fat, crusted with mud and probably searching the woods for acorns.

"Looks like the same beast I danced with last night," said Wolfgang.

The pig snorted, then faced them. Susannah squatted down and gave it a quick snort of her own. The pig scuttled back into the trees.

Susannah stood and ironed out her dress with her hands. "Lincoln needs to learn how to keep those beasts locked up proper."

Wolfgang began walking again. "Suppose they don't want to be cooked."

Just then Lincoln came running and huffing from the trees to their right. The letters *WHS* were stenciled in white above his left shirt pocket. He leaned over, hands against his thighs, breathing heavily. "I'm too busy in the morgue to deal with this every morning."

Susannah patted him on the back. "Keep 'em penned, Lincoln. Can't have our dinner running the hillside."

Lincoln scratched his wispy hair. "Which way'd it go?" They both pointed toward the left side of the footpath. Lincoln took a flask from his pants pocket, downed a quick swig, and then offered it to Susannah. "Want a squirt?"

"No, Lincoln. I don't want a squirt."

"Wolf?"

Wolfgang shook his head, glanced at his wounded hand, and then surveyed the woods. "Too early for illegal whiskey, Lincoln."

He screwed the top back on. "Suit yourself." Lincoln disappeared into the trees.

They had nearly reached the clearing where a grassy field rolled downward from the façade of the sanatorium. A hammering sound echoed from the nearby workshop, a single-level barn nestled in the trees. Wolfgang ducked his head inside and the smell of wood chips welcomed him.

A dozen patients, those healthy enough to test their endurance, worked on various crafts. This workshop was a popular activity among the patients, because it allowed them to release tension. A giant farm boy named Jesse wore goggles and gloves while he repeatedly smashed a ball-peen hammer against a sheet of copper foil, denting it into some kind of shape. He took a break to wave and Wolfgang waved back. A young man in the back corner screwed wheels into a small wooden toy car. A bald man attached leather to the seat of a chair. A group of women sat behind wooden frames, working together weaving a colorful rug. One of them snickered at Wolfgang, who ducked back outside with Susannah.

"What?" asked Susannah.

"Nothing." Wolfgang sniffed the air. "I smell breakfast."

A tall black man with thick dark hair and bulging muscles walked away from the main sanatorium, pushing a loose-wheeled wooden cart stacked high with food and supplies. Apples, oranges, and bananas. Wheat bread and cucumbers and tomatoes. Beneath the cart rested a dozen glass jars of white milk. Steam rose from beneath a beige towel at the front of the cart. Fresh breakfast.

"Morning, Big Fifteen." Wolfgang lifted the towel and snatched a piece of bacon.

"Morning, Boss." Big Fifteen rested on the cart for a moment and wiped sweat from his forehead. He nodded at Susannah. "Miss."

Susannah nodded without smiling and walked on across the lawn.

Wolfgang patted Big Fifteen on his thick shoulder. "First trip of the morning?" Three times a day Big Fifteen trekked the property with a cart full of supplies for the colored hospital that lay lower down the hill. And when he wasn't pushing supplies, he helped with the maintenance, everything from chopping wood to cutting grass.

Big Fifteen nodded. "Gots to feed my people, Boss." He stared toward Susannah, who stood facing a cluster of crows eating bread crumbs. "Why don't she talk to me, Boss?"

"A little shy, I guess." Wolfgang inhaled the pleasant aroma wafting up from the cart. "What else they cook up this morning?"

"Bacon…and some eggs and sausage."

Susannah folded her arms across her chest and spoke over her shoulder. "We'd have more of the bacon if Lincoln would keep the pigs bottled up."

Big Fifteen lifted the cart. "Reckon so, Miss." He smiled. His muscles flexed beneath his long-sleeved gray shirt and he continued down the hillside.

"Good day, Fifteen." Wolfgang watched him descend the uneven terrain, hardly straining on the downhill. Big Fifteen stood at least six foot six, and his hands were enormous, big enough to palm the largest of pumpkins from the patch on the north side of the hillside. They called him Big Fifteen because of the size of his boots.

Big Fifteen, a patient at Waverly for two years, had been cured of TB in 1916 when the hospital was a mere flicker of the size it was now, and he'd insisted on staying at Waverly to help the patients at the colored hospital. He'd never say it, but Wolfgang could tell by the looks Big Fifteen would give Dr. Barker that he wasn't satisfied with the conditions down there. It was cramped, dark, and over-crowded. And if indeed it was fresh air that helped cure the disease, the white patients got the best of it, perched as they were at the highest point in the county, where the Waverly wind was found in abundance. The colored hospital caught everything downwind—the air, the smell of the pigs and cows, the smell of the freshly baked food before it was transported, along with the flooding from the heavy rains.

"Abel seems to be doing better every day," said Susannah, as they walked on. Abel Jones, the poor little boy; he'd arrived at Waverly in 1926 from the German Protestant Orphans Home. No family, no visitors, no pictures from loved ones. Susannah had become like a mother to him, and at times Wolfgang felt like he'd become the boy's father too, a position that left him at once uncomfortable and yet pleased.

Wolfgang glanced at her. "Abel has you to take care of him."

The comment drew a smile from Susannah. "Miss Schultz spoke of you before I left last night. She hopes you'll play for her today."

"Dr. Barker thinks my music therapy is a waste of time."

"Has he told you that?"

"No, but I can tell."

Susannah waved her hands. "Dr. Barker is a bore who's mad at the world because his wife won't sleep with him anymore."

"She's afraid of catching TB," Wolfgang said. "I'd be careful too."

"Would you?"

"You know what I mean."

She watched him curiously. "You know Barker's wife moved out."

"No, I didn't know that."

"Moved off the hillside and took the kids with her," said Susannah. "Heard they're staying with her family in the Highlands, near Cherokee Park."

They were twenty yards away from the entrance portico on the south side of the sanatorium, where a cluster of visitors met with some patients on the lawn. One of the visitors stared at the building while the patient talked. The portico had archways with alternating sections of brick and stone that gave it a mosque-like appearance, although the building itself looked more like it was stolen from an Ivy League college campus. It was a five-story monster made of brick and stone, ornately fashioned by Gothic architecture from the first floor all the way up to the rooftop and bell tower. Solarium porches stretched the length of the building on each floor, six hundred feet long. Every room on the south side opened to the sleeping porches, where the patients who still had a chance at survival stayed. The terminal cases were on the other side of the hallway, behind the rooms that opened up to the solariums. The building was designed in the shape of a boomerang, with the idea that it could catch the breeze and keep fresh air on the patients at all times.

Rest and fresh air supposedly helped tuberculosis, but the pressure to find a definitive cure led to experimental treatments such as pneumothorax—collapsing diseased lungs—and another surgery called thoracoplasty, in which Wolfgang and Dr. Barker removed several rib bones from the chest wall. They also performed lobectomies, in which they removed parts of the lung, and in some cases the entire lung. Phrenicotomies cut the nerve supply to one of the diaphragms in hopes of allowing the disabled lung to heal. They used heliotherapy, or sun treatment, because they believed that sunbathing killed the bacteria that caused tuberculosis. But these were all treatments, not cures, and the procedures, bloody and dangerous as they were, often only delayed the ultimate outcome.

Recently they'd been losing almost one patient per hour, and the menace showed no signs of slowing. Waverly held its full capacity, and the waiting list was growing. While Waverly bulged at the seams, the town shrank. The disease consumed entire families. Wolfgang spent much of his day now hearing confessions, regardless of faith or denomination. But he refused to allow the dying to exit the world without cleansing their souls, and the patients never seemed to mind.

Father, bless me for I have sinned…

"Wolfgang?"

"Yes?"

Susannah grinned. "Where were you just now?"

"Contemplating whether or not to open the door for you." He

stepped forward and opened it. They stood in the center of a hall-way that stretched three hundred feet on either side of them. Shiny black and red tiles formed a checkered pathway down the center of the hallway. The walls were gray, the woodwork a dark brown. Globe lights hung down from the white ceiling. You could smell how clean it was.

Coughing echoed down the hallway, reminding Wolfgang that it was still a home for the dying. Yet the doctors, nurses, and vol-unteers made it as much like home as possible. A retired farmer from Bardstown ran Waverly's hillside farm, raising cattle, hogs, and chickens to provide meat, fresh eggs, and dairy products for the patients and staff. Those who turned to faith could visit the non-denominational chapel that Wolfgang oversaw on the second floor. Children could attend school in the pavilion building, and there were playgrounds there as well. The library contained hundreds of donated books, newspapers, and magazines. Waverly's theater offered movies and plays, and patients could partake in activities from weaving rugs and making toys to the popular copper hammer-ing and furniture manufacturing, and everything made was sold to the public to raise money for the hospital.

And then there was Wolfgang, who brought them music.

"Dr. Pike!"

Susannah and Wolfgang turned. Dr. Evan Barker was dressed in his white lab coat buttoned all the way up, covering his usual three-piece suit. His gray hair showed hints of the blond it had once been. Blue eyes moved behind the wire-framed glasses, positioned in such a way that he always seemed to be looking down on the unfortunate souls before him. His thin, upturned nostrils flared.

"Morning, Dr. Barker," Wolfgang eventually managed to say.

Dr. Barker glanced at Wolfgang's bag of instruments. "I see you have your *healing* supplies."

"I don't go anywhere without them."

He handed Wolfgang a clipboard full of charts. "After rounds I need you to tend to these patients. They came in very early this morning."

"Yes, sir."

"Medical tests, Wolfgang." Dr. Barker said. "Not their theories on music." He glanced at Wolfgang's black bag again and then stared at Susannah, who was not so smoothly disguising a smile behind her hand. Dr. Barker started to say something else but then stopped to exhale a breath he must have been holding onto all morning. He nodded, spun on his heels like a soldier, and hurried away.

"He's still wearing his wedding ring," said Susannah.

"It's none of our business, Susannah."

Wolfgang and Susannah went off in opposite directions. She stopped suddenly and looked over her shoulder. She'd caught him staring. "Lunch?"

"Cafeteria at noon," said Wolfgang. "I just happen to know the cook."

Susannah smiled. "Good luck with McVain today. And watch out for the mud."

CHAPTER 4

McVain, the new patient on the fourth floor, had yet to utter a word to Wolfgang since his arrival two days ago during the rainfall. Wolfgang had been fascinated by McVain ever since. There was something about the man. Wolfgang could see it in his eyes. He was a man of stories and secrets, a man of *opinions*. And, of course, the bigger mystery: the three missing fingers on his left hand.

He wasn't a mute; that much Wolfgang knew for sure. On the afternoon of McVain's arrival, Wolfgang had seen him chatting with some of the other men on the fourth-floor solarium porch. He'd spotted him on several occasions talking to Lincoln, and McVain had started responding to the nurses when they asked him their daily questions.

Even Susannah had managed to open him up on one of her visits. "How are you feeling this morning, Mr. McVain?"

"I'd feel better if there were women on the fourth floor, doll face."

She'd tapped him on the shoulder. "I'll see what I can do, Mr. McVain."

"Just 'McVain,'" he'd said grumpily. "Mister makes it sounds like me and you have got no chance."

As Susannah had walked away, she heard the men around McVain's bed cracking up. "Women," he'd muttered, just before she turned the corner. "Can't live with 'em. Apparently can't die with 'em either."

Later, when Wolfgang approached McVain's room for afternoon rounds, he noticed five of the beds on the solarium porch were empty. The sunlight was shining perfectly, yet no patients? Then he heard laughter from McVain's room, and McVain, in a Chicago accent: "So I bust the door down. Me and my boys move in to find him with his pants around his ankles and two broads on the bed—"

Wolfgang moved in at that point, knocking on the doorframe. "Party's over, gentlemen."

The men looked up from their folding chairs. "Hey, Father," one of them said. "Father," said another.

"Come on." Wolfgang motioned for them to get up. "Enough fun and games. I'm your doctor now." He grinned and then eyed McVain. "Back to the sunlight. Mr. McVain probably needs to rest that voice, since he's been using it so much."

McVain grunted and stared up at the ceiling as the men filed out. Wolfgang patted a couple of them on their backs. Every room in the sanatorium had the capacity for two beds, and each bed was equipped with a radio, phone, bell signal, and an electric light socket. McVain's roommate was a man named Mr. Weaver, a forty-year-old man whose gray hair made him look twenty years older—that and the sickly pale color that masked his face. He was on his back, lying very still in his bed. Weaver smiled every time Wolfgang entered the room, because he cherished their conversations about music, but today it seemed that McVain had already brought about Weaver's smile, with some story of ill repute.

"Guess what today is, Doc?" Weaver said, his throat raspy.

"Your birthday?"

"Nope. My one-year anniversary here."

"Congratulations, Mr. Weaver." Wolfgang put on a smile that he hoped appeared genuine. "Maybe we'll get you out of here before year two." Then he added four more ounces of shot pellets to the bag that rested on Weaver's right collarbone. The shot-bag method was typically used on patients with infections in both lungs. Several weeks ago, Wolfgang had begun the procedure by placing a one-pound bag of shot on both collarbones. He increased the weight by about five ounces a week. The weight restricted the excursions of the lungs, made them quiescent, and taught the patient correct breathing.

Weaver was a good patient, and he was always careful not to move around when he had the bags on him. Only his beady eyes roamed. "What are we up to?"

Wolfgang squinted. "Four and a half pounds."

"That good?"

"It's better."

Wolfgang glanced over at McVain, who lay in bed only a few feet away, staring blankly toward the gray wall, or maybe at the sunlight out on the solarium porch. Other than his coughing spells, he was quiet when Wolfgang was present, his lips in a scowl. McVain's nose was flat and bent slightly to the left side up near the bridge, as if it had been broken several times and not set correctly. Wolfgang wondered if he was once a boxer. Probably not. His hands seemed too delicate.

His hair was uncombed, perpetually tousled by the constant breeze, and fiery red. With his green eyes, he looked Irish, possibly Catholic, not that it mattered. Either way Wolfgang would welcome him at Mass, which was neither official nor regimented in any way and often included a mixture of Protestants, Catholics, Jews, and a few who clung to no distinct faith at all. Mass at Waverly Hills was more or less just a nondenominational gathering of patients who needed to pray, talk, and discuss the Bible and the scriptures. The chapel was never full except during Christmas or Easter, in which case Wolfgang would have the bread and wine sent out to a local church for the transubstantiation so it could be changed officially into the body and blood of Christ for Eucharist.

Wolfgang stared at McVain's hands, his left one in particular. Was that the reason for his foul mood?

"Doctor?" It was Weaver again. Wolfgang carefully placed the last few ounces of shot on his far shoulder. Weaver stared up at him with kind, trusting eyes. "Or should I call you Father, like some of the others? I've been here for a year and I've never called you Father. I'm Baptist, you see."

"Call me whatever you like, Mr. Weaver. But I am not a priest yet, just in training on leave from the seminary. My parents were strict Protestants."

"How'd you become Catholic?"

Wolfgang smiled. "The ultimate rebellion, I guess."

Weaver stared, perplexed, and Wolfgang was careful to avoid his gaze until Weaver moved on to the next subject, which he did almost immediately. Weaver wasn't one to pry. "Do you like jazz?"

"I don't dislike it." Wolfgang straightened the supplies on his cart. "I'm sure it would grow on me."

McVain coughed painfully loud and then spat onto the floor. He ratcheted up another clump and expectorated it next to the first.

Wolfgang looked over his shoulder. He saw the blood on the floor. "You okay, McVain?"

McVain looked away.

"There's a pail beside the bed," he told McVain. "For the sputum."

McVain grunted.

Wolfgang faced Weaver again but nodded toward McVain, speaking loud enough for both men to hear. "Does he ever talk to you?"

"Sure," said Weaver. "He claims he knows Al Capone."

"That's something to be proud of, McVain."

McVain didn't respond.

Weaver tilted his head. "Hey, McVain, you like jazz?" No reply. McVain lifted up his right hand and produced his middle finger, holding it ramrod straight for at least ten seconds before lowering his arm back down to the wrinkled sheets that enclosed his body like a cocoon.

Weaver looked up at Wolfgang. "Sign language?"

"An enigma," Wolfgang whispered to Weaver. "But I'll crack him. I always do."

"Can you plug me in?" Weaver lifted his headphones from beside the bed. "I like Mozart."

"Ah, Mozart," said Wolfgang. "His music put me to sleep every night as a child. It always put everything else in the background."

Wolfgang plugged the wire into a receptacle between the solarium's double doors. "My parents named me after Mozart. My mother wanted me to become a preacher. My father demanded that I become a composer."

"So what'd he say when you became a doctor?"

"He died long before I ever made the decision." Wolfgang chuckled. "But he would have been furious. He was a strict believer that only the Lord could heal."

"And your mother?"

Wolfgang hesitated. He and his mother hadn't spoken for almost ten years. Weaver started to put on his headphones but stopped. He motioned for Wolfgang to lean down. "McVain's fingers," he whispered. "They move at night."

Wolfgang shot McVain a glance and then whispered. "Move? How so?"

Weaver lifted his hands and forearms from his sides, careful not to dislodge the bags of shot, and wiggled his own fingers. "Goes on for hours." Wolfgang helped Weaver put on his headphones. "Perhaps I'll start learning a few of your instruments," Weaver said. "What do you think? How about the violin, the piano, and the cello?"

"I'm afraid that has always been my curse, Mr. Weaver. I'm an expert at none. I suggest you stick to one and master it."

Weaver pursed his lips. "Nurse Susannah says you play the piano like Mozart."

Wolfgang grinned. "She's kind."

Weaver turned the volume up on his headset, closed his eyes, and smiled as jazz tunes poured into his ears. "Ahhh…like heaven."

Wolfgang turned toward McVain again. "Anything I can get you, Mr. McVain?"

Again, there was no reply. McVain didn't even shake his head. Wolfgang used his right foot to unlatch the lock at the wheels of McVain's bed and rolled it from the room, through the double solarium doors, and toward the sunshine, where dozens of other patients lay in their beds up and down the porch. There were more than a hundred patients on each floor, and many of them were out now, facing the trees and sunny landscape that surrounded the building.

A swift breeze vented through the screens; it was a warm day for January—an odd twenty-degree change in temperature overnight, and a treat for the patients who were wheeled outside every day regardless of the temperature. It was easy to spot the rooftop dwellers, especially on the sunny days: their skin burned from the wind and sun.

Wolfgang patted McVain on the shoulder. "I could play you a tune if you'd like."

McVain waved him away as if disregarding a fly.

"Very well." Wolfgang pursed his lips. "Good day, McVain." McVain shifted in his bed but said nothing. Wolfgang stared at his hands briefly and then walked away.

On the first-floor solarium porch, Mary Sue Helman sat up in her bed and squinted in the sunlight. She had a room to herself lately, a good distance from the other patients. Mary Sue was on the mend but still months away from leaving Waverly Hills. Now they had to do everything possible to protect the baby, which was due any day. Wolfgang sat beside her bed, and together they stared out toward the woods.

"Who will deliver him?" Mary Sue asked.

"Probably Dr. Barker," said Wolfgang. "He delivered his two children, you know? Here at Waverly."

"Have you ever delivered a baby?"

"I…yes, I have," he said, and then added, "in medical school."

Mary Sue looked at Wolfgang and touched his arm. "Tell me about Frederick."

"Frederick is fighting the disease just as you—"

She squeezed his arm. "Tell me the truth. Out of all the people on this hillside, I can expect that from you. Or Dr. Waters. Why is Frederick not returning my letters?"

Wolfgang sighed. They were under orders to keep Mary Sue's blood pressure down, and Dr. Barker feared that the truth about her husband would upset her too much. They didn't want the baby to come too early. Wolfgang looked at her swollen belly. They were past the fear of her delivering too early, and as painful as it might be for her to hear, she deserved to know the truth.

"He is simply too weak to write, Mary Sue."

Mary Sue relaxed her grip on his arm and returned her hands to her belly. "Then at least he is still alive. That much you can tell me?"

Wolfgang nodded. "I'm sorry. I know some of the rules here seem crazy, but trust me. Every rule has a reason, even though I might not agree with them all."

Mary Sue wiped a tear from her left eye. "I must confess, Frederick and I didn't report to Waverly when we were supposed to." She chuckled softly. "We were supposed to come in immediately to start treatment."

Wolfgang was well aware of their story. Frederick and Mary Sue Helman were only four weeks into their marriage when they'd gotten the devastating news that they both had tuberculosis. Mary Sue was twenty years old and Frederick twenty-two.

"It's not a death sentence," Frederick had told Mary Sue at the time, in an attempt to lift her spirits. "Jeffrey Cheevers...from church...he survived tuberculosis."

"Yes, well, name another."

Frederick had just stared at her, searching his brain for another.

"You see? And Jeffrey Cheevers is always alone in his pew, Frederick," she'd told him. "He's shunned now. I don't want to live like that!"

"But live we must, Mary Sue."

Reminiscing, Mary Sue rubbed her stomach again. "Everyone knew about Waverly Hills," she told Wolfgang. "The castle on top of the mountain, the fortress on the hillside, the colony for the diseased. Well, we took our time getting here. We strolled hand-in-hand along the riverfront for hours, taking in the Ohio River. I can still remember the smell of the barges and riverboats. I can hear the water lapping against the wharves. The dock workers hauling boxes. The passengers unloading with their luggage and fancy hats.

Bicycles and horse carriages bouncing along the banks. That night Frederick took me dancing at the Brown Hotel. We stayed the night and dined like king and queen."

Wolfgang patted her hand. "Good for you."

"And then we spent half of the next day at Fountaine Ferry Park." Mary Sue grinned. "We shared a kiss at the top of the Ferris wheel. We could see the tip of the Waverly Hills bell tower in the distance." Mary Sue looked away. "Frederick assured me that we would be okay."

Wolfgang reflected back on the day Mary Sue and Frederick had arrived at Waverly. They didn't know they would be separated, taken to different floors. Maverly had welcomed them to the sanatorium from her window. Even before Mary Sue entered the building, she looked up at the strange voice and started crying. They wrote letters every day, and Wolfgang and the nurses delivered them. It didn't take long to make friends on their floors, and they weren't the only ones writing letters. Many of the single patients had developed friendships—some romances had formed too.

Mary Sue shifted to her side, facing Wolfgang. "I was ready to crawl out of my skin after a few weeks. I'd seen Frederick in the cafeteria on several occasions, but I needed to be alone with him. I just didn't feel gravely ill. I became friends with Charlotte. You remember Charlotte, don't you?"

Wolfgang laughed. "I think everyone will remember Charlotte."

Charlotte Reecer was a twenty-one-year-old waif of a girl who'd been a patient at Waverly for nine months. She had a boyfriend on the fourth floor named Chip, and they wrote as many letters as Frederick and Mary Sue. One night Charlotte and Chip were caught having relations on the rooftop. Rumor had it they'd performed the act on the swing set—while swinging. The next day they were both released from the sanatorium, deemed healthy enough to leave, since they were, according to Dr. Barker, "healthy enough to be acrobats."

"Charlotte told me about Lover's Lane." Mary Sue eyed Wolfgang for a reaction. "And how some of the patients liked to sneak out at night to neck."

All the staff knew about Lover's Lane—all except Wolfgang at one time—but they simply couldn't justify using needed staff to police it. Susannah had informed him of its existence years back on a walk through the woods toward the pumpkin patch just before Halloween. Susannah chuckled and then said, "Better close your eyes, Wolfgang." When he'd asked why, she'd told him, "We're about to pass through Lover's Lane, and I don't want you to see anything you shouldn't."

A parallel run of trees on the north side of the property between the pumpkins and the tomatoes, Lover's Lane offered some real privacy. Columns of bark for the walls and leaves for the ceiling. There were logs to sit on and plenty of room to be alone.

Mary Sue went on. "I informed Frederick about it in one of our letters. We began to sneak there in the middle of the night. It was stupid, I know…" Mary Sue's eyes moistened. "Five months later I missed my period." Tears trickled down her cheeks.

It was Wolfgang's turn to grip her hands. "Frederick has had a very rough time of it the past several months. For whatever reason, he has continued to grow sicker just as you continue to improve."

"Can he not even write?"

"No," said Wolfgang. "Believe me, he barely has the strength to speak more than a few words. A month ago, we were forced to collapse his left lung, hoping it would help it heal."

She bit her lower lip. "Have you removed ribs?"

He looked her in the eyes. "Yes, three of them. And now I'm afraid that on the last x-ray a small lesion showed up on his right lung."

She began crying.

"I'm sorry. I can't imagine how difficult this all must be."

"Where is he now?"

"He's on the fourth floor, Mary Sue."

"Is he on the porch?"

Wolfgang shook his head. "No, he's on the other side of the hallway."

"The terminal rooms, huh?" she whispered.

"We must not give up hope," Wolfgang said. "We're doing all we can to help him."

"Not all," she said.

Wolfgang knew what she wanted.

"I must see him."

Wolfgang stood. "I'll see what I can do, Mary Sue."

The life in her eyes all but died. "I know what that answer means."

"You know me better than that." Wolfgang placed his hand on her forehead. "Now please rest."

"Until then, Doctor."

He nodded. "Until then, Mary Sue."

CHAPTER 5

Miss Schultz was probably Wolfgang's biggest fan. He played his harmonica for her, one of the hundreds of short tunes he'd come up with over the years. The song had no title and, like many of the others, it changed depending on the day or the instrument chosen, the notes existing only in his mind and therefore never right or wrong. He pulled the harmonica from his lips and leaned back in his metal folding chair. Miss Schultz was lying back on her fluffy white pillow, staring at him with two rheumy eyes glazed by cataracts. Her charts said she was seventy, but her skin looked younger. Only her eyes dated her, but when she smiled her youthful side always won out.

"Thank you." She gazed out toward the woods from her third-floor spot on the solarium porch. Wolfgang put the harmonica inside his black bag, placing it right next to a piccolo his father had given him when he was five years old. "You had a nice homily this morning," she said. "It made me appreciate what I have."

Wolfgang's hair blew in the light breeze. It was beautiful out, sunny and mild. He felt as if God had rewarded them for enduring the roller-coaster weather at the beginning of the month.

Miss Schultz tugged on the sleeve of his lab coat. "You think I need a haircut?"

"It looks fine to me." Her hair was brown with hints of red and gray, pulled back from her pale forehead with a black clip.

"Oh, applesauce!" She waved her hand at him. "You're just being kind."

"The color in your cheeks is better," he said. "You look stronger. And your weight gain has been consistent for the first time in years."

She touched her hair, checking for bounce. "Is the new barber very good? I'll miss Anna Mae. She knew exactly how I liked my hair, and I'm very particular."

Wolfgang stood. "I think you'll be pleased with the work Dolores does, Miss Schultz." He touched his own hair. "She cuts mine, you know."

"With those bangs you could be a Roman Caesar, you know that?"

A slight chuckle. "Get some rest."

Miss Schultz touched her hair again. "I've been considering getting it bobbed."

Wolfgang blinked. He took a deep breath, hoping Miss Schultz didn't notice how her harmless comment had struck him. "I think a bob would look nice."

"Father?" She nodded downward. "You know Mr. Jenkins on the second floor? Your music helps him relax at night. He misses his wife."

Wolfgang sighed. "I'll see if I can pay him a visit."

"See if it doesn't make him smile."

"I will pray for him as well."

"Where do we go when we die?"

"I'm asked that question often," he said. "Where do we go when we die?"

"That's not what I'm asking. What do you do with our bodies when we die here? The ones who don't Make the Walk."

"Don't worry yourself with such details, Miss Schultz. By the looks of your improvement, you aren't likely to be among them. But I assure you they're properly taken care of."

"Do you believe there really is a heaven?"

"Why, yes, of course I do."

She shook a finger at him and gave him a wry smile. "A priest shouldn't hesitate when asked that question."

Nurse Cleary, a perpetually slow-moving nurse with wide hips, hurried with flushed cheeks toward Wolfgang. It was uncommon to see her moving so quickly, and the sight of it started Wolfgang's heart racing.

"Dr. Barker needs you," she said. "Quickly. Room two-oh-seven."

Dr. Henry Waters was dying.

Wolfgang hadn't been summoned to Room 207 as a doctor or a friend but as a man of the cloth. Lincoln moved hastily about the crowded room as sweat dripped from his hair. The room's bright light glistened off Dr. Barker's high forehead, making the red in his face more prominent, the strained veins in his neck more visible. "Dr. Pike. Hurry!"

Henry's chest rose from the bed. Blood spewed from his mouth and rolled down his convulsing neck. His lungs were probably on fire, his chest feeling like it was about to explode, his throat closing up. His lungs had already begun to disintegrate. His roommate, a new patient whose name Wolfgang had failed to memorize, watched in horror from his bed across the room. It was in his eyes. *Is that going to be me next?*

Wolfgang pointed. "Roll him outside, Lincoln—now." Lincoln quickly pushed the roommate's bed out to the solarium porch.

Wolfgang gripped Henry's hand. He showed no signs of feeling the touch. Some patients, shortly before death, had said they heard a buzzing in their ears—a dizziness caused by constant fever and lack of oxygen to the brain. Henry choked on more blood, some of it landing on Wolfgang's hand.

Dr. Barker felt for a pulse.

Henry's face was pale, ashen. His eyes were red, opened wide. "I see—" And then he stopped moving. His hands fell limp, and he stared unblinking at the bright ceiling.

Dr. Barker wiped his hands on a towel and dropped it to the floor.

Wolfgang drew the sign of the cross over Henry's body and closed his eyes. "*Requiem aeternam dona eis, Domine, et lux perpetua eis.*" Wolfgang looked upward. "Grant them eternal rest, O Lord."

He touched Henry's forehead. "And may everlasting light shine upon them."

Dr. Barker walked toward the solarium porch and stopped at the threshold. He was tall; probably six three or six four, and the top of his head nearly reached the frame over the doors. "Wolfgang," he asked. "Where were you?"

"Upstairs. With Miss Schultz."

Barker shook his head. "What was it this time? The violin, the trombone?"

Wolfgang was silent.

"These patients need medicine, Wolfgang. They need rest, not music."

"I got down here as fast as I could."

Dr. Barker pointed his long finger toward the bed. "Henry said he had sins that needed to be cleansed."

"I played for him last night. He mentioned nothing."

"Perhaps you couldn't hear him over the sound of your *harmonica*." Barker was practically sneering. "You are their doctor," he said. "Just—stop wasting time." Barker pulled a small flask from his coat pocket and tossed it to Wolfgang, who caught it awkwardly. "I found that under Henry's pillow. Know anything about it?"

"Henry liked his bourbon," said Wolfgang. "It was a dying wish."

"Of course he did." Dr. Barker left with a swift turn that spun his white coat in a dove-like swirl.

Lincoln stepped back in the room.

Wolfgang handed him the flask and sighed. "Help me clean him."

Lincoln was usually a jokester, but now his face just sagged as he stared at the bed, Henry's body, and the bloodstained sheets. They'd all lost a dear friend in Dr. Waters, and the hurt was no less painful for Lincoln just because he was lower down on the totem pole. A big part of his job was to see to the bodies after they were dead. Lately, if not chasing after escaped pigs, he spent most of his time in the morgue. "The morgue is full, Wolf. I need more help in the chute."

"I'll see that you get it."

"I'm calling it the Death Tunnel now," he said. "I spend all day in there. It never stops. The smell is getting to me, Wolf."

Wolfgang nodded as if he understood, but he didn't. He wasn't stuck in the chute all day long, accompanying the dead as they descended the hillside, unseen, all hours of the day. Wolfgang handed Lincoln a clean towel, and together they began to wipe blood from Dr. Waters's neck.

CHAPTER 6

Wolfgang spent the rest of the bright day in a somber mood. He had an afternoon gathering in the chapel, where he gave a sermon on hope to seven patients—three Catholics, two Protestants, a Jewish woman, and an atheist searching for answers. Susannah showed up afterward to help two elderly patients back to their rooms. Before leaving the chapel, she waved to Wolfgang and smiled.

Wolfgang returned the gesture and then eyed a patient in the back row, a hulking farm boy with a crew cut named Jesse Jacobs. The baby-faced young man, who appeared barely over twenty, had been with them at Waverly for almost four months with not one appearance in the chapel. Every morning during rounds, though, he'd ask Wolfgang to pray for him and his roommate, Ray, a dark-haired young man who was as thin as Jesse was large, a man whose name never failed to escape Wolfgang's overtaxed brain.

Jesse's skin was naturally pale, his cheeks pink and scattered with freckles. He had a toothy grin that filled out his box-like jaw. Jesse had already gained much of his pre-tuberculosis weight back. His arms were thick, strong, one of those kids who could lift a Buick over his head but still look fat doing it.

Jesse approached Wolfgang and offered a hand. "Hello, Father."

Wolfgang grinned, and shook it. "Not quite 'Father' yet, I'm afraid." Wolfgang lowered his arm, flexing his hand and wiggling his fingers to make sure they hadn't been crushed by the young man's grip. "Don't tell me. Jesse Jacobs, fourth floor. You prefer to call the violin a fiddle, if I remember correctly."

"That's right...Doctor." Jesse reached down toward the seats and grabbed a copper cross about two feet tall and textured with carefully placed dents throughout. "Made this at workshop. It's for the chapel."

"Thank you, Jesse. I'll find the perfect place for it." Wolfgang held the cross at arm's length as if analyzing the artwork. "Haven't noticed you in the chapel before." Wolfgang had to lift his gaze upward to meet Jesse's eyes. "Glad you could join us. You're welcome any time."

"Well, I like how you play music here...for the patients." Jesse rubbed his hands together, as if nervous. "I was wondering, since I'm starting to feel a lot stronger, if you needed any help in the chapel. I've prayed for my recovery and He seems to be listening. I'd like to give back somehow."

Wolfgang sized him up. "If nothing else I could use you to intimidate my boss. He doesn't believe in my musical medicine."

Jesse looked downward, perplexed.

Wolfgang waved it away. "Oh, never mind. Of course, Jesse, I would be happy for any help you could give in the chapel."

Jesse nodded, smiled. "Thank you. I once thought about becoming a priest myself. You know, after I'm fixin' to get out of here."

"Great," said Wolfgang. "I'm not sure I'm the best role model yet for a budding priest, but I'll do my best."

"Okay, then," said Jesse, but instead of moving to the side, he just stood there.

"I have an extra Bible." Wolfgang pointed to the back of the chapel. "Under the altar over there. Feel free to borrow it any time you like. I've got theology books back at my cottage as well."

"Only I don't know how to read, though, Doctor."

"You don't know how to read," said Wolfgang, his voice trailing away while big Jesse stood there with an innocent grin. "So it's safe to say you don't know Latin?"

"Is he a patient here?"

Wolfgang stared for a moment, and when he realized the young man wasn't joking, he said, "Let's meet here tomorrow, Jesse, and I'll show you around."

In the evening, Wolfgang granted Miss Schultz's request and stopped on the second-floor solarium for a visit with Mr. Jenkins. He played the harmonica for ten minutes while Mr. Jenkins listened silently with a smile, his spotted hands clutching and releasing his bed sheets, clutching and releasing. His fever was high. His skin was chalky, his eyes dark around the sockets. He was an old man who seemed ready to go.

"Thank you." Mr. Jenkins craned his head toward Wolfgang's chair. He coughed. Blood trickled from the left corner of his mouth. He wiped it on his shirtsleeve and settled his bald, spotted head on a flat pillow. Behind them the woods were silent. The night was dark, the moon concealed by layers of cloud cover. It was much cooler now. Dozens of patients remained out on the porch, some sleeping and some talking. Plumes of steam escaped from their noses and open mouths.

"The night has a chill to it." Wolfgang was lost for words. The patients looked to him for conversation, comfort, even wisdom, but often he felt empty and fake, like an impostor. And then he'd remind himself that he'd assisted on surgeries before he'd officially become a doctor. Was this any different?

Mr. Jenkins looked up at the ceiling. "When I was a boy, my father used to take us to the Ohio River to fish. I loved to sit and watch the barges."

"I was in awe when I first saw the *Idlewild* dock when I was a boy," said Wolfgang. "It was so big and it held so many people. The paddle wheel spinning that water like foam. And with all the steam coming out, I thought it was on fire."

Mr. Jenkins smiled. "Nothing like the river noises. At night we'd sit around the campfire. We could hear the water crashing from the falls in the distance. I'd go to sleep to my father playing the harmonica."

Wolfgang thought of his own father and how he'd play the violin and piano at night and how their living room was full of musical instruments. And how his father, despite all his faults and eccentricities, had been taken from him too early.

Mr. Jenkins's hands shook noticeably. That was why he was clutching and releasing the bed sheets. To give his hands a job. To keep them from shaking. Wolfgang opened Mr. Jenkins's left hand, pushed the harmonica into his palm, and closed his fingers around the small instrument. The old man's hands stopped shaking. All the lines in his face seemed to soften.

Wolfgang started to get up.

Mr. Jenkins touched Wolfgang's arm. "I'm not a Catholic."

"And I'm not technically a priest yet," Wolfgang said.

"Well, can you hear my sins?"

Wolfgang sat back down. "Of course."

"I've never been to any kind of confession."

"Contrition is the beginning of forgiveness," said Dr. Pike. "I can see the sorrow in your eyes. You must regret your sins, resolve not to repeat them, and then turn back to God."

He looked Wolfgang in the eyes. "I used to drink a lot." He moved the harmonica inside his grip. "I hit my wife one night when I was drunk. She has forgiven me, but my daughter never will. We don't speak. She won't see me." He sighed, still watching Wolfgang. "I can't go to my grave without the forgiveness of my little girl."

Wolfgang extended his right hand toward the elderly man's head. "I absolve you from your sin in the name of the Father, and of the Son, and of the Holy Spirit." Wolfgang lowered his hand. "The absolution may take away the sin, Mr. Jenkins, but it does not fix all that the sin has caused. You must—"

"There's a box in my room," he said. "On a shelf above the bed. I write to her every day. Her name is Amy. And in the box… are letters."

"You don't send them?"

He shook his head. "Can you see that she gets them?"

"Of course." Wolfgang placed his hand on Mr. Jenkins's frail shoulder.

"Will I be forgiven, you know, when I'm gone?"

"The Lord has freed you from your sins. Go now in peace."

"Am I supposed to say something here?"

"Most would now say, 'Thanks be to God.'"

"Thanks be to God, then." He wrinkled his brow. "What about some kind of penance?"

"Those letters you've written to your daughter are penance enough, Mr. Jenkins. I'll see that she gets them. Your heart is pure."

Mr. Jenkins made the sign of the cross, more than likely because he'd seen Wolfgang do it at the beginning of the confession. His eyes were wet. He closed them. Without another word Wolfgang stood and walked away.

In the hallway, Susannah stepped out of the shadows. "Wolf?"

Wolfgang jumped back.

"Sorry. Didn't mean to startle you."

A little boy stood by Susannah's side, a brown-haired, ten-year-old patient named Abel Jones. Abel with the dimples. Wolfgang gave him a wink. "How's it going, Abel?"

"Swell." He licked on a lollipop.

The three of them walked along the second-floor solarium. With each bed Wolfgang passed, his mind wandered back to the brick crashing through his window. Could any of these men have been the culprit?

Abel walked near the edge of the porch, looking down toward the front lawn below and the woods beyond. Like many of the children, he'd shown improvement since his arrival at Waverly.

"Wolf," Susannah whispered as they passed a male patient who was snoring loudly. The noise coming from his clogged nostrils sounded like a whistle. Susannah covered Abel's mouth to keep the boy from laughing. "Wolf, you gave Mr. Jenkins your harmonica."

"I've got several." He walked on. "I need to make a stop before we go."

"Where to? I'm tired."

"McVain."

"Wolf, do you have to befriend every patient who arrives here?"

"He pushed me in the mud."

She laughed.

"And he's missing fingers," Wolfgang said. "I'm curious is all."

"You just can't stand it when someone doesn't like you."

"Who's McVain?" Abel asked.

"A mute," Wolfgang said.

Abel chuckled. "What's a mute?"

"Same thing as a McVain."

"What's a McVain?"

"You'll see," said Susannah.

Wolfgang whispered to Susannah. "You're not completely correct, by the way. I can stand it as long as that someone has a reason for not liking me."

"So as soon as you have a reason, you'll leave him alone?"

"Of course."

They took the nearest stairwell to the fourth-floor solarium and quietly passed the beds lining the porch. Some patients slept. An old man with very little hair waved. A middle-aged man stared out the windows, oblivious to everything around him. Wolfgang found Mr. Weaver asleep on the porch, snoring in a much deeper octave than the man two floors below. Even so, Abel thought it funny and stifled his laughter with his own hands this time. Susannah gently placed her hands on his shoulders and he continued to lick his lollipop. Wolfgang looked inside the room and found McVain on his bed in the far corner, still in civilian clothes. He'd seen it many times before, patients thinking if they dressed the part, somehow they would remain healthy. A subtle denial. Wolfgang inched closer. It was dark, but he could still make out McVain's hands.

Abel and Susannah stepped closer. "Where'd his fingers go?" Abel whispered.

Susannah put her finger to Abel's sticky lips.

Wolfgang watched McVain. "I'll be damned..." McVain's eyes were closed. His hands were raised above the covers, slightly bent at the wrists. His fingers, long and arched, moved side to side, up and down—precisely, gracefully, with authority. Even the nubs from his three missing fingers moved ever so slightly from muscle memory. It was as if he were playing a piano.

Wolfgang backed away with his mouth open.

"What is it?" asked Susannah.

Wolfgang tiptoed from the room and they followed.

Abel looked over his shoulder toward McVain's room. "Is he a monster?"

"No," Susannah said in a hushed voice, although it had a twinge of humor in it. "He's not a monster."

"My Lord, did you see that, Susannah? He was playing the piano."

"Yes, I saw it."

"Now we should have something to talk about."

"And what if he continues to ignore you?" Susannah had taken off her nurse's cap. Her hair had lost some of the morning's curl, but it was still enough to get Wolfgang's attention.

"Look," he said. "I have a plan for tomorrow night." As he leaned closer and whispered in her ear, a tinny sound floated up from a floor below.

Mr. Jenkins had begun to play his new harmonica.

CHAPTER 7

Walking with Susannah back through the woods had become a nightly ritual. At first they had seemed to meet accidentally, leaving at the same time only occasionally, for many times Susannah left with the other nurses—especially during Wolfgang's early days at Waverly Hills, when he and Susannah first met. However, both had somehow settled on the same unspoken schedule each evening. The fresh, untainted air of the wilderness, mixed with the crickets and the wind, seemed to ease the tensions of the solarium behind them. They'd discuss the new patients, the children, or the funny incidents; any talk of death on this walk home was taboo.

But tonight Wolfgang walked with a quicker pace, his eyes on alert. They'd dropped Abel off at the children's pavilion, where several of the kids were already asleep on their little screened porch. Susannah had walked him inside and returned looking a bit sad. She'd see him in the morning, but of course there was always her greatest fear: that one morning he wouldn't wake up, that he'd become one of the growing, unstoppable statistics that had long ago made the sanatorium the talk of the city.

Wolfgang normally stood a careful pace aside from her, keeping a respectful distance. But tonight, if there was someone prowling about who was willing to throw bricks through windows, they were probably capable of more. So he walked closer by her side. Susannah seemed preoccupied with her thoughts too, and to Wolfgang, the woods around them had never appeared so ominous.

Come after me if you must, he thought, *but leave my friends in peace.*

"Wolf, what's eating you?"

Wolfgang hesitated. "McVain. He was a pianist."

"You said so earlier."

"I don't just mean he plays the piano, Susannah. Didn't you see him?"

She folded her arms against the cold wind. "I saw him the same as you did."

"His arm movements, how his fingers moved. Even the nubs. Piano wasn't just a hobby for him."

She smirked. "The real McCoy, huh?"

They stopped outside the nurses' dormitory, a two-story rectangular brick building that housed thirteen women, including nurses, laundry women, and cooks. The nurses split the two daily shifts, seven days a week. Susannah was a veteran of the crew and was fortunate enough to have her own room on the second floor. Wolfgang had overheard tales among the nurses of life in the dormitory: drinking after hours, smoking and playing cards, laughing, pillow fights, chatter about men half the night—but of course Susannah would not discuss such matters with him.

Wolfgang shoved his hands into his pockets and stared at the dormitory. "I need to get to McVain."

"Why?"

"I don't know yet." Wolfgang stared at the ground, thinking of his plan for tomorrow night. He hoped Susannah wouldn't back out. He could have asked Lincoln, but he couldn't trust Lincoln to keep his mouth closed.

"There's…something I'd like to show you," said Susannah.

Wolfgang looked up. "Show me? Where?"

"Inside," she said.

"Susannah… I can't—"

"It's something I've been working on for a long time. Two years, in fact. I'd like you to see it."

"What is it?"

"It's kind of a surprise. Not a gift, but…it's something I'm proud of. You'll see. It's no big deal, really…"

Wolfgang watched the silhouette of a nurse pass by an upstairs window. "Um, can't you bring whatever it is out here?"

"Well, I guess I could."

His instincts told him to run. "You know, I wouldn't want rumors getting started, Susannah."

She seemed amused by this comment. Or was it something else? "It'll only take a minute. And then you can get back home to your work. I'll be right back."

He waited outside as Susannah hurried toward the small porch. When she opened the door, a wave of giggling came forth from the nurses inside. Wolfgang glanced up toward the second-floor windows again. A form that could have been Susannah moved behind a drawn shade and then disappeared. But there was no way she could've made it upstairs so quickly.

What happened next was so sudden he didn't have time to cover his eyes. The dormitory's door burst open and an auburn-haired nurse stumbled out onto the porch, giggling, a white towel over the mounds of her breasts. The flesh of her exposed shoulders was pink from the heat of a recent shower and still slightly wet by the glistening look of it. The bottom of the towel barely covered the opening between her thighs. Wolfgang turned and covered his eyes. But then she screamed, surely not expecting a man to be standing out in the middle of the woods, let alone a budding priest. And so because of the scream he looked up again. She slipped on her way back inside and the towel shifted, exposing her right breast. Another burst of laughter followed.

"Oh, dear God," he whispered, moving away from the dorm.

"Wolf," Susannah called after him from the porch, struggling to contain her amusement.

Wolfgang stopped. "Did you set that up?"

"No, of course not." She shushed the girls and closed the door. "Don't be silly. I didn't even make it up to my room."

Wolfgang felt his face burning. "I'd better be going. Another night maybe."

She nodded. "Well, sure. Okay."

"Good night, Susannah."

Wolfgang heard laughter again, but it faded as he penetrated deeper into the woods. He felt like a fool. He'd seen breasts before. The art world was full of naked women and bare breasts—paintings, murals, statues. And he was a doctor; he had studied anatomy for years. It wasn't anything he hadn't seen before.

And after all, he was once married for five years.

Wolfgang moved as briskly as his limp would allow down the rest of the hillside to his cottage and locked the front door behind him. His heart raced, partly from the walk but mostly from the lingering images of Marlene's right breast. That was her name. It had come to him halfway home.

Not that it mattered.

But it did matter. He couldn't get the image of her lone nipple from his head, and the way the breast slipped from the confines of her towel. Lincoln had told him on several occasions about the shower room in the nurses' dormitory. He'd joke about the hole in the wall on the back of the building that stood several feet off the ground, just high enough that Lincoln needed to stand on a log to get eye level with it.

Lincoln seemed to delight especially in sharing such details with, of all men, a future priest. "Just make sure Nurse Beverly ain't the one naked," he'd say, as if Wolfgang had any intention of sneaking over to the nurses' dormitory in the middle of the night to spy. "Marlene's the one you want to catch."

Little did Lincoln know, Wolfgang had plenty of experience. He'd spent his childhood looking through such a peephole—spying, curious, frightened—and what he'd seen through that hole one night had changed everything.

Marlene's the one you want to catch...

Wolfgang moved from candle to sconce and back to candle, lighting the wicks until his cottage was aglow. He lit the candle atop the piano and then the one beside his bed. More light. That's what he needed. More light. He removed his lab coat and loosened a few buttons on his cassock.

He grabbed his rosary beads from his bedside table, knelt beside his bed, and prayed. He would channel his thoughts—to the Lord first and then to his music. He imagined he was back in the seminary, the abbey at Saint Meinrad, hearing the bells every morning for the wake-up call. Five o'clock. They had a half hour to get to the abbey church for matins, and then Mass. A plain breakfast of milk, oatmeal, and Meinrad's brown bread would follow. Then class from 7:30 until noon, where they studied Latin, Greek, theology and some science. Lunch in the refectory and then afternoon classes. Vespers before dinner. They were allowed some free time after dinner until lights out at ten, when the Grand Silence would begin. No talking. It was during this time that Wolfgang did his best thinking. Oftentimes he missed the schedule of his days at Saint Meinrad. The peace and tranquility without the fears of Waverly Hills: of illness and blood and disease. He missed the clanking of the radiators as the steam revved up every morning, what Wolfgang told his mother—on a rare visit home—was "the abbey's bang-clank symphony."

Wolfgang sometimes wondered if he'd made a mistake coming back to Waverly when his heart often longed to return to Saint Meinrad, to officially return and complete the studies needed to become ordained. Training from afar had proved to be more taxing than he'd imagined. But he just couldn't leave with how widespread the tuberculosis was becoming, and so what he originally thought would have been several months had by now turned into years.

Wolfgang prayed for ten minutes before dropping the rosary beads on the bed. He still felt unsettled, like he needed a night of meditation in the crypt chapel of the abbey church, or an afternoon chanting from his *Liber Usualis*. He pulled the black box from under the bed, removed the pages, and put them atop the piano. He poured a glass of wine, swirled it repeatedly, the meniscus sloshing expertly to the rim of the glass but no higher. He never spilled a drop. He let it breathe, swirling, smelling, and then he took a sip. He savored the warmth as it barreled down his throat and spread out through his stomach.

The window next to the piano had been repaired during the day. The new panes were still smudged with remnants of fresh putty, but they fit well enough to keep the cool air out. Wolfgang sipped his wine again and placed it on the piano bench. His right foot throbbed as it did near the end of every day, so he dragged it across the room to the fireplace. There was no shame in dragging it while he was alone. A few more glasses of wine would help numb the pain, and then he would hardly care.

Next to the fireplace was his father's Edison phonograph. It was the Gem, the smallest of the Thomas Edison models. Beside it was Wolfgang's canned music collection, stacked ten rows wide and six high, some taken from his father's collection when he'd left home, the rest acquired over the years. The music ranged from Mozart to ragtime, from Beethoven and Bach to Gregorian chants Wolfgang had been given by one of the Saint Meinrad monks, the chants recorded at a German monastery in the late 1890s. The cylinders were all protected and labeled in cardboard tubes. Wolfgang chose the Gregorian chants, popped the lid, and removed the cylindrical record. He was careful not to touch the outside surface as he fit it inside the phonograph. He touched the stylus down on the grooves of the rotating cylinder and, moments later, fighting through the static, male baritone voices burst forth from the arched horn.

At the piano, he warmed his fingers with Beethoven. Soon the wine took hold. Susannah, Dr. Waters, McVain, Marlene—the day was all fading into distant memory. He dipped his quill into the inkwell and scribbled notes, tested a few keys, and then scribbled some more.

Thirty minutes later, Wolfgang sat with elbows propped on the keys, his fingers interlocked around his drooping head. He could see the pages he'd crumpled into balls and tossed on the floor minutes ago.

They just were not right.

Five years and he'd yet to complete a simple requiem Mass.

Not that it could be so simple; the requiem had to be perfect. Rose's memory demanded so, and if nothing else in this life, Wolfgang was a driven man. His mother told him when he was eight that he'd never walk again. He did. His father was convinced that he'd never learn the piano. He did. His mother said he'd never become a doctor. He'd never amount to anything without the King James Bible. And look at where he sat now.

Wolfgang saw that the rose atop his piano was wilting, the petals no longer bright red and flowering. They'd darkened to rust, hard and crisp. He limped across to the front door and stepped outside, where the cool temperatures made his arm hair stand on end.

Behind the cottage was a birdbath full of dirty leaves and water. Wolfgang knelt beside it. Spread before him, in the embrace of the candlelight, was a small rose garden. Dozens of red roses stood there, protected from the cold by heat lamps and metal mirrors that reflected the sun's rays. Lincoln had put the contraption together, borrowing everything from the sanatorium without Dr. Barker's knowing. Wolfgang had not believed it would work. Roses would not continue to grow in the winter. But Lincoln had been adamant. So Wolfgang had blessed the garden the day it was planted, even scattering some of Rose's ashes behind the cottage. And voila— Lincoln, it turned out, had a bit of a green thumb.

Wolfgang perused the choices and found the rose he wanted. Its sturdy stem was upright and scattered with thorns and tiny green leaves. He clipped it, lifted the candlestick from the grass, and returned inside.

A fresh rose for the vase atop the piano. He felt better now.

He worked for another hour before his eyelids grew heavy. He finished his third glass of wine and blew out all the candles. At the side of his bed, he said a prayer for the patients. He prayed for McVain. Wolfgang lay in bed, staring at the ceiling and listening to the night. Then he did what he always did when he couldn't sleep.

He thought of Rose.

It had all started with a glance on the steps of the Cathedral of the Assumption in downtown Louisville. But in truth, his love for her had started weeks before, when Wolfgang took his seat in the back of the cathedral and spotted her arrival. Or, rather, heard her arrival. She was a few minutes late, and the clicking sound of her heels on the marble floor drew his attention. In that moment, a tug-of-war began in Wolfgang Pike: between Rose Chandler and the Lord.

He was twenty years old, with two years of major seminary under his belt and home for the summer from Saint Meinrad, where he'd been schooled for the past six years, through high school and into his college studies. That summer he couldn't wait to go to the cathedral and listen to the choir. He loved listening to the monks chant at the abbey, but he missed the harmony of female voices. When her slender fingers and red nails dipped into the baptismal pool, he was mesmerized—but not by the choir this time. Instead, he followed her fingers as they touched her forehead, the shallow valley between her breasts, her left shoulder and then her right, motioning the sign of the cross. She wore a red dress that conformed to her figure and ended just above her knees. Her black hair had faint swirls of auburn, cut in a bob that hovered like a small black curtain around her neck. She hurried to the row in front of Wolfgang, genuflected, and then sat on the first seat. What had Brother Blackstone told them before they'd left for the summer? To just move along and go on your merry way if confronted by someone of the opposite sex. Wolfgang quietly removed himself from his row and relocated to the other side of the church. But that advice proved useless.

He still watched her throughout the entire Mass. He watched her lips move as she sang along with the choir. Father Peterson had told them to carry their *Liber Usualis* with them everywhere they went, and if confronted with temptation, put eyes and mind to word and prayer. Wolfgang didn't have his *Liber Usualis*. He'd left it at home on his desk. So his eyes stayed on her every time she stood, sat, and kneeled. Friar Garney had laughed when he'd given Wolfgang advice on women, which was to blur the eyes and pretend they were monsters. Wolfgang tried that as well, but no amount of blurring could mask her beauty.

He couldn't get her out of his mind after that day. Every

afternoon he returned to Mass at the cathedral with hopes of seeing her again.

Two weeks later on a Sunday, a light rain fell. Wolfgang hurried
along the slick sidewalk with an umbrella, hobbling more because of
the rain, and his left foot got too far ahead of his right. He slipped
just before the cathedral steps but managed to catch himself with his
outstretched hands, avoiding injury. He felt like a fool and quickly
wiped his hands off on his pants. Lowering his head against the rain,
he moved up the steps. He opened the cathedral door and spotted
her coming up the sidewalk, moving hurriedly in a blue dress and
heels, protecting herself with a black umbrella. Wolfgang held the
door open at that moment, allowing the wind to blow rain inside
the front of the cathedral. Finally a cluster of people moved inside,
thanking him as he soaked himself in the rain. But he hadn't been
holding the door for them.

She lowered her umbrella when she reached the first step. Her
hips moved beneath the tight blue dress and an urge swept over
Wolfgang. He resisted. He never expected her to talk to him, but
she looked up. They locked eyes.

"Are you okay?" she asked.

"Me? Yes…"

"I followed you up the street." She clutched his left forearm with
her right hand and led him inside. "I saw you slip and fall."

"I'm fine, thank you." Wolfgang wondered if she would have
touched his forearm so easily if she'd known that he was a student
at Saint Meinrad and that he'd been wearing the Roman and Jesuit
cassocks for two years now.

Once inside, she ran her hand over the front of her dress, flick-
ing off tiny beads of rainwater. She shook water from her hair and
smiled at him. Her eyes were blue, her lips full, and her smile framed
by dimples.

"You had a chance earlier to close the door, on the steps back there."

Wolfgang blushed.

"You waited for me, didn't you?" Another smile. And then she
touched his arm again. "I thought it was sweet." She extended her
hand. "I'm Rose."

"I'm Wolfgang." He shook her small hand, his palm memorizing the feel of every bone, ridge, and knuckle in her grip.

"Do you mind if I sit with you today, Wolfgang?"

His heart raced. Sweat had already begun to wipe away the residue of her grip on his palm. "Of course."

"Of course, you mind?"

"No, no, I mean—"

She laughed. "Wolfgang, I'm kidding."

He started off toward his seat in the back, and she held on to his arm as if being escorted. Wolfgang looked down to his right foot, aware of his pace and the awkwardness of his steps with another in tow.

"Don't be ashamed, Wolfgang," said Rose. "I like your limp."

"Really?"

"Not everyone has one, you know." She squeezed his elbow, and the pressure helped to ease his speeding heart. They sat side by side during Mass. Wolfgang sat with his legs straight and his feet flat on the floor. Rose sat with her right leg crossed over her left, exposing part of her thigh. At some point during the Mass she whispered in his ear, "I love the Coronation Window. Don't you? The colors are beautiful."

Wolfgang turned his head toward her, their faces less than a foot apart. She smelled of something exotic and pure. "Yes," he told her.

Rose patted the top of his hand, and they both returned their attention to the priest and the altar.

In his mind, Wolfgang still talked to Rose, almost nightly. He knew it was silly; in fact, it was just the kind of reaction he saw at times with intensely grief-stricken relatives of his patients. But he desperately clung to the intimate details of her face. He'd had nightmares of not remembering what she'd looked like. He asked her questions. He laughed about their memories.

Rose never answered back.

CHAPTER 8

Swaths of dusty sunlight hit the shiny floor of the Grand Lobby, where a bright red cardinal fluttered around the white columns, frantically searching for a way out of the sanatorium. Wolfgang's footsteps echoed off the tall ceiling as he hurried toward the north wing, oblivious of the trapped bird, and of Susannah and Dr. Barker standing behind two of the columns with towels in their hands. The front door was propped open. The warm weather had returned for another day. The bird dove and nearly took Wolfgang's head off, but he ducked just in time.

He squatted on the ground and spotted Susannah a few feet away.

"That was close." She watched the bird as she spoke to him. "You in a hurry?"

"I'm looking for Lincoln." Wolfgang ducked again as the cardinal swooped low and then back up toward the ceiling.

"You're heading in the right direction." Susannah made a play for the bird when it stopped on the floor a few feet away. She attempted to cover it with the towel and actually thought she'd been successful, only to turn the towel over and find it empty. She looked back toward Wolfgang. "Last I saw Lincoln, he was in the morgue. About twenty minutes ago. Something wrong?"

"Mr. Jenkins passed away during the night." Wolfgang stood, careful of the flying bird. "I wanted to catch him before he sent the body away."

Dr. Barker's voice rang out. "I got it. I got it." He took off toward the front door and opened the towel. The bird was hesitant at first but then took off toward the trees. Dr. Barker returned a moment later, towel in hand. He smiled at Susannah. "How about that? I did it."

Susannah nodded. "Very impressive, Dr. Barker. Lincoln now has competition."

"That he does." Dr. Barker moved on toward the east wing, folding the towel as he went. To help circulate more air, Waverly's doors were often left open, especially when the weather was mild. Sometimes birds accidently flew into the sanatorium. And if not through the doors, they oftentimes slithered in through creases or holes in the solarium screens. When it happened, Lincoln was usually called in to catch the bird, but this time Dr. Barker had insisted on trying it himself.

Susannah knelt down next to one of the columns and wiped bird droppings from the floor. "*Othello* is playing in the theater in an hour."

"I'm sorry I'll have to miss it."

"Your new helper in the chapel. Jesse." Susannah stood up. "He's volunteered to play Cassio."

"He doesn't even know how to read."

"This isn't exactly Broadway, Wolfgang."

"True." Wolfgang started off toward the north wing. He waved without turning around and then headed down the hallway. He ducked his head into the morgue, which reeked of cleansing solution. The floors had recently been washed. Dead bodies lay under blue sheets on all six tables. The three trays on the far side of the room were occupied as well; the corpse on the middle tray had long red hair that reminded Wolfgang of his mother. Curls fell from the end of the tray, the tips scraping the wet surface of the floor. He looked away.

No Lincoln.

Wolfgang checked the freezer room next. It was a cold storage for Waverly's dairy, meat, vegetables, and fruits. And it probably wasn't too far away from being used as cadaver storage if the death rate didn't slow.

Wolfgang continued down the hallway and through a pair of

metal doors. The large roll-up gate that led directly to the body chute was open. Amid the darkness and cobwebs he heard footsteps. He stepped into the chute and spotted Lincoln kneeling down beside a coffin.

"There you are."

Lincoln, his face half concealed by shadows, looked up from his kneeling position on the floor. He grinned. "Peeping Tom." His voice echoed in the cool, dank air. "You sly devil. I told you. Marlene is the one you want to see naked."

Wolfgang ignored him.

"Well, how did she look?"

"Dr. Barker just caught a cardinal bird in the lobby."

"What? That's my thing."

Wolfgang shuffled fully into the tunnel and squatted down to help Lincoln position the wooden coffin on the pulley system to the right side of the chute. "So Mr. Jenkins didn't make it through the night?"

Lincoln stood, knees popping, and tapped the top of the coffin. "Couldn't pry the harmonica from his grip. Had a smile on his face, though."

Wolfgang sighed. Darkness filled the chute. There was no electricity. On the left side of the chute, a set of elongated platform stairs ran alongside the winch system that gradually lowered the coffins downward and toward the hearses that idled next to the railroad tracks, awaiting pickup. The same reversible system brought supplies up the hillside on delivery days. Drop-off was right outside the bottom of the chute. Lincoln and a few other orderlies were responsible for getting everything up into the main building, and the winch system was the easiest way to go. In years past, some of the men who delivered to Waverly would stop and chat and even help get the supplies up the chute. But the current team would be in and out like phantoms, petrified of tuberculosis. Afraid that any moment the Waverly wind could swoop down the chute and invade their lungs.

Wolfgang had been inside the chute with Lincoln one morning when the delivery truck arrived. They'd waited in the shadows at the bottom of the chute and watched as two young men hastily unloaded the boxes from the back of their truck. "They were practically tossing them inside the chute," Wolfgang had told Susannah later in the day. "They wore white masks over their noses and mouths, and their fidgety eyes followed every sound. They flung a receipt atop the pile as if the boxes were going to explode." Just as they turned back to the truck, Lincoln had stepped out of the shadows with his arms outstretched like a creature of the dead. "Maverly at Waverly," he hissed. "Maverly at Waverly."

One of the young men slipped on some gravel. The other one shouted, "It's one of them," and quickly locked himself in the truck. "He actually started driving off before the other one could make it!" Wolfgang had told her, laughing uproariously.

Wolfgang remembered the incident every time he entered the chute. Waverly needed more young men like Lincoln. He could be obnoxious and crude, but he was a treasure, and loyal to a fault. Lincoln's father and grandparents had all battled tuberculosis—and lost—so Lincoln was determined to fight it off, especially after his two older sisters had succumbed to the disease in the early 1920s.

It was his stubbornness that had brought Lincoln to Waverly, despite the pleas from his mother to stay away, not to run into the lion's den and chase the beast responsible for wiping out half of their family. His mother had told him numerous times that he had no medical training. "Don't go looking for it. It'll kill you like it killed your sisters." But that didn't matter to Lincoln, and it didn't stop him from marching up the hillside one April morning in 1926 with a bag in each hand, prepared for the long haul. And when Dr. Henry Waters had stopped him in the lobby to ask if he needed to be checked in, confusing him for a new patient, Lincoln had said calmly, "No, sir, but I'm a volunteer ready to go to war."

Wolfgang had heard the story of Lincoln's arrival from Dr. Waters, and they'd both admired the boy's grit, immediately feeling at ease with his sense of humor. Months later, they invited him to Dr. Waters's cottage for a game of cards. Just before shuffling the virgin deck, Lincoln pulled a bottle of brandy from his bag. With a cautious look, he said, "You two aren't prohibitionists, are you?"

To which Dr. Waters replied, "We're Catholic. I'll get the glasses. You start pouring."

So far, and for no reason other than luck and sheer willpower, Lincoln had managed to keep the white death from entering his body. He'd never had a positive x-ray in nearly four years of labor on the hillside, and the staff was checked every year.

Wolfgang stood beside Mr. Jenkins's coffin, careful not to look Lincoln in the eyes and invite a deeper discussion of last night's incident with Marlene on the porch. Wolfgang touched the top of the coffin and imagined Mr. Jenkins inside, resting peacefully, eyes closed, the harmonica in his grip, his hair neatly combed for the trip downward.

A few months ago, in the beginning of October, Wolfgang had stopped at the doorway of the morgue. Lincoln was crying. Maybe not crying, but sniffling. He was working on a male patient he'd befriended at the beginning of the summer. Wolfgang saw the black comb in Lincoln's hand and how carefully his young assistant was dividing the part on the left side of the dead man's hair. Wolfgang left him alone, for the interruption would have embarrassed him. Only he knew that Lincoln combed the hair of each and every victim, male or female, before their final descent from Waverly down the chute.

Wolfgang motioned the sign of the cross over the wooden box and then whispered a quick prayer for Mr. Jenkins.

They sat silent for a moment before Lincoln burst out with laughter.

"What's so funny?" asked Wolfgang.

Lincoln tapped the top of the coffin. "I sent Mr. Jenkins down twenty minutes ago. You just blessed our newest shipment of alcohol." Lincoln arched his fingers under the lid and pried it open. It creaked and wood splinters fell to the concrete floor. Bottles of bourbon, wine, and beer rested in pockets of hay. "Want one?"

"No…not now," stammered Wolfgang.

"Haven't you ever wondered how I got the booze in here? Your extra wine?"

"I gave up on the notion long ago, Lincoln," said Wolfgang. "This isn't going to help my inability to sleep, you know."

Lincoln sat back down and patted Wolfgang's knee. He stared

down the dark chute for a moment. "I know it was my choice to work here, Wolf, but it don't change the fact that sometimes I feel like a prisoner."

"You're not alone in that regard."

Lincoln let out a quick laugh. "You know what I'm craving?"

"What?"

Lincoln stared at the coffin. "A Hot Brown from the Brown Hotel."

"That does sound good," said Wolfgang. "Rose and I had one when they first started making them."

"Open-faced with that turkey." Lincoln's eyes grew large. "Cheese and bacon under the broiler. And that special sauce."

"Mornay." Wolfgang laughed. "Rose tried making her own."

"And?"

"I told her I loved it." Wolfgang grinned as he reminisced. "But it was pretty bad." He chewed on the memories for a moment. "Did you find a bundle of letters in Mr. Jenkins's room? I promised I'd get them to his daughter."

Lincoln stood. "His stuff's in a locker. Barker wanted his room cleaned out right away. Someone else is already moving in."

During his morning rounds, Wolfgang managed to scratch off over half of the morning's request list, with most of the tunes requiring the violin. By noon his right shoulder hurt from all the playing, but he was determined to finish the list by the end of his shift, which he was able to do most every day, even if he had to abbreviate many of the requests.

He took a break at noon to meet the farm boy and *Othello* star in the chapel to go over how to make communion bread. A budding thespian Jesse was not, according to those who had seen him in the morning on stage. Word had made it back to Wolfgang within ten minutes after the shortened play. He'd missed his lines. His timing was impeccably bad. He overacted. But he apparently had fun doing it, and the crowd of tuberculosis patients had been amused. The tragedy had been turned into a comedy of sorts. And was that not the entire purpose, Wolfgang thought, to be entertained? He regretted not seeing Jesse live on stage.

He found Jesse hunched over the altar, staring down at a piece of paper, as if trying to read. He looked up, startled, as Wolfgang approached.

"What do you have there, Jesse?"

Jesse handed him the note. Wolfgang read what had been printed in blank ink: *We know about the alcohol, Father. This Klan hangs bootleggers from trees.*

Wolfgang looked up. "Where did you get this?"

Jesse pointed to the altar. "On top there. It was weighted down by the rope when I come in."

Wolfgang lifted the thick rope, which had been tied into a noose.

"Somethin' wrong, Doctor?"

Wolfgang placed the noose back on the altar and shoved the note into the pocket of his white coat. "No," he lied. "Everything is fine. Let's start with the bread, shall we?"

Jesse seemed eager to learn, although all Wolfgang would let him do was watch. He couldn't allow a TB patient to handle bread that would at some point make it into the mouths of other TB patients. Wolfgang worked quickly because he was preoccupied: he was thinking about the note and about his plans for McVain after his shift was over.

Jesse watched from a safe distance with a goofy smile on his face as Wolfgang demonstrated how to warm the honey and mix it into the dry ingredients. He explained how long to bake it, how to cut a cross into it, how many pieces to break it into, and how to refrigerate some and store the rest in the freezer. How to take his time and not rush. And how to do it all with a pleasant smile because the Lord would be watching him prepare the very bread that would be consecrated into the body of Christ.

As Wolfgang worked on the bread, Jesse was full of questions. Yes, the abbot was in charge of the abbey, and the monks taught the classes, and there were priests and brothers, and, yes, I'd be happy to take you there once you get out of Waverly, Jesse.

Wolfgang left Jesse to clean up the mess, which he began to do with the same goofy smile. *God love 'em*, Wolfgang thought as he'd hurried up to the fourth-floor solarium to find McVain resting with his eyes open.

Wolfgang sat by his side, gazing out at those same trees, as if having the same focal point would help him tap into McVain's thoughts. *If I can't coax him into a conversation*, Wolfgang thought, *maybe I can bore him into it.* So ten minutes of meaningless—unanswered— questions soon turned into a droning monologue about his Edison records and the new blue cylinders that held four minutes instead of two, leaving McVain on the verge of sleep, or perhaps it was nausea.

Wolfgang continued on. "I'm sorry you have tuberculosis, but Waverly is the place to be if you've got it. You know thousands are traveling to the Arizona desert for the sunshine and dry air. Pitching tents and building cabins. They're calling them 'lungers.' But they underestimate the heat out west. Be glad you are here."

McVain wasn't amused. His eyes were nearly closed.

"You used to play the piano, didn't you?"

McVain flinched slightly. He attempted to hide his mangled left hand beneath the sheets. He closed his eyes.

"My father played the piano. He loved Mozart." Wolfgang watched him for a reaction. "Maybe we should start over. No mud to push me into this time."

McVain opened his eyes and coughed into his hand. Then he resumed his gaze out toward the trees.

"I saw your fingers last night." Wolfgang shifted on his seat and leaned forward with his elbows on his knees. "They moved as if you were playing the piano."

McVain clenched his jaw.

"I know I shouldn't have been prying, but, look, I consider myself a composer. I'm working on a requiem." Wolfgang folded his hands. "It started out as a simple Catholic funeral Mass, but I've begun to expand it and make it grander. It'll be a concert requiem. I have a full orchestra with piano in mind. And wonderful singers." He leaned back and straightened his lab coat.

McVain's eyes never wavered from the woods.

"I could use your opinion, Mr. McVain. I've come into a bit of trouble, you see, and I can't seem to finish it with an ending it deserves. It all ends up in my garbage can or wadded up on my floor. Would you like to see it?"

McVain's fist struck Wolfgang across the right side of his jaw. It caught Wolfgang totally off guard—he'd never been in a physical altercation in his life and was slow to react. Wolfgang rocked back. His chair toppled. He landed on his side and rolled to his knees, feeling for missing teeth. They all seemed to be in place, but his jaw felt numb.

Several patients leaned up from their beds but were apparently too shocked to say anything. They stared. McVain grinned and looked back out toward the trees again.

Wolfgang wiped his mouth with the top of his hand and it came back with a smear of blood on it. "So you *can* smile."

McVain said nothing.

"TB hasn't ruined that." Wolfgang backed away. *You stubborn ass,* he almost said.

A grin spread across McVain's face. "Possum-eatin'" was what Wolfgang's mother would have called that look. He waited, then turned and left McVain alone, touching his sore jaw as he hobbled away.

CHAPTER 9

Wolfgang waited until most of the patients were asleep and Dr. Barker had walked the trail to his own cottage shortly after ten o'clock. His plan would not be deterred tonight, despite the headache and bruised jaw McVain's fist had given him earlier in the day. The cut on his lower lip had formed a healthy scab that felt twice as big as Susannah said it really was.

Susannah followed Wolfgang into McVain's dark room, where the cantankerous man snored like a hibernating bear. "I don't know about this, Wolf."

Wolfgang put a finger to his lips and then winced upon the touch. He stopped a few feet from McVain's parked bed. Luckily, Mr. Weaver was sleeping out on the porch, so they'd have plenty of room.

"Barker will fire us," she whispered.

"He'll fire me." Wolfgang winked. "I made you help me, okay?"

Susannah rolled her eyes and mumbled under her breath. "You don't *make* me do anything, Wolfgang Pike."

"Why don't you ever call me Father, like some of the others?" He said it without looking at her.

She brushed past him and headed toward the foot of McVain's bed. "Let's get this over with."

Wolfgang rolled a wheelchair next to McVain's bed. Weaver had told him that McVain was a solid sleeper, so Wolfgang hoped he was right. He snaked his left arm under McVain's neck and locked his hand beneath the man's left armpit. McVain grunted but didn't awaken. Wolfgang did a silent count to three and nodded. He lifted McVain's torso while Susannah lifted his feet, and McVain continued snoring as they lowered him, as gently as they could, into the leather seat of the wheelchair. Suddenly McVain snorted awake, but by the time he was alert enough to understand that his doctor and nurse were indeed tying him to a wheelchair, it was too late.

"What…what shit is this?"

"He just spoke to you, Wolf," said Susannah, seemingly upbeat now that they'd gotten him locked in the chair.

"Quiet," Wolfgang said.

McVain wrestled against the makeshift restraints, grimaced, and then allowed his body to settle. He was too weak to fight.

Wolfgang rolled McVain from the room and out onto the crowded solarium porch, where Mr. Weaver lay asleep with one arm dangling. Susannah draped a shawl over McVain's shoulders, covering the restraints.

"Where in the hell are you taking me?"

"I can gag you if you like." Wolfgang plodded along, his foot hurting more the faster he moved, weaving behind and around the scattered beds, hoping no one called out for him. No musical requests or confessions tonight.

They made it to the elevators and down to the first floor without anyone seeing them. It wasn't as if Waverly were a prison, but Dr. Barker had made it clear that they weren't supposed to leave the hillside, and that went double for the patients. But they weren't taking McVain off the hillside anyway. Wolfgang's heart pounded as the wheels of the chair sped over the checkered tiles in the center of the hallway. He hadn't done anything this mischievous in years, not since Rose was alive, and he felt himself smiling. He dared Dr. Barker to show up now just as they were leaving. He imagined the confrontation. He imagined knocking his boss aside.

Susannah held the doors open. Wolfgang didn't break stride outside as the wheels sped from tile to concrete and then finally to grass. Moonlight lit the clearing. An owl hooted from a nearby tree. Bats circled the bell tower in a frenzy. Crossing the grassy knoll that rolled down toward the woods meant lots of bumps for McVain. His neck lolled. He grunted every time the wheelchair plummeted down from an exposed root. He moaned when the wheels slammed into and up every incline, and it only got bumpier in the woods, with the uneven ground of brambles, twigs, leaves, acorns, and deadfall. Susannah jumped ahead to kick away a few branches, and Wolfgang pushed as quickly as he could, knowing if he slowed his pace he might not be able to muster enough strength to get the wheelchair moving again. McVain was heavy.

Susannah straightened the shawl around McVain's shoulders. "I can't believe I'm doing this."

"Where are you taking me?"

"It was her idea," said Wolfgang.

Susannah slapped Wolfgang's shoulder. "Don't believe him."

McVain surveyed the trees and the darkness beyond. "You should be fired for this."

McVain was stronger than Wolfgang had thought, certainly stronger than a man with his condition should have been. He'd managed to wriggle his left arm free from the chair, flinging the shawl from his shoulders. From the lingering pain in Wolfgang's jaw and the spasms that shot up his cheek every time the wheelchair caused a jarring movement, he didn't know why he'd doubted McVain's strength. "Wherever the hell I'm going, I can walk there. Untie me, God damn it."

After a short hesitation, Wolfgang untied McVain's right arm. The patient nudged Wolfgang away before he had a chance to untie his ankles. McVain bent at the waist and worked on the ankle ropes. His fingers moved effortlessly, as if he'd escaped from restraints many times before. "So what happened to your leg?"

Wolfgang watched the top of McVain's head move. He finished with the ropes and then shot Wolfgang a glance. "Well?"

"Well what?"

"What happened to your leg?" asked McVain. "You walk like a three-legged mule."

"Polio," Wolfgang said. "When I was eight."

McVain didn't seem to care. He stood from the wheelchair,

stumbled as if drunk, which triggered a tiny squeal of panic from Susannah, and then righted himself against the trunk of an oak tree. He straightened his pajamas and ran his left hand through his orange hair. Wolfgang thought it amusing that he'd used the hand with the missing fingers for such a duty.

"What's so funny?" asked McVain, running his maimed hand through his hair again.

"Must be like raking leaves with a pitchfork."

"What the hell are you talking about?" McVain looked up the hillside. The rooftop and bell tower of the sanatorium were visible between the swaying tree limbs. "Never thought I'd get kidnapped from a TB hospital in the middle of the night."

Susannah walked by his side, but not too close. "Consider it a field trip."

McVain gave Susannah an angry sneer. "Do I scare you, doll face?"

"It's Susannah, and no, you don't scare me, Mr. McVain."

"Didn't I warn you about calling me Mister?"

She giggled. "Sorry. It's just a habit when I speak to my elders."

McVain called up to Wolfgang. "Where did you get this mouthy broad?"

"Gift from God, I'm afraid." Wolfgang pushed the empty wheelchair, and McVain and Susannah followed. McVain kicked various rocks down the hill like a kid would probably do, and he walked with his hands in the pockets of his pajamas. He looked up when they neared Wolfgang's cottage. The lone window on the side of the house glowed with a fiery warmth not found in the hospital.

Wolfgang extended his arm. "Shall we go inside?"

Susannah gripped McVain's elbow and walked him inside. McVain didn't pull away from her touch. Wolfgang lit several candles to go along with the snapping flames in the fireplace. It was warm and the windows were steamed.

"No electricity?" asked McVain.

Wolfgang lit a candle above the fireplace and caught a glimpse of Susannah's right wrist, which had a purple ring around it. "Where'd you get the bruise?"

Susannah looked at Wolfgang. "Where did you get yours?"

Wolfgang touched his jaw and nodded toward McVain, who now wore a smirk on his face. "You're dodging my question. Your bruise?"

Susannah pulled her sleeve down to cover it. "It's nothing."

"It doesn't look like nothing."

"It happened this morning." She shook her head. "I was up on the rooftop. Something spooked Herman. I tried to calm him and he grabbed me. No big deal."

"Who's Herman?" McVain asked.

Susannah and Nurse Rita had the unfortunate job of tending to the mental patients daily, and Herman was a loose cannon inside Room 502. Susannah could hold her own with most men, but Herman was twice her size.

"Was this the first time he touched you?"

"Who the hell is Herman?" McVain asked again.

"I'll be fine." She walked McVain deeper into the room and stood beside him in the center of Wolfgang's dwelling area—piano to the east, bed to the south, couch and fireplace to the west and kitchen to the north. She turned toward McVain. "He prefers candlelight to electricity. Which is probably why his eyesight is going bad. But it's all part of the nostalgia. Right, Wolf?"

"All part of the freak show," said McVain. "I half expect to hear some Gregorian chant coming from the dark corners of this cave."

"He told you about his cylinder collection?" asked Susannah.

"Nearly fell asleep." McVain finally pulled from Susannah's grip. "What am I doing here? I want to go back."

"And do what, McVain?" Wolfgang asked. "Sleep? Rest like you've been doing for the past month? Go back to ignoring your doctor?"

"Ain't the doctor part I got a problem with, Padre."

Wolfgang could tell he'd seen the piano but was purposely avoiding it. Wolfgang placed a candle on top of the instrument, highlighting the rose beside it.

"This some kind of joke?" asked McVain.

"Therapy," said Susannah. "Therapy we think will do you more good than rest and fresh air."

Wolfgang held up a finger. "A happy McVain would do us all a favor."

"Breeze off, priest." McVain turned away from the piano and headed for the door.

Susannah blocked his path and stood rigid, her arms folded. "Please stay." Her voice quivered, but she didn't budge.

McVain clenched his jaw. "I hate both of you. You know that?"

"We can discuss your anger in confession," Wolfgang said. "But don't hate the music."

Wolfgang propped a few sheets of music on the piano, sat down and began playing a Mozart piano sonata. He stopped and glanced over his shoulder at McVain, who looked sad and angry at the same time. His red hair was aflame in the candlelight, his deep-set green eyes rested in pockets of darkness. Wolfgang rose from the piano, urging McVain on with his eyes.

Slowly, McVain walked through patches of shadow and light, approaching with small, shuffled steps. Wolfgang watched him sit and wondered how long the man had repressed this. McVain coughed. He straightened his back and stretched his fingers. He touched a low key with the pinkie on his left hand. When the sound faded, he struck another key with his left thumb. Again he waited until the sound faded. He looked at the music and began to play. He hit a few clunkers and stopped. "Needs tuning," he said.

"Keep going," Susannah said.

"I'm missing three of my fucking fingers, Miss Susannah." McVain continued to face the piano. His shoulders relaxed. His tone softened. "I just can't hit the right keys."

Wolfgang stepped into light that shrouded the piano. "Then the remaining two fingers will have to work that much harder." Now that Wolfgang had heard McVain's talent, it made him more persistent. "Please, keep playing."

McVain focused on the piano again. He played for ten seconds and then messed up. He played again. The fingers on his right hand flowed over the keys, gentle yet demanding, and he milked every note and tone. But his left hand lumbered, stiff and plodding, his wrist at the wrong angle. Tight. Wolfgang's father would have hit him atop the hand with a violin bow for such technique, but Wolfgang could empathize with McVain's difficulty. He needed to learn how to adapt.

Wolfgang tapped the sheet music. "Mozart's piano sonata in C minor."

"I know what it is." McVain pushed the music to the floor. "I don't need this." His hands hovered above the keys at the center of the piano. First the right one dropped softly, then the left. He played, but the left hand lost pace quickly again. He stared silently at the keys.

"Try to make the adjustment," said Wolfgang.

McVain raised both hands and brought them down as fists, hard. "How's that? Huh?" He banged against the keys again and again, looking over his shoulder, his anger focused on Wolfgang. "How's this adjustment?" Bang. Bang. The shrill sound of the keys was painful. Across the room, Susannah winced. Bang. Bang. Bang. McVain stood and faced his two kidnappers. "I'm tired. I'm ready to go back now."

"But—" Susannah started.

"I'm ready to go back!"

"Yes, of course." Wolfgang's skin tingled. "But if I may ask, how long has it been since you've played?"

"Over ten years." McVain looked to the floor. "Not since the war."

CHAPTER 10

Wolfgang had filled the bathtub so high, even the slightest of movements sent water trickling over the lip onto the bathroom floor. He wanted nothing more than to soak his weary bones after the outing with McVain. He rested against the edge of the tub, doing his best to stay still as the water sloshed over his body. A sliver of moonlight found its way through the trees outside into the bathroom.

Wolfgang's first vivid memory of his childhood was of a bath. He had been five years old. He'd accidentally knocked Charles Pike's latest fugue from the Llewellyn piano, scattering the pages to the floor and completely out of order. When he took off running, he tripped on one of the house's numerous throw rugs and banged his face on a dining room chair. That he didn't remember. His father's screaming voice he remembered, as well as the bath his mother had given him to calm him down.

Wolfgang still remembered the feeling of sitting naked in the tepid water, shivering, his teeth chattering. He sat with his legs drawn in and his knees upright, his lowered chin resting on bony knees. He stared below at his penis as it buoyed in the water, not wanting to look anywhere else but down. He needed to pee but didn't want to get out of the tub. The blood from his nose hit the water in red swirls, spreading out between his thighs. His nose throbbed. On the corner of the sink was the Bible. His mother had read from it while the bath water was running. Her voice blended in with his father's ranting from the other room, and the combination made him want to cry even more.

His mother, Doris, hovered above, leaning so far over the side of the tub that her long red hair grazed the water. Her nightgown hung loosely from her body. Her barely concealed breasts drooped inches from his face, hanging in the folds of that nightgown he'd become so accustomed to smelling every morning when she'd hug him. She plunged the washrag into the bath water, squeezing it and wetting his hair, rinsing it free of suds. She washed his back, humming one of her made-up tunes.

She always hummed after one of his father's tirades; they never spoke about it, but the melody was her way of calming Wolfgang. She would smile for him, too, but behind the smile there was sadness. Even at age five, he'd known.

Louisville's Central Park, designed by the famed architect Frederick Law Olmsted, the same man who designed New York City's Central Park, rested on seventeen acres that included a colonnade, a wading pool, and walking trails. Wolfgang's childhood home rested on the outskirts of the park. It was a two-story structure with stucco siding, a steep roof, and arched doorways. To Wolfgang, it looked almost like a medieval cottage from a fairy tale, especially the small dormer windows and the brick chimney rising above the roof. Wood dominated the interior of the house: the old flooring, with its whorls, splintered planks, and tiny holes and cracks, most of which Doris had covered with various throw rugs. The wall separating Wolfgang's bedroom from his parents' was wood as well.

Every sound and smell carried throughout the house—bacon frying in the morning, potato soup in the evening, and most certainly the sound of his father's music. The sound of the Bach and Beethoven fugues from one of his eight violins, Mozart resonating from the piano, and Charles's own creations on the clarinet and flute. These were the two constants of Wolfgang's early life: his father's music, which, like his father, could go from soft to raging in a matter of seconds; and then his mother's humming, always dependable, always calm.

Wolfgang had pieced together his parents' history as he grew older, though they rarely talked about the past. Doris Pike was a pretty woman, slight of build and twenty years of age when she'd given birth to her only son in the winter of 1898. Charles cried the first time he held his newborn boy and immediately named him Wolfgang after his favorite composer. "He held you for ten minutes, rocking you, playing with your fingers, so tiny!" Doris had told him once.

But then, as babies do, Wolfgang started crying.

"Stop that," Charles told him. "Stop that sound." Wolfgang continued to cry. Charles glanced over his shoulder toward his wife. "Why does he do this? I don't understand. I've done nothing to him…." Wolfgang began wailing. Charles stood, on the verge of dropping the newborn baby, and placed him on the bed beside Doris. "Here, you take him." And then he wiped his hands on his slacks and exited the hospital room.

When Charles did hold Wolfgang as a baby, he'd hand him off as soon as the crying started. He just couldn't take it. He'd walk around the house with his hands over his ears, and many times, he'd open the front door and leave them alone. Doris would never admit as much, even when Wolfgang pressed her, but he imagined how his father must have raged when Wolfgang cried at night.

Wolfgang had never seen his mother cry in front of them. She only cried behind closed doors, alone in their bedroom when no one was watching. After Wolfgang was born, Charles often left them alone at night. He became consumed with his new membership at the Pendennis Club, the city's prestigious men's social establishment. Every Monday and Wednesday night, he'd told Doris he was going to have drinks with colleagues at the club on Walnut Street. He even mentioned their names, how they'd play cards and smoke pipes and cigars and talk politics. He was moving up that social ladder. He was going places. But his apparent success left her feeling alone and vulnerable, because it brought with it a coldness between them, colder than before their child was born.

At night, Wolfgang would spy on his parents through the hole in his bedroom wall. He would spy on both of them while they were in bed, his mother reading while Charles wrote his compositions, his inkwell placed carefully in the folds of the unmade bed. On most nights they were silent. Not a single word passed between them. Occasionally Doris would look up from her book and watch Charles write, but Charles was too involved in his own world to look up. She'd return to her book, and all Wolfgang heard through the wall would be the turning of her pages and the scribbling of his pen.

But on other nights his father was different. As Wolfgang grew older he realized those nights coincided with the ending of whatever his father had been writing. Those nights made Wolfgang smile. If his father ever found out he'd been spying, oh, what trouble he'd be in—but he couldn't help himself. It was part of the thrill, the fun, the danger. He'd lie on his stomach, prop his elbows atop his stacked pillows, and peer through the hole in the wall. Some nights, Wolfgang watched his father lovingly hold his mother as they danced along the limited floor space of their bedroom—from the bed to the dresser, from the dresser to the bathroom door, and then back to the bed—moving to a rhythm Charles would hum, smiling as he'd clutch her small hands and hold her close. The sound of their feet shuffling across the dusty floorboards always stayed with Wolfgang, as would his mother's giggle.

Charles was tall with a thick chest, strong forearms, and a head of black hair always worn pulled back from his forehead. He had large, droopy ears like an elephant. His eyes were magnified by dark, bushy eyebrows that hung wildly above them. Charles always dressed in a suit, morning, day, and night, changing only before bedtime. When they danced, Doris came up to his chest. Often Charles rested his head atop hers. Some nights they would laugh. When his father tickled his mother, Wolfgang always sprang back. At that point, even he knew his secret spying must stop. He'd rush to bed and clasp his hands over his ears until the grunting ceased.

But most nights it was silence.

The Light of Christ Church was only a few blocks from their home, and they attended as a family three times a week. His mother often prayed with her eyes closed. Wolfgang knew she wasn't asleep only because her lips moved. His father prayed so loudly during the services, it was as if he was trying to pray over Minister Ford, who was pretty boisterous himself. In hindsight, Wolfgang realized that his father probably thought he could out-preach Minister Ford. Probably figured he could do it louder and more clearly than the robust man in suspenders. One Sunday, Charles had leaned down during the service and whispered to Wolfgang, "I don't think he's saving as many souls as he thinks he is." He looked out the window. "The city is teeming with heathen Catholics badly in need of saving. That's who he needs to be preaching to."

Wolfgang always sat in between his parents; one loud, the other silent. He liked going to the weekly services because, unlike at home, Charles was engaged in what was going on at church, and thus his moods were much more predictable. And there was something about hearing Minister Ford's voice reading the scripture that made Wolfgang feel safe. Minister Ford might not have been saving enough souls to make Charles happy, but the deep pitch of his voice never failed to draw Wolfgang into the scripture, even at a young age. When most of the other kids his age were daydreaming or sleeping during the service, Wolfgang was focused on the words. And when the congregation wasn't praying from the Bible, they were praying through music. Wolfgang liked the purple robes of the choir, and he one day envisioned singing with them. By age seven he not only wanted to sing with the choir, but he also imagined himself leading them. And he wouldn't have minded touching those giant organ pipes while he was at it.

One Sunday, while they walked home from church, Wolfgang asked his father about singing with the choir.

But of course Charles Pike only laughed. It was Wolfgang's opinion that his father tried to out-pray Minister Ford, but it was *everyone's* opinion that Charles Pike thought himself better than the choir leader and that he was too good for the job.

Charles was a musician and composer, and though Wolfgang loved the music he played throughout the house, he realized as he grew older that his father was a frustrated man: never quite good enough, apparently, to make a living with his art. Instead, he spent his days working for Henry Pilcher & Sons, manufacturing pianos and other musical instruments. "Just until my career takes off," he always said, promising Doris repeatedly that one day they would move to Vienna to open his music store, one of his many dreams. But the local venues he booked somehow never translated into bigger opportunities. It wasn't him, Charles would mutter, it was them. They were all fools. They were simply not on his level. When he was denied a spot in the Louisville Quintet Club, he raged at Doris about the hack who was chosen instead. When the Philharmonic Orchestra did not call him back after his third, his fifth, his tenth audition, he blamed everyone but himself.

Wolfgang knew it wasn't for lack of talent; his father was a man with brilliant ideas. To a boy like Wolfgang, his father's music could certainly rival Mozart and Beethoven! But even Wolfgang could see his father was often his own worst enemy. His intensity was off-putting at best, frightening at worst. So there Charles's brilliance stayed, buried deeply.

He'd drink more, and the more he drank, the more distant he seemed to get. And paranoid. The curtains over the downstairs windows were always closed, but Charles would peek out numerous times each night. At least twice every hour, he'd walk away from his writing, push the curtain aside, and watch the dark street. When Wolfgang was seven, he asked, "Is someone coming over, Daddy?"

"I don't know, Wolfgang."

"Then why do you keep looking out the windows?"

Charles knelt down and placed his hands on his son's shoulders. "You never know if someone will come by and steal your ideas."

"How can somebody steal your ideas?"

Charles returned to the piano. "Go to your room and read the Bible, Wolfgang. The King James Bible will explain how stealing is a sin."

Charles evidently didn't see lying as a sin. He'd been telling lies for years, lies about why he was excluded from certain orchestras, why his work wasn't being performed, and his most incredible lie: his membership at the Pendennis Club.

One winter evening when Wolfgang was six, Doris bundled Wolfgang in a coat and scarf, and they followed far behind Charles as he strolled along the downtown streets, wandering aimlessly in and out of the fuzzy glow of scattered lampposts. His arms moved as he walked, conducting to tunes in his head. But when he turned on Walnut Street, he passed the Pendennis Club, stopping in the middle of the street to stare up toward the lit rooms of the mansion, where shadows passed like phantoms. He continued on toward Green Street, where he didn't even look up when propositioned by two ladies. That street was full of women, and Doris attempted to shield Wolfgang's eyes from most of them, though he couldn't quite understand why. Meanwhile, Charles continued without hesitation. He entered an establishment called the Baroque, a two-story brick building, and sat at a table next to the foggy front window and ordered a drink as if he'd been doing it every Monday night for years.

"I knew it," Wolfgang's mother had muttered. Then she looked down at her son and smiled, as if everything was just fine. "Wolfgang, I don't believe your father is ever telling the truth. Do remember this evening." They stood there for a few moments, Doris peering into the Baroque as the men played cards and dice, as Charles drank alone.

Then she turned and led Wolfgang home.

Every evening, Wolfgang got down on the floor of his bedroom. On his hands and knees, he pulled back the woven throw rug and peered through the cracks in the planks. The living room was directly below. It was his father's work area, his life earnings saved in the form of music. Musical instruments were scattered everywhere like discarded clothing—a piano against one wall, his eight violins sitting like little children across the cushions of the couch, two cellos propped against another wall, a trombone resting on the seat of a straight-backed reading chair, two clarinets and three flutes in the middle of the floor, and a piccolo atop the piano next to three lit candles and his well of ink. Atop his podium sat his latest symphony or fugue, his latest opera or requiem, all weighted down by a harmonica he'd play when all else failed.

From the crack above, Wolfgang watched his father. Charles dipped the quill of his pen into the ink and carefully scrawled notes on the page, starting and stopping abruptly, then placed the pen sideways between his teeth and lifted one of his violins to play. He waved the bow of his violin like a sword, facing imaginary attackers, frustrated, happy, or drunk. During these times, Doris stayed in the kitchen or read in her bedroom as her husband shuffled around the cluttered floor, pulling and pushing the bow at every conceivable angle against the taut violin strings, sweating profusely, strands of hair coming undone from his braid and dangling over his unblinking eyes, his face red with strain. The face of a crazed man, Wolfgang had thought.

But that was also why Wolfgang loved his father. He was a man of such passion. His father had given him music! The vibrations of the stringed instruments as they'd hum through the floor like a current; the sound of the piano keys under his father's delicate fingertips, flowing like honey; the clarinet reverberating off every nook of the house. Despite all the letdowns he'd experienced, Charles never failed to get excited when he finished scribbling down yet another row of notes he believed would carry him to greatness. Pages still locked in his hands, he would hurry upstairs to find his wife and son.

"Doris… Wolfgang…" He'd scurry from room to room until he located them. "I've got it. This is the one. You have to come and listen."

Those were the evenings when a smile and giggle would return to his mother's face. Life surged to her cheeks, and her eyes would glow as she and Wolfgang sat on the couch, waiting eagerly as Charles readied his violin or straightened his posture at the piano. He winked and smiled at them. "You ready? Here it goes." No matter what it sounded like, they applauded. Charles stood and bowed and waved to the vast imaginary crowd around them.

"Well, is it not brilliant, Wolfgang?"

"It is brilliant, Father." Then he would hug Charles around the waist and Charles would ruffle his hair. They would laugh and dream, and soon, just like his father, the music consumed Wolfgang too. Soon he couldn't live without it. He spent most of his early childhood indoors, learning how to play all the instruments. He understood that the same passion that caused the sadness and silence in the house also caused the happiness in his heart. Without the music, he would have been lost.

Every day when Charles returned from the factory, Wolfgang begged for a lesson on one of the instruments. Most days his father obliged, working with him on the piano and violin until dinner. They were the only times he could remember his father allowing him to sit close. "Here, Wolfgang," Charles would say, placing his hands over Wolfgang's on the piano. "Like this." Or "Stronger, Wolfgang," gently prodding Wolfgang's shoulder as he held the violin. "Feel it there," Charles said, rubbing his son's throat, as Wolfgang tackled the harmonica.

So music became Wolfgang's life, the invisible bond with his father, until a few weeks before Wolfgang's eighth birthday, when Charles Pike was killed. And Wolfgang saw it all through the hole in his bedroom wall.

Second Movement

Andante moderato

CHAPTER 11

Wolfgang slept through the night. His body was exhausted from wheeling McVain out of the sanatorium and down the hillside. He dreamt of the small ensemble he had started in his later years at Saint Meinrad, up in the choir loft of the abbey church with three other students. One of them had played the flute, and as he slept he could hear the sound resonating as clearly as if he'd journeyed back in time. His eyes didn't open until after the sun rose over the trees and the sound of music woke him up.

At first he assumed it was the birds, but it sounded more like... a flute?

Wolfgang tossed the covers aside. He felt the erection before he saw it. He reluctantly looked down and immediately wondered what kind of dream the flute had lured him from. Glimpses of Marlene's breast teased him again.

With Rose dead, he'd been determined to focus on the Lord and his patients. But he was also a man, and a doctor at that, who knew there were urges that couldn't just be turned off like a faucet. All the more reason to remain strong in his vows to the Church and to his music. Wolfgang forced himself from the bed and thought about birds, food, music, God—anything but.

He rubbed his eyes. The flute continued. He slipped on his bathrobe and stepped outside into the cool morning. The flute music was louder and clearer.

Where was it coming from? Whoever was playing had talent, he thought. He surveyed the woods and eyed a cluster of squirrels as they sprinted down the hill, falling over one another and crisscrossing seamlessly around the trees.

Susannah came walking around the corner wearing a long brown coat. He looked over his shoulder and did a double take before realizing what time it must have been. She giggled. "That's what you're wearing to work now?"

Wolfgang pulled the lapels of his robe together. "Do you hear the music?" He pointed down the hill where portions of the colored hospital were visible through the naked trees. "It's a flute."

Susannah folded her arms. "Someone's been playing for an hour now. Come on. We're going to be late. Get dressed. And please do something with that hair."

Outside, near the tree line, the combination of wind and damp hair made Wolfgang's skull feel like an icy ball, but his brain was full of optimism. The sound of the flute reminded him of Dr. Waters, and specifically what he'd said days before his death, something about never seeing where Wolfgang's music would take him. Wolfgang's pace quickened. Susannah had to hurry to keep up with him, and then suddenly Wolfgang stopped.

"What would you think if I formed an orchestra here?"

She looked up through the trees. "At Waverly?"

"We have a theater," he said. "Why not a music program?"

"Anyone can pretend to act, Wolf, but unskilled music is just painful noise."

"Maybe not a full orchestra..." He continued walking. "Never mind."

"No, tell me."

"What if I taught the patients to play? And sing?"

Susannah looked amused. "A choir and an orchestra, here? This isn't Carnegie Hall. They're too tired, Wolf. They lack the energy."

"Not all. And some of them already know how," he said.

Susannah sidestepped a narrow dip in the ground where water had collected in a puddle. "Is this because of McVain?"

"No." He walked for a moment in silence, staring at his shoes, and then his chin popped up again. "But watching McVain last night, it sparked ideas."

"I like the idea," she said, "but Barker won't."

"At Saint Meinrad, the only instrument we had during Mass was the organ. All that room up in the choir lofts and only one organ- ist. I convinced the monks to allow me to play the violin, and they allowed it."

"But this is a hospital, Wolf, not an abbey."

"A few months later another student volunteered to play the clarinet with us. And then another with the flute. Soon the choir loft was alive with music. I want to do the same here. I'll handle Barker. I just need to get McVain."

Big Fifteen made his way toward them, maneuvering his cart while he popped something into his mouth. He chewed. He passed right through the steam wafting up from his covered food, inhaling it as he angled the cart downward. "We got sausage this morning, Boss. Want one?"

Wolfgang waved. "I'll wait, thank you."

Susannah stepped away from them. "I'll meet you inside."

Wolfgang nodded and then approached Big Fifteen. "I heard music coming from the colored hospital this morning. A flute."

Big Fifteen eyed Susannah as she reached the entrance portico and entered the sanatorium. "Heard it m'self, Boss."

"Who is it?"

"New patient, I reckon. Group of 'em come in yesterday."

"Could you get a name for me?"

"Sure could try."

Wolfgang patted his shoulder, lifted the towel from the cart, and grabbed a piece of sausage. He half jogged up the lawn toward the sanatorium, crazy notions flirting with his mind.

Only eleven patients attended Wolfgang's early Mass that morn- ing, and he even found himself pushing his own heart to focus on the homily. He couldn't get the flute out of his head.

After Mass, he was summoned to Dr. Barker's office. Nurse Marlene, of all people, had been sent by Dr. Barker into the chapel to get Wolfgang. He'd managed to avoid looking directly at her when she'd spoken to him. Foolishly he'd stared at her white shoes and shapely calves, and then her bare knees just below the bottom of her skirt. Finally he turned away, as if something else had caught his attention. He'd thanked her and she'd moved on.

Wolfgang knocked on the large pane of frosted glass inside Dr. Barker's office door. After knocking a third time, Barker invited him in.

Dr. Barker's gaze remained on a set of files spread out atop his cluttered desk. A toothpick danced across his teeth. He looked up at Wolfgang and said nothing. He just sat there, gnawing on the toothpick. Then he said, "I warned you, Doctor."

"Sir?"

Dr. Barker leaned forward. "I know what you did last night. You took a patient out of this hospital. A highly contagious patient. You deliberately—"

"I brought him back, sir."

"This isn't a joke." He took the toothpick from his lips and tossed it into the trash can. "What kind of doctor acts this way?" He smirked. "Or is this the action of a priest? Deception?"

Wolfgang moved closer, placed his black bag of instruments on the corner of Dr. Barker's desk, and sat down in a chair opposite Barker's. "I'd call it more of a revelation. McVain's speaking to me now."

Dr. Barker pursed his lips, ran his hands through his hair, and sighed. "He's been speaking to the rest of the patients for days now. They love him because he was in the war. It's not as if you had a sudden breakthrough."

Wolfgang remained silent.

"They need rest," Dr. Barker said, his tone rising a bit. "They need fresh air. They don't need to be walking through the woods in the middle of the night in the dead of winter." He stood from his chair and leaned with splayed fingers on his desk. "You're too friendly with the patients. Too lax with our rules."

Wolfgang stood with him, eye to eye. "This isn't a prison. And I'm searching for other options besides our medicine. I'm sorry if you don't understand—"

"I understand music, Wolfgang." Dr. Barker lifted Wolfgang's bag of instruments and tossed them into Wolfgang's lap. "Don't tell me—"

"Then why do you keep fighting me?" Wolfgang leaned forward. "Henry believed in what I'm doing."

"Henry is no longer with us." Dr. Barker walked around his desk. "This disease is killing more people than we lost in Europe during the Great War. Five years ago Waverly Hills was a two-story wooden building. The overflow slept in tents. And now we have this grand place. But even still, half of our schools have vacant seats. Churches are empty." He pointed out the window, in the vague direction of Louisville. "People are afraid to leave their homes. They think the white wind is going to come down and infect them. My wife is afraid to be around me."

"Music can be contagious too. It—"

Barker rubbed his eyes impatiently. "Don't speak to me of music, Wolfgang. Not until you can speak to me of a cure."

"I'm closer to a cure than you, sir." Wolfgang spun away and stepped out into the hallway, where he found Susannah, most assuredly listening to the entire conversation.

"I'm on my way upstairs," she said softly because Barker's door was still open.

"To check on Herman?"

"And the others."

"I'm going with you."

"It's not necessary, Wolf."

The bruise on her wrist was lurid in the morning light. "Yes, it is."

At times, the wind on the rooftop was enough to knock over a well-balanced man. Wolfgang and his deformed foot managed to stay righted as he followed Susannah. His lab coat rippled in loud snaps. Susannah held on to her cap as she walked across the graveled roof and then onto the terra cotta tiles where most of the heliotherapy patients spent their time in the sun. Farther down the rooftop, inside the nurses' station and bell tower, Herman's bellow carried from the open windows of Room 502.

"I want my cakes! Give me my cakes!"

"I wonder what's got him wound up." Susannah approached a group of men lying on lounge chairs. Three of them, despite the thirty-degree temperature, sat with their sleeves rolled up to their shoulders, their skin absorbing the sun's rays, which, at the moment, remained hidden behind a cluster of puffy white clouds. The men looked up politely. A thin man with sunburned shoulders nodded toward Wolfgang. "Morning, Father." He tipped an imaginary cap toward Susannah and smiled. "Miss." Three of his front teeth were missing. Wolfgang studied how the men all looked at Susannah—she was clearly flattered.

The doctors prescribed sun treatment for TB of the glands, bones, joints, skin, eyes…there was really no stop to where the white death could spread after it entered the lungs. The heliotherapy patients spent nearly every sunny day on the roof, and when it rained, some were treated with radiation by means of mercury lamps. Today, the men were in the middle of a game of cards, but they were struggling to keep the cards and chips on the table.

"Little windy for cards, Geoffrey." Wolfgang bent down, picked one up off the floor, and handed it to Geoffrey's buddy, a chubby man with a sunburned forehead named Cletus Janks, who, for whatever reason, winked at Wolfgang before he began to shuffle the deck. The wink was followed by a nodding of his head in Susannah's direction, as if the man was trying to tell him something.

Wolfgang glanced at Susannah.

Herman screamed again. "My cakes! Who stole my cakes?"

In the background, over the ornately capped rooftop wall, the treetops danced with the wind. Susannah and Wolfgang stepped into the shadows of the bell tower and opened the door to the nurses' station. What had once been a sleeping station for the nurses now held a handful of mentally ill, and Herman was the worst of them all.

"Susannah!" Herman screamed as she entered, as if he could smell her. Nurse Rita sat pale and very still behind the main desk, her eyes frozen in a daze across the room toward 502. Wolfgang touched Rita's shoulder. "Rita...Rita!" Nurse Rita didn't respond.

"I hear the music!" Herman shouted from behind the closed door, locked in but not restrained.

Susannah turned toward her fellow nurse. "Rita...?"

Slowly Rita turned toward Susannah.

The two young nurses stood silently for a moment, one calm and unflappable, the other completely on edge, too frightened to even talk. "Are you okay, dear?" Susannah asked again.

Rita looked back at Room 502 but said nothing.

Wolfgang lifted the food tray from the counter, but Susannah snatched it from him. "I'll get it." She walked toward Herman's room, balanced the tray on one knee, and unlocked the door. Wolfgang followed behind her. The room had two beds and a large screened window. It smelled of urine and feces. Herman sat naked on the floor, slapping his belly and hairy chest repeatedly with the palms of his hands, which appeared to be smeared with excrement. His clothes rested in a bundle at the foot of the bed. He stood, fully exposing himself to Wolfgang and Susannah. Wolfgang wanted to cover Susannah's eyes, but she remained calm. Her eyes didn't waver as she pointed at Herman. "It's time to eat, Herman. Put your clothes on."

Herman looked toward the door for a split second, just long enough for Wolfgang to catch a glimpse of his dark eyes; it reminded him a little of a rat he'd seen scurrying across his porch early in the fall. Herman's tangled hair and scraggly beard hung down toward his hairy chest in one matted plait. Somewhere within was a mouth that, when he spoke, caused the entire hairy contraption to move.

"Can you hear the train coming? Rita can hear it." Herman hunkered down again, moaning with his right hand between his legs, the flesh around his eyes turning red. "The train's a-coming." He moaned, stopped abruptly, and then slumped over toward his bed.

Susannah remained calm but finally did look away. The fact that she wasn't completely unnerved by the entire episode interested Wolfgang in a way he couldn't truly explain. Herman wiped his hands on his bed sheets, coughed, and spat at the window. Yellow phlegm dripped slowly down the screen, filling the tiny holes with pockets of his saliva. He sat up with his back against the pea-green wall and faced them, smiling.

Susannah had her stern face back on. "Clean yourself, Herman. And put your clothes on now. You're going to wake up Benson."

Something moved beneath the covers on the other bed, and a high-pitched voice emerged from the tangle. "Shut up…shut up… shut up…shut up…No, I cannot hear the train. I do not hear it coming down the tracks…I love my dog…I would never hurt him… her…hurt her…so shut up, Herman. Shut up—"

"I want cake for my birthday!" Herman screamed.

Maverly Simms joined in on the madness from Room 504, shouting as if in competition. "Maverly at Waverly. Maverly at Waverly. Maverly at Waverly…"

"It's not your birthday, Herman," said Susannah.

"When *is* his birthday?" Wolfgang asked. "And why do they never use the toilet? There's a bathroom right over there."

Benson stuck his bald head out from the covers and then quickly ducked back under. His words faded to a whisper. "Shut up…I let the dog out…shut up…"

"Maverly at Waverly…Maverly at Waverly…"

Herman was a huge man with a thick chest and a deep, powerful voice. His hands and feet were huge, probably second only to Big Fifteen's on the entire hillside. Although fat hung in rolls beneath his droopy chest, he could easily pick up Susannah or Rita and throw her, or worse. Tuberculosis hadn't seemed to deplete his strength.

Susannah stepped farther into the room with Herman's tray of food. Wolfgang grabbed her arm. "What are you doing?"

"I'm taking him his food."

"Just leave it there on the floor."

"He won't eat it unless I bring it to him." Susannah carried the tray to the bed and placed it where the covers weren't rumpled. Herman's beady eyes watched her like a jackal. She kicked his clothes toward him. "Get cleaned up and get dressed, Herman. Don't disgrace yourself."

"No one listens."

Susannah moved toward the door. "I listen plenty, Herman."

"But you don't hear me." Herman looked directly at Wolfgang. "I'm like you, Father. I have secrets." A laugh emerged from Herman's mass of hair and lips.

What odd words. Wolfgang turned away from Room 502, wondering what Herman could have meant. When the other patients called Wolfgang "Father," he never minded, but hearing Herman utter the word made his skin crawl. When Wolfgang looked back over his shoulder before exiting the nurses' station, Rita's eyes were following him.

The cafeteria at dinnertime echoed with the sound of silverware clanking off plates piled high with meatloaf, mashed potatoes, and green beans. Wolfgang sat with Susannah, Abel, and Lincoln at a table near the back of the cafeteria, where most of the staff preferred to eat. Fifty tables with six chairs per table, but easily expandable to over four hundred seats if needed. A quarter of the chairs were occupied by patients mobile enough to be there, and the rest were currently empty. The staff was supposed to eat during the downtime. The cafeteria was a picture of cleanliness, white and bright and optimistic. The walls were decorated with paintings and drawings made by the patients during workshop and occupational therapy. Proper diet was essential to beating tuberculosis, and when the current building was completed in October 1926, they'd designed the cafeteria to be as welcoming as possible. It was open at all times, and more than two thousand meals were served daily. In an average meal, the cooks went through 140 pounds of bacon, one hundred dozen eggs, thirty pounds of cottage cheese, thirty gallons of ice cream, 140 pounds of ground beef, and 190 pounds of liver.

Abel attacked his food as if he hadn't eaten in days. Susannah watched him proudly, knowing that a healthy appetite often meant improved health. His exuberance was starting to show more every day. His color was better. *If only the adults had the same success rate as the children,* Wolfgang thought. One day it would happen.

Between bites of meatloaf, Lincoln puckered his face and furrowed his brow in a crude imitation of their boss. "Stop wasting your time on tunes, Wolfgang."

Susannah laughed and then gave Abel a quick glance. He laughed as well. Dr. Barker had yelled at Abel a few times in the past for being up too late.

Lincoln ratcheted it up a notch. "I bet his wife is a stiff too."

"She's a nice woman," said Susannah. "They're in a rough patch, though."

Lincoln took a bite of potatoes. "Shocking."

"Barker is a decent man," Wolfgang said. "He has a stressful job here."

"He took my bird. It's my job to get the birds." Lincoln put his fork down and wiped his mouth with a napkin. He looked over his shoulder and then leaned forward over the table toward Susannah. "Brought some hooch up the chute."

Susannah rolled her eyes. "How on earth do you get this whiskey?"

"I got my ways."

"That he does," said Wolfgang. "He got roses to bloom in the dead of winter."

"But don't tell Barker, Susannah," Lincoln said. "He doesn't know we borrowed his stuff."

"You scare me, Lincoln." Susannah leaned back in her chair and folded her arms. "Somehow, Prohibition doesn't affect you, and I don't care to know the reason why."

"Prohibition doesn't affect you either, does it, Father?" Lincoln winked at Wolfgang. "I got plenty of ciggies too."

Abel put on a miniature man-of-the-world face. "That's not illegal."

"That's all we need," Wolfgang said. "One of our staff smoking in a TB hospital."

"What's that got to do with anything?" asked Lincoln.

"Wolf thinks those cigarettes you smoke kill your lungs," Susannah said.

Lincoln waved a hand at them. "Horsefeathers." He leaned forward with his elbows on the table. "I heard Al Capone and some of his gangster friends frequent the Seelbach downtown. They've been pushed out of Chicago, so they do their bootlegging down here. Chicago of the South."

"Nonsense," Wolfgang said, more for Abel's ears than anything else. It was a common belief that Prohibition had caused more problems that it had solved, and crime was a major product—a new type of crime that was organized and frightening. The most recent note from the Klan was a glaring example.

"McVain said he knows Capone," said Lincoln. "Knew him in Chicago before he moved south to Louisville. I bet McVain's a gangster."

"He's a pianist, Lincoln."

"So? He can be a lot of things."

"Like a pervert," said Susannah, mouthing the word "pervert." "He's still trying to get me to wheel some of the women up to the fourth floor."

"And how does that make him a pervert?" asked Lincoln.

Susannah winced, glancing at Abel.

Lincoln grinned. "Makes him a man if you ask me."

Susannah rolled her eyes.

Abel snickered, hanging on Lincoln's every word. Lincoln looked across the table at Abel. "Hey, little fella, what are you doing here anyway? Aren't you supposed to be with the other children?"

Abel lifted his chin. "Miss Susannah said I could be here."

Lincoln stared at him. "Not contagious, are you?"

"They're all contagious, you buffoon." Susannah sipped her tea. "Leave him be."

Lincoln let it drop. Wolfgang could tell Lincoln was getting on Susannah's nerves. He always did. Lincoln fidgeted in his chair and looked around the cafeteria until he found Rita sitting at a table all alone. Her food was untouched. She stood, left her tray, and hurried out, holding her mouth clamped shut as if trying not to throw up. Lincoln saw it too. "What's wrong with Rita lately? She's not talking to me anymore."

Susannah sighed. "She must be depressed."

"She hasn't been here long enough to get depressed."

"It doesn't take long in the mental ward," Wolfgang said, knowing where this was going.

"Try working in the Death Tunnel all day."

"This isn't a competition," Susannah said.

"What's the Death Tunnel?" asked Abel.

"You bring Herman his birthday cake yet, Susannah?" Lincoln laughed and then picked at his teeth. "Benson let his dog out?" Another laugh. "Maverly at Waverly. Maverly at Waverly."

Susannah stood and slid her chair back. Abel followed her to the counter where they deposited their trays and left the cafeteria.

"When *is* Herman's birthday?" Lincoln asked Wolfgang.

"Good job," Wolfgang said.

"What?"

"It can be dangerous up there on the roof," Wolfgang said. "Make jokes if you want, but those women have a tough job." Lincoln stared over Wolfgang's shoulder as he chewed another bite of meatloaf, and eventually his eyes settled on Wolfgang. An unreadable smirk crossed his face.

"What?" Wolfgang asked.

"Susannah. She laughs at everything you say."

"So?"

"You're not that funny a guy, Wolf."

Mary Sue Helman's eyes opened when she felt her bed moving. Wolfgang's face hovered above as he hurried toward the elevators.

"Where are we going?"

"Somewhere I should have taken you weeks ago, Mary Sue." He smiled down at her. "Now, put your head back down on the pillow and relax."

Mary Sue's hands gently rested on her pregnant belly. "You could have at least given me time to fix my hair."

Wolfgang helped her into a wheelchair and they took an elevator to the fourth floor. He pushed Mary Sue quickly down the hallway that cut a border between the rooms on the left and the solarium porch on the right. Even though Dr. Barker was gone for the night, he still felt the need for haste. Plus, she was on the mend; she was walking outside, taking basket-weaving classes. He wanted to get her in and out as quickly as possible. She probably should not be visiting the "terminal rooms," but Wolfgang had weighed the options and allowing her a few moments with her dying husband seemed worth the risk. The baby would be fine. In fact, a baby born to tubercular parents was apt to have more immunity.

Frederick's room was near the middle of the hallway. The bed on the left side of the room was unoccupied, the sheets pulled taut, prepped for a new patient. Cool air filtered in through the screen. Frederick lay on his left side, facing the far wall. His skin was pale, his hair disheveled. Weak breaths pushed from his only operating lung.

"Oh, Frederick." Mary Sue pushed herself closer to the bed as Wolfgang gave them a little space. Frederick's right arm was limp against his right hip. She looked over her shoulder toward Wolfgang. "Can he hear me?"

"I believe he can, Mary Sue, but he doesn't even have the strength to eat." Wolfgang squatted beside her wheelchair. "We've been feeding him for weeks now."

"I need to see his face." Her lower lip quivered. "Can you turn him?"

Wolfgang carefully repositioned Frederick's body so that he faced the ceiling. His eyes were open. His lips were slightly parted. He blinked, but even that appeared difficult. "His chest is slightly sunken in on the left side where we collapsed the lung and removed the ribs."

Mary Sue sniffled, wiped moisture from her eyes, and then grabbed Frederick's right hand. She kissed the top of it, held it against her lips, and then kissed it again. Then she placed his hand against her belly. "Frederick, can you feel your child kicking?" She blinked away tears. "He keeps me up at night. He can't seem to get comfortable, and I'm the one who pays for it. I think he will have your stubbornness, Frederick."

No response.

"I said 'he,' didn't I?" Mary Sue smiled. "A boy. He'll have blue eyes and brown hair just like his daddy." She watched her husband.

"I'm sorry, Mary Sue." Wolfgang stood behind her wheelchair. "We better get you back to your floor."

She kissed Frederick's hand again and lovingly positioned his arm on the bed. "Until next time, Frederick."

In the hallway Mary Sue asked, "Will he die soon, Doctor?"

He hesitated. "It is very likely, Mary Sue."

"But not a certainty."

"No, nothing is ever a certainty. Not with prayer."

"Can we visit him again tomorrow night?"

"Yes, we can."

"Will you play music for him?"

"Of course."

She grinned. "Until then."

"Until then, Mary Sue."

CHAPTER 12

Wolfgang was in his high school years at Saint Meinrad when the war in Europe began, and even though the action seemed worlds away, isolated as they were at the seminary, the priests and brothers kept abreast of what was happening on the European continent. And close by at home. It became real to them all when a fellow student named Heinrich Becker, a German and a roommate of Wolfgang's, had been called back home for duty. He'd left the campus with tears in his eyes, explaining to Wolfgang that "all German nationals have been ordered back home for war duty." Friar Haas was the next to go a week later, and the departure was even more solemn than that of Heinrich Becker. There was a look of fear and sadness in Friar Haas's eyes that none of them had seen before. In Louisville, the French consulate countered by summoning all the French nationals.

The Louisville newspapers took sides. Henry Watterson's *Courier Journal* began its daily attacks on the Central Powers led by Germany and Austria-Hungary. But Louisville had a large German American population, which leaned heavily toward what the *Louisville Anzeiger* was printing in support of Germany. Even the Irish tended to lean toward the *Anzeiger*, because they were so anti-English. But when the *Lusitania* was sunk by a German U-boat in May 1915, several local residents nearly lost their lives and public opinion shifted toward the Allies.

As time moved on, even though most Americans wanted no part in the conflict, it became harder to remain neutral. In 1917

Woodrow Wilson asked Congress for a declaration of war against the Central Powers. After a Louisville-owned wood and timber vessel was torpedoed by a German submarine on its way to Africa, patriotism heightened. Wolfgang followed it all from his southern Indiana seminary, eighty-five miles west of Louisville, part of him wanting to be back home to witness the excitement of the marches and parades that filled the streets. Women volunteered in abundance for the Red Cross. Recruiting stations in Louisville swarmed with men wanting to enlist. Many from the German and Irish communities enlisted as well, and even the *Louisville Anzeiger* claimed devotion to America. Several banks and insurance companies dropped "Germany" from their names, replacing it with "Liberty." At Saint Martin of Tours Catholic Church on South Shelby, which had been threatened with being burned to the ground in 1855 by the Protestant mobs during the Bloody Monday riots, English replaced German as the language for services and sermons. But the *Courier* still questioned the loyalty of the German Americans and warned all to be aware of the "Kaiserists" hiding around the city.

When the government announced that Louisville would be the site of one of the nation's largest army training facilities, the American sentiment swelled. More men enlisted. More women volunteered back home in the factories and for the Red Cross. Forty-five million feet of lumber later, Camp Zachary Taylor was quickly built between Preston and Poplar Level, housing about fifty thousand troops in barracks and tents. Named in honor of President Zachary Taylor, who had been raised in Jefferson County, the camp first became home to the 84th Division, the 159th Depot Brigade, a field artillery training school, and several other military units. It would become the largest artillery training camp in the country and eventually would be used as a demobilization center and hospital for the troops.

So was the scene when twenty-year-old Wolfgang returned home after his sixth year at Saint Meinrad, where he met Rose Chandler, a young woman and recent graduate of the Louisville Girl's High School, and also one of the first to volunteer for the war effort at the local Red Cross.

Everything with Rose moved in fast-motion, so fast, in fact, that Wolfgang never had time to think about where his love was heading. He struggled to keep up with what it all meant. They'd seen each other every night since they'd met at the Cathedral of the Assumption. Immediately he'd felt comfortable with her, comfortable enough to talk about not only his high school and early college years in the seminary and his devotion to the Lord, but also about his relationship with his parents, his passion for music, and even about what had happened to his father.

Rose's parents, Wilma and Thomas Chandler, owned a successful clothing and jewelry store on Main Street, which was actually run by an old Jewish couple who doubled as store managers and as Rose's nannies as she'd grown up. Thomas Chandler was a member of the Pendennis Club in which Charles Pike had so badly sought inclusion. The Chandlers had friends in high places. Thomas was well-mannered, educated, sophisticated, and a heavy drinker of bourbon and scotch. He came from old money, and he and his wife, according to Rose, their only child, traveled out of the country most of the year. But what they were unable to give Rose with their time (she'd been an accident and only complicated their travel and social outings), they made up for in her allowance. So in the summer of 1918, when Wolfgang balked at the notion of their going out every night because he had no money, Rose shushed him and started paying for everything.

The work at the Red Cross was at times stressful, and she needed to have some fun. The city was still alive with patriotism, the streets at night teeming with soldiers from Camp Taylor, and Rose often went out of her way to engage them in conversation. She loved to ask the soldiers about their plans after the war. One soldier told her he wanted to open a factory for boots. One soldier dreamed of owning his own farm. Another soldier named Fitzgerald talked to Rose about writing novels.

Rose and Wolfgang ran into several soldiers watching a movie at the Strand and ended up sneaking that same group of soldiers into the Gayety for a burlesque show two nights later. The Baroque had nightly bourbon specials for the soldiers, although a sign outside the front door did call for well-mannered soldiers only. And the sign had an arrow pointing next door to the Rue de Lafayette: GO TO THE RUE IF YOU FEEL THE NEED TO ROUGHHOUSE.

When they passed the Baroque on one of their many walks, Wolfgang told Rose about how his father would drink there on Monday nights after passing the prestigious Pendennis Club.

She waved as if swatting a fly. "The Pendennis Club is for snobs, Wolfgang. Your father missed out on nothing, I assure you." And then she peered inside the Baroque, where tables of finely dressed patrons and several soldiers played cards and downed whiskey. "The Pendennis doesn't have the charm of this place. Look at the art on the walls." She hooked his arm in her own and led him away from the window. "You know the Baroque is half brothel, don't you?"

"No, I'm afraid I didn't know that."

"Yes, indeed," she said. "This is the red-light district, after all. It's on the second floor. It's called Babylon."

For an instant Wolfgang wondered if his father had ever ventured up the stairs to Babylon on his Monday night excursions.

Rose walked on. A beer bottle shattered against the inside of the Rue's window and she gave it little attention. "The city agreed to shut down all the brothels while the soldiers are here. Or the government would never even start building Camp Taylor."

Wolfgang looked inside the Rue, curious. "You think they obeyed?"

Rose giggled. "Of course not, Wolf."

At night they walked hand-in-hand along the walkways of Central Park, watching their distorted reflections in the wading pool and laughing at how their bodies shimmered in the moonlight. He wondered what the monks would think. He'd completed two years of college work as a major seminarian but was not yet a theologian. What he was doing may have been frowned upon by a few of the monks, but it was not forbidden. He still had three years of schooling to become a priest. So he continued to spend his time with Rose.

They enjoyed rides at Fountaine Ferry Park and got stuck atop the Ferris wheel. At the Magnolia Gardens pavilion and beer garden they danced until Wolfgang's legs hurt. Wolfgang was convinced that his father would have been impressed, and even moved to

dance. They bet on horses at Churchill Downs, and every time they
went there, Rose wore colorful hats with wide brims and fancy bows.
Sometimes they lost and sometimes they won. But it didn't matter.
Rose loved watching the powerful horses round the turns, kicking
up mud in tiny thunderclaps.

One clear night that summer, thousands of stars watched them
on their walk, along with a moon that was nearly full and illuminating the night as if it were day. Rose clung to Wolfgang's arm, giddy.
"Pick any restaurant and we'll go tonight."

He suggested the Vienna Model Bakery on South Fourth but
then added that it was too expensive. His parents had always discussed going there because of their fondness for Vienna, but they
never managed to go. Rose rolled her eyes at any mention of cost.

"But I don't have anything nice to wear," said Wolfgang.

Rose gripped his hand and walked him to West Market. She
bought Wolfgang his first suit at the well-known men's store M.
Cohen and Sons. They dined on roasted duck and fine pastries for
dessert. They talked a lot about the war. Even though men across
the country were enlisting by the thousands, the country still needed
twice as many for the war. The Selective Service Act had begun to
pluck the men they needed. Rumor was that the draft was going to
be changed to include eighteen-year-olds soon. Rose was nervous for
some of her friends. Wolfgang was nervous himself, even though he
would be ineligible for the draft because of his deformed leg. And
he was on his way to becoming clergy, making him twice ineligible.

"But not yet, right?" Rose had asked him.

Wolfgang was already having trouble sleeping at night as a future
with Rose seemed inevitable. He had begun to flirt with notions of
leaving the seminary. Even if he did return to the abbey at Saint
Meinrad, his mind would not be fully committed. He could not
give the monks his full, undivided attention knowing that Rose
was back in Louisville, waiting to be swept away by other men.

When he was a child, his days had been so regimented: breakfast, school, music, church, prayer, and then bed. And his schedule at Saint Meinrad had been no different—his mornings, afternoons, and evenings revolving around prayer and study. And now, for the first time in his structured life, he planned the day as it developed, adjusting on a whim with every ebb and flow of Rose's unpredictable personality. The summer days passed so quickly. He'd begun to volunteer his services to the Red Cross, as well, working with some of the wounded at Camp Taylor with Rose. He began toying with crazy thoughts of what it would feel like to be a doctor and to be able to help people all the time as he was helping at the army camp. Since he couldn't fight in the war, it gave him a sense of worth as far as the war effort was concerned.

Even though he was sleeping at home, he rarely saw his mother. He awoke early every morning to meet Rose and arrived home late every night. One day, he brought Rose home to meet Doris. She eyed Rose from several paces away, her condescending gaze an affront to the way Rose was dressed, with a hint of makeup and a skirt that showed her knees.

"I assume you're Catholic?"

"Yes, ma'am," said Rose.

Doris didn't even shake her hand. Instead, and in perfect Charles Pike fashion, she'd turned away from Rose's offer of a handshake and left them alone in the living room. Wolfgang took Rose's hand and stormed out of the house.

That night Wolfgang returned for a suitcase and some clothing. It was the same suitcase he'd taken with him to the seminary. He hadn't planned on packing and leaving with it for several weeks, but the circumstances now demanded it. The wedge between him and his mother had been driven too deep. He couldn't understand her stubbornness and refusal to accept anything Catholic, and her attitude had gotten worse during his time at the seminary. He didn't know where he would stay, and he didn't care—as long as he could be with Rose and away from his mother. Rose's father had a Model T that he'd allowed them to take, and Wolfgang stuffed his suitcase and belongings inside of it, along with every instrument that had belonged to his father. Doris Pike screamed at him as he carried each instrument from the house, from the violins and cello to the harmonica, piccolo, and flute. He took them all while Doris knelt on the floor praying to God to save him. The piano he left, only because it would have been impossible to remove on his own.

Doris Pike pounded her fists on her thighs and raised her Bible in the air. She pleaded to God. What had happened to her son since his father had passed? Why was the devil taking her son away from her? "Wolfgang, how dare you disgrace your father's memory," she yelled at him, "running off with a Catholic girl who dresses like a whore from Babylon."

Wolfgang moved into a spare bedroom at the Chandlers' house, temporarily, as he still planned on returning to Saint Meinrad at the end of the summer. A few days later, Rose's parents were away for a weekend trip. He and Rose were alone in the Victorian home just south of Central Park at Saint James Court, which, with its central esplanade, cast-iron fountain, and luxurious homes, was reminiscent of the fancy residential areas of England. It was home to many of the city's elite, and Rose's family had purchased one of the initial lots in the 1890s. Rose convinced Wolfgang to come up to her bedroom. He knew he shouldn't be doing it, but he wanted her. He'd dreamt of seeing her naked since the day he'd met her.

He played her a tune on his father's flute, and when he turned to face Rose, she took the instrument from him. They kissed. She slid her tongue into his mouth and began to unbutton his shirt. This they had done on several occasions, but never had they gone further. Moments later, Wolfgang was almost naked on her four-poster bed, wearing only his underwear and black socks. His skin was alive. His heart pounded inside his chest. His mind was swimming with terrifying visions of his mother and father making love on the other side of his bedroom wall. His focus was fully restored when Rose, sitting atop his waist, still in her yellow summer dress, leaned down and kissed him again. And then all of a sudden she slithered off of him and stood beside the bed, giggling.

She took the straps of her dress and lowered them down over her shoulders. The dress gathered in a yellow puddle around her ankles. Her breasts appeared heavy behind the cups of her bra.

Wolfgang sat up in bed. "We shouldn't be doing this."

"Is that you or your mother speaking?"

"God will know. We aren't married, Rose."

Rose stepped closer, the flat of her stomach inches from Wolfgang's face. She bent down and kissed his lips again. "Maybe we should be." She kissed the stubble of his beard. "This isn't a sin."

Her newly bobbed hair shimmered in the light of a nearby lamp. She squatted down so that her face was between Wolfgang's knees.

"Rose…"

She put a finger to her lips. "Shhhhh."

She surprised him by rolling down his left sock and sliding it off his foot. She looked up at him, as if asking for permission to expose the deformed foot. Wolfgang nodded. She carefully began to remove the sock from his right foot. It would be the first time anyone other than his mother had seen his deformity caused by the polio—the twisted part of his lower calf, the arched thrust of his shinbone near the top of the foot, the thickness of the flesh and bone and tightened ligaments and joints that resulted in one big skeletal mess, uncorrectable with a mere splint or brace.

Rose slid the sock off and dropped it to the floor. Wolfgang forced himself to watch as her fingers ran down his shin and across his calf. She lowered her head and kissed his shin. She kissed the top of his foot, his ankle, his calf, and the part of his foot just before the toes.

Rose stood before him again. Wolfgang leaned forward and gripped the waistline of her underwear.

"Go ahead," she said.

Wolfgang pulled them down and felt the firm roundness of her buttocks giving the slightest resistance against the waistband. He pulled them the rest of the way down and let go, allowing them to slide down into the folds of the yellow dress around her ankles. She crawled on the bed with him.

Rose. That beautiful, stylish, brash, hedonistic young woman with short skirts and bobbed hair. She loved him. She'd told him as much every day. But was she saving him from the priesthood? Or was it the devil sending him one final test?

CHAPTER 13

Wolfgang couldn't watch a silent film without thinking of Rose. They'd seen so many together, but none as controversial as D. W. Griffith's *The Birth of a Nation*, released in 1915 and based on the novel *The Clansman*. He and Rose watched the film in the summer of 1918 and found the racist themes appalling and untrue—portraying the Ku Klux Klan as heroic while white actors in blackface attempted to pan blacks as stupid and sexual predators of white women. Riots broke out in Boston and Philadelphia. Widespread protests led to many cities banning the film altogether.

On the hillside, the films slanted more toward humor. Charlie Chaplin's *The Circus* was Waverly's movie of the week. Wolfgang stood with his arms folded in the back of the dark theater, behind dozens of patients and a handful of staff members as they sat in rows, eyes glued to the screen. Wolfgang chewed his lower lip, eyeing the clock on the wall, his mind second-guessing his decision to wheel Mary Sue up to the fourth-floor terminal rooms to see Frederick. He couldn't undo it now. Rose would have done the same thing.

He forced himself to watch the silent movie. One center aisle split ten rows of comfortable chairs and faced a wall where the picture was shown, and except for a few coughs and bits of contained laughter, the first-floor theater was quite silent as everyone focused on the screen. The Little Tramp was being chased by a policeman at a circus, and the ringmaster thought his antics were hilarious. Mary Sue laughed from her wheelchair near the back of the room.

Wolfgang had kept his promise. Hours ago, he'd given Mary Sue another short visit with Frederick, and he'd played them a few songs on his violin. Although there was no change in Frederick, Mary Sue's spirits had been lifted by seeing him. It was good to hear her laughing at the film.

Wolfgang couldn't muster up that same urge to laugh. He thought of the brick crashing through his window and the note left on the altar in the chapel. Both brought back memories of Rose and watching *The Birth of a Nation* with her that summer. The movie helped inspire the second era of the Ku Klux Klan, and rumor was the Klan used it as a recruiting tool. He feared that the Klan had arrived at Waverly's doorstep and, what was worse, that he was partly responsible.

Susannah stood beside Wolfgang, stifling her laughter with a closed fist. She looked at him. "You're not laughing. What's wrong?"

"Nothing." He kept his eyes on the screen. "I'll be back."

"Where are you going?"

"To see Big Fifteen." Wolfgang ducked out into the bright hallway. Someone down the hillside was playing the flute again. He could hear it more clearly as he approached the exit and stepped out into the cool air, where the sun barely lingered in the west, smearing the sky in swaths of purple and gold. He inhaled the fresh air as he entered the line of trees and hurried through the woods. It was dark amid the trees, but he knew the paths like the back of his hand. He hummed along with the flute: Mozart's *Requiem*?

About forty yards downhill and northwest of the main sanatorium, Wolfgang stopped at a two-story clapboard building where the colored workers lived. He tossed a pebble up at a closed, grimy window. It sailed several feet from its target and bounced off into the undergrowth. He found another pebble. This one hit the edge of the window. Moments later, Big Fifteen stuck his head out. "Boss, that you?"

Wolfgang stepped into a small clearing where the ground was hard and free of grass. "You hear the flute?"

"Course I do."

"Will you take me to it?"

Big Fifteen sighed. "Be down in a minute, Boss." The window

closed with a thwack. A few minutes later Big Fifteen stepped outside, buckling a large black belt that cinched his overalls at the waist.

The colored hospital was another thirty yards down the hillside,
and the flute became louder as they neared the entrance to the two-
story brick building. The entrance was little more than a slanted
tin roof with sagging gutters held up by four wooden posts—a glori-
fied lean-to. Two folding chairs flanked the double glass doors. A
stray cat looked up from the chair on the right and meowed as they
passed. Wolfgang ruffled the fur behind the cat's ears. Big Fifteen
opened the door and ducked inside, where the air was thick with the
damp vapors of mildew. The colored hospital had taken the brunt
of the rainfall. Not only had it been soaked because of the holes
and crevices in the weathered roof, but the basement had quickly
flooded from the rain and mud streaming down the rest of the hillside. Mud, water, and remnants of backed-up sewer gunk had stood
three feet high against the basement walls. Big Fifteen led a bucket-
by-bucket chain gang and had the basement emptied in two days.
Much of the first floor had flooded as well, and puddles of water still
remained in the lobby.

Wolfgang wanted to hold his nose, but he resisted the temptation. The colored patients breathed it in, so why shouldn't he? If
he were to close his eyes, the moaning and coughing would have
sounded much like up in the main sanatorium, but seeing this awful-
ness made it worse. Beds in the shadows. Children sleeping in dark,
musty corners while long-legged bugs skittered along the walls. The
modest sleeping porches were too crowded to fit everyone at the
same time, so they took turns.

Big Fifteen took it in stride as he passed through the lobby. Three
children jumped up from the shadows and excitedly shouted his
name. Big Fifteen smiled and waved, slapping low fives like some
hero. To them, Wolfgang saw, he *was* a hero: a strong, strapping TB
survivor who had come back to help. "My people," he called them.
His presence alone gave them hope while the main sanatorium
loomed over the trees like an unattainable beacon of light.

Wolfgang followed Big Fifteen up a narrow stairwell, where they
sidestepped a skinny man blowing his nose into the sleeve of his

yellow pajamas. Wolfgang touched his shoulder and gave it an affectionate squeeze. Wolfgang had been to the colored hospital before, but not usually at night, so the patients viewed him with curiosity as he and Big Fifteen made their way upstairs.

The second-floor sleeping porch was much smaller than the porches up the hill, but at least the air was moving. Dozens of beds filled the porch. Screens kept the biggest insects out. Spit buckets sat beside each bed. The patients were either asleep or resting with their eyes open, listening to the flute, which appeared to be coming from a room about twenty yards ahead to the right.

Big Fifteen ducked inside, leaving Wolfgang next to an adolescent boy in a white T-shirt and baggy tweed trousers. He had big brown eyes and dark skin. His black hair was cut close to his scalp. The kid had a toothy grin, and he tugged on Wolfgang's lab coat. "You like baseball, Father?"

"Well, I'm…" Wolfgang changed course and motioned toward his right foot, where the toes of his black shoe angled to the floor. "Never been much of an athlete, but yes, I do follow baseball."

The kid lifted his right thumb and pointed to his chest. "I'm gonna play pro ball someday. Soon's I get outta here. I'm gonna be the black Babe Ruth."

Wolfgang knelt beside the bed and rubbed his hand over the kid's coarse scalp. "I'll pray that you do." Wolfgang looked him in the eyes. "What's your name?"

"James. Friends call me Smokey."

Wolfgang patted the kid's shoulder and stood up. "All right, Smokey. Perhaps one day they'll make a Louisville Slugger with your name on it."

Smokey smiled widely and leaned back on his pillow. The flute music stopped. Somewhere a baby wailed. Coughing mixed with the wind. Big Fifteen ducked out of the room, and beside him stood a squatty black man in blue-and-red-checkered pajamas under a brown coat. The man had short hair and a chubby face free of stubble. At a glance he appeared in his forties, although no wrinkles or age marks marred his caramel skin. He smiled, but Wolfgang sensed a twinge of reluctance behind it.

"I'm Dr. Pike."

Big Fifteen patted Wolfgang on the back. "He likes to be called Boss."

"I'm Rufus." The man sat on a wooden bench and started to offer his hand but then pulled it away. "I've heard stories of you. You play music for the white people. They call you Mozart."

Wolfgang sat beside him. "They call me all sorts of things." Wolfgang spotted the flute in Rufus's thick, callused hands. "You like Mozart?"

He nodded.

"I heard you playing his *Requiem.*"

"Seems to fit." Rufus put the flute to his lips and played a few bars. His pudgy fingers and hard nails danced effortlessly over the keys. He slowly lowered the instrument.

"I play the piccolo," Wolfgang said. "But not anywhere close to the perfection with which you do."

"It's peaceful out here on the porch." Rufus rotated the flute in his hands. "The music carries."

Big Fifteen sat on the edge of Smokey's bed and yawned. Smokey was still smiling, staring up at the ceiling with his hands behind his head.

Rufus turned his head and coughed into his fist. "Excuse me." He wiped his mouth. "Luckily I still have some power in my lungs. Don't know what I'd do without this."

"Perhaps it is keeping your lungs vibrant. Where...where did you learn to play?"

He chuckled and his belly shook. "Thought I'd like jazz, didn't you? Or ragtime? My grandpappy was a slave for a family in Georgia. The owner treated them well. Taught them to read and write. Gave them this flute when they let them free."

"Can I see it?"

Rufus hesitated. "Don't you worry 'bout getting TB?"

"Not anymore." Wolfgang took the flute, turned it in his hands, tried the keys, and gave it back. "Good instrument."

"He taught my grandpappy to play. And my father when he was a boy."

"If I call on you to play one night, will you come?"

"Where?" Rufus looked skeptically up the hillside and pointed toward the main sanatorium. "Up there? Oh, no, sir." He shook his head.

Big Fifteen stood from Smokey's bed. "Boss seems all proper 'cause he's a padre. But he ain't a stickler for no rules."

"I don't know. Why can't we play here?"

Wolfgang patted his knee. "I've got someone I'd like you to meet. He's a pianist."

"Up there?"

"Will you come play with him?"

Rufus rotated the flute in his hands. "I think I'd like that."

"That means you'll do it?"

Rufus stood with a grunt. "It means I'll think about it. How would you like to be the only white man in a building full of Negroes?"

"Isn't that where I am now?"

"It isn't the same." Rufus turned away and disappeared into his room. Seconds later he began playing again.

Wolfgang wasted no time deliberating how he'd make the proposition to McVain; planning a conversation with someone completely unpredictable was an exercise in futility. He marched up to the fourth-floor solarium porch, clutching his lab coat tightly against his chest as the evening temperature continued to plummet. The purple clouds above moved quickly across the dark sky.

He found McVain sitting up in bed. Wolfgang immediately told him about Rufus and then waited for an answer he feared would never come.

"Well?"

"What?" McVain looked at him as if he truly didn't remember what Wolfgang had just asked him.

"Would you consider playing with someone else?"

"What does he play?"

"I told— The flute, McVain. He plays the flute. I'm sure you've heard it."

"Who is this guy, where is he?"

Wolfgang hesitated. "He's on a different floor."

McVain grunted, stretched his legs out on the bed.

"You were a concert pianist, right?"

McVain exhaled a deep breath and glanced over at Weaver, who had his eyes closed, earphones over his head, and a copy of the *Waverly Herald* on his chest. "I wrote three symphonies before the age of twenty. And had them performed. I was a different man back then. I don't play anymore."

"You played the other night," said Wolfgang.

"I was terrible."

"But with more practice—"

"That quack Barker isn't going to let me out those doors again." McVain leaned forward and glared at Wolfgang. "What you did was cruel—*Father*. You dangled the carrot. You probably give drunks a spoonful of booze and then smash the bottle." He held up his fingers. "Might as well cut the rest of them off. I'm going to die here. Neither your God or your confessions can help that."

"I wasn't planning to—"

McVain held up his mangled hand, palm stiff, his two fingers spread, nubs suspended. Wolfgang stood, frustrated, and turned away, disappointed but not finished. He checked Mr. Weaver's charts.

McVain shifted toward Wolfgang. "I saw Dr. Barker walking one of the patients up and down the hill this morning."

Wolfgang pretended to be busy with Weaver's charts. "Is there a question somewhere in there, McVain?"

"Might have been, Dr. Pain-In-My-Ass."

Wolfgang sighed. "They were Making the Walk. The patient you saw this morning is being released from this sanatorium tomorrow. She's been here for eighteen months, and now she gets to go home to her family." Wolfgang knew the woman's family would be initially excited to have her home, and then they would begin to wonder if she'd brought some of the disease back with her. They'd wipe down everything she touched when she wasn't looking; they'd wonder if she'd carried the Waverly wind.

Wolfgang stepped toward McVain's bed and lightened his tone.

"It's what all the patients here are working toward, walking down and back up the hillside and not being completely out of breath. Generally, if you can Make the Walk, you go home."

McVain let it sink in, chuckled slightly. "Make the Walk, huh?"

Down the solarium Wolfgang spotted Susannah hurrying into the stairwell. Children screamed from the rooftop. He took off after Susannah and caught a glimpse of her calves as she bounded up the stairs to the next platform leading to the rooftop. His eyes followed her flesh to just above the back of her knees, where the hem of her skirt fluttered in waves as she sprinted upward.

"Susannah!"

She looked down over her shoulder. "Something's happened with Herman."

"What?"

She continued and Wolfgang chased behind her. "You know, you don't always have to accompany me up here."

A dozen kids had gathered near the swing set. Nurse Marlene stood in the middle, calming them. Two of the kids spotted Wolfgang and Susannah and pointed to the bell tower and nurses' station. A few snowflakes spiraled through the air. Herman was out and standing next to the ledge beside the tower, staring off toward the trees behind the sanatorium. His hair blew back from his head in wild strands. His beard clung to his chest.

"My cake!" Herman screamed.

"What on earth is he doing out?" asked Wolfgang.

Susannah shook her head and slowly approached Herman. He craned his head and stared her down. "My cakes!" Saliva dabbed the corners of his lips. Moisture pooled in his eyes. He faced the bell tower. "Miss Rita. The train finally came for her."

Susannah took a cautious step toward him. "What about Miss Rita, Herman? Herman?"

"Her feet don't touch," Herman said softly.

Wolfgang gripped the large man's right elbow and led him along. "Let's get you back inside."

Herman kept his wild eyes on Susannah. He gnawed the fingernails on his left hand, his fingers lost in the growth that concealed his mouth. "Her feet don't touch."

"Did you do something to her?" Wolfgang asked.

Susannah opened the door to the nurses' station and screamed. Wolfgang, directly behind her, saw the horror over her shoulder. Nurse Rita hung by a rope from the ceiling pipes. Susannah lurched backward, covering her mouth with her hands. She fell into Wolfgang's arms, knocking him slightly off balance. He braced their weight with his stiff left leg and then walked her inside.

Herman entered behind them. "I told you. Her feet don't touch the floor."

Rita's white shoes dangled a few feet from the floor, swaying slightly under the weight of her body. The chair she'd used lay on its side a few feet away. Her eyes stared straight ahead. As the rope crinkled and twisted, Rita's gaze met Wolfgang's for a moment and then passed on. The sound of the rope pulling against the pipes was like an ice shelf preparing to crack. Benson was out of his room, as well, walking in a daze around the station, passing Rita's body as if nothing had happened. "I let the dog out. He didn't shit on the carpet. He didn't. He didn't. The train won't come for me. Because I let him out. He didn't shit on the new carpet."

Wolfgang covered Susannah's eyes, and they both hunkered down against the wall. Her tears trickled through his fingers. He wiped her cheeks and hugged her shoulders and told her repeatedly that it was going to be okay. He couldn't take his eyes off Rita's body. Such a young girl.

An envelope rested on the floor next to the overturned chair. Susannah reached it with the heel of her right shoe and reeled it closer. Wolfgang rested his chin on her shoulder as she pulled out a note. Susannah started to read but then stopped when Herman approached. She slid the note back into the envelope to read later, in private.

Herman stepped closer to Rita's swaying body. "Benson, you

shut up. Her feet don't touch! Can't you see? She'll never bring me my cakes."

Maverly Simms stood at the doorway to her room. "Maverly at Waverly," she said, lacking her typical enthusiasm. "Maverly at Waverly."

Wolfgang took it all in. "Quiet," he said. Then when they ignored him, he screamed it: "Be quiet!"

Herman and Benson froze. Maverly looked up, startled. Wolfgang pointed at them, one by one. "Back into your rooms."

Herman inched his way back into Room 502, and Benson followed, still mumbling. Their door closed. Maverly backed away and slithered into her dark hole.

Wolfgang held Susannah close. He felt Susannah's warm breath against his neck. "Cut her down, Wolf. Please, cut her down."

Herman, Benson, and Maverly were quiet as mice as Lincoln and Wolfgang worked. The rope was thick, and Lincoln needed a tree saw from the basement. Lincoln held Rita around the waist as Wolfgang stood on Rita's chair and worked on the rope. Lincoln was silent. Pale. Of course, Wolfgang realized. Lincoln was a young man; giving Rita a hard time about the mental ward had been his way of flirting. And now she was dead.

When the rope snapped, they lowered her body to the floor. Her neck was blue and swollen. Her hands and legs were blue.

Lincoln fingered Rita's hair.

Wolfgang could still picture Rita's blank eyes staring him down as he'd held Susannah on the floor. It was as if he could read her final confession in her reddened eyes.

Father, forgive me, for I have sinned…

Lincoln cradled Rita's head on his lap. "We were…" He looked up. "Rita and I. You know."

Wolfgang patted Lincoln's shoulder. "No, I'm sorry, Lincoln. I didn't know."

"Will she still go to heaven, Wolf? Even though…"

Wolfgang sighed. Heaven. The question had haunted Wolfgang ever since his childhood, and here he was, a doctor and almost a priest, two professions that faced heaven daily despite the fact that he still couldn't answer this question. "I don't think you have anything to worry about, Lincoln. Rita was a loving person. One of God's own. She will be forgiven."

Wolfgang touched Rita's dark hair and thought of Rose. He'd held her in much the same way when she'd died. He closed Rita's eyelids and whispered a quick prayer for her soul.

Lincoln was staring at Wolfgang's right hand. "You still wear your wedding ring."

Wolfgang moved his hand away. He knew Lincoln had seen it many times before, yet he'd never asked until now. Wolfgang turned the gold band, slowly rotating it. "After I decided I'd return to serving the Lord, I moved it to my right hand. I refused to stuff it in a box or some dusty drawer." He sat up straight and touched Rita's hair again. "Let's get this over with."

Dr. Barker's office was empty. Surely he'd heard the news. Wolfgang made his way to the chapel, walking slowly, not ready to confront anyone. He grieved for Rita. But he was thinking about Susannah too, the weight of her slender body in his arms, cradled against him. The fresh smell of her hair against his cheek. His fingers interlocked and holding tight against her stomach. How the buttons of her dress had brushed against his palms.

His pace quickened. *What am I doing?* he thought. He hurried into the chapel at the corner of the second floor where the east wing joined the north. Rows of candles rested on every window sill, lit by patients honoring the dead or praying for the living. The flames cast shadows against the white Roman support columns that melted into the white plaster ceiling. Wolfgang leaned against a column, arms folded. He wasn't alone in the chapel. Dr. Barker stood in the center aisle facing Susannah. He spoke in a hushed voice, placed a supportive hand on her right shoulder, and then gave her a hug. Susannah didn't return the awkward embrace. Her arms hung at her sides. Dr. Barker left her alone, his footfalls echoing off the tall ceiling. Wolfgang ducked behind the column until Barker was gone.

Inside the chapel, Susannah was on her knees, facing the life-size crucifix on the back wall, her hands folded on top of a pew. Wolfgang gave her a moment alone before limping down the rug that stretched the length of the center aisle. She sobbed. She'd lost a dear friend, a friend who wasn't even sick with the disease all around them but apparently still touched by it. Susannah didn't turn around. *Perhaps she didn't hear me*, he thought. She continued to stare ahead while Wolfgang purposely looked everywhere *but* at the cross. He reached out for her shoulder but stopped inches away. His hand hovered. Then he reeled it back to his side. Instead, he knelt beside her. They said nothing for a while. She stared at the cross while he stared at the floor.

Finally he spoke. "I'm sorry."

Susannah glanced at him and then faced the crucifix again. "Thank you."

Wolfgang stood and left her alone.

Wolfgang and Susannah walked home together as usual just before ten o'clock. They remained silent until they reached the line of trees where they usually parted. Susannah spoke softly. "I don't think I can sleep alone tonight."

Wolfgang hesitated just long enough to make it awkward. Susannah turned away, her face red. "You...can sleep on my couch," he said.

"Thank you."

Wolfgang peered over his shoulder as they walked deeper into the woods. He convinced himself that he was doing the right thing, comforting a dear friend in a time of need. Wolfgang's heart fluttered. His palms sweated despite the cold.

"You look nervous, Wolf."

"Just cold." He hugged his arms. "Should have worn a heavier jacket."

As soon as his cottage was within sight, he hurried ahead and unlocked the door. Inside, he lit several candles. He took her coat, hung it up in the closet, lit two more candles, glanced into the kitchen, and closed the bathroom door, stretching out the mundane actions to fill the time.

When he stepped back into his living quarters, she stood inches from his face. She was only an inch or two shorter than Wolfgang, her eyes elevated to find his. She reached up to his collar and unlatched the top button of his cassock. "You seem tense."

"What are you doing?"

She didn't answer. He stepped away.

She sat down on the couch. "Maybe some wine would help."

He quickly disappeared into the kitchen, moving as if he'd prayed for such a request. He leaned against the counter and took a deep breath. He pulled a bottle of unmarked wine from a rack beside the sink and pulled the cork. He poured two glasses, spilling a few drops on the counter. He wiped them up with a towel. He lifted the glasses and turned away from the kitchen. In the other room, his piano stood against the wall, and beyond that was his bed. He eyed the neat half of the bed—Rose's side. Was this why he'd craved the priesthood again after Rose's death? So that moments like these could be reconciled with a single statement and oath? So that he could not be tormented by his promises to her?

No, he was not so shallow. His faith was the only thing that could have kept him afloat.

"Wolf?"

Susannah was just around the threshold, on the couch. He wondered how she was positioned. Both feet on the floor? Legs crossed? Had she taken off her shoes? He entered the room. She sat barefoot, her legs tucked delicately beneath her.

"Can we light a fire?"

Wolfgang handed her a glass of wine. "Of course." Then he dove into another distracting chore, adding logs to the fireplace, stuffing newspaper under them, igniting the paper and logs with a candle from the mantel. Within minutes the wood, slivers of which had already begun to glow a shade of amber, began to snap and pop. The warmth was immediate.

Susannah took off her cap, rested her head on the arm of the couch, took a sip of her wine, and then closed her eyes. She opened them again and swirled the wine in her glass. Her technique was good, Wolfgang noticed, wondering how often she drank. He knew that Lincoln's bootlegged alcohol also made it to the nurses' dormitory on a regular basis. Susannah smiled at him. "Lincoln winked at you when we spoke of bootlegging."

Wolfgang laughed, still standing in the middle of the room. "Sacramental wine is exempt under the Volstead Act."

Susannah sipped her wine. "Is this sacramental wine?"

If it were, he thought, would it sanctify the moment for her or make him seem a piker? "Let's call it leftover and leave it at that." Wolfgang turned away and poked at the logs.

"How's your requiem coming?"

Wolfgang squatted near the fire and continued to prod the logs. He looked to his left. Her lips touched the rim of the glass. Red wine wet them. In the seminary, fellow priests discussed past friendships with females. Women were often open and rather forward with priests, in fact, because they weren't threatened by them. In a way, it made Wolfgang feel used. Was Susannah using him now? Was she testing him, as Rose had?

"Wolf—your requiem?"

He stood. "I'm afraid I'll never finish."

"Would Rose have expected perfection?" Susannah sat up on the couch, both of her feet flat on the floor. Wolfgang didn't answer her. Susannah sipped her wine and surveyed the bare walls. She spotted his Edison phonograph beside the fireplace. "They have newer ones now, much larger."

"And they play longer too. But this works fine. It was my father's."

"As were all your instruments," she said. "What was he like?"

Wolfgang sat on the piano bench and scratched his forehead. "It's complicated. He was a tough man to love. He wasn't a bad person. I do think he loved me."

"And you?"

"I fear that I love him more now that he's gone." Wolfgang chuckled. "He wanted me to be a famous musician."

"And you think you let him down?"

"No. I'm putting my music to good use. I let my mother down by running off with Rose."

"She didn't approve?"

Wolfgang was beginning to feel the warm, familiar rush from the alcohol. His tongue loosened. "Rose was a modern woman. Short dresses, bobbed hair."

"Ah! A flapper," she said. "Why did your mother disapprove?"

Wolfgang stared down into his wine. "She disapproved of my becoming a doctor. She knew I became a doctor to spite my father. He detested science. He believed only the Lord could heal."

"Why *did* you become a doctor? Out of spite?"

Wolfgang pointed to his right foot. "For answers. To help cure disease. Out of spite, I guess. Not because of my father, but my mother. She was Protestant. I was raised Protestant. Not just Protestant but anti-Catholic. My parents were true 'Natives,' descendants of Know-Nothing Party members. Equated the pope with the devil. She wanted me to become a Protestant preacher."

Susannah's left hand touched her mouth in shock.

"I was determined to torture my mother." Wolfgang finished off his glass of wine and noticed that Susannah had managed to down only half of hers. "Rose was Catholic. She deepened my love of the Catholic Church. We met at the Cathedral of the Assumption."

"So after she died you ran back to the priesthood?"

"I'm here, aren't I?"

"I meant figuratively, Wolf. We know why you're still here. But otherwise you would be there?"

"I…" Wolfgang buried his thoughts. He tilted his glass until the last drop hit his tongue.

Susannah cleared her throat and winced as if her head ached. She looked tired, her eyes finally touched by the wine. "Will you play for me?"

Wolfgang spun quickly around and faced the piano. "Love to."

He looked over his shoulder and noticed she'd stretched out on the couch, lying as if ready to be painted. "What shall I play?"

She closed her eyes. "You choose."

Wolfgang played bits of Beethoven, Bach, and Chopin for nearly an hour, occasionally checking over his shoulder to see if she was asleep. Her eyes stayed closed, but every so often she'd shift and give off the slightest sound. Her glass of wine rested empty on the floor before the couch. He wasn't sure when she'd finished it. The firelight cast a halo around her torso and head. He smiled and faced the piano again, and just before his fingers eased down on the keys once more, she spoke.

"Wolf, how did your father die?"

CHAPTER 14

In September 1905, when Wolfgang was seven, he guessed
something was wrong with his father. Charles Pike normally
played his violin four hours without tiring, but he began taking naps in the middle of the day. Wolfgang wasn't used to seeing
him rest. Three days in a row his father had slept in late, skipping
daily Mass, something Wolfgang had never seen him do. Wolfgang
had watched him from the hole in the bedroom wall, wondering
when he would wake up. When Charles did finally get up, he failed
to get dressed. Instead, he sat at the kitchen table for an hour,
drinking coffee.

On an afternoon in October, Charles came home from the factory, sweating and holding his stomach. He removed all eight of
his violins from the couch, one at a time, and leaned them against
the far wall. He dropped to the cushions and stretched out while
Wolfgang watched from the dining room. Charles blinked as he
stared at his son and then doubled over into a fetal position.

Wolfgang took a step toward the couch. "Daddy?"

Charles grunted and straightened, wincing. "Play the piano for
me, Wolfgang."

Wolfgang sat on the piano bench, still watching his father.
Seeing him in pain made Wolfgang want to cry. Charles had shown
his son nearly every emotion over the years except pain. Often
Wolfgang had wished pain on his father, when Charles would slap
him across the wrist with a violin bow every time he missed a key
on the piano. Or when he'd spy on his mother and see her crying.

Wolfgang would secretly pray some kind of small pain on his father, nothing too harsh, just enough to get his attention.

He'd only fully begun to understand prayer months before, when he'd asked his father why Minister Ford's wife, Cecelia, hadn't been at church two weeks in a row.

"She's sick, Wolfgang," Charles had told him. "Which is why we pray for her every day. Go ahead, talk to God and tell Him you want Mrs. Ford to get to feeling better."

And so Wolfgang prayed for Mrs. Ford, along with everyone else in the congregation. He missed seeing her at church. She was wide with a hefty bosom, and every time she hugged him she pulled him close. And she smelled good. Every night for a month he prayed to God for Mrs. Ford to feel better. And it worked. Cecelia Ford walked into church one morning looking the same as if she'd never gotten sick. Wolfgang felt as if he'd been involved in the greatest miracle on earth. That night Wolfgang went home and prayed that his mother would fry bacon in the morning. When the sun rose, the smell of frying bacon came with it.

Wolfgang looked to the cross on the wall above the piano and held back tears. What had he done, wishing pain on his father?

"Play, Wolfgang." His father winced on the couch.

Wolfgang focused on the white and black piano keys before him. He started to warm up with scales.

"Good," coached Charles. "Good...tempo...tempo..." He screamed out. Doris was at the grocery. It was just the two of them. Charles gripped his stomach. His eyeballs bulged.

Tears formed in Wolfgang's eyes at the piano. "Daddy—"

"Keep playing," hissed Charles Pike. "And God damn it, watch your tempo."

Wolfgang looked to the cross above the piano. *Stop it*, his mind cried. *God, please stop my father's pain. I should never have prayed for such a thing. I take it all back.*

"Damn it!" Charles screamed.

"Daddy—"

"Keep playing."

Wolfgang glared at the cross. *Stop it...stop it...stop it.*

Wolfgang prayed for his father to feel better. The next week Charles seemed to improve. The lethargy had passed. He stood with Wolfgang in the center of the living room floor. Wolfgang had the violin craned between his neck and left shoulder. He held the bow in his right hand and awaited the next instruction. Charles had his hair down, and it fell over his shoulders and hid his loopy ears. His red cravat hung loosely around his neck. He'd taken off his jacket and vest, so all that remained was his fluffy white shirt rolled to his elbows. In his left hand was his favorite violin, the one with the carefully burned letter *P* on the base of the wood—a signature-type letter, sprawling and slanted, a letter he'd spent hours practicing. It was how he would sign all of his instruments in his Vienna music store—such a dreamer. He slapped the violin bow across Wolfgang's knees and warned him about his posture.

Just as Wolfgang raised his bow across the strings, he noticed a look in his father's eyes. The same look he'd seen on the couch the previous week. Charles dropped his violin and bow, doubled over, and ran that way into the bathroom down the hall. Wolfgang, still clutching his own violin, followed his father until the bathroom door slammed in his face. On the other side of the door, Charles grunted in discomfort and breathed heavily. A minute later Charles screamed. "Jesus. What the— Doris! Doris!"

Wolfgang's mother ran down the hall, wiping her hands on a dish towel. She backed Wolfgang away from the door and tried the knob. It was locked. "Open up, Charles." The lock clicked. Doris Pike grimaced and forced her way inside. Wolfgang heard her gasp: "Charles, you're bleeding."

Over the next several months, Charles lost weight at an alarming rate. There were mornings when Wolfgang hardly recognized his father from the day before. During school Wolfgang often lost focus as his mind drifted to his father's health. He prayed when he should have been studying. He'd imagine his father getting better during the day, the Lord's hand reaching down through their roof and healing him. But he'd return home and his father would look much the same. His face showed the angled form of the skull underneath his skin. His eye sockets darkened. His hair began showing signs of gray. Still he refused to see any doctor. "The Lord will heal me if he so chooses."

Wolfgang cursed his father's stubbornness, and he couldn't understand why the Lord was waiting so long. He'd been praying to Him for over a month. By November Charles had stopped going to work. He was too weak to play his instruments. He and Doris fought over money. They fought over his declining health. Every day she urged him to go see a doctor, but still he refused. His clothes hung from his thin frame. He'd had Wolfgang cut a new notch in his leather belt to keep his suit pants from falling. Charles spent most of his evenings in bed, especially after the nausea began to set in. He'd lay with his legs under the covers, his composition on his lap and his inkwell propped in the folds of the bed sheets beside him.

One night Wolfgang knocked on his parents' bedroom door. His mother was in the kitchen and would have scolded him had she known he was disturbing Charles while he was writing.

"Come in," he said weakly.

Wolfgang slid inside the cramped room, which smelled thick with sickness—sheets that needed to be washed, clothes that needed to be cleaned, and pillows stained. Wolfgang wore a stethoscope around his neck. He'd been secretly playing doctor. Charles gave him a warm smile and beckoned him closer. His fingernails needed to be clipped. Wolfgang approached slowly, staring at the man he'd once known as his father. Charles put his pen on the top page of his work and ruffled Wolfgang's hair. "The greatest fugue ever written." He tapped his work with a crooked index finger. "Right here." His favorite violin, the model for Pike Music, rested on the pillow beside him.

Charles reached out and yanked the stethoscope from Wolfgang's neck. He stared at it and then dropped it to the floor. "I don't need a doctor, Wolfgang. God will do with me as He wishes. Nothing science or medicine can do." Charles laughed. "From monkey to man? Can you believe that, Wolfgang? From monkey to man." He pouted out his lower lip and scrunched his face. "Do I look like a monkey to you?"

Wolfgang didn't know whether to laugh or be afraid. "No, Father, you don't look like a monkey." It was during the time of sickness that Wolfgang had begun to call Charles "Father" instead of "Daddy." This sick man wasn't his daddy. "Did God make you sick?" asked Wolfgang.

Charles nodded. "Yes, He did. But He had his reasons, Wolfgang. He always has his reasons." He ruffled his son's hair again. "Do you have dreams?"

Wolfgang shook his head.

"Someday you will."

Wolfgang stared at him, confused.

The vomiting started in December. And the fevers after that. His mother cried a lot when she thought Wolfgang wasn't looking. Sometimes she'd cry at night, knitting in a rocking chair next to their bed while Charles worked by candlelight. Wolfgang would watch them from his bedroom wall. Whenever his father would lean his head back against the headboard and moan, she would stand up and wipe his brow with a wet cloth. When he'd lean over the side of the bed and vomit into a metal pail, she'd empty it and wipe his mouth. Sometimes his mother would leave at night and return a few hours later with food. Fruit and vegetables. She'd fix him a plate of carrots and celery, apples and oranges, and take them up to their bedroom so he could nibble on them while he composed.

One night Wolfgang heard her feet on the stairs. He knelt on his mattress, peered into their room through the hole and watched her enter with a plate of vegetables. It was all she could get Charles to eat. She placed the plate on the bed beside him, but she was clumsy taking her hand away. Her fingers clipped the well of ink, spilling some of it on the sheet. A few spots splattered on his work. He grabbed her hair, yanked her down, and shoved her nose in the spilled ink. He lifted the inkwell and rammed it against the side of her head, cutting her above the left eye. She staggered back with ink covering her face.

It was the first and last time Charles had ever raised a hand in anger to either one of them. Perhaps if he had, at least his behavior over the years might have been easier to understand. But later, before they went to bed, he kissed her forehead and told her he loved her. And that they would jump on a boat and sail to Vienna as soon as they had enough money stashed away. He would open his own music store. Doris nodded obediently, some of the ink still staining the creases of her face. Charles moved a strand of her red hair from her eyes, kissed the cut he'd made above her left eye, and tucked the hair behind her left ear. "You've got ink in your hair."

As if he never remembered hitting her.

A few days later the stench from his parents' bedroom was nearly toxic. Charles lay in bed. His inkwell and papers were still on the bedside table. His feet were bare, the bottoms facing Wolfgang. Wolfgang heard his mother in the hallway. He quickly hopped into his bed and pretended to be asleep when she quietly stuck her head into his room. When she left, he returned to the wall and peered through.

His mother closed her bedroom door, paused for a moment with her nose against the grains of the wood, and locked it. She approached the bed and kissed Charles on the forehead. She stroked his hair for a moment and said something to him that was not audible to Wolfgang. She handed him the King James Bible, and he clutched it tight against his chest. Then she took a pillow and, with both hands, pressed the pillow down over her husband's face. Wolfgang could see her back straining. She let out a soft grunt. She stood on her tiptoes. Her calf muscles strained as her slight body pressed down on the pillow. Charles moaned and grunted against the pillow, his right hand held on to the Bible while the fingers of his left hand clawed at the tangled bed sheets. His bare feet rose several inches off the mattress, kicking and falling, kicking and falling, until finally they stopped.

Wolfgang watched, wide-eyed. What was she doing? He tried to scream, but the sound got caught up inside his throat. He froze. He couldn't breathe. His mother moved the pillow from his father's face and dropped it to the floor. She checked for a pulse at his father's neck. She knelt to the floor, rested her face against his chest, and started crying.

That night, Wolfgang lay in bed, his covers pulled up to his neck, and stared at the ceiling. His mother cried on the other side of the wall for hours. He watched the tree limbs outside his bedroom window. Shadows moved everywhere. He was too scared to close his eyes. He felt like he was wheezing. He prayed for his own safety. How could she? He'd been praying for him. It could have worked. It had taken some time with Mrs. Ford, but eventually praying had worked on her. He waited all night for his bedroom door to creak open and for his mother to walk into his room with a pillow. He waited, but she never came. When he finally fell asleep, he startled awake.

Do you have dreams? Someday you will…

Even after the sun shone into his room, he was slow to get up. He'd convinced himself that it had all been a dream. A terrible nightmare. His father would be alive and writing in the living room when he came downstairs, his favorite violin tucked to his neck, the bow moving back and forth over the strings.

But the living room was empty and silent. Wolfgang found his mother sitting alone at the kitchen table. Maybe he'd gone to work? Or off to the Baroque for an early drink?

Doris Pike sniffled into her fist as Wolfgang showed himself. "Come here, honey." She patted her right thigh. Her eyes were red and swollen from crying. Wolfgang didn't budge. He stood ten paces away from her and stayed there. She sniffled again. "I'm sorry, honey, but you know how sick your father was?"

Wolfgang nodded.

"Well, God took him away during the night."

Wolfgang sat on the piano bench with his hands folded between his legs, staring down at the floor of his cottage, the splintered slats between his boots. Only Rose had known. And now Susannah.

Wolfgang waited for her to say something, but the room was silent. She sniffled much like his mother had that morning in the kitchen. Flames snapped against the charred stones of the fireplace. His face felt slack. He didn't look up, afraid to look into Susannah's eyes.

The couch creaked as Susannah shifted her position. Her bare feet padded against the wood floor, coming closer, her shadow combining with his own. He didn't look up. She draped her arms around his shoulders and kissed the top of his head. His face brushed against the buttons of her dress, pressed against her chest. Her heart beat into his ear.

Susannah touched the top of his head. She sunk her fingers into the fluff of his hair momentarily before moving back to the couch. Only then did he look up, watching her from behind—the way her sandy hair fell in curls between her shoulders, the way her nurse's dress conformed to her narrow waist, the way her hips moved beneath it. He turned to face the piano as she sat again.

"Shall I play some more?"

She sniffled. "Please."

Wolfgang faced the piano keys. His arms relaxed. His shoulders sagged. He began playing, moving from Mozart to Beethoven and back to Mozart before pausing to see if Susannah had fallen asleep. Before even the last note had drifted to silence, Susannah's soft voice came from across the room. "Keep playing."

He could have played for her all night. He touched his fingers to the keys again, periodically glancing toward the rose atop the piano. For the next hour he played Chopin, Liszt, and Brahms, and finished with the Mozart *Fantasia* in D minor. After the sonority of the final chord faded to nothing, another soft sound found his ears.

Susannah snored on the couch. He watched her for a moment. *No hole in the wall here,* he thought. She was lying on her side, her chest rising and falling in rhythm, her left hand resting on the curve of her left thigh, her legs bent at the knees. Wolfgang covered her with a blanket and then got himself ready for bed. He contemplated changing into his pajamas but decided against it. He'd sleep in his pants and shirt. He blew out all the candles, then limped his way to his side of the bed. He watched the fire dwindle to ash. He stared at the ceiling, and glimpses of the city outside of Waverly Hills flashed through his mind—the growing downtown buildings and hotels, Macauley's Theatre, an orange-and-red-smeared river sunset, the wooded parks, the brick-making kilns that created that noticeable haze over Smoketown, the hogshead barrels on the sidewalks of the Tobacco District, the Irish in Limerick, the Germans in Frogtown, the prestigious houses at Saint James Court, poor blacks and whites living in darkened alleyways, horse farms on the outskirts of the city where the grass was so green in the spring that it appeared blue.

Wolfgang glanced at the cross on the wall as the wine continued to work on his brain. His hands fondled the bed sheets below his waist—what was he doing? Now he was helpless to stop it. He was still too aware of Susannah's presence in the room. He thought of the patients on the hillside, black and white. He thought of the brick flying through his window. He thought of McVain and Rufus, and an idea suddenly hit him like a fist in the face. He closed his eyes and blocked out Susannah's breathing.

Finally he slept.

CHAPTER 15

Wolfgang had a hangover from the wine, but the headache wasn't so bad as to cloud the memories of Susannah spending the night on his couch. She was gone now. He'd heard the door close sometime after sunrise, and she'd left the blanket neatly folded on the arm of the couch, along with a note.

I'll be back at 7:30. It's a workday, you know.
    S.

Wolfgang thought about tossing the note into the trash can, but what if it was found? Lincoln would have years' worth of fun if he found out she'd spent the night. Instead, Wolfgang slid it beneath a stack of music atop his piano. He should burn it.

In the bathroom he filled the tub with cold water. He sat on the edge of the tub and said the rosary as the waterline grew closer to the lip. The temperature reminded him of the Holy Water fonts near the entry doors of the abbey church during the winter, when they could literally feel ice crystals, it was so cold. He eased himself inside, trembling, shivering until his teeth chattered. He washed quickly.

All out of love for God.

Wolfgang started the morning off with a baptism in the chapel. A thirty-year-old man in the final stages of TB had lived what he'd called a faithless life, a moral but faithless life. He'd never believed in God, and the closer he got to death, the more he began to wonder, as they all did, what would happen after his death. Where would he go? Was there really a heaven? Wolfgang explained to the man that he wasn't a priest yet so the baptism technically wouldn't count, but the man insisted anyway.

"You have doubt?" Jesse Jacobs had asked him with Wolfgang listening from behind, preparing the baptismal water.

"Yes," the man said.

"Faith is doubt, my friend," Jesse said, patting the man's shoulder.

Wolfgang stepped in. "Very well put, Jesse." And so Wolfgang baptized the man Catholic, with Jesse as witness. They'd managed three pieces of cake and three glasses of milk from the cafeteria as a celebration before Jesse and the newly baptized man returned to their respective solarium porches.

Wolfgang found Susannah waiting in the hallway outside the chapel, arms folded. She giggled and then attempted to hide it with a fist.

Wolfgang touched the top of his head. "What is it?"

"You haven't heard?"

"About what?"

"We have women patients on the fourth floor now."

Wolfgang smiled. "Surely, you're joking?"

"Go look for yourself," she said. "McVain was playing cards with them when Barker arrived this morning."

"And how did that go?"

"He didn't show it in front of the patients, but he was irate." She prodded him with her finger on his chest. "He blames you, of course. Said McVain is *your* patient."

"My patient? He barely speaks to me."

"Well, I just spent the past hour rolling the women back to their floors."

"How did the women get up there?"

Susannah shrugged. "They wouldn't say."

"Who wouldn't say?"

"McVain," she said. "The women just said they all woke up on the fourth floor."

"I'm sure that's half the truth," Wolfgang muttered. He went right up to the fourth floor to see McVain and found him standing on the solarium porch, his face inches from the screen. Down below, an orderly chased two pigs across the lawn.

"Fool. Can't keep a pig in its pen." McVain sat down on his bed with a dramatic sigh. "What do you want, Amadeus?"

"How did you do it?"

"Do what?"

"How did you get the women up here during the night, McVain? There's no way you could have physically rolled all of those beds."

"I'm very persuasive."

"Evidently."

"Am I in trouble, Your Holy Fatherness?"

"Not from me, but possibly from—"

"Don't start spouting God on—"

"From Barker, McVain. Personally, I thought it was clever. I'm more curious than anything else."

"Well, I ain't talking." He rested back on his bed and winked. "Might want to try it again. There are actually some lovely broads in this hellhole."

"This is the nicest sanatorium in the country, McVain." Wolfgang motioned out toward the woods. "It's new. It's clean. Look at those trees. Smell the air. What you see as a hellhole, I see as beauty." Wolfgang opened his bag, pulled out a bundle of paper, hesitated, then handed it to McVain.

"What's this?"

"The requiem I'm writing."

McVain flipped through it carelessly and then tossed it on a chair beside the bed. He rested his head on his pillow. "I'm tired and nauseous."

"I've got a surprise for you tonight."

"Sending me home?"

"No, but it should keep us both out of trouble."

McVain closed his eyes. "Can't wait."

By mid-afternoon the sun ducked behind the clouds and the temperature dropped several degrees. Wolfgang's hands turned numb
while he searched the hillside for Big Fifteen, and after twenty
minutes of wandering about, he spotted him playing with a group of
kids outside the children's pavilion. The children of Waverly loved
Big Fifteen. He'd lost valuable years of his childhood in a hospital
bed because of tuberculosis, so he claimed he had time to make up.
Rarely a day went by that Big Fifteen couldn't be found in his time
off playing—at the colored hospital or the main playground outside
the children's pavilion—throwing a ball or pushing the children on
the swings. The current game was one they called "Airplane." Big
Fifteen ran across the lawn holding Abel high above his head. Abel
was stiff with his arms out like airplane wings.

"Dat's it," Big Fifteen told Abel above him. "Hold out those
arms! Breathe in dat good air!"

Wolfgang watched from the line of trees, proud.

In the fall, Big Fifteen dressed up as a scarecrow and took the
kids—the ones who were healthy enough—on hay rides around the
Waverly Hills property. He was the Easter Bunny in the spring, the
Tooth Fairy all year round, and at Christmas, he was the big black
Santa Claus.

Big Fifteen spotted Wolfgang watching them. He slowed to a
walk and lowered Abel to the ground. Abel ran toward four other
boys who'd been watching, and they all slapped low fives.

Wolfgang shook Big Fifteen's hand. "Thank you, Fifteen, for
playing with *all* the children."

Big Fifteen nodded. "The color of the child makes me no never
mind, Boss. They all smile the same, don't they?"

"Yes, they sure do." A deer sprinted through the growth and
then jumped over a small ditch and out of sight. "Come join us for
lunch, Fifteen."

Big Fifteen's eyes grew large. "Probably shouldn't, Boss."

"Nonsense." Wolfgang waved him along. "I need your help with something tonight. You're the strongest man I know. And you know every undulation of this hillside."

Big Fifteen followed Wolfgang into the cafeteria and nodded sheepishly toward the scattered tables, where nearly a hundred patients currently dined, although the room held twice as many. Some offered kind smiles, but others, Wolfgang could tell, wondered what the big black man was doing there. "Ignore them," Wolfgang said. Big Fifteen sat beside Lincoln, who wore a pin-striped fedora that Wolfgang had never seen before. Wolfgang and Susannah sat across the table from them. They listened intently as Wolfgang revealed his plan. Susannah rolled her eyes throughout.

Lincoln leaned over the table. "Sounds fun. Count me in. Your place. Midnight."

"Me too, Boss."

Dr. Barker walked by their table and eyed Big Fifteen. "Lincoln. Room two-eighteen needs prepped." He gave Wolfgang an extra-long glare and moved on.

Lincoln got up from the table, and Big Fifteen took that as his cue to leave as well.

Lincoln tipped his hat. "You like it?"

"It's McVain's, isn't it?"

"Was. He gave it to me," Lincoln said proudly.

"For doing his dirty work, I'm sure."

"Makes me look like a gangster, doesn't it?" Lincoln and Big Fifteen moved on.

After they'd gone, Susannah spoke up. "Moving the piano, Wolf? Really?" She dropped her ham sandwich to her plate, having eaten only two bites from it. "It's a foolish idea. And I'm not giving you last rites if you die."

Wolfgang grinned. "You haven't eaten much."

"I don't have much of an appetite."

Wolfgang watched her. "Don't worry, we'll have plenty of muscle."

She looked away. "How much can you lift on that foot of yours?"

Wolfgang sipped his vegetable soup. "Did you read Rita's note? Lincoln was asking."

"Lincoln? Why does he want to know?"

"I think he was sweet on her, is all."

Susannah wiped her mouth with a napkin. "I read it this morning. She was depressed. She felt suicide was the only way out."

"It seems…"

"What?" she snapped.

"A bit selfish." Wolfgang wished he hadn't finished his thought. He was out of practice reading women's moods. "All these people here, dying. Sick people fighting until the end, freezing on the porches at night in hopes of getting well."

"I forgot," she said. "You're a man of the cloth. What she did was a mortal sin. Completely unforgivable."

"Susannah—"

"She felt trapped, Wolf."

"We all do at times."

She dropped her napkin. "Then why do you stay?"

Wolfgang looked away. "I'm needed here."

"Of course you are, but there's more to it than that."

"Like what?"

Susannah rubbed her eyes and sighed deeply. "Rita was pregnant."

Wolfgang's heart thudded in his chest.

"She was afraid," Susannah said. "Having a baby on her own. And afraid for its health. She made a terrible mistake, but don't condemn the poor girl."

"I'm sorry."

Susannah folded her napkin and then unfolded it. Folded it, unfolded it.

"Was Lincoln the father?" Wolfgang asked.

Susannah pondered it, then let out a breath. "We'll never know that, will we?"

"No, I guess we won't."

"Lincoln doesn't need to know what was in the letter, Wolf."

He nodded. "You feel trapped here too, don't you?"

Susannah glanced to her side, where Wolfgang ran his spoon through his soup. She chuckled sarcastically. "One day I'll get married and have a family. With a washer and a refrigerator and a Model T in the driveway."

"What's stopping you?"

"What a stupid question. How am I supposed to find a husband here, on this hillside, surrounded by death?"

"Well, why do you stay?"

Susannah stood up, waited for a nurse to pass, and then stepped closer. "All you do is spend time at that piano, writing something you'll never finish. I'm sorry about your father—and for Rose. But all your life you've been searching for an answer you won't get until you die. I'll give you the answer, Wolf. No one knows what happens when we die. That's the answer. Running to the priesthood won't get you closer to the truth."

Wolfgang's mouth dropped open. What happened since last night? "Have I said something to upset you?"

"Everything about you is stuck in the past, Wolf." She started to walk away but stopped to look over her shoulder. "Do be careful tonight."

"Mother, where do we go when we die?"

It was the first question Wolfgang had asked his mother after his father's funeral. They sat at the kitchen table eating bread with butter.

She looked up, surprised. "We go to heaven." She took a bite of her bread and wiped a spot of butter from the corner of her mouth. "To live with the Lord."

"So Father is in heaven?"

"Yes."

She was always so confident with her answers. So sure of it all. For so many years, her confidence and her warm embrace—the smell of her nightgown—had been the welcome respite from his father's moods. But not anymore. Since the funeral, his shoulder pushed her away until eventually she treated him in kind. The house became a cold place where they did nothing more than sleep and eat.

Wolfgang played his music, not because she asked him to, but because his father would have wanted him to. He prayed to God, not because she wanted him to, but because God and music were his only friends. He cut the grass and did the chores because he was taking his father's place in the household. He attended church but sat next to her in silence and refused to discuss the readings with her afterward. Ever since the Lord had failed to heal his father in time, there had been a disconnect between Wolfgang and his parents' church, and he didn't know how to explain that to his mother. Nor did he feel like trying. But it had something to do with how Minister Ford had said at the funeral, "The good Lord has called one of his sons home early…and now Charles Pike sleeps with the angels." Something about the way he'd said it made Wolfgang feel sad, and the sadness came back every time he entered the Light of Christ Church with his mother.

Wolfgang watched her chew the bread. "Can Father hear me when I talk to him at night? Even if I talk to him in my head?"

"He hears you, Wolfgang."

"Then how come he never answers?"

He saw the hesitation. For a moment, she was baffled. "He answers you, Wolfgang." She'd attempted to touch his hand, but he pulled it away. "He hears you in ways that we just can't understand."

That night, Wolfgang rushed to answer the knocking at his door. It was midnight. Right on time. Lincoln and Big Fifteen hurried inside and quickly closed the door. "Did anyone see you?"

Lincoln moved to the left side of the piano. "Relax, it's not like we're stealing anything." He squatted, lifted the side of the piano a few inches off the floor, and then dropped it with a clang.

"Careful," said Wolfgang.

Lincoln straightened his gangster fedora. "This baby's heavier than I thought."

"Will you take that silly hat off?"

"Can't." Lincoln flexed. "Gives me strength."

"Good," said Wolfgang. "You doing okay?"

"Yes, why? Do I look like I'm not?"

Big Fifteen took the other side of the piano. "Ready, Boss? I gots to get up b'fore the sun does." He hunkered down, laced his thick fingers beneath the wood of the piano bottom, and lifted his end with an ease that challenged Lincoln to roll up his sleeves and try again.

Lincoln grunted. "You are twice my size. You know that, Hercules?"

Lincoln and Wolfgang lifted the left side while Big Fifteen handled the right, and together they walked it out the door with shuffled, strained steps. They put it down on the porch and stared up the wooded hillside.

"This is crazy." Lincoln leaned on the piano. An owl hooted. "What was that?"

"A dog." Big Fifteen looked at Wolfgang. "Or maybe a wolf."

"It was an owl." Wolfgang urged them onward. For the next fifteen minutes they sidestepped, duck-walked, backpedaled, squatted, cursed, and nearly toppled in a heap as they carried the piano through the woods. Wolfgang started to think he'd set up an insurmountable task, one that would more than likely have them leaving the piano for the forest animals to play on.

They took a brief sit-down in the middle of the woods as the breeze blew the tree limbs into a rickety song above their heads. Lincoln breathed heavily, lounging on the ground with his back against the sappy bark of a pine tree, complaining about the temperature and his aching fingers. Big Fifteen seemed ready to move again. He cleared sweat from his forehead and pushed out plumes of air.

Lincoln mumbled from the ground. "Work smarter, not harder. Smarter, not harder. Smarter—"

Wolfgang stared him down. "That your motto?"

"Smarter, not harder." Lincoln straightened his hat and popped up with a sudden burst of energy. "The chute!"

Big Fifteen leaned against the back of the piano. The front left wheel was bent. Something groaned inside. "He got a point, Boss."

So they started back down the hill, and the task proved more strenuous than going uphill because of how they had to angle their backs and shuffle their steps. Big Fifteen did the bulk of the backpedaling downward and was sweating so profusely that Wolfgang feared for his health. He never complained, though, unlike Lincoln, whom Wolfgang would have liked to fit for a muzzle. At the bottom of the hill, near the opening of the chute, they rested again as a train rumbled past, shaking the piano. After the train vanished and the piano stopped vibrating, Lincoln stared across the dewy grass that sloped toward Dixie Highway. A fuzzy light approached, about forty yards away, bouncing about five feet off the ground.

"What is that?" asked Lincoln.

"A lantern." Wolfgang squinted. "And it looks like a horse."

"Shit." Lincoln hurried to open the doors at the bottom of the chute and then took his place at the piano. "Hurry. Into the chute. It's a policeman."

Big Fifteen hoisted his side of the piano and Wolfgang did likewise. They practically ran the piano into the chute, and Lincoln quickly closed the doors. Moments later they heard the clip-clopping of horse hooves over the hardened ground next to the train tracks. An orange glow penetrated the cracks around the chute's doors.

They all waited, quietly.

"Lincoln," whispered Wolfgang. "Why would the police be sniffing around the hillside?"

Lincoln shushed him. Outside, the horse neighed and paced, and then moments later it moved on. The glow around the doors vanished.

"Did I go blind?" asked Big Fifteen.

"Give it a minute," Lincoln said. "Eyes will adjust."

A minute later Wolfgang could see them both, as well as the piano and the bottom of the winch system. Thirty yards ahead, moonlight shone down through an air vent.

"Lincoln…the police?"

"Might have heard rumors, is all," said Lincoln.

"What kind of rumors?"

"Bootlegging."

"Bootlegging," Wolfgang said, flabbergasted. "That's just great, Lincoln. Why don't you just have the police help us get the piano up there?"

"Don't worry." Lincoln tapped the piano top. "They're Prohibition sharks. They get tipped off by someone, they're required to check it out. They'll circle and move on. TB is like a ring of fire around this place."

"Uh-huh."

"They'll sniff, but they won't get closer than that."

"And you know about this how?"

"They're been sniffing on and off for years."

"Let me guess," said Big Fifteen. "Ever since you been here?"

Lincoln scratched his head. "That's about right."

In total, it took them nearly three hours to get the piano from Wolfgang's cottage to the sanatorium, but for the final leg of the journey, the winch system worked like a charm. Lincoln was especially happy to use the chute for what it had initially been designed, as a supply tunnel, instead of a slide for dead bodies. Big Fifteen had braced himself behind the piano as it ascended the chute, holding it in place in case it decided to shift or slide backward. Lincoln and Wolfgang followed beside it on the elongated steps as the system pulled the piano upward. By the time they entered the north wing of the first floor, they were all near collapse, even Big Fifteen.

Wolfgang's finger joints ached. His legs were sore. His wrists were scraped and his back had begun to tighten up. Lincoln was on the floor in the middle of the hallway, on his back, cursing under his breath. Big Fifteen sweated profusely as he leaned against the piano but appeared ready to move on.

Lincoln looked up from the floor. "I hate you for this."

"He don't mean that, Boss. He smilin' when he say it." Big Fifteen started pushing the piano down the hallway, broken wheel and all.

"No, I meant it." Lincoln walked beside Wolfgang, pushing along with them.

Wolfgang pointed down the hallway. "To the elevators."

Upstairs, McVain's eyes opened and followed the squeaking sound as Wolfgang and Lincoln grunted their way across the fourth-floor solarium porch, pushing the piano, which by now had developed an annoying rumble near the base. The left side partially scraped the floor. Big Fifteen had left them at the elevators, determined to get a few hours of sleep before he had to get up and push his food and supply cart. He'd also told them he was nervous about being seen too often in the main sanatorium. Wolfgang and Lincoln took it the rest of the way.

A few patients were awake and they watched amusingly as the two passed. One man said aloud, "Am I dreaming?"

"No," Wolfgang answered. "This is very real."

They parked the piano near the foot of McVain's bed and in front of the screen window. Wolfgang stood at one end, quite proudly, and Lincoln stood on the other, hunched over at the waist and breathing heavily.

"So this is the surprise?" McVain's head never lifted from his pillow. His lips quivered in the cold.

"What do you think?" Wolfgang asked. "It'll need a few cosmetic repairs, but you can play whenever you need to."

"You wasted your time."

Lincoln shook his head and hobbled away.

Wolfgang pointed toward Lincoln, who had already disappeared into the shadows. "They risked quite a lot bringing this piano here—for you."

"I didn't ask them to."

Wolfgang bit his lip. "You stubborn mule." He pointed a finger at McVain. "What is your problem with me, McVain?"

"Ain't got a problem with you as a doctor."

"So that's it," said Wolfgang. "What are you, an atheist?"

McVain scoffed. "Why do you care, anyway? What does it matter if I ever play the piano again?"

Wolfgang couldn't sleep the rest of the night. His mind jumped from pain to worry and back again. Would Susannah knock on his door in the morning? He couldn't sleep knowing she was still mad at him. Would McVain ever get up from his bed and approach the piano?

He looked across the room, and beyond the patch of moonlight the wall was empty without the piano. His candle and vase stood on the floor. He stared at the ceiling and tried not to move. Every movement caused a different kind of pain. He hadn't felt so immobilized since polio had kept him bedridden for nearly six months when he was eight years old.

It had started three months after his father's funeral. His mother felt sure he'd gotten it from another child at school. It started with headaches and a fever. His neck became stiff, his muscles sore and painful to the touch. Wolfgang was convinced he'd become sick like his father, but his mother repeatedly said he was not. How could she be so certain? But he was too exhausted to fight her when she held damp washcloths to his forehead.

A few days later, on his way to the kitchen, Wolfgang fell to the floor. He could not stand back up. His mother had gone off to the store, promising to be back soon. He'd crawled along the floor like a slug for about ten feet before giving up. He punched his thighs and slapped his legs but felt very little sensation. His mother came home an hour later and screamed when she found him on the floor. Finally she brought in a doctor, a sterile man with narrow eyes, white hair, and a small, white mustache. The doctor confirmed that he'd been infected with polio. He'd know more after analyzing a stool sample, but after listening to Doris Pike explain the symptoms, he felt sure.

"He could continue to shed the virus in his stool for the next three to six weeks," the doctor had said. "Until then he needs rest. And a lot of fluid."

Is that it? Wolfgang thought.

Doris managed to get him up to his bedroom. The polio virus had attacked the nerve cells that controlled the muscle movements in both of his legs. Only time would tell if the paralysis would be permanent. Wolfgang had no choice but to let his mother stay close to him. He couldn't push her away. His arms were too tired, and his legs couldn't move at all. Every time his bedroom door opened and she walked in with a tray, he feared the pillow. At night he'd awaken from nightmares of being suffocated. On several occasions he awoke to find that he'd fallen out of bed in meager attempts to run.

But the pillow never darkened his vision. Instead, his mother took care of him with frequent baths of water and almond meal, mustard applications and massages. One night he opened his eyes and found her sitting next to his bed. He was so startled, he pushed himself back against the wall beside his bed. She was holding a violin. She attempted to play something but quickly stopped. She held out the violin and the bow toward Wolfgang and said, "Sit up, son. I know your arms work." Wolfgang grabbed the instrument. He stared at her, waiting until she left the room, and then he lifted the violin to his neck. He played until he tired, and the next day he reached for the violin again. In time, his mother carried him downstairs to the piano.

Two months later the feeling in his left leg returned, first the thigh and then a few days later below the knee and into his foot. Sensation started to come back in his right leg days later. The following week he tried to walk but collapsed on his bedroom floor. His mother helped him back into bed and cautioned him that he may not be able to walk again. He was determined to prove her wrong, and he'd told God as much every day when he prayed for his legs to come back.

So many weeks he'd slept on his back with the hole in the wall above his head, but he'd been unable to get up on his knees and look through it. He could hear his mother crying at night. Did she cry for him? For his father?

His left leg recovered fully, but some of the nerve cells in his right ankle and foot had been completely destroyed. They tried splints, rigid braces, and uncomfortable corrective shoes. The doctor called it equinus foot; the muscles in his right leg that pulled the toes downward worked, but the muscles that pulled them upward did not. So his foot tended to drop toward the ground. His Achilles tendon at the back of the foot had retracted to the point where his foot couldn't take on a normal standing position. His left foot could stand flat on the floor, but his right foot could not. He couldn't put his right heel on the ground, so it remained permanently raised. He'd walk on his right toes for the rest of his life and drag them when he tired.

But he'd survived, and with the help of a cane and miles of Louisville streets, he'd learned to walk again. In fact, he still had the cane in his closet, as a reminder of what he'd endured.

As Wolfgang lay in bed, he contemplated getting up for a glass of wine. If he still felt this sore in the morning, he feared he would need that childhood cane to get up the hillside.

Then something caught his ear.

The piano.

The music carried down the hillside from the fourth-floor solarium porch. Wolfgang got back into bed and listened with a broad smile etched into his face.

He knew it. McVain had caved.

CHAPTER 16

As Wolfgang walked across the drafty floor, his muscles screamed, but he'd managed to gain his balance by the time he made it to the bathroom. He braced himself against the wall as he urinated. He winced as he dressed, but the more he moved, the more his muscles loosened.

At seven o'clock he heard Susannah's familiar rapping on the door. He jumped up so quickly he nearly spilled his coffee down the front of his lab coat. Not only had she come, but she'd arrived early. He opened the door. She stood at the bottom of the steps, as always, smiling.

"Morning, Wolf."

As they walked side by side through the woods, he did his best not to appear too stiff.

"I want to apologize for the way I spoke to you yesterday," she said.

"Think nothing of it."

"Rita got me thinking of my family."

"Of course." Susannah's parents and both of her brothers had been taken by tuberculosis, all within a span of seven years, all but her father passing away at Waverly Hills. She was the only one not infected. Wolfgang suspected it was another reason she felt so attached to Abel. Both of her brothers had been younger.

Susannah grinned on their way up the hill. "You're hobbling more than usual."

"It's nothing… Well, all right." Wolfgang gave in and allowed his shoulders to sag. "I'm in severe pain, and my back is so stiff I could hardly tie my shoes. I'm sure I'm quite a sight."

She giggled. "So the piano's up there? No one got hurt? Arrested? Fired?"

"Not yet," Wolfgang said. "Lincoln survived."

"Not without a few complaints, I bet."

"We never would have made it without Fifteen."

Susannah folded her hands as she walked. "He always seems helpful."

Wolfgang did his best to keep up with her, but his legs were not dependable. Her comment about Big Fifteen surprised him. She'd barely spoken a few words to him in all the years she'd known him. Wolfgang knew it wasn't prejudice. She didn't have a hateful bone in her body, but he'd noticed the way she carried herself, the way she became withdrawn over the years whenever they ran into a Negro.

"We're early, Wolf."

"Yes…yes, I've noticed."

"The other night I wanted to show you something that I've been working on."

Wolfgang rubbed his forehead. "Yes, and I've been too pigheaded and self-involved to remember."

"I can't deny that." She smirked. "And Marlene's already at the sanatorium."

"Very funny."

"It wouldn't take me a minute to show you."

Wolfgang extended his right arm. "Lead the way."

After they traveled half the distance to the nurses' dormitory Susannah caught Wolfgang smiling. "What are you thinking about?"

"Barker's reaction when he sees that piano."

Susannah was right. The dormitory was empty when they arrived. No one emerged from the showers and onto the porch half naked. No one watched him suspiciously as he walked inside, but it didn't stop the butterflies from swirling when they climbed the steps to the second floor and entered her room. Unlike his room, her walls were decorated with pictures of her family members and a few oil landscape paintings. Her bed was neatly made and fit snugly in the corner next to the window. Beside it was a wooden dresser painted white and covered with more pictures and two stuffed animals—one bear and one puppy dog with a missing left button for an eye. She grabbed his arm and walked him across the room to her desk, which was cluttered with stacks of paper, pens, and medical books. A large black typewriter—the kind in which the type bars struck upward and the typist could not see the characters he or she had hit until the subsequent lines scrolled into view—took up much of the desk's surface.

She pulled out her chair and lifted a stack of pages that was about two inches thick. She appeared nervous as she handed it to him. "I'm not finished yet, but that's most of a first draft."

"What is it?" Wolfgang flipped through it with interest and then returned to the top page, which read: *White Death by Susannah Figgins*.

"Is this a novel?"

She shook her head. "No, it's a book on tuberculosis. I've been working on it for five years, reading medical books, studying treatments. I'd like to eventually publish it and help find a cure."

Wolfgang flipped through it again, read a short passage about sun treatment, and closed it. "This is wonderful. I had no idea."

"I'd like to become a doctor."

Wolfgang smiled.

"I know. You laugh—"

"No, no, I'm not laughing. I think it's great. I'm just shocked."

"My father would be as well," said Susannah. "I loved him dearly, but let's just say he was not of the opinion that women should vote. Or have any kind of equality in the workplace." She took the manuscript from him, placed it back on the seat of her chair, and pushed the chair back in the well of the desk. "Well, now you know why I stay here."

"I'd like to read it sometime."

"Give me a few more months." She looked at the clock on the wall. "We better get going. Barker's probably thrown the piano overboard by now."

Dr. Barker stared at Wolfgang pensively from behind his desk. His deep-set hawkish eyes glared through his thin glasses. Wolfgang waited for the eruption, but what came instead was an attempt at a controlled temper. "Need I ask what your piano is doing on the fourth-floor solarium?"

"An act of God, sir."

"Don't mock the Lord. You of all people." Now came the eruption. He stood and pointed at Wolfgang. "You did this behind my back."

"Look, you refused to let me take him to the piano, so I brought the piano to him. What else could I do?"

"I'm sure Lincoln had a hand in this as well?"

"It was my doing."

"And Susannah?"

"She was against it."

"Big Fifteen?"

"Just me."

"Why does he call you Boss?"

"Maybe he calls everyone Boss." Wolfgang knew that Fifteen addressed Barker simply as Doctor. "Repairs are badly needed at the colored hospital. It's overcrowded, dark, and—"

"Do you think I don't know that, Dr. Pike? I can't do anything without more funding." Barker sat on the corner of his desk. "We can't have McVain playing the piano in the middle of the night, not when everyone is trying to sleep."

"See if his mood doesn't improve."

"Don't play innocent. You know this isn't only about him. We have hundreds of other patients to worry about. We have occupational therapy, movies, and all kinds of activities—"

"But not a piano."

Dr. Barker pounded his fist against the top of his desk. Papers scattered to the floor. "They need their rest. We can't have him playing at all hours of the night."

Wolfgang stood eye to eye with the older man. "McVain already has fans. When I arrived this morning, dozens of patients asked me who was playing the piano and if he'll continue. They smiled."

Dr. Barker turned away. "Don't bank on it."

Wolfgang gripped Dr. Barker's elbow and spun him back toward him. Barker pulled away violently and shoved Wolfgang against the wall, where his head hit a picture of Barker's wife, Anne. The picture dropped to the floor, cracking the glass inside the frame. Barker gave it no attention. Instead he stuck his finger in Wolfgang's face. "Don't tempt me. The Church doesn't make you invincible. We have rules—"

"Always about rules."

Dr. Barker sidestepped Wolfgang and stopped next to his door. "And don't involve Nurse Susannah in this. She has aspirations that go higher than your music. Don't bring her down with you."

"What do you know about Susannah?"

Dr. Barker folded his arms. "You're lucky the piano didn't crush you."

"The piano stays." Wolfgang slammed the door and left.

Snow flurries spun frantically in the wind. The night's frost had settled in, and the wet grass hardened to a crunch underfoot. It seemed as if January had finally found its cold weather, and it was here to stay now. Wolfgang navigated the downhill by himself, using his Babe Ruth Louisville Slugger as a makeshift cane. In his other hand he held his black bag of instruments. He found the colored hospital only slightly less depressing than he had the other night. The cold temperatures seemed to dampen the stench and bring with it a façade of crisp cleanliness.

He played the piccolo on the solarium porch for a group of patients while Rufus followed along with his flute. Off to the side, standing atop his creaky bed, Smokey playfully swung the Babe Ruth baseball bat, hitting probably a hundred imaginary home runs in the short amount of time that Wolfgang and Rufus had played together.

Wolfgang lowered the piccolo from his lips. "Cold."

Rufus stared up the hillside. "I heard him playing last night. He's not bad."

"He's missing three fingers." Wolfgang held up his left hand and wiggled his middle three fingers. He hoped McVain could hear the playing up the hill. "He's learning to adjust."

"What happened?"

"That's what I'd like to find out."

Rufus nodded. "Your offer still stand?"

"My offer?"

"To play up there."

Wolfgang's eyes lit up. He stood from his seat. "Of course. We can go now if you'd like. Dr. Barker has left for the night."

"What should I wear?"

Wolfgang viewed Rufus's attire—plaid pajamas, a brown coat, and black boots. "Come as you are."

Wolfgang started down the porch, thanking several of the patients for letting him play. He checked over his shoulder. Rufus was slow, hobbled by a limp of his own, and burdened by his hefty size.

When they passed Smokey's bed, the kid held the bat out for Wolfgang to take back. "Thank you, Father."

Wolfgang gripped the barrel of the bat and pushed it gently back Smokey's way. "Oh, no, Smokey. It's a gift. The bat is for you. Go and become the…the black Babe Ruth is what you called it?"

"Yep, the black Babe Ruth." Smokey swung again. "That's right, Father."

No cold feet for Rufus. He played the flute as he walked. Once he'd decided to journey up the hillside, he moved at a brisk pace, stopping only when they'd reached the entrance to the Grand Lobby, where he stood in awe of the beautiful décor and pillars that stretched from floor to ceiling. He tested the shiny floor with his shoes, swiping over it like a baseball player clearing the dirt in the batter's box.

"It's huge." Rufus waddled beside Wolfgang, his flute tucked under the weight of his right arm. The first-floor hallways were clear. Wolfgang took Rufus on an elevator to the fourth floor. On the way up Rufus drummed his fingers against the length of his flute, his eyes darting, ears perked by the mechanical sounds of the elevator. The door opened and Wolfgang was the first to step out to the fourth-floor solarium. Again, Rufus moved behind him in awe, peeking through the screened window and down to the lawn four floors below. McVain was playing the piano from his spot down on the porch. Many of the patients slept. Others seemed to be relaxing to the sound of McVain's playing. A few gave Rufus unfriendly looks as he and Wolfgang passed the foot of their beds.

"I feel like I shouldn't be here," said Rufus.

An old man lifted his head from his pillow and hissed. "What's the Negro doing here?"

"Ignore them," Wolfgang said, quickening his pace. As they approached McVain and the piano, Wolfgang had Rufus wait in the shadows. Susannah stood next to the piano, turning pages for McVain as he flew through a piece by Chopin. When he stopped playing, several of the nearby patients applauded. McVain shrugged off the attention and turned to face Wolfgang.

"You know Chopin was a victim of tuberculosis," said Wolfgang.

"I'm tired," said McVain. "What did you want to show me?"

Wolfgang extended his hand, and Rufus stepped toward the piano, gripping his flute like a child would hold a blanket. He nodded politely. "McVain, meet Rufus. He plays the flute like he invented it."

McVain stared at Rufus as if he were an alien. "He's a nigger."

"So?" Wolfgang said.

"So they've got separate hospitals."

Wolfgang crossed his arms. "I should have known."

"He's no different than you," Susannah said. And then she smirked, whispering to McVain, "You're both probably dying anyway."

"And you both love music," Wolfgang said quickly. "McVain, you played Bach earlier. Rufus, you know any Bach?"

"I do, but I'm perfectly content playing by myself...down with my own." Rufus turned away and began walking back down the solarium toward the elevator.

McVain called after him. "Stop by the cafeteria on your way out. Have a banana on us."

Wolfgang glared at McVain and then went after the black man.

Later that night, Wolfgang attempted to mask his anger when he approached Mary Sue's bed, but every time he tried to calm himself down, his facial muscles tensed up again. How dare McVain. What a fool!

Mary Sue gave him a familiar smile. "What is it, Dr. Pike?"

"Oh, nothing I need to trouble you with, Mary Sue." He began to wheel her bed across the solarium. Her spirits had begun to improve the night he'd first taken her to see Frederick. Many nights since then, she'd had quick, clandestine visits with him, no longer than ten minutes, where she would sit next to Frederick's bed and hold his hand while Wolfgang played a few songs on his violin. She would hold Frederick's hand against her belly to feel the baby kick. Despite the fact that Frederick was still mostly unresponsive, Mary Sue was convinced they were making progress. A few times when she'd squeezed his hand, he'd squeezed back, albeit slightly, but a reaction nevertheless.

One night when Wolfgang had played a familiar tune on the violin, Frederick's head had rolled slightly toward the music with the hint of a smile on his chapped lips. When Mary Sue spoke to him, his eyes more or less stayed focused on her, not nearly as glazed over as they had been.

Mary Sue leaned forward and kissed Frederick's forehead. "Until tomorrow night, Frederick." When she straightened in the wheelchair, she screamed out.

Wolfgang leaned toward her, placed his hands on her shoulders. "Mary Sue—?" And then it hit him. "Oh! Your water just broke." Mary Sue screamed out in pain again, and Wolfgang hurriedly pushed her out into the hallway. "How long have you been having these contractions?"

"Since this morning."

"This morning? Mary Sue, why didn't you tell anyone?"

She moaned as Wolfgang ran her down the hallway. "Wanted to get my visit in before I had him."

"What if he's a girl?"

"He's not." She screamed again. "He's a he. Now, hurry."

Susannah ducked her head out of a room on the other side of the hallway. "Oh, my. I'll go get Dr. Barker?"

"Not enough time, Susannah." Wolfgang motioned with his head. "Come on. We're about to deliver a baby."

While Wolfgang scrubbed his hands, Susannah gathered as many pillows as she could find and as many clean sheets as she could hold. She made a soft pallet on the floor of the operating room and helped Mary Sue from the wheelchair. They propped several pillows under her head and a couple under her hips. Mary Sue screamed out as another contraction hit her. Susannah gripped Mary Sue's hand and dabbed her forehead with a wet washcloth.

Mary Sue grimaced. "Father…"

Wolfgang looked up from his spot between her legs. "Mary Sue, at this point could you refer to me as Doctor?"

"Doctor! Why are we on the floor?" Another contraction hit her and she screamed out again.

"The one thing I remember from the baby I delivered in medical school was how slippery he was." Wolfgang rubbed his hands as if for warmth. "I don't want to drop your baby, Mary Sue."

After another twenty minutes of pushing—and much screaming on Mary Sue's part—Wolfgang's eyes lit up. "I see something. We're crowning, Mary Sue."

"What does that mean?" she screamed. "And what do you mean, we?"

"I can see the baby's head." But the head wasn't as visible as it should have been. Wolfgang leaned forward. On closer inspection, the amniotic sac hadn't broken as it should have. He leaned in and pinched the slimy membrane, releasing a gush of amniotic fluid. Mary Sue moaned and squeezed Susannah's hand. The baby's head was more visible now. The uterus contracted again, and Mary Sue pushed on cue. The head came out first, and then the rest of the body came out in waves, very quickly once the shoulders popped free. Mary Sue panted and breathed heavily as Wolfgang guided the baby into his arms.

"Susannah," said Wolfgang. "Bring the towel." Susannah did so with a smile on her face, carefully wiping the fluid and membranes away from the baby's airways. And then she cleaned the rest of the baby's body. When the baby started wailing, it seemed to Wolfgang the most pleasant sound he had ever heard.

Susannah bundled the baby in several towels to keep him warm. Minutes later the placenta came out, adding to the soaked blankets under Mary Sue's body. Wolfgang had Susannah cut the umbilical cord while he held the wet baby in his arms. The baby was still wailing, a high-pitched ululation that echoed off the cold, sterile walls of the fourth-floor operating room.

They were all exhausted, but no one more so than Mary Sue. Her face was pale, her breathing coming out in gasps. But she was grinning. Her baby was crying; he was alive. Wolfgang stood with the baby in his arms. He couldn't help but share glances with Susannah, who stood leaning over the table with a cool compress on Mary Sue's head. Their eyes met for a few awkward moments before Mary Sue's voice lured them both away from each other.

"Well, is it a boy?"

Wolfgang walked the baby over toward Mary Sue. "Yes, Mary Sue. He is a he."

Mary Sue stared at her baby's head, which was oddly misshapen. At first she held him like he were made of glass, but she soon relaxed and melted with her embrace.

"Don't be alarmed." Wolfgang wiped sweat from his forehead. "His head will go back to normal shape in a day or so."

Susannah wiped Mary Sue's forehead once more and began to clean up around the operating table. Wolfgang stole another glance at Susannah, who glowed as she worked.

The baby's cries began to soften as Mary Sue held her close.

A Waverly baby.

CHAPTER 17

The rooftop was crowded with sunbathers. Men with their shirts off played cards and shivered in the cool air, the sunlight an illusion of heat. Women with their sleeves rolled up huddled together and played dice games on the terra cotta. Even Herman had requested an hour outside, which he spent alone, facing the swings, watching the children play. He'd been on his best behavior since Rita's death. Wolfgang had begun to believe there was a real person inside that confused mind. Every time Wolfgang came near, Herman would watch him with an unreadable gaze, which, had he known better, could have been mistaken for some kind of jealousy.

The patients, especially the two women's floors, were excited about Mary Sue and Frederick's baby. The news had spread rapidly. Mary Sue spent most of her time since the delivery resting. After all, she was on the mend but still a tuberculosis patient. The delivery had taken its toll, so Susannah and the rest of the nurses were taking turns watching the baby, which she'd named Fred. They'd set up a makeshift nursery inside the laundry room, where Susannah thought the rumbling of their new electric clothes dryer could act as background noise while the baby slept—something to drown out the sound of sickness all around. Dr. Barker was as thrilled as everyone else that the baby was born healthy, although he had asked Wolfgang and Susannah why the delivery had taken place on the fourth-floor operating room and not the one on Mary Sue's floor.

"Mary Sue wanted to be closer to Frederick," Wolfgang told him.

Barker looked a bit suspicious. But the answer made sense and seemed to appease his curiosity. He just nodded.

Wolfgang had spent most of the morning avoiding the fourth floor, but when it was time to add shot to Weaver's bags, the confrontation with McVain was unavoidable. He'd been so angry at McVain last night that he'd felt his blood pressure rise. Of course, the delivery had worked wonders in distracting him and improving his mood since then.

But as Wolfgang worked on Mr. Weaver, he did his best to avoid looking at McVain, which proved difficult, for he was constantly in Wolfgang's line of vision. And when McVain rotated on his side, he reached across to his chair and grabbed Wolfgang's requiem. That McVain was a sly creature. For a brief instant, the two men locked eyes. Then Wolfgang looked away, as if repelled.

McVain flipped through the pages, loudly, methodically. No one had ever seen Wolfgang's work before, and he was already having second thoughts on whether the bully-gangster should be the first. But the requiem needed to be fixed, and he would take the help even from the likes of McVain.

Mr. Weaver was hot with fever and rather quiet, probably aware that Wolfgang's attention had been turned elsewhere. Wolfgang finished with him and moved on toward McVain.

"'The Requiem Rose,'" McVain said obnoxiously loud. He flipped through the pages some more, shaking his head at random parts, quite aware that he had Wolfgang's full attention now. "It's choppy. Like here..." He pointed to a page near the beginning. "And here."

That was it? Choppy?

McVain tapped the front page. "The harmony needs filling out. More notes."

"I'm happy with everything but the ending," said Wolfgang.

"Do you want my help or not?" McVain asked. "And what ending? You have no ending. It just rambles on to this...this..."

Wolfgang pursed his lips. "Go on."

McVain began leafing through the pages again without preamble. "I've marked places where it needs more improvement, and there are many. The second movement...I think needs a double bass to give it a darker feel." McVain sighed, placed the music on his lap, and rubbed his eyes. "I'll help, but we'll need to start over."

"Start over? I've spent years on this." Wolfgang stared at him, but McVain didn't budge. It was too much for Wolfgang to grasp. He turned away, walked a few paces, and then stopped. "I'll bring the black box up later."

"What box?"

"I keep the requiem in a black box," said Wolfgang. "Only you and I will have a key."

McVain laughed. "A key, huh?"

"Yes, McVain, a key." Wolfgang turned his back and moved along.

"And get that damn piano tuned!" shouted McVain. "It sounds like a pig at a slaughterhouse. A tone-deaf pig."

Wolfgang fumed his way across the solarium, staring down so the patients could not see his frustration. Up ahead it was hard not to notice Nurse Cleary and her considerable bulk calling his name.

"Father Pike." Nurse Cleary waved both arms, apparently excited about something. Father Pike. Dr. Pike. She was the only one who never stuck to one name, as if terribly confused, and sometimes she'd utter both within a ten-second span. "Dr. Pike. Father Pike. There's a patient on the second floor who wants to see you. His name is Josef Heinz. Room two-eighteen."

Wolfgang hurried down the stairwell, clip-clopping to the second-floor solarium. Josef Heinz. The name sounded familiar to him. Wolfgang had met nearly every patient in the building, but with the high turnover, meeting them all was becoming increasingly difficult. Inside Room 218, an old man lay on his bed. Wolfgang knocked on the doorframe. "Josef Heinz?" The old man pointed out toward the solarium. Outside, dozens of beds were clustered together in a bunch. "Josef Heinz?"

A slender man with long arms and yellow hair raised his right hand. He appeared to be about forty years old, possibly younger. Tuberculosis had a way of prematurely aging the skin. Wolfgang maneuvered among the catty-cornered beds and stood at the foot of Mr. Heinz's, on which a newspaper lay open to the cartoon comic strip *Thimble Theatre*.

"One of my favorites," Wolfgang said. "I like that new character, Popeye the Sailor." Mr. Heinz's toothy smile was kind and inviting. He held a small chalkboard on his lap and a piece of chalk in his right hand. Wolfgang sat beside him on the bed. "I believe we've met before. TB of the throat?"

Josef Heinz nodded. Physically he could still speak, but the doctors and nurses didn't permit it except for emergencies. They preferred he used his chalkboard to allow his throat to heal.

"You asked to see me?"

Josef wrote one word: PIANO?

"You heard him playing?"

Josef nodded.

"Two floors up," said Wolfgang. "He's a patient here. Tad McVain."

TALENTED.

"You're one of many fans."

Josef erased his board and wrote another word: FLUTE.

"You've got quite an ear, Mr. Heinz."

"Josef," he hissed.

"Use the board. But Josef it is."

I'M A CONCERT VIOLINIST. DO YOU HAVE ONE?

Wolfgang couldn't believe what he'd read. "At home. I have several in fact. I could bring one to you. Will you play with us?"

I'D BE HONORED.

Wolfgang's first inclination was to march Josef Heinz up to the fourth floor and have him meet McVain as soon as Dr. Barker left for the night, but minutes before his boss left, Wolfgang thought of a better idea. He'd take Josef down the hillside to the colored hospital. Josef was excited about the clandestine trip and greeted Rufus and Smokey as if they were long lost friends.

Smokey sat on the edge of his bed with his Babe Ruth Louisville Slugger propped against his thigh, listening as Josef and Rufus played the violin and flute in beautiful harmony. Wolfgang sat beside

Smokey, declining to play the piccolo with them, preferring instead to listen. The violin he'd given Josef was one of his father's old violins, not the famous *P*, but one of the better ones. It delighted Wolfgang to hear music coming from the instrument again—true music, not Wolfgang's typical ramblings. As the duo finished a short piece by Brahms, the small crowd that had gathered applauded.

Wolfgang clapped as well. "Bravo." He pointed up the hill to the main sanatorium. "Now louder. I want McVain to hear. Stick the dagger in and twist it."

January weather in the Ohio Valley was unpredictable. The sun was gone the next morning. Instead the sky was crowded with dark, billowing clouds that appeared confused about whether to rain or snow or sleet. The clouds rolled in so low, the tip of the bell tower pierced them like a knife through a feathered pillow. The temperature hovered near the freezing mark, but with the wind gusts it felt ten degrees colder.

Shortly after lunch the first drops fell as sleet, pounding the rooftop like dice. On all the floors, dozens of patients headed for the solarium porches to watch the heavy precipitation. Wolfgang could hear the tumult from the fourth floor and the chatter from the patients. It was a soporific sound, the rain falling as ice pellets. All across the woods, the boughs and branches cowered and swayed. The grounds became covered with dancing shimmers of silver, and then it all changed into a cold rain. Wolfgang approached McVain's room on the solarium for the first time that day, determined not to say anything about last night's party at the colored hospital. But he had to make his rounds, so seeing McVain was inevitable.

McVain was the first to speak. "Hey." Wolfgang continued to walk along as if he hadn't heard. "Hey."

Wolfgang stopped. "I'm busy, McVain. What is it?"

"I heard the flute last night. And a violin."

Wolfgang clenched his jaws together, squashing a smile. "You refused to play, so I found someone else."

McVain stared for a few seconds and scratched his chin with the two remaining fingers of his left hand. "Tell the nigger I'll give him another chance."

"His name is Rufus."

"Okay, Rufus, then. But get that piano tuned first."

Wolfgang tuned the piano himself, as his father had taught him years ago, with a beat-up tuning lever and a few rubber wedges to mute the strings he didn't want to hear. McVain listened as Wolfgang set the temperament and periodically referenced the pitch from a tuning fork he'd found inside a chest of his father's musical devices. He tested the keys repeatedly, and after an hour of tinkering they both seemed satisfied with how it sounded.

The rain decreased as the night moved in and then gradually transitioned to snow flurries. Shortly after ten o'clock, Barker left through the woods toward his cottage, and the grounds were covered with a dusting of snow. The coast was clear. Susannah escorted Josef up to the fourth floor while Wolfgang retrieved Rufus from down the hillside. Introductions between the men were brief. One wasn't allowed to speak, one felt out of place, and one put everyone else on edge when he did speak. The most eloquent moment was the wide-eyed expression on Josef's face when he first saw McVain's left hand. Luckily McVain hadn't seen him, or more than likely there would have been a confrontation.

They began playing, and their music became the conversation; they meshed quickly, with McVain as the centerpiece in the three-man ensemble—four-man, if you counted Wolfgang as the conductor.

For half an hour they played different movements from Mozart's *Requiem*. Although the piece was written for an entire orchestra and chorus, the three of them made it sound full and complete. At some point, each took a solo before the other two would join back in. They spoke with their eyes, their hands, by nodding their heads, never breaking stride. The awed audience grew by the minute, crowding the fourth-floor solarium with what seemed like most of the healthiest patients in the sanatorium, men and women, braving the inclement weather and the sanatorium's rules to listen.

It all came to a halt when McVain stopped. He flexed his fingers, rolled his bullish neck, and pushed away from the piano. Josef was standing beside the piano, smiling as he lowered the violin from his shoulder. Wolfgang watched McVain's eyes. Suddenly he was nervous.

"So what kind of a name is Heinz?" asked McVain.

Josef grabbed his chalkboard: GERMAN.

McVain stood abruptly.

Wolfgang grabbed his arm. "What is it now?"

McVain wrestled his arm away from Wolfgang's grip. "First a nigger. Then a Kraut. Next you gonna send me up a Jew?"

"If I could find one," said Wolfgang.

Josef cleared his throat. He showed them a new message. I AM A JEW.

Rufus grinned. Susannah chuckled. As much as he tried not to, Wolfgang burst out laughing.

McVain walked off.

CHAPTER 18

The journey of Wolfgang's requiem had been a long one. He had started writing it in the latter days of 1918, weeks after the war in Europe had ended and days after he and Rose secretly married at Saint Patrick's on West Market Street—a sudden and private ceremony spurred on by the patriotic fervor that spilled onto the Louisville streets for days after the armistice was signed. Of course, it had been Rose's idea to get married that night (not that Wolfgang hadn't been dreaming of it since the day he'd left Saint Meinrad), and so Wolfgang had contemplated it in front of her for all of three seconds before throwing his arms around her waist and lifting her off the sidewalk, smothering her with kisses as dozens of neighbors walked along the street with American flags draped over their shoulders.

At the time, the requiem had been the beginning of a symphony. It had also been the longest piece of music he'd ever attempted to write. He met the challenge at full steam, inspired as he was by a life-time with Rose. But even then he couldn't conceptualize it properly. He'd run into the same roadblocks his father had; it just wouldn't come out on paper as it sounded in his head. So Rose's symphony sputtered to a halt soon after it had begun, and Wolfgang all but abandoned it during his medical school studies. But Rose never allowed him to completely let it go; Wolfgang needed the music, Rose understood that. When his studies in medicine grew intense, she urged him to take a break at the piano. When they attended church together, she smiled at him as the organ played, squeezing his hand. "Listen," she said between humming along with the music. "You can do that, too," she told him. And so she convinced him to keep trying, week after week, all throughout medical school—until her death five years later, when Wolfgang set it aside yet again.

For weeks after her funeral Wolfgang was lost. He slept all day, rarely ate, his heart beating slower with every passing of the sun, as if an invisible weight had come down to suffocate him, sucking him dry of all tears and breath. He missed his father, he'd been estranged from his mother for over five years, and he prayed for the chance to hold Rose's hand just one more time. The grass grew tall in the front yard of their Portland neighborhood home, two miles northwest of downtown, where many of the working class were buying houses and raising their families. The mail overflowed the box next to the driveway. Newspapers piled up on the front porch.

And then one morning the sun rose. Birdsong penetrated his windows from a nearby tree. In the few moments it lasted before the birds flew off, he thought of his six years at Saint Meinrad and of the friends and mentors he'd left behind there, the peace and tranquility of the farmland, so far removed from the city. He reflected on one of his times of private prayer there, and the memories of it warmed his heart. He'd been alone in the crypt chapel beneath the abbey church, kneeling at a pew in his Roman cassock, staring at the cross on the wall, confused and praying for guidance about his summer with Rose. And at that moment he heard some of the monks chanting from the church above, plainsong, the Gregorian chanting that was such an integral part of the Benedictine prayer. Their combined voices had perfect harmony, and the timing of their chanting was an answer to his prayers—perhaps not an answer at the time but proof that someone was listening. It had given him the strength and courage to talk to Friar Christian about his relationship with Rose.

For the first time since leaving the abbey to be with Rose, he felt the urge to return and complete his studies to become a priest. He felt the calling again. The pressure on his heart eased somewhat, enough so that he found it more cleansing to breathe, and the beats no longer felt marred in molasses. Music had nourished him as a boy, and it would do so again as a man. The Lord's music. He imagined joining the organist in the abbey's choir loft and starting a fledgling choir. Beautiful music would soar above as the monks chanted from their choir stalls below, flanking both sides of the altar. And more importantly for himself, Rose's symphony needed to be opened up again. It needed to be changed: now it would become her requiem, a musical composition for the dead. Rose's funeral Mass.

He wrote to Friar Christian and told him of his plans to return. Ten days later Wolfgang received a letter from the abbey: he would be welcomed back to Saint Meinrad with open arms.

But while Wolfgang waited for the letter, he'd sat on his porch one afternoon, opening all the newspapers he'd ignored for the past weeks. Every day there were headlines about the tuberculosis epidemic that ravaged the country, and Louisville had the worst death rate of them all. He and Rose had been to Waverly Hills before, but now a new building had been constructed, a massive brick and stone structure that housed nearly five hundred patients. And, according to the article in the *Courier Journal*, they were in bad need of doctors and clergy. If the birdsong had been a calling, the newspapers had been a sign of another sort.

He thought of Rose and of their experience at Camp Zachary Taylor with the Spanish flu during the war, and he knew what he had to do. He wrote Friar Christian another note: he was fully committed to returning to the abbey, but with the current health crisis back home, he felt he had to fulfill his duties as a doctor and a man of science first. He would return to Saint Meinrad as soon as the tuberculosis died down.

The next day, with his Portland house on the market and a suitcase in hand, Wolfgang walked up the steep road to Waverly Hills, catching ominous glimpses of the monstrous sanatorium through the trees. But he never wavered. He spoke to Rose all the way up, and the thought of her strength in life propelled him. Dr. Barker hired him on the spot.

The patients at Waverly inspired him—he'd found a new home. For months the requiem moved along so clearly, practically writing itself.

As he'd learned weeks before, the sanatorium was short on

staff and had no religious figurehead. He quickly, and without an agenda, began to fill the voids of both jobs, at least to an extent on the latter—guilt often left him fearful of overstepping his bounds. The staff had already artificially ordained him as priest and, jokingly or not, Wolfgang lost sleep contemplating it. So again he'd put pen to paper and wrote to Friar Christian with a proposition. Again he said he would return to the abbey as soon as the tuberculosis showed signs of slowing. But this time he added that while he was working as a doctor, if they agreed to send him his cassocks, his lessons, and the theology books, he would continue his training as a theologian at Waverly. Of course he understood that the years studying on his own would not count toward becoming a priest, but the experience he would gain, he told them in the letter, could be immeasurable. After all, many of the patients at Waverly were already calling him Father.

On the same evening McVain had stormed away from Rufus and Josef, Wolfgang decided to return to the sanatorium after walking Susannah to her dorm. Like it or not, the fourth-floor solarium was Wolfgang's new composing area. He couldn't complain, because it was his own doing, and he convinced himself that cool temperatures helped him think more clearly. His cold fingers on the keys were just another obstacle to overcome. His frozen earlobes only pushed him to focus more closely on sound. After starting the requiem over, as McVain had requested days ago, Wolfgang's mind began to flow with optimism: certainly the work would be improved. The positive attitude reminded him of the time he'd made the decision to change it from a symphony to a requiem shortly after Rose's death. But the creative flow had been short-lived back then. Perhaps with McVain's guidance it would be different now.

He blew into his hands to warm them and continued on, composing, trying to ignore the fact that he was still at Waverly while his theology books sat in a stack against the inside wall of his cottage, covered by a thin but recent layer of dust, used but not often enough. Four years the patients had been calling him both Doctor and Father, and the secondary title felt no less artificial than it had the first time it had been uttered as a mistake. *Focus on the music, Wolfgang! The music.*

Near midnight a quiet snow began falling, drawing his attention from the requiem only momentarily for a quick glance toward the woods. Wind blew flakes against the screen, and a few of them filtered in through the tiny holes and melted on the concrete solarium floor. McVain lay behind Wolfgang and the piano, fountain pen in hand, reworking a portion of the music. He'd said very little since his abrupt exit from their ensemble earlier in the evening.

Several of the surrounding patients slept, but not soundly due to the cold. None of them minded his composing late at night; in fact, they preferred it. Many, even with his constant stopping and starting, considered his playing something akin to a lullaby. Wolfgang blew into his hands again, rubbed them together, and softly played the new opening, which was to begin with the deep, rumbling tone of a bow gliding across the thick strings of a double bass. Minutes later a viola would enter, and then the three would blend into a piano trio.

Wolfgang imagined a woman's soprano voice singing the introit. He could hear it clearly. He mouthed the words as he played. A song for the angels. A song for Rose. He glanced over his shoulder and found McVain crossing out and scribbling. If the man felt any guilt over his treatment of Josef and Rufus, Wolfgang couldn't see it. He acted as if nothing had happened.

Wolfgang checked his pocket watch—two in the morning. His eyes were getting heavy. Just as he was about to stand, he heard someone shuffling through the shadows. Josef emerged in slippers and pajamas, walking slowly with his chalkboard.

Wolfgang jumped up. "Josef, it's late. What are you doing up here?" He stood between Josef and McVain.

McVain dropped the requiem to his lap and glared at Josef. "Scram, Kraut."

"Blarney," Josef hissed. Upon his board he'd written a long

message: LET ME GUESS. YOU WERE A SOLDIER IN THE GREAT WAR. A GERMAN BLEW YOUR FINGERS OFF.

McVain read the board and looked away.

Josef erased the board with a rag he'd brought with him and wrote again: I FOUGHT FOR THE GERMANS. I'M AN AMERICAN NOW.

Wolfgang said nothing. This was between McVain and Josef.

Josef didn't give up: WHERE ARE YOUR PARENTS FROM?

McVain stared at him with his ornery green eyes before finally speaking. "Ireland."

THEN WE'RE BOTH IMMIGRANTS. He erased and wrote again. AND WE'RE BOTH DYING OF TB. He erased, wrote. I'D BE HONORED TO PLAY WITH YOU IN THE MEANTIME.

McVain grunted, looked away, and fingered the bed sheets that he'd pulled up to his waist. "Same time tomorrow." He rolled over in bed and faced the other way.

Josef leaned down toward McVain's exposed left ear. "Rufus too," he whispered. "Bullets don't care what color the skin is."

Wolfgang stumbled wearily down the hillside to his cottage shortly before 3:00 a.m. Yet he tossed and turned in bed, his mind full of everything except sleep: the requiem, his new little orchestra, McVain, Josef, and Rufus…and then Susannah. His mind kept drifting to her legs on the stairwell, her bare knees on his couch, the curve of her hip, her chest gently rising and falling to the flow of his piano music. Her eyes fluttering behind closed lids as she slept, lips slightly parted.

He thought of Lincoln's bootlegging and joking about the peep-hole in the nurse's dormitory. How different would life have been, Wolfgang wondered, if he had never peered through that hole in the wall of his childhood bedroom. He would have believed his mother's lie. Charles had been deathly ill, after all. Wolfgang would never have turned against her. Would he still have sought comfort under the folds of Catholicism? Would he have met Rose? In spying through that hole, he had traded his mother's life for Rose's, and in that, Wolfgang had no regret. He would not have traded Rose for anything, including his parents.

What would Rose think of Susannah?

Wolfgang forced it all from his mind. It was four in the morning. He felt chilled. He was to become a priest someday. A man of the cloth. He grabbed his rosary beads from the dresser, knelt beside the bed, and began to pray. "Hail Mary, full of grace, the Lord is with thee—"

Something thumped against his front door.

A splat. Then laughter.

Wolfgang tossed the rosary on the bed and ran to the door. He opened it and jumped back. The severed head of a pig faced him, its blood trickling through the cracks in the porch. A knife had been stuck in the animal's skull, pinning a piece of paper to the muddy flesh on top. Its eyes were open and slightly yellowed. Its ears had been sliced off, the tongue cut out.

Wolfgang ran down the porch steps. Footsteps sounded up the hillside, crunching over the dusting of snow, amid the dark trees, fleeing, but Wolfgang was determined to catch them. If they were indeed patients, he should be able to catch them, even with his gimp foot. He half sprinted and half hopped into the trees, ignoring the soreness that still lingered. The footsteps scattered. Laughter. Male laughter from two different angles. Flashes of white confused him, and before he could react, one of them was upon him. The attacker wore a white garment, not too unlike the vestments Wolfgang wore at Mass, yet atop his head, covering his face and most of his neck, was a pointed hood with eyeholes.

"You're gonna die."

The second man, dressed in the same white attire, jumped at Wolfgang from the opposite direction. One of them hit Wolfgang hard in the stomach with a thick club. He doubled over. A knee collided with his jaw. He tasted blood. He dropped to the ground to protect himself.

Another voice bellowed from down below. "Hey, Boss! Hey!"

Upon hearing Big Fifteen's voice, the attackers took off into the darkness. Instead of giving chase, Big Fifteen stopped next to Wolfgang, knelt by his side, and rolled him over. "You okay, Boss?"

Wolfgang leaned on his right elbow and dabbed at the blood running from his lips. "The Klan."

He saw a look in Big Fifteen's eyes that he'd never seen before. Was it fear? Big Fifteen helped Wolfgang to his feet. "There's a burnin' cross down by the colored hospital."

By the time they navigated the downhill to the colored hospital, the flames had been doused with water. A black, charred cross, built crudely with two planks of splintered wood, stood on the grassy rise before the hill plummeted down to the hospital. Wolfgang stopped about twenty yards away, clutching his stomach. Acrid black smoke spiraled from the burnt cross. The boards used for the cross looked like those Wolfgang had seen on the woodpile next to the maintenance shed, which supported his theory that the culprits could have been two of the Waverly patients. Or possibly employees?

Big Fifteen kicked the makeshift cross. It held together stubbornly with a few bent nails. He kicked it again and the planks dropped to the wet grass. Dozens of patients stood outside the entrance to the hospital, staring at the broken cross. Smokey leaned on his bat, his smile nonexistent.

Wolfgang attempted to straighten. "We'll find who's responsible." Wind shifted the smoke away from the hospital and toward Wolfgang. He choked and slumped over in the grass. He waited there with Big Fifteen's hand on his shoulder, fought back the dry heaves, and wiped his mouth. Only then did he realize how cold he was in his pajamas.

"Why they afta' you?" Big Fifteen helped Wolfgang back to the footpath, gripping his elbow the entire way.

"The new Klan is radically anti-Catholic," he said. "They're also Prohibitionists."

"Then why ain't they after Lincoln?"

"Lincoln's too clever," said Wolfgang. "And I have the feeling he's got pull on the outside. His family. He's got family with muscle."

"But so are you, Boss. Clever like Lincoln."

"Hardly, but thank you." Wolfgang watched for movement

between the trees, but all he could see was darkness. "My attackers. I think they're patients here."

Big Fifteen chuckled. "Then maybe they gonna die soon."

The pig's head was still on the porch when Wolfgang returned. The wide yellowed eyes watched him go up the steps. Removing the knife lodged in its skull proved to be more difficult than he'd expected.

He yanked the note from the knife, nearly ripping it in half:

ONLY WARNING, FATHER.

NO MORE NIGGERS IN THE HOSPITAL.

"Cowards." Wolfgang crumpled the paper and stuffed it into his pocket.

He thought of McVain. No, it wasn't possible.

Neither attacker had been McVain's size. But McVain did have a lot of influence in the sanatorium. They considered him a war hero. Wolfgang squatted down over the pig's head and pondered the task before him. After a few seconds of twisting, he pried the knife free and set it aside next to the cottage wall. He lifted the head in both hands, heaved it into the brush, and watched it roll down the hill for about ten yards until it stopped against the trunk of a tree.

Then he limped inside, where he sat by the fire until his hands and feet thawed. He just needed to close his eyes and rest.

Someone knocked on the door.

His eyes shot open. His mouth felt more swollen than it had before he'd closed his eyes.

"Who is it?"

The door creaked open and Susannah's head popped in. She stepped quickly inside and closed the door behind her. "Oh, Wolf, look at you." She knelt beside him. "I came over as soon as I heard." She sniffled as if she'd been crying.

"I'll be fine." He attempted to get up, but her hands pressed firmly against his chest and forced him back down to the cushions.

"Rest." She raked her fingers through his hair and down the

side of his beard. She leaned down and kissed his forehead. He was reminded of his mother's kisses and he blinked, swallowing a mixture of saliva and blood. He coughed heavily. Susannah was up in a flash, her navy blue skirt swirling behind her as she turned for the kitchen. She brought a glass of water and stuffed a pillow from the bed behind his neck. The water was cold but felt good. He was sure he could have managed to hold the glass himself, but he didn't stop her as she helped him. He swallowed two large gulps, wincing.

"Enough?"

"Yes, thank you."

Susannah reentered the kitchen. Cabinets opened. Dishes and utensils clanked. The faucet turned on. She returned with a bowl of water and a washrag. His throat felt raw, the taste in his mouth was rancid, yet...

Susannah was taking care of him.

She dabbed the wet cloth to his chin, leaning close enough for him to see the slight imperfections in her skin—a few freckles, a tiny white scar about a half inch long above her arched left eyebrow, a couple tiny pockmarks on her right jawline. Her eyelashes were longer than he'd thought.

"Open your mouth," she said. "Oh my, your lip is swollen." She leaned closer to examine. He gazed into her eyes, noticing for the first time the tiny flecks of blue around her pupils. He felt the gentle pushes of breath coming from her nose, and he truly believed, despite his pain, that he could have stayed in his current position for days. "One of your teeth is missing." She handed him the glass of water. "Wash your mouth out with this."

Wolfgang took a mouthful and spat into the bowl. She dried his neck and then combed his hair with her fingers again. She caught him staring and looked away. Wolfgang found the spot against the wall where his piano had been. Rose's vase rested on the floor next to a lit candle. "Thank you."

Susannah scooted down the couch toward his feet and removed his left shoe and sock. He flinched when she began to remove his right shoe. "Please," he said. "Leave it on." At first she appeared hurt by his insecurity, but she gave him a quick smile and lowered his foot back down to the cushion. Rose was the only woman other than his mother who had seen his withered right foot.

He reached down and tugged the note free from the pocket of his pajamas. "They left this note."

Susannah read it and immediately crumpled it again. She dropped it to the floor. "I assume they mean Rufus? It's harmless, isn't it, his playing for a few hours a night?"

Wolfgang shrugged. Susannah carefully lifted his legs, sat on the couch, and then dropped the weight of his feet on her lap. She massaged his bare left foot. "You'll warn Rufus?"

"Of course."

"And Barker?"

"I don't know."

"He's sure to know what happened."

Wolfgang lifted his head. "But he doesn't have to know about that note." He watched Susannah's hands and slender fingers rub the top of his foot. "Perfect excuse to shut us down for sure."

"You'll be taking a chance, Wolf. It worries me." She stopped rubbing.

"I'll live." He rested his head back on the pillow and peered down the length of the couch, where his left heel sunk slightly into the meat of her skirt-covered thigh. "I'll leave it up to Rufus if he plays or not. He'll be my only concern."

"And you?"

"I'll take my chances." He couldn't say this aloud yet, but in the many years of service for his faith, this new trio of musicians was the closest thing he'd ever seen to God's intervention. Wolfgang felt as if He'd placed them all here for a purpose. "I won't allow the threats of the weak to interfere with my plans. Perhaps it is selfish, but I want it for the three other men as much for myself. They need it."

Susannah started to argue but stopped. Her grip on his foot became stronger. He turned on his right side to hide his arousal.

"What is it?"

"Nothing." He hoped she would continue to touch him. She did. The rosary beads he'd tossed on the bed earlier caught his attention. Was God watching? Was this worse than wearing a white hood and beating a man? Or burning a cross? He wondered if Rose could see him. Could she hear his impure thoughts? Susannah closed her eyes and eventually fell asleep with her hands on his legs. He watched her until his eyes grew heavy, and he too succumbed to slumber.

At some point before sunrise he felt Susannah's lips on his left cheek. "I'll be back in a few hours," she whispered. And then she was gone.

CHAPTER 19

Wolfgang searched for footprints the next morning, but the night's dusting of snow had already melted and the wind had scattered the leaves. In the middle of his rounds, and a third of the way through his growing request list, he took a pause on the first-floor solarium to survey the woods. His face stung from last night's attack. With his swollen tongue, he felt the hole in his gums where his tooth should have been.

Down the hillside, next to the barn, the cows were especially agitated, mooing, some in unison.

"They actually sound quite good," Susannah said, coming up behind him.

Wolfgang looked over his shoulder. "Who?"

"The cows."

Wolfgang laughed. Susannah moved on.

In the chapel just before Mass, Jesse approached Wolfgang, gripped his arm, and pulled him aside. "If you want me to, I can stand outside your place at night. Like a bodyguard. I know where it is and all. Wouldn't be no trouble."

"Thank you, Jesse," Wolfgang said, "but it won't be necessary. A few prayers would suffice."

Jesse nodded and then ushered an elderly woman to the front row near the altar.

Wolfgang waited until after Mass to see Dr. Barker, and when he did, he heard Susannah's voice inside his office. He'd evidently called her in as well, because he doubted she would have ever gone there voluntarily. Wolfgang waited just outside the door and listened.

"I saw you last night," Dr. Barker said to Susannah. "Entering Dr. Pike's cottage."

"He was assaulted," said Susannah. "I went to check on him."

"People will talk, Susannah."

"Let them."

"Wait." He paused. His tone softened. "Wait. Perhaps when you're finished with your book, I can be of some help in getting it published. Maybe a medical journal."

"You would do that?"

"If the work merits it," he said. "We can both work on it. I'm going out of town for a week, but when I get back, I'd like to see it."

"Oh, okay. Really?"

Wolfgang stepped closer to the open doorway.

Dr. Barker sighed heavily. "What should I do with Wolfgang? He continues to defy me. Just the other night we had patients from other floors up there listening to McVain play the piano."

"I'm not sure I'm the one you should be asking," said Susannah. "I'm in favor of what—"

"He thinks he's giving them hope, but it's a mirage, Susannah. Music can't cure disease."

"He's lifting their spirits. And it's taking Wolfgang's mind off Rose."

"And you think that's important?"

She paused. "I think he truly believes God has sent him those musicians. It can't stop now, sir."

"But this isn't about him. It's about the patients."

"Exactly, Dr. Barker. The patients." Susannah paused. "I was with Frederick this morning on the fourth floor. He's gotten stronger. He actually opened his mouth to swallow chicken broth this morning. I think he'll live to hold his baby soon."

"We can only pray that he does, Susannah," said Dr. Barker. "It's a miracle he has not gone down that chute. I thought we'd lost him."

"Dr. Pike plays for him every night. You know that, don't you?"

Wolfgang waited out in the hallway through a lull in their conversation. It seemed as if Susannah had struck a chord with their boss. And then Dr. Barker said, "I'll look forward to reading your work, Susannah, after my return."

"Thank you." She gave Wolfgang no time to backtrack down the hallway, leaving as abruptly as she did. So instead of pretending he hadn't heard their conversation, he gave her a smile on her way out and then knocked on the doorframe.

Dr. Barker looked up from his desk and waved him in. He carefully placed a stack of files inside a briefcase as he eyed Wolfgang. "I'm sorry this happened. How's your face?"

Wolfgang touched his lip and chin. "Sore."

Dr. Barker snapped his briefcase closed. "We'd hoped the brick would be an isolated incident. I've contacted the police."

"I believe the two attackers are patients here."

"What makes you think that?"

"One of them has a TB cough." By the light of day, Wolfgang's decision not to risk the music by telling him about the note seemed irresponsible but irrefutable. "I've heard it on both occasions."

Dr. Barker grabbed his briefcase from the desk and held it with military-type stiffness by his left side. "I doubt anyone at Waverly Hills is affiliated with the KKK."

"We'd be naïve to think that everyone here is a saint…sir."

"I guess McVain is a perfect example of that." Barker walked past Wolfgang to the door. "I have to go out of town for a week. My mother is sick."

"I'm sorry."

"I think she'll be okay, but she says my presence comforts her."

"Is Anne going with you?"

"Anne? No," he said softly. "Dr. Pike, see to it that there are no problems while I'm gone."

As the day drew on, Wolfgang tended to the patients, listened to confessions, and played bedside music for those who requested it. Mary Sue was regaining her energy since the delivery, and the baby was doing very well, sleeping almost four hours at a time before needing to be fed. Wolfgang promised he would take her to see Frederick soon. She glowed when he told her of Frederick's slight improvement.

It was a gray, freezing day, typical of late January in the valley, the type of day when all the plants, shrubbery, and grass seemed to shrink as if curling up to preserve heat. More snow flurries fell—the clouds full of uncertainty. Sometime after lunch Wolfgang got word from Lincoln that Big Fifteen had found the rest of the pig's body in the woods, not far from where the cows were kept. The cows had evidently spotted the carcass, and they'd mooed until someone came to find out what the commotion was about.

Jesse, in Wolfgang's medical opinion, was a month away from Making the Walk. So when he volunteered to help Susannah and Wolfgang question the rest of the patients about the attack on the hillside, Wolfgang agreed to let him roam the floors with them, especially since Dr. Barker was not around to reprimand. Wolfgang was convinced the attackers were from Waverly, but after analyzing everyone, he began to have doubts.

Except for a bearded brute on the second floor named Edward Bryne—whom everyone called "Teapot," because his persistent cowlick on the top of his head resembled a handle—they all seemed so innocent, and sick, and he felt guilty for suspecting them in the first place. Edward Bryne wasn't shy about his opinion of blacks; he referred to them as spearchuckers, but when Wolfgang questioned him further about his whereabouts during the attack, Bryne pulled the bed sheet away from his lower half to reveal that his right leg was missing from the knee down. He'd lost it in the war. "Unless the Klan man you saw was a cripple," said Bryne, "it wasn't me." By sundown they still had no answers, so Wolfgang told Jesse to return to his room and rest.

It was time to play some music.

As Wolfgang expected, Rufus refused to let the threatening note scare him from entering the sanatorium. "I been given a dose of medicine," he told Wolfgang, "and I need more." Wolfgang retrieved Rufus shortly after sundown, and when they arrived

McVain and Josef were already playing, McVain apparently warming up to his German chalkboard-writing enemy. Susannah listened under the warmth of a wool quilt while Wolfgang conducted at his new podium, an apparent gift from Lincoln's uncle.

Maverly's cries carried from her room on the rooftop, but she was mostly ignored, her voice drowned out by the music. The ensemble played for two hours—portions of Wolfgang's evolving requiem, along with pieces from Handel and Mendelssohn—and stopped only because they were exhausted.

McVain blew into his cupped hands. "Can't feel my damn fingers."

Rufus lowered his flute. "And you ain't got that many to feel."

Wolfgang nearly gasped, staring at Rufus. McVain looked shocked. But he merely grumbled, "Well, it's fucking cold, I know that much."

They called it a night, and after Wolfgang escorted Rufus down the hill, he returned to the fourth floor to work on his requiem. The cold helped to numb his busted lip. He found McVain still sitting at the piano with a blanket draped over his shoulders. At first he appeared asleep, but as Wolfgang approached, McVain looked up from the keys, his eyes red. He shivered in bursts. His red hair squirmed in the breeze, and he wiped his nose on the blanket. The skin above his upper lip was red and chapped.

"It wasn't me," McVain said.

"What do you mean?"

"The burning cross." McVain faced the piano again and ran his left pinkie across one of the black keys. "It wasn't me."

Wolfgang sat on the edge of McVain's bed. "I never said it was."

McVain turned to face him. "You wear your emotions on your sleeve, Wolfgang."

It was the first time McVain had called him by name. He noticed that beneath the blanket McVain had changed into pants, a nice white shirt, and a pair of Buster Browns. "Going somewhere?"

"Take me to the colored hospital."

"Why?"

"Because I don't know how to get there, that's why." McVain stood from the piano bench and lifted a brown sack from the floor.

McVain snuck out of the sanatorium this time on his own free will, accompanied by Wolfgang instead of kidnapped, and Dr. Barker would know nothing about it. Wolfgang decided not to risk spoiling the mood by asking what McVain was carrying in the sack. McVain's eagerness to reach the colored hospital was a pleasant shock, and he didn't hesitate to stand beneath the lit porch and wake up whoever was sleeping above.

"Hey, Rufus!"

Wolfgang stood in the shadows and leaned against a tree. It was McVain's business. He would give them privacy to talk unless invited.

A portly lady with caramel-colored skin pressed her face against the screen and called downward. "My lands, man, what could you possibly want this time of night?" She glanced over her shoulder and spoke to someone. "It's a white man."

"I'm looking for Rufus," called McVain. "Is he there?"

"What's in the bag there, mister?" the lady asked.

He raised the brown bag. "Beer."

"Got one for me?"

"No."

Crickets chirped. One minute passed, then two. McVain appeared ready to give up and return up the hill, so Wolfgang delayed him: "How'd you get the beer?"

"Lincoln." McVain glanced over his shoulder. "Said he can get anything up the tunnel."

"Lincoln looks up to you," said Wolfgang.

McVain shrugged.

"Lincoln seems to have a limitless supply of giggle water."

McVain grunted. "He's infatuated with Al Capone. Told me Capone hangs around the Seelbach Hotel. I told him I know; I've played cards with him before."

They shared a laugh, and then Wolfgang watched McVain's face harden again. "You were serious just then? About knowing Al Capone?"

"Yeah. Is that a problem?"

Just then, Rufus stepped out in his pajamas, slippers, and a dark coat. "What do you want?"

McVain held up the brown bag and removed the two beer bot-tles. "Could only manage two."

Rufus watched him for a few seconds. McVain stood only a few paces from where the cross had burned. As if he'd read his mind, McVain looked down, spotted the charred grass, and respectfully stepped farther away. Rufus took a few cautious steps forward.

McVain handed Rufus a bottle that had already been opened. "No problem keeping it cold."

Rufus grinned, barely, and took a swig. He wiped his mouth with the sleeve of his coat. McVain walked down the slope and sat on a concrete bench next to the brick building. Rufus found room beside him. Wolfgang sat down in the grass about twenty feet away. Their voices carried.

McVain took a swig of beer. "My father hated Negroes."

Rufus looked at McVain's hand. "My father hated cripples."

McVain smirked. He took a swig and coughed into his left hand, which did little to stop the mist that flew from his mouth.

Rufus lifted his pajama shirt and showed McVain a circular wound on the left side of his stomach. "I was shot at Saint Mihiel."

Wolfgang knew that McVain had been in the war and that he'd probably lost his fingers there. It was the perfect opportunity to offer how he'd lost them, or where, but McVain said nothing. Their conversation just rolled on, and they soon invited Wolfgang over, making room for him on the bench.

Rufus was one of nearly two hundred black soldiers to receive the French Medal of Honor. He was in the 93rd Division of the United States Army, an all-black division that was kept apart from the white soldiers. They were sent to France, wearing U.S. uniforms, to fight side by side with the French troops. They'd volunteered by the thousands, their opportunity to express patriotism and bravery, Rufus said. They fought at Argonne, Chateau-Thierry, Saint Mihiel, Champagne, Vosges, and Metz.

McVain and Rufus talked about music, about the war, about buddies killed in action, and about war stories thought long bur-ied. But every time the conversation began to approach the end of McVain's service in Chateau-Thierry or its aftermath, he quickly

202 ❧ James Markert

changed the subject. Wolfgang was surprised McVain had opened up as much as he had, but now the bottle had been opened and he wanted to learn more.

Long after the beer was finished, Rufus wished them a good night and returned to bed. There were no handshakes involved in the departure.

Wolfgang helped McVain back uphill, and into bed. In the silence, Wolfgang said, "My foot kept me out of the draft."

"That doesn't surprise me," McVain said. He mimed Uncle Sam's stern poster expression and pointed at Wolfgang with his mangled hand. "I want *you*." He lowered his hand. "Son of a bitch."

Wolfgang listened to McVain's labored breathing for a moment. "What was your wife's name?"

"Who told you I had a wife?"

"Lincoln."

McVain sighed. "Jane."

"Where is she now?"

"We divorced years ago. She moved to Virginia. Remarried." He stared down at his fingers. "I would have given both of my legs to keep my fingers."

Wolfgang patted his shoulder. "Your playing is getting better."

McVain said nothing.

CHAPTER 20

D r. Barker's absence was like a vacation. McVain, Rufus, and
Josef played to near exhaustion, taking breaks only when
Wolfgang demanded, which was every thirty minutes. But
as soon as Wolfgang walked away, they'd start up again. One night
Josef fell asleep in a chair next to McVain's bed and Susannah left
him there.

Extra medical duties had fallen in Wolfgang's lap and he'd shared
them with Susannah. Whenever Barker was gone, Susannah was
used as an extra doctor. This time he allowed her to assist on a nerve
crush, and she'd been by his side when he'd removed two rib bones
from a woman who'd been a patient at Waverly for seven months
when her lungs stopped functioning properly. They kept so busy
they rarely had time to join the ensemble, but the music carried on.
Patients on every solarium remarked to Wolfgang about the music,
and the days passed quickly. Bouts of snowfall graced the sanatorium
every day.

Mary Sue began to pace up and down the solarium porch with
little Fred in tow. She was getting stronger. Wolfgang had wheeled
them both up to visit Frederick, but only for a few minutes. Mary
Sue held the baby in the doorway and Frederick smiled from his bed
across the room. He'd managed one word: "Beautiful." And then
they'd left him alone to rest.

Mary Sue was an avid fan of the fourth-floor trio, and she insisted
on listening up close every time they played. She wasn't the only
one. The audience swelled. The trio played Mozart and Haydn,

Beethoven and Schubert, Baroque and Classical, Renaissance and Romantic, and by the fourth day of Dr. Barker's absence, they'd begun to dabble with their own original pieces. No longer restricted to playing at night, the trio flourished. Three instruments became one. Their minds fused. Josef's wife, Steffi, visited and brought chocolate-chip cookies. They played for her, and between pieces, she told them stories of Josef's past—about his clumsiness in the war, his inability to fire a gun the first time he'd tried, his violin performances in Austria, his concerts on stage in front of hundreds, embarrassing moments in their fifteen happily married years, and their immigration to the United States.

The Great War had crippled Germany's economy. Josef's music store in Berlin had gone out of business. Propaganda began to circulate through the cities, some of it blaming the German Jews for losing the war and for the state of the country afterward. They'd fled the growing anti-Semitism and came to a new life in America in the summer of 1925. On the boat trip across the Atlantic, Steffi told them with a smile, Josef had thrown up seventeen times!

McVain listened intently. He laughed along with them. He no longer appeared disgusted around Josef and had been quite cordial to Josef's wife.

And no new threats had come from Rufus's daily presence in the sanatorium. "Wonder if it was Barker in those robes," Lincoln joked to Wolfgang.

Wolfgang was amused but didn't drop his guard.

Every night he worked on the requiem, collaborating with Rufus and Josef, for both proved valuable as well. But McVain was the catalyst. Whatever may have happened to his fingers had not touched his mind, and every comment he made, every note he gave showed Wolfgang that when it came to music, he was just the student. McVain was clearly the teacher.

Once the piece gained momentum again, Wolfgang found himself unable to push it aside. His wine consumption increased. It was becoming increasingly more difficult to separate music from work. On the fifth night of Dr. Barker's absence, he paced the floor of his cottage, his hands moving to the sound of music in his head—violins and violas, flutes and clarinets, double bass and piano, woodwinds, strings, and brasses together. Just as his mind had nearly become lost in a violin solo, a knock interrupted.

"Who is it?"

"Open up, it's freezing out here." It was Susannah.

Wolfgang opened the door. He had escorted her to the dormitory less than an hour before. Why was she dropping by after midnight and waving a newspaper in his face?

"What is it?"

"Hello to you, too." She pushed the paper into his hands, pointing at an advertisement. "New Steinite radio. Thought you might want to take a look."

"A hundred and eighteen dollars. I can't afford this."

Susannah snatched it back. "Start saving." She pointed to the small table beside the fireplace where his phonograph rested like the fossil it had become. "It would look great in place of that monstrosity." She sat down on the couch. "Think how it would sound."

"Rose loved that phonograph."

"Of course she did."

Wolfgang sat beside her on the couch. "Susannah, what are you doing here?"

"You want me to go?"

"No, no, I just mean…it's late."

She clapped his shoulder and stood. "You stay up all hours of the night working and studying those theology books. It's not late for you and I'm not tired."

"Have you been drinking?"

She rolled her eyes and spotted the open bottle of wine on the floor. "No, but I see that you have."

Wolfgang walked to the window and leaned against the sill. A cool draft blew over his hands. "Did anyone see you?"

"What does it matter? This is just an innocent night with a friend."

"Exactly." Wolfgang nodded in agreement. "This is as harmless as if Lincoln visited me in the middle of the night."

Susannah pretended to look deeply offended for a second,

and then her smile returned. "What were you working on? Rose's requiem? Can I hear some of it?"

Wolfgang hesitated before grabbing his father's P violin that rested on the stone hearth of the fireplace. His eyes drifted to the swell of her breasts beneath her red dress, and then he focused again on the violin. He fit it between his shoulder and neck and lifted the bow. "I'm not terribly good at the violin."

"You play it for the patients every day, Wolf. Just play."

He played. It sounded much better in his mind than what resonated from the instrument's F-holes, but it was a work in progress. He stood in the middle of the floor, lightly tapping the toes of his right foot against the floor while maintaining his balance on his left leg. He focused on the fingers of his left hand as they danced over the strings. He concentrated on his right arm, making sure the bow slid across the strings at the correct angle on every touch. Susannah didn't seem to mind his awkwardness on the violin, wincing only once when he hit the wrong note. What stole Wolfgang's attention, five minutes into his playing, was when Susannah closed her eyes, leaned back on the couch, and began to hum. Her humming turned into soft singing. Her voice was lovely. He pulled the violin from his shoulder.

She opened her eyes. "I like it."

"I didn't know you had such a nice voice, Susannah."

"Sorry, it just came out."

"I had no idea you could sing."

She sat up straight. "I can dance too. And cook. And sew."

And then it hit him. His eyes widened nearly as much as his smile.

"What is it, Wolf?"

He sat next to her on the couch, not completely unaware that their legs were touching. She didn't move away. "I write for the piano and violin and flute," said Wolfgang, "but in my head I always hear a soprano singing too. What's a requiem without a choir?"

He looked at her. "But forget the requiem." He pointed out the window, toward the main building. "Our little ensemble up there, it needs a choir, a chorus."

She leaned away from him playfully. "Doctor. Priest. Conductor. And now choirmaster?" She laughed. "Just where will you find a choir, Wolfgang?"

"From the patients, of course."

Third Movement

Scherzo

January 23rd, 1929

Dear Friar Christian,

I hope all is well at the abbey. Though our letters have grown less frequent over the years, I hope you have not lost faith in me, for my faith in God remains strong, as is my intention to return. But the patients at Waverly Hills continue to arrive, and my duties have come to involve much more than medicine. God has blessed me with a surge of music on this hillside, and in that way I see Him and sometimes I can even see my Rose again.

But I do carry a burden that is growing more troublesome. We are without clergy at Waverly. Even though it was not my intention, the patients have claimed me as their source of spiritual light. Some even call me "Father," which at first seemed a harmless comfort, but I fear that in their eyes it has been accepted as truth. I try to deceive no one, but when men and women are on their deathbed and they need to confess their sins, I simply can't turn them away.

And so I remain, as ever—

Yours in Christ,
Dr. Wolfgang Pike
Waverly Hills

CHAPTER 21

I t was the sixth day of Dr. Barker's absence, and the mood was optimistic on the hillside—the perfect atmosphere for recruitment. Snow covered the grounds with an inch of accumulation, a wet snow that clung to the top of every tree branch and rested in the pockets of every bough, pretty enough to engage smiles in even the sickest of patients. Wolfgang and Susannah, along with Lincoln, spoke to every patient and staff member, searching for people who were willing to sing and still had the lungs to belt out a tune. Rumor grew throughout the day until talk of a choir was on everyone's lips.

By nighttime they'd collected twenty-seven volunteers, two of whom Big Fifteen and Rufus recruited from down the hill—a man and a woman. Abel, to their delight, surprised them by grabbing five eager kids from the children's pavilion. The turnout was better than Wolfgang had expected. They gathered on the fourth-floor solarium around nine o'clock that evening. Several neighboring patients, including an ailing Mr. Weaver, had volunteered to scoot their beds aside to make room for everyone. Susannah arranged them in groups—men, women, and children—and positioned them to the right side of McVain's piano. Josef and Rufus stood to the left of the piano while Wolfgang took a position in the center so that all eyes could follow his conducting; he knew most would not have a clue what each movement of his arms meant. He needed to teach them.

Susannah situated a ten-year-old girl next to Abel in the front row and then bounced over toward Wolfgang. "They're ready. A few have really lovely voices."

"Then let's get started," he said.

Susannah spun away to join the women's section on the right side of the choir. The men stood to the left. Wolfgang faced them all and spoke over the bitter wind that fought the screen windows. "I admire everyone's courage on this cold winter night." They stood silent, focused on every word. "Don't be shy with your voices. I understand that some of you simply want to be involved and admit not to be the best of singers, but that doesn't matter to me. The fact that you're here is all that counts."

The patients stared back at him with haunted faces. Some had sunburned cheeks, others were deathly pale. A few scattered coughs filtered through the choir, but something new now burned in their tired eyes.

Wolfgang raised his arms. "We'll start with the *Cantate Domino* of Hans Leo Hassler." They continued to stare at him, even Susannah. McVain rolled his eyes. Josef, without hesitation, gripped his bow and readied himself. "I'm kidding," said Wolfgang. "We'll get to that eventually. We'll begin by warming up our voices with some simple scales." He nodded to McVain, who began playing the scales on the piano, apparently bored by the simplicity. He sat like a hunchbacked troll. "Women first," Wolfgang shouted. "Open up your voices. If the other floors hear, it could get us more recruits."

The thirteen women opened their mouths to sing. They started slowly, reluctantly, struggling to vocalize in the freezing weather, but after a few minutes their voices grew stronger, despite weakened lungs, and became warm and lyrical. Clouds of steam puffed like smoke from every opened mouth. After the women, the men sang, and finally the children. When Wolfgang had them all sing together and began to tinker with different ranges, experimenting with different combinations of voices, the choir's confidence grew. Specific roles were defined. He divided the women into sopranos and contraltos, and the men into tenors, countertenors, and a couple of baritones. They lacked that one deep bass that would have made it perfect. Nevertheless, after only forty-five minutes of practice, the choir had already passed Wolfgang's expectations and showed an eagerness to learn more. He'd handed out sheet music for those who knew how to read it. The rest learned by following the movements of Wolfgang's arms and by listening. They caught on quickly.

Just before ten o'clock, when Wolfgang was ready to rehearse a short section of a Mozart Mass, Lincoln, who had been busy in the chute during most of the rehearsal, hurried by his side. "Barker," he said, breathing heavily. "He's back early."

It took a second for the words to register, but when they did, Wolfgang moved frantically, motioning for the patients to return to their rooms. But it was too late. Dr. Barker's voice boomed from somewhere on the solarium. The crowd of spectators parted like the Red Sea, and Moses walked on through.

"What's the meaning of this?" Dr. Barker stood a few feet away from Rufus and Josef, who quickly stepped aside.

Wolfgang nodded toward Susannah and the choir. With Susannah directing them, they began to return to their beds and floors. Dr. Barker stared at him with contempt. But he was silent, letting everyone clear out, all except McVain, who simply stood from the piano, shuffled to his bed, and pulled up the covers. Finally, Dr. Barker—who was puffing so hard, Wolfgang thought a fire smoldered inside his head—said, "I want the piano taken down."

"It's too heavy," Wolfgang said. "And we recently had it tuned."

Dr. Barker looked baffled. "Sick patients standing out in the cold? In the heart of the winter?"

"They'd be lying in their beds in this same cold air. At least the singing keeps them warm."

"The standing puts strain on them."

"We'll get them chairs."

"And what about those children? This is a school night."

"Do you think these children worry about school, Dr. Barker?" Wolfgang pointed to where the children stood moments before. "They're here because they're sick. They care more about figuring out how not to die on this hillside. The children are the strongest we have."

Dr. Barker stepped closer. "Our city fears this place like a leper colony. Yet it's the most sought-after TB hospital in the country, and not because of our"—he practically spat—"*music program*. I won't have you damaging our reputation. Or our patients. Prove to me that music can cure TB."

"Prove to me that it can't."

"Dr. Pike, I studied at Johns Hopkins—"

"Did you see their faces?"

Dr. Barker clenched his jaw. "They're tired."

"Did you see their faces?" Wolfgang asked. "You can't deny them—"

"How dare you speak to me this way." He glared at the cassock visible beneath Wolfgang's lab coat.

"We have a patient here. She asks me every day, 'Where do the bodies go?' I lie. I change the subject. I don't tell her about Lincoln's Death Tunnel."

"Lower your voice, Wolfgang." Dr. Barker looked around at the patients, many of whom had been listening to their quarrel. "They need rest and fresh air."

"That's what we tell them, but they're still dying. At times it's at the rate of one an hour." Wolfgang stepped forward, daring Dr. Barker to shove him, both of them too irate to stop this public argument. "My only cure is to make them happy. Make them look forward to opening their eyes the next morning. That is my mission now."

Suddenly, McVain's voice came from his bed. "Shut us down and you'll regret it."

Dr. Barker spun to face him. "Are you threatening me?"

McVain sat up in bed, resting his weight on his elbows. "I've done much worse things in my life than threaten someone. But if I have to, I will."

Wolfgang didn't give Dr. Barker time to muster a retort. "Do you realize the talent we've stumbled across here? This is no coincidence. This is fate." A notion hit Wolfgang, an ally whom Dr. Barker couldn't touch. "God has put these people here. The music is from God. The choir has a calling from Him."

"Don't hide behind your cloth." Dr. Barker shook his head. "That's sacrilege."

"You can tell me what to do as a doctor, but not with the Lord."

Dr. Barker started to turn and then stopped. "I'll go above you. To the diocese."

"On what grounds?"

"Prohibition keeps you from buying your wine in stores." Dr. Barker pointed to his chest. "I track every order that comes into this place, *Father*. And I know about the extra stuff you get from Lincoln. But it seems the consumption of sacramental wine has risen quite substantially since you've been here. Yet the church attendance is falling off."

He stormed off without another word.

Wolfgang stayed on the fourth floor that night and played softly. He played for the patients. He played for Rose. Could she hear him? He played for McVain, who appeared restless, tossing and turning, the mattress springs groaning with every shift of his weight. Every ten minutes McVain would punch his right fist into the center of his pillow and then plop his head inside the dent. Nothing seemed to work.

When Wolfgang's fingers ached, he stood. He walked the requiem over to McVain's bed and locked the manuscript in its black case.

McVain's eyes were open. "You really believe this is fate?"

Wolfgang flinched. "I thought you were asleep."

"It's twenty-five degrees out here and you expect me to sleep? I asked you a question."

Wolfgang dropped down on the cold folding chair beside the bed. "What do you think?"

"Coincidence," said McVain. "There's no other explanation. You believe in God because it makes you feel better about where you're going after you die." He looked Wolfgang in the eyes. "We're going nowhere except the ground we're buried in."

"You don't believe in God?"

McVain laughed. "Do you? I mean really?"

"Of course."

"Then why the look in your eyes?"

"What look?"

McVain sighed and laughed a soft, cynical laugh. "Why are you convinced that joining the priesthood is the right answer to your wife's death?"

"It's a calling from God."

"You say that as if you rehearsed it." McVain's breathing was labored, pushed out in shallow bursts followed by bouts of calm. "So why all the nonsense?"

"What nonsense?"

"If it were a calling from God, then you wouldn't be here. You'd be there. You can't have it both ways."

"I'm here because…I'm needed here. Look around," he nodded to all the other patients. "And this music is God's work too."

McVain chuckled. "What about heaven and hell? Do they exist?"

Wolfgang paused and stared down the solarium. "There is a heaven, McVain, and one day I'll see Rose in it."

"With the angels, huh? Floating around above the clouds in pure bliss with wings and shit?"

Wolfgang stood. "Good night, McVain."

McVain held his head upward, his voice strained. "Do you really think there's a hell?" His head settled on his pillow again. "A place of fire where the sinners go? Like me. Or was it concocted to keep people straight? Be a more dangerous world without the fear of consequence, wouldn't it?"

"What have you done that's so bad that you belong in hell?"

"Maybe one day I'll pour my confession out to you. But what would it matter?"

"It would empty the bitterness in your heart."

"Don't you have bitterness?"

Wolfgang opened his mouth to speak as thoughts of his mother consumed him, but nothing came out.

McVain smiled. "The bitterness keeps me going. I wouldn't know what to do without it." Wolfgang started to leave, but again McVain stopped him with another question. "Would God keep a moral man from heaven's gates?"

"I shouldn't think so."

"Even if he doesn't believe in God anymore?"

Where was this heading? thought Wolfgang.

McVain said, "There was a time when I thought I'd been blessed by God."

"When did you lose this belief?"

McVain held up his left hand and wiggled his pinkie and thumb. "Was it coincidence that sent me to European soil? Or was it fate?"

"I don't have all the answers, McVain."

McVain's jaw tightened. "I made a decision while I was over there. I lost these fingers as a result of it. If it was a punishment from God, then I hate him for it."

"God doesn't punish—"

"It's easier just not to believe," he said. "What kind of God would give something like this and then take it away?"

Wolfgang immediately thought of Rose. "Good night, McVain. I'll pray for your answers tonight."

He turned away, unable to shake the vision of Rose from his mind—how she looked, how she talked, how she breathed when she slept, how she smelled, how she tasted, the feel of her skin...

CHAPTER 22

Wolfgang referred to the years after his recovery from polio as the "walking years." He had insisted that his mother allow him freedom from the bed. "I feel like a prisoner in this bed," he told her.

To which she responded, "What do you know of prison, Wolfgang?"

"I'll prove to you that I'll walk again."

She stared at him for a moment before putting on a smile. "I'll get you a cane at the store today."

Doris returned an hour later, opened his bedroom door, and propped the cane against the wall of the hallway outside so he could see it. "Well, there it is. Go ahead and grab it. I won't baby you anymore."

After he'd heard her descend the stairs, he crawled out of bed and then out into the hallway to retrieve the cane. He started off with the upper floor, walking up and down the hallway ten times that first day before tiring. On his first attempt he fell after only two steps. Doris hurried up the steps to help, but he insisted that he do it on his own. "I don't need your help, Mother."

She returned to the kitchen and moments later he heard her crying. Thoughts of the pillow closing in on his father's face fueled his drive to walk. He wanted more than freedom from the bed, even at eight. He wanted out of the house and away from her. He'd used the cane so often that the grooved feel of it would always be ingrained in the palm of his right hand.

Next he'd used the stairs to strengthen the muscles of his legs. Up and down he'd travel them, twenty times a day, before and after school, from the living room to his bedroom until he'd begun to wear the shine from the wood on the middle of each uneven step. He'd step up with the left foot, drive the cane down on the same step, and then lift the right foot up next, the sound of each movement distinct, like a ritual, like a song. He pounded every inch of the sidewalk up and down their street, his daily presence as common to the neighbors as the milkman and mail carriers. Neighbors waved, and sometimes, depending on his focus, Wolfgang waved back. Mostly he'd nod and keep to his business, venturing outside more than he ever had in his life, loving the freedom of it, away from his mother's increasingly extremist remarks and teachings of her religious thinking.

In the eighth grade Wolfgang pushed the limits and ventured down the road to Central Park. He walked the seventeen acres of the park throughout each week, he and his cane clip-clopping around the winding walking trails, careful not to place the end of his cane in any patches of sunlight that bled through the overhanging tree limbs. It was a game. His cane couldn't touch the sunlight, and his feet couldn't step on any crack. On some sunny days he'd appear to be dancing as he sidestepped and maneuvered his way around the patchwork of light and shadow, watching the squirrels and dogs chase each other, watching the women push babies in strollers, and waving to the horse carriages. Some days he'd stop to skip rocks across the wading pool or stare at his reflection in the shimmering water, sighting the first curls of black hair on his chin that would later become the beard he would never shave from his face.

One morning at breakfast, Doris said to her increasingly unresponsive son, "Mrs. Hammerston down the street. She saw you walking the park the other day."

"I walk the park every day," said Wolfgang.

"Well, I'd like you to keep it at that," she said. "You've no business on the streets by yourself."

That afternoon, Wolfgang figured it was time to expand his horizons. He'd finally gotten rid of the cane and decided it was time to venture farther downtown. He stretched it a block or two every day until his daily jaunt had reached nearly ten miles. He'd pack a canteen full of water on his trips, sipping and rationing it out so as not to run dry too early. Hurrying across streets, he'd slow his steps on the sidewalks. He would slow even more when he'd curiously pass a bar or whorehouse on Green Street where the men liked to drink to crudeness and dirty crib girls were known to give themselves for money. He'd imagine them in the throes of passion and then hurry on, snickering inside his head at the dirtiness of it all. And then he would silently apologize to a God he befriended on a daily basis.

On several occasions he stopped outside the Baroque and peered through the window, imagining his father alive and slurping from a beer mug. Men played cards and dice games and drank bourbon. In the back, half concealed by smoke, a man played ragtime on the piano. A thin young man painted with oil paints at a table just inside the front window. The walls of the Baroque glowed with dozens of framed oil paintings. Along the wall next to the fireplace stood a marble statue with nude figures, a replica of Giambologna's *Rape of the Sabine Women*—a man and a woman upright and inter-twined, coiled, their arms reaching up toward a ceiling covered by smoke. Wolfgang never hesitated to stare at the statue, at least for a few seconds before moving on, past the Rue de Lafayette next door, where the sound of drunken laughter always permeated the walls.

He liked to pass storefront windows and watch his limping reflec-tion, a boy without a care, a boy with no destination. Until he hit Fifth Street one fall day and noticed the tall spire extending from the pitched roof of a glorious building down the way. Clouds passed above it. Wolfgang's heart began pumping. Something seemed to be calling him; a throbbing in his gut, a warm feeling he could only compare to the one he'd get after his father occasionally patted his back after he'd successfully played a complete piece on the piano. His pace quickened as he limped toward the building. He walked so fast his right foot began to drag, the toes of his black shoe like a broom sweeping across the dirt-covered concrete. A horse carriage rumbled down the street. He pretended to race it.

When he reached his destination, he stood for a moment with his hands on his knees, staring at the tall façade and large arched doors. Two women in pretty dresses and artfully arranged hairdos walked up the wide steps and opened the massive doors, and what emerged from the belly of the building was the angelic singing of a choir, singing in a language he'd never heard before yet felt drawn to. He took out his canteen and drank more water. He stared at the building for a good five minutes before inching closer to the steps. A man in a top hat brushed past him and apologized on his way into the building. Wolfgang knew it was a church of some sort. He surprised himself by speaking out at the man.

"What place is this, sir?"

The man stopped on the church steps and faced Wolfgang. "Why, this is the Cathedral of the Assumption."

"Cathedral? Is it Protestant?"

The man chuckled. "No, it's Catholic. Try coming in someday." He tipped his hat. "Good day."

Wolfgang watched the guy disappear into the church. Catholic? He didn't know what a cult was, but it was the most common word he'd heard his parents associate with the word "Catholic." If his parents were telling the truth about the Catholic Church, the man he'd just spoken to would have had devil horns, a tail, and a pitchfork. But instead he'd had straight white teeth and a handsome smile. He couldn't quite put his finger on the appropriate words, but being there just felt right. And the music sounded as if it had come down from heaven itself. Wolfgang spent the next two hours sitting on the steps, contemplating entering. On that day he didn't, and when he got home he spoke nothing of it to his mother. Over dinner she said to him, "You have a smile on your face, Wolfgang. I'd like to know the cause, but I'm sure you won't tell me."

Four weeks later he did enter the cathedral. He arrived at a time when there was a rush of people coming for daily Mass. He limped hurriedly to funnel inside with the herd, and once he entered he knew he'd found the part of his life he'd been missing. He was swept away by the vastness of the building, the grandeur of the architecture, the colors of the tall stained-glass windows that dominated the side walls, the height of the ceiling that hovered over what he would later learn was the nave. Upon entering he stopped without thinking to gawk and was nearly trampled by the incoming people. He stumbled back toward the baptismal pool and font that stood before the length of the center aisle. He righted himself and sidestepped out of the way, watching as the people poured in and the choir practiced singing in the choir loft above the entrance. Everything looked so different from the church he'd grown up attending with his parents, which was minuscule in comparison.

Wolfgang faced the body of the church. So many seats filled the expanse. Marble and granite everywhere. One large center aisle flanked by two side aisles. Giant pillars stood like endless tree trunks along the center aisle, stretching up to sweeping arches and a curved rooftop highlighted by a painted fresco of cherubs surrounding Mary at the time of her assumption into heaven. At the far end of the church behind the altar was the massive Coronation Window that took up much of the back wall and supported the fresco's theme. Sunlight penetrated the stained glass, illuminating the purple, gold, and deep blue that dominated the window. The colors shone brilliantly, prism-like, across the altar and marble floor. Dust motes hovered in and out of the light. Mary was being crowned as queen. God took her body into heaven—the eternal goal. Wolfgang would dream of that window at night, and the vision would save him from the pillow that suffocated him in every nightmare.

He sat in the back row of the cathedral, captivated by that window. He listened to the priest at the pulpit, how his voice reverberated off of everything it touched. Later, during a silent lull in the Mass, he asked a neighboring woman, "What language is he speaking?"

"Latin," she said.

Latin. He'd heard his parents refer to the language during several of their rants on the Catholic Church and the pope and Rome's influence in the States. *One day*, he thought, *perhaps one day I will speak Latin and preach from a pulpit while others listen.*

The cathedral felt like home. If he could have placed a physical form on his faith, that form had been floating aimlessly in the air ever since his father's funeral. Minister Ford's church no longer conformed to it. But Wolfgang's faith fit that cathedral like a glove. As soon as he'd entered, he'd felt as if the wound had begun to heal. Cells were changing, the skin was transforming, and the scar would begin to fade.

It was just a fleeting notion at first, not something he could fully understand, but over time it began to make sense. Protestants and Catholics were both Christians. His parents' church just seemed to have a much more literal interpretation of the Bible, and that, in Wolfgang's mind, was the beginning of the many differences, along with how they viewed the pope, confession, purgatory, and how they prayed in general. But they both prayed to the same Christ, and because of that Wolfgang couldn't understand the animosity that existed between the two branches. For Wolfgang, one of the most intriguing aspects of the Catholic faith was the role of the Virgin Mary. His parents had always criticized the Catholics for praying to Mary, referring to it as idol worship, claiming that nowhere in the Bible did it say that Mary was greater than any other Christian.

But on Wolfgang's second visit inside the cathedral, the statue of Mary in the back of the church called to him. He approached it slowly. Mary with her head tilted, eyes closed, so at peace holding the newborn baby Jesus. Wolfgang imagined being held in Mary's arms. In his mind, he spoke to her and immediately felt a motherly comfort he had not known in years.

He kept his daily walks a secret for months until one day Doris decided to follow him. Part of him had been hoping for weeks that she would follow him much like she had years earlier with Charles and the Pendennis Club. She followed him around Central Park and eventually to the cathedral, where he'd bounded up the steps with an enthusiasm that had nearly made her nauseous. When he'd exited the cathedral after Mass, she'd stood horrified on the side-walk, so angry she couldn't look him in the eyes.

"Hi, Mother," he'd said, when he found her. They walked home together until Wolfgang finally broke the silence: "I've found my calling. I'm going to attend high school at the abbey at Saint Meinrad. I'm going to become a Catholic priest."

Doris Pike dropped to the sidewalk and wept.

So six years later as a twenty-year-old seminary student returning back to those same wooded hills after that confusing summer with Rose, he knelt beside his bed for what seemed like hours, searching for answers and reminiscing. He questioned whether God was still calling him to a life of celibacy and prayer. Had Rose been a test?

He thought back to how nervous he'd been the first week at Saint Meinrad at fourteen and how new it had all been, entering the quiet church every morning to pray before the sun rose, the *Liber Usualis* heavy like a brick in his hands—never going to prayer or the abbey church without it. But Wolfgang knew the instant he'd arrived at the abbey at Saint Meinrad that it was the place for him, just as the monks had decades before when they'd founded the priory in the hills that reminded them of Switzerland. God had called him to the secluded seminary to pray amid the wooded, rolling landscape with the friars and monks. It was so peaceful, so far removed from a city that was growing louder and more polluted every year. He loved the predictability of the schedule, the simplicity of the lifestyle, and the lack of conflict that he'd been so accustomed to with his mother.

He cherished the memories of his four years in minor seminary, from age fourteen to eighteen. Despite the rigidity of the atmosphere, boys were still boys. They told jokes, they played pranks, they tossed balls on the lawn, and they fished in the lake. He chuckled as he remembered how fast they'd run after Trevor Kane had thrown a rock at the cloister's front door, and then Trevor, ever the clown, falling in the grass and rolling down the hill to be seen by Friar Bennett moments later.

Wolfgang and his friends would sneak into the church spires and race up the three-story spiral staircase to the top and overlook the grounds. They'd race back down, Wolfgang always coming in last (unless chubby Franklin Ferbough joined them), and all became dizzy by the time they reached the bottom, where they'd stumble out the door and fall in the grass and stare up at the sky. In the winter, when snow covered the grounds, they'd sled down the hills toward the lake. And when the lake was frozen, they'd coast right on out over the ice.

Christopher Schmiltz, a major seminarian who had almost been kicked out twice (once for smoking and another time for having a picture of a woman on his wall), showed Wolfgang's group of minor seminarians how to make ketchup-flavored alcohol. They added yeast and a little sugar to the monks' homemade ketchup. Then they pushed the cork in really tight and placed it in the windowsill so the sun could hit it. It would be ready when it popped its cork. And on that day, Christopher Schmiltz, who ended up leaving the seminary a year later and starting a family, was long gone by the time Friar Christian heard the cork pop and confiscated the bottle.

Wolfgang had met Friar Christian the first day at Saint Meinrad and had instantly taken a liking to the man. He taught Latin, and he was Wolfgang's favorite teacher. He had an appreciation for music and liked to tease Wolfgang, calling him Saint Meinrad's young doctor, for Wolfgang often found himself playing doctor to his fellow classmates. When Jimmy Hatcher broke his hand in the carpentry shop and when Chester Tankersly sliced his leg open pulling some farm equipment out of one of the barns, Wolfgang had taken care of them, stabilizing and administering to the wounds until Brother Allcut, the seminary's designated medic, could get there with his wooden container of wraps, gauzes, and creams.

"Latin will be especially important for you," Friar Christian liked to joke. "You'll need it to memorize all those medical terms." He was a stocky man with a head of curly hair, but the hair wasn't confined to his head. It sprouted from his nostrils and ears with equal zeal, and it was so noticeable that Ronald Middleton had joked one night that Friar Christian had a bird nest inside his skull and the leaves and twigs were growing out his ears and nostrils. You could hear the nest moving like a dry-leaf whistle every time he inhaled and exhaled.

Good old Friar Christian.

As a minor seminarian Wolfgang always looked upon the major seminary students with admiration as they moved across the grounds in their Roman and Jesuit cassocks and the birettas on their heads. So when his time came to enter major seminary, at age eighteen, he was honored to be wearing the cassocks instead of the regular trousers and shirts they wore as high school kids. He'd felt so proud when he'd first walked up the big marble steps that led up to the abbey church, wearing those sacred garments.

After his summer with Rose he questioned whether he was worthy of the cassocks. Twenty now, torn and confused, Wolfgang prayed beside his seminary bed and stared up toward the tall ceiling, remembering all the monks as if he'd made up his mind to leave Saint Meinrad. But he hadn't made that decision. Not yet. He convinced himself that he was still weighing his options.

But the Spanish flu had come to Camp Zachary Taylor, and they needed help in Louisville. And Rose was back home, waiting. How could he leave her behind when her flesh and her scent had already become so ingrained in his senses that he craved them like a drug?

CHAPTER 23

R ose rested on the bed, naked, her left leg lost in the sheets, the rest of her backside in perfect view.
	Wolfgang emerged from the bathroom and sat next to her on the bed. "Rose, what are you doing?"

"Helping you study, Wolf."

"Is that so? Looks more like a ploy to convince me not to study."

She rolled over and handed him a wooden baton Charles Pike had used while conducting his imaginary choirs and orchestras. "Here, it's the first thing I could find."

Wolfgang laughed as he took the baton. "And what would you want me to do with this, Rose?"

"Use it as a pointer, Wolf." She rolled onto her side. "Go on. Review. You have a test in the morning on the human body, do you not?"

He ran the tip of the baton softly along her exposed hip. "Yes, I do."

"Then what are you waiting for. Start studying."

As much as Wolfgang wanted the dream to be real, as soon as he blinked the weariness from his eyes, the vision of Rose faded. A cruel trick of memory. And by the time he reached the sanatorium that morning, he could barely remember what his mind's eye had rehashed during the night. He was in a hurry to see if Dr. Barker had removed the piano. But, no, it was still there. Wolfgang found McVain playing it as if nothing had occurred last night. Lincoln sat in a chair beside the piano with his fedora on, turning pages for McVain.

Shortly after lunchtime, Dr. Barker stopped Wolfgang in the

second-floor hallway, his face solemn and his voice surprisingly non-combative. "These are my rules, Dr. Pike, and you will obey them or it's all over, whether *God* allows it or not."

Wolfgang stood with his black bag of instruments and waited.

"You and the choir can meet three times a week," he said, "but for no longer than an hour. Choir members must sit in chairs—I can't have them standing that long. And you're to finish before sundown. I can't have the children up late." He sighed. "And we shouldn't have the colored patients up here. It could anger some of the other patients."

Wolfgang wondered if Barker had heard about the note stuck to the pig's head. "Have you heard specific threats?"

"He's not supposed to be up here."

"It can only be complete with Rufus. The healing."

"You've already caused enough tension with your *healing*, Dr. Pike."

Wolfgang started to walk away but then stopped. He tempted fate by opening his mouth. "You mentioned my sacramental wine the other day."

"What of it?"

"You like whiskey, Dr. Barker. That's no secret, so let's not deny it because of the times."

"I like whiskey. I like bourbon." Dr. Barker checked his wrist watch. "Please tell me you have a point to this."

"I read that doctors made millions last year writing prescriptions for whiskey to patients."

"I can assure you that I'm not one of them."

"And neither am I."

"Don't allow the rehearsals to interfere with your work, or I *will* go over your head. I hear priests can be moved quite easily."

"I am not yet a priest, Dr. Barker. You know that."

"Yes, of course I do, and so does the diocese. But wouldn't they be interested in what you've been doing here…unofficially?"

For the next few weeks Wolfgang strictly followed Dr. Barker's rules and met three times a week to practice with his choir and musicians. They gathered typically near the end of the afternoons when the weather was warmest. He was careful with the time, because he knew Barker would be monitoring. The situation with Rufus was not ideal for building chemistry and harmony with McVain and Josef, but Rufus practiced with them from the colored hospital down below while they rehearsed above. It was better than not having a flute at all, at least until Wolfgang could think of an alternative. The chorus came along quickly, most of them memorizing the words and the music on their own so that they could spend every moment of rehearsal on harmony. Wolfgang had almost everything he needed now except that strong bass singer.

They'd been hit by a string of days that refused to climb above twenty degrees, so Wolfgang took it upon himself to cancel five rehearsals. He didn't want to take any chances in the below-freezing temperatures. He had too many ideas brewing, too many patients who seemed to be responding to his music medicine, and he didn't want any of it curtailed by Barker.

Mary Sue was now strong enough to walk with baby Fred around the grounds for a half hour, without assistance but supervised. Wolfgang continued to allow her a visit to Frederick every night, and Wolfgang always brought his violin. Frederick's battle with the disease was growing unpredictable. Some days he could barely move without assistance, and others he could manage to sit up in bed, yet his name always appeared on Wolfgang's request list.

He'd yet to hold his son.

Wolfgang made his rounds. He heard confessions. He listened to their questions and gave them answers that would ease their passing. While doing so he came up with another idea. On a sunny day near the end of January, he asked Susannah to gather the choir a few minutes early because he had an announcement to make. Even she didn't know what he had planned.

Wolfgang cleared his throat, stood by McVain at the piano, and faced the choir. "We've set a date."

Abel shouted from the front row. "For what?"

"A date for our first concert, Abel. A little over two weeks from today. On Valentine's Day."

Susannah half raised her hand. "Valentine's Day?"

"You have plans, doll face?" McVain asked.

"No."

"Well, now you do," Wolfgang said. "We'll throw a party better than New Year's and play for everyone here. From the rooftop."

McVain coughed. "What about Barker?"

Someone else coughed in the background, and when Wolfgang turned he spotted Susannah covering her mouth. It was so cold. Her cheeks were pink.

"Dr. Barker doesn't know yet," Wolfgang said. "But I believe I can convince him. If the temperature is decent and, God willing, it doesn't snow, we'll have lawn chairs out on the grounds for all the patients and we'll play from above."

Susannah raised her voice above the wind. "What will we perform?"

"A bit of everything. We'll decide in the coming days." Wolfgang pointed to the chorus. "With your input, of course."

Abel raised his hand. "We need a name."

McVain rolled his eyes. "And what name shall that be?"

Abel shrugged. "I don't know. The Orchestra of Waverly Hills."

"Sounds reasonable enough." Wolfgang surveyed the crowd. "Any objections?" There were none, not even from McVain, who appeared more tired than normal as he slumped lower against the piano. "Very well then. On Valentine's Day, the Orchestra of Waverly Hills will present its debut performance."

Wolfgang's enthusiasm about the concert made the night's work go by much more quickly. When his rounds were finished he searched every floor and solarium porch but couldn't find Susannah. He couldn't wait to see what she thought of his surprise announcement. She'd appeared happy, but there was something in her departure after the rehearsal that made Wolfgang think she was preoccupied. Like she was hiding something.

He ran into Nurse Marlene on the third floor thirty minutes before midnight. He was finally able to approach her without feeling uncomfortable. "Have you seen Susannah?"

"She left a few minutes ago," Nurse Marlene said. "She told me to tell you she'd see you in the morning."

Wolfgang sighed and walked over toward the porch screen. It didn't make any sense. They always told the other when they'd be unable to walk the hillside at night. He looked down the slope of the snow-dusted hill below but didn't see her walking toward their trail in the woods. He breathed in the frigid air and inched closer to the window, the cool screen clipping his nose. Down the hillside to the left some movement caught his eye.

Susannah's white dress blew behind her as she carefully stepped over the frozen ruts in the muddy road near the sanatorium's entrance. Her left hand held her white cap pinned to her head while her right arm clutched something against her chest. He strained to see but couldn't tell what it was. She entered the line of trees on the far side of the road, navigated a grassy downhill toward a narrow footpath, and disappeared under a canopy of low-lying limbs.

Where was she going? He walked down the solarium, his face nearly brushing the screen window as he peered down into the woods. And then he saw the only cottage on that side of the hill about thirty yards deep in the trees. He knew where the footpath would take her.

A light was on in Dr. Barker's cottage.

CHAPTER 24

I t was the summer of 1918, the summer of Rose, and Friar Christian and Wolfgang sat side by side on a concrete bench outside the monastery. Friar Christian rested his elbows on his knees, leaning forward, fingers interlocked with his lowered chin resting upon them. Wolfgang attempted to read the face of his favorite monk, but as usual, Friar Christian just looked serene. That was how Friar Christian prayed, eyes open and slightly glazed, staring at something no one else could see. He inhaled deeply, and his squatty face seemed to shrink in upon itself. And of course Wolfgang could hear the dry-leaf whistling sound of his breathing, the air fighting through the hair inside his nose.

Wolfgang smiled inside.

A breeze ruffled Friar Christian's unruly hair. The grass on the hillside was growing brown in spots from the heat of the summer and lack of rainfall. Many of the leaves on the surrounding trees had turned colors early. Wolfgang found himself staring at them when Friar Christian finally spoke.

"Would you believe me if I told you I was once in love, Wolfgang?"

"I would," said Wolfgang.

Friar Christian smiled. "Her name was Julie. She had brown hair and freckles, and she lived next door to me when I was a teenager."

"Was she in love with you?"

"Oh, yes." Father Christian's façade thawed. "She wanted to get married. And she was a delightful girl. I did love her. But the spark for me was not as great as my love for God. Or this place."

Wolfgang looked down. "I see."

"No, I don't think you do, Wolfgang." He was teacher again. "Distancing myself from her was the test for me. I proved my love for God by doing so, and I don't regret it. Not once did I think I'd made the wrong decision. But that was my greatest hurdle. It eventually faded away. Julie married another man, who made her much happier than I ever would have." He patted Wolfgang on the shoulder. "But we all are different, are we not?"

"Yes, Father."

"I am not you, and you are not me," said Friar Christian. "And Julie was not Rose. She sounds like a truly remarkable woman."

Wolfgang looked up. "She is. Unlike anyone I've ever known."

Friar Christian laughed. "How old are you, Wolfgang?"

"Twenty."

"Go to her. You've been back in classes for two weeks now. Clearly not yourself, though. The Wolfgang I know doesn't mope about or doubt." He watched two squirrels scamper across the lawn. "I hear the Spanish flu has hit Camp Taylor very hard. I've seen you with the others here. You have a good bedside manner, Wolfgang. Go back to Rose and help the soldiers defeat this illness before it spreads throughout the city."

"Thank you, Father."

"You see, you didn't need my advice," said Friar Christian. "You knew in your heart what you were going to do. You only needed my permission." Friar Christian stood. "But you didn't even need that, Wolfgang. Not really. I'm certain you would have made a wonderful priest, and the doors here are always open for you. But I think you have another calling."

Wolfgang looked at him.

"You should become a doctor, Wolfgang." Friar Christian walked him toward the abbey church as birds chirped from the transepts. "Love the Lord with a scalpel in your hand. And communicate with him through your music."

Wolfgang returned home to Rose and Camp Zachary Taylor the next day, where the Spanish flu continued to spread. She gave him a quick kiss on the lips and immediately pulled him to work. The conditions at the camp were far from sanitary, and the tents were overcrowded. The virus struck the camp hard and fast. The men returning from action were believed to be carriers of the virus that would hit nearly 20 percent of the country's population. Many of the barracks had been converted to hospitals for the thousands of soldiers who had become ill.

At its height, forty per day were dying inside the camp. Rose and Wolfgang and dozens of other volunteers spent their days tending to the sick, changing bedpans, washing sheets, wetting towels, and assisting the doctors with whatever was needed. Despite their futile attempts to keep it contained, the virus spread outside the camp, turning up in thousands of cases across Jefferson County. One evening Wolfgang hurried past a cot where Rose sat, holding a wet cloth on the forehead of soldier who was so hot with fever he didn't know who he was. He trembled with his eyes closed, moaning.

"Wolfgang." Rose stopped him. "Get the violin in our bag."

"I didn't pack my violin, why would—"

"I packed it this morning," she said. "I had an idea. Just hurry and get it, please."

Wolfgang returned a few minutes later with one of his father's violins and a bow. Rose stood and offered her seat to him. Wolfgang looked at her and then toward the open seat next to the suffering soldier. Finally he sat down. "I don't want to disturb the others, Rose."

"Play, Wolfgang." Rose squatted next to him. "Just play something. See if it doesn't help calm him."

Wolfgang eyed the other occupied cots inside the cramped barrack and then positioned the violin against his neck. He slid the bow across the strings and began to play a snippet from Vivaldi's *Four Seasons*, softly. Moments later the soldier's arms and legs began to settle. The fever was still burning him from the inside out, but his face appeared calmer, more at peace.

"See, Doctor?" Rose winked at Wolfgang. "Keep playing."

Wolfgang continued. Ten minutes later, the soldier managed to find slumber. On the far side of the barrack, another soldier cried out. Wolfgang tucked the violin under his arm, hobbled across the barrack, and played.

The epidemic eased by November, and by that time Wolfgang had gained a reputation at Camp Taylor for his musical medicine; the soldiers began calling him Music Man. Rose entered Saint Helena's on South Fourth Street, a Catholic college for women, and set her sights on studying to become a nurse. Thoughts of the lingering Spanish flu were overshadowed by the announcement in November 1918 that the war was ending. An armistice was signed, and the telegraph operator at the *Courier Journal* was the first to spread the word. Church bells sounded and factory whistles blew in the middle of the night. Sleeping Louisvillians jumped from their beds and hurried to the streets, where they celebrated well into the next day.

Wolfgang was shirtless when Rose pulled him from beneath the covers and tugged him to the street. She tiptoed and kissed him on the mouth. "The war has ended, Wolf." They stood arm in arm for a few minutes and watched as their neighbors took to the pavement on foot, on bicycle, on canes, walking dogs, all of them hooting and hollering and waving their arms joyously in the air. They hurried downtown to dive right into the middle of it all. Men and women waved American flags and tossed confetti. Others had draped the flags across their bodies. Patriotic songs were belted out, one blending into the next. Stuffed dummies depicting "Kaiser Bill" hung in effigy from the Courier-Journal and Louisville Times building. Bands played. Couples kissed on street corners. Mothers hugged their children, and fathers walked with little boys and girls hoisted on their shoulders so they could see over the crowds. City leaders and politicians gave speeches from makeshift stages.

Two weeks later Louisville had the largest parade in its history as most of the residents stood to watch ten thousand soldiers from Camp Taylor march in lines along Broadway en route to Central Park. Rose and Wolfgang stood on the curb along Fourth Street, waving to the soldiers as they passed in their seemingly endless rows, recognizing so many of them. The young soldier Wolfgang had first played the violin for spotted them alongside the street and shot them a sharp salute, which Wolfgang and Rose returned.

The Medical School at the University of Louisville welcomed Wolfgang with open arms. He had experience and a high school diploma, which instantly put him on more solid ground with the professors who had their share of students with only two years of high school, or less. Many were students because their parents wanted them to become doctors and were willing to donate more money. The teaching staff immediately singled out Wolfgang because they knew he was there for the right reasons, and he was motivated.

Professor Montgomery Philpot, a sixty-year-old doctor with a reoccurring case of gout in his left leg, was particularly intrigued by Wolfgang's musical medicine. He'd read an article in the *Courier Journal* about a young man playing the violin for the soldiers at Camp Taylor. One afternoon after his pathology lecture, the professor asked Wolfgang about it, and Wolfgang admitted that he was indeed the young man from the newspaper article.

"I know it was popular with the soldiers." Professor Philpot scratched his rotund belly as he sidled along with Wolfgang, both of them limping across a sidewalk that was covered with fallen leaves. "But do you believe this musical medicine to have purpose?"

"I do, Professor." Wolfgang walked with books in his arms. "It is not the answer as far as cure, but I do believe it helps the soul, and when the soul is at peace, healing can take place."

"Spoken like a man of the cloth." Professor Philpot laughed. "Most of the staff here would think you crazy, young man." He scratched his bald dome, which was covered with liver spots. Wisps of long white hair stuck out around his ears.

"I agree it's unorthodox, Professor, but—"

"I for one think it's brilliant, Wolfgang."

Wolfgang let out an anxious breath. "It was my wife's idea originally."

"Of course it was. What are we without our wives, Wolfgang? Dogs chasing our own tails." Professor Philpot patted Wolfgang on the shoulder and pointed toward a brick building across the lawn. "Come, tell me about your experience at Camp Taylor. And your music. I've got a cadaver in Dissecting Room A that hasn't totally been plucked by our second-year vultures, if you care to take scalpel to hand."

The stench Wolfgang expected, but not the dozen chickens clucking around the legs of the dissecting tables. The shelves along the walls were full with boxes, files, bones, skulls of various shapes and sizes, and jars with things floating inside of them. A broom leaned against the closest shelf. Philpot used the broom to corral the chickens to the far corner of the room, where a cage rested with its door wide open, the floor covered with hay, dirt, and feathers. Once he had them inside the cage, he closed the door and moved a box of bones in front of it to keep the chickens from escaping again. He leaned the broom against the wall and grunted as he faced Wolfgang. "Dr. Jennings." Philpot wiped sweat from his brow. "The chickens are his. He's doing an experiment on embryology, and they're constantly getting loose."

According to Professor Philpot, many of their cadavers were, as he called them, "indigent" Negroes, and it appeared that the body currently lying on the dissecting table had been badly hacked by the second-year students. The man's heart was missing, as were most of his ribs and his liver. The right lung was still intact, and Wolfgang immediately got to work analyzing it, taking notes, sketching his own diagrams. "Make friends with the lungs, Wolfgang. With tuberculosis running wild, we're going to need our share of doctors who are competent with them."

While Wolfgang worked on the cadaver, Professor Philpot waddled around the room, rearranging things, looking for things, clanging things, his head moving not unlike the chickens inside the cage as he talked about the woefully underfunded medical school and the state of medicine in general ever since Abraham Flexner's infamous report in 1910. "'Quite without resources,' Flexner writes." Philpot grabbed a scalpel off a cart. "How can we expect to have resources without proper funding?" he scoffed. "Flexner was on the nose,

Wolfgang. Blunt and a tad harsh, but on the nose. Not one university across the country went unscathed by that report. Things have improved here, there is no doubt about that, but our classes are still far too big, the labs are overcrowded, and the staff is undermanned."

Finally Philpot got to the reason he'd brought Wolfgang into the lab in the first place—the music, which Philpot took to like a bee to honey. He even encouraged Wolfgang to write a paper on it, using his experience at Camp Taylor as an example. And then the professor motioned Wolfgang to the head of the table. "Care to take a look at the brain?"

Chapter 25

Wind blew snow against the solarium screens, scattering pages of concert notes from Wolfgang's podium. The choir barely broke stride, pausing only for a second when their choirmaster squatted to grab the first sheet from the floor. Wolfgang continued to conduct with his free hand, hopping and conducting like some deranged frog, all while keeping his eyes on the choir. Ever since Dr. Barker's reluctant approval, they had been practicing with great enthusiasm.

He moved back to the podium, his face red, and his hair dotted with snowflakes. He mentioned canceling the rehearsal due to the inclement weather, but the choir wanted to hear nothing of the sort. They demanded to sing, and the musicians never once stopped performing, despite the numbness in their hands. Rufus must have heard them playing, because after only a few minutes into their first piece, he'd joined in, blowing his flute from down the hillside, practicing from afar as he'd been doing for weeks now.

Wolfgang conducted like an orator, his vision roaming the choir from side to side, leaving no one out. On each pass he made sure Susannah was in view. For two days he'd wanted to ask her about her clandestine visit to Dr. Barker's house, but he feared upsetting her. Other than leaving him to walk the hillside alone that night, she'd acted no different around Wolfgang. She'd knocked on his door the very next morning as usual—her eyes a bit heavier than normal—and apologized for leaving without him the night before, although he'd noticed that she'd conveniently not offered any explanation. It was none of his business. That was her attitude, and that was how he'd left it—an irksome mystery.

Halfway through the rehearsal Wolfgang spotted Dr. Barker standing in the shadows at the end of the solarium porch. He stood there listening, watching. Spying. And then he was gone. After they finished a Haydn piece, Susannah stepped away from the choir, eyeing the spot where Dr. Barker had stood. "Did you see him watching?"

"I think he's up to something." Wolfgang watched Susannah carefully, wondering if she knew something more.

Susannah folded her arms. "He pulled the case files on all the musicians and choir members today."

"What for?"

"I don't know." Susannah looked upward as a voice soared over the weather.

"My cakes… My cakes…"

"How long has he been carrying on?" asked Wolfgang.

Nurse Cleary came running across the solarium, panting and calling for Susannah. She'd taken on Rita's hours in the mental ward and had been none too pleased about it. "It's Herman," she cried. "He's going mad. I can't take it anymore."

Susannah brushed quickly beside Wolfgang. "You don't have to come."

"I don't trust him."

Susannah hurried to the stairwell, her feet pounding the steps in rapid motion, her hand gliding up the rail. Wolfgang had to hustle to keep up. When she reached the rooftop, she held on to her hat and never broke stride as she lowered her shoulders into the wall of wind that threatened to push them back down the steps.

"Susannah," Herman shouted. "I want my cake! Bring me my cake! Susannah!"

Wolfgang could have strangled him. Susannah opened the door to the nurses' station and stormed inside, fumbling for her keys. She quickly unlocked Room 502. "My Lord, Herman. What is wrong with you?"

Herman sat cross-legged on the floor beneath his window, yelling through the screen. He looked up when Susannah entered. He was fully clothed this time. Benson's bulk was concealed on the bed but unmoving beneath the covers. Wolfgang wondered how he could even breathe under there. No wonder Benson had been at Waverly for five years. He breathed his own diseased air all the time.

Herman unfolded his long legs and braced his hands on the wall to stand. He faced Susannah, his voice under control. "Nobody listens." Tears welled in his eyes. "Nobody hears me." He stepped closer to the doorway. "Nobody ever listens to me."

"Stay back," Wolfgang told him.

Susannah stepped in front. "He's not a criminal, Wolf."

Benson poked his head out from beneath the covers. "I can hear him. I can most certainly hear him. I ate my dog. They let him out, but I ate him. Rita's feet…they dangled…" Benson ducked his head back beneath his turtle shell of blankets and stopped talking.

"I'm better than all of them," Herman said. "Don't you see?"

"Better at what?" Susannah asked.

Herman sat on his bed, defeated and tired. "I want my cake."

Susannah sat bravely beside him. "What is it, Herman?" She lifted his hand and looked into his dark eyes. "Better at what?" Herman stared past Susannah at Wolfgang and then whispered something into her left ear. Susannah's eyes widened and she spoke to Nurse Cleary, who stood behind Wolfgang in the doorway, panting. "Go to the kitchen and get me a cake. Any kind of cake."

"But—"

"Just do it," Susannah yelled. Nurse Cleary turned away, and seconds later the door to the nurses' station flew open and slammed against the outside wall. Wolfgang closed it, but not before the wind had scattered the papers atop the desk in the center of the room. He left them where they landed and returned to Room 502, where Susannah continued to comfort Herman. Wolfgang couldn't believe how she'd tamed the man. Well, yes, he did believe it. She had a way of controlling any man. And what had he whispered in her ear? How dare he get that close to her? And what was he talking about, "no one listens"? How could they not, as loud as he was?

"No one listens," Herman said softly.

Susannah touched his shoulder. "We'll listen, Herman." Wolfgang saw a look of determination in Susannah's eyes that wouldn't be squashed by his fear and distrust of Herman. She stood from the bed and tugged on Herman's elbow. Herman stood beside her, dwarfing her by at least a foot, the top of her head barely reaching his shoulders. She walked Herman out of Room 502 and into the body of the nurses' station. She left him standing in the middle of the room while she hustled around to the back of the desk for a folding chair.

"Susannah," Wolfgang said. "What on earth are you doing?" It was the same chair Rita had used to hang herself. Seeing it in her grip made him uneasy.

Susannah placed the chair behind Herman and told him to sit. He did, lowering his body slowly down to the small seat that creaked under his massive bulk. Susannah tied a towel around his neck. Not once did he ask what she was about to do to him, not even when she reached across the desk for a pair of scissors.

"Susannah?" Wolfgang said.

She gave him an annoyed look. "Relax, Wolf. I'm just going to cut his hair."

"Cut his hair?" Wolfgang stared at the top of Herman's head, where strands of hair stuck out at odd tangents like plant growth. "That could take days."

Susannah rolled her eyes and worked like the barber she wasn't. "He's been ignored his entire life, I bet." She lifted a tangled patch of Herman's dirty brown and gray hair. Snip—the clump fell to the floor with a slight bounce. "But not anymore." Herman stared straight ahead into Room 502 as if they weren't discussing the man right in front of him. Susannah clipped another patch of hair.

Lincoln opened the door to the nurses' station and stuck his head in. "Wolf, you better come down. It's Frederick."

Wolfgang looked at Susannah and then specifically to the scissors in her right hand. Herman was calm now, but Wolfgang didn't trust him. The big man had bruised her before.

"Go, Wolf," said Susannah. "I'll be fine."

Wolfgang turned and left. He trusted her.

Wolfgang found Frederick Helman in the middle of the fourth-floor hallway, on his stomach, his left cheek against the floor, his eyes facing the wall. Wolfgang knelt down and felt for a pulse at Frederick's neck. He found one.

"You left him like this?" he asked Lincoln.

Lincoln squatted next to him. "Of course not. He was in his room, but he was crying hysterically." Lincoln fingered the rim of his fedora. "He's getting stronger. He was letting it out pretty good for just one lung."

"What was it about?"

"Wouldn't talk to me," said Lincoln. "That's why I came and got you."

Wolfgang looked down the hallway toward Frederick's room on the right. "Apparently in the time it took you to find me he'd made it this far on his own." Wolfgang snaked his arms underneath Frederick's torso. The poor young man was so slight compared to what he had weighed upon his arrival at Waverly. Lincoln helped Wolfgang by grabbing Frederick's feet, and together they carried him back to his bed.

"What do you think he was trying to do?" asked Lincoln.

"See Mary Sue and the baby, no doubt." Wolfgang propped a pillow on Frederick's bed and gently settled his head down on it. He leaned down and listened to Frederick's breathing with his stethoscope. "He is getting stronger."

Frederick's eyes opened. He looked up at Wolfgang and Lincoln and then, on his own, turned away from them and faced the wall.

Wolfgang touched Frederick's head with an open hand, silently blessing him. "Rest now, my friend. I'll come back and play for you later."

Frederick didn't respond.

In the hallway, Lincoln said, "He looked sad."

"He must have learned the news."

"What news?"

"Mary Sue and the baby are being released," said Wolfgang. "She's due to Make the Walk in the next few days."

Wolfgang and Lincoln ran into Nurse Cleary on the stairs leading to the rooftop.

"Dr. Pike," she shouted. "Come quickly."

"What is it now?"

"Susannah, she—"

Wolfgang didn't even hear her finish. All he could think about was the scissors slicing Susannah's throat or the sharp blades piercing her chest. His heart raced so quickly he feared it would jump from his rib cage. He sprinted to the stairwell and took the steps two and three at a time, ignoring the pain that shot down his right leg with every step, unable to block out the horrible visions that assaulted his mind. He could see her now, lying on the floor in a pool of blood, the scissors sticking from her slender neck. He hated himself for trusting her, for leaving her alone with Herman. He hit the rooftop with a wild burst of speed, lunging with his left foot while dragging his right. A pig snorted near the doorway to the nurses' station. Wolfgang gave it only a second's glance—why the hell was it up on the rooftop?—before he rushed inside.

"Susannah!"

"What is it, Wolf?" Susannah smiled at him. She stood with her arms folded, leaning against the desk. A man sat in the chair, young and handsome, with trimmed hair and neat beard; Wolfgang blinked. It took him a moment to realize…

"Doesn't he look great?" she said.

Wolfgang nodded like an idiot. Herman's face was long, his jaw sculpted, his cheekbones high beneath dark eyes. Wolfgang touched his own beard and wondered, given the choice and a razor, if Susannah would have shaved his as well? Herman looked at Wolfgang and grinned. In his right hand he tightly clutched a fork. Before him, resting on a small rounded table, was an entire chocolate cake Nurse Cleary must have retrieved from the kitchen. A good chunk of it had already been eaten. A tall glass of milk stood next to it. Herman took another bite of cake and washed it down with a loud gulp of milk.

Nurse Cleary stepped inside. "Well, what do you think?"

"I think you should have told me that everything was okay."

"Relax," said Susannah.

"You ran before I had the chance," said Nurse Cleary.

Wolfgang stepped closer to Herman. "He looks like a new man."

"No, about the surprise," Nurse Cleary said.

Wolfgang looked at Susannah. "What surprise?"

Susannah laughed. "Herman. Show Dr. Pike what you're better at than the others."

Herman scooted his chair back from the table and stood, slowly, dramatically. It seemed to take forever for his long frame to unfold from the chair and straighten, but he faced Wolfgang with a military alertness.

Then he cleared his throat and began to sing.

Wolfgang's knees buckled. Susannah hurried over to him. He couldn't believe his ears. This giant lunatic sang an aria from Mozart's *Magic Flute* with one of the strongest, deepest voices Wolfgang had ever heard, the sound resonating from the unseen cavern inside the man's massive chest.

Wolfgang's choir had been missing its bass for weeks.

Now God had sent him.

They wasted no time hurrying Herman down to the fourth floor, where McVain was in bed, eyes closed. Susannah skipped her way down the solarium, stopping at the piano with a playful hop. Herman waited patiently with a fork clutched in his right hand. Wolfgang struck one of the piano keys and McVain's eyes snapped open. He sat up in bed, staring at Herman's towering figure. McVain's jaw dropped when Herman began an aria from *Don*

Giovanni. He easily had the best voice of the entire chorus, barely hampered by the tuberculosis. McVain nearly broke into a grin.

Susannah rubbed her hands together joyfully. Herman stopped abruptly and stood as stiff as a board, staring over McVain's piano toward the bed, fork in hand.

Wolfgang, too, looked to McVain for a verdict. They all did.

McVain craned his head for a better look. "What's with the fork?"

Wolfgang walked Susannah home that night, wondering every step if she would veer off in the direction of his cottage and decide to sleep on his couch again. Or would she venture up to Dr. Barker's residence after he dropped her off? They continued toward the nurses' dormitory. *As it should be*, he thought, relieved and disappointed at the same time.

"I knew there was something hiding inside of him," Susannah said.

"And the fork?" Wolfgang asked.

"Herman spent ten years singing opera in Italy." Susannah was in a playful mood, stepping carefully over twigs that had fallen on the footpath, maneuvering in a way that reminded Wolfgang of how he used to avoid the cracks on the sidewalk on his way through Central Park as a kid. "After his girlfriend left him for a baker, he stabbed the baker with a fork, half a dozen times, claiming, get this"—she slapped Wolfgang on the shoulder—"claiming that he'd stolen his cake."

Wolfgang raised his eyebrows. "So he *is* a little crazy." Wolfgang pictured the fork in Herman's tight grip, the same fork he'd taken with him back into Room 502. "Hopefully he doesn't use it on Benson."

"If he wanted to hurt Benson, he could have done it long ago," she said.

Wolfgang watched her hop on one foot over a fallen tree branch, balance herself for a second, and then hop to the other foot. It was her childlike nature that he loved about her. "That was a beautiful thing you did tonight. For Herman."

"It was long overdue," she said.

Wolfgang reached down and gripped her right hand as they walked. She looked at him with surprise. Wolfgang averted his gaze and stared straight ahead, expecting her at any moment to move her hand away from his grip, but she didn't. She even swung her arm slightly, which was enough of a reaction to give Wolfgang the confidence to not let go and run into the woods from embarrassment.

"This is long overdue as well," he said.

Soon, as they approached Susannah's dormitory, she removed her hand. She stood on her toes and kissed his cheek, pressing just above the hair over his beard.

Wolfgang ran his fingers over his chin. "I was wondering if I should shave my beard."

"Why would you do that?"

"Well...I don't know..."

"I happen to like your beard." Susannah giggled. "Good night... Father."

Wolfgang's sleep was restless.

He heard the gravel beneath his feet before he saw it, and then the driveway opened up to him. And beyond the upward bend around the apple trees, their old home was visible. The anticipation of seeing her face forced him to move faster. The intoxication of the moment still held the same feeling of giddiness he'd had the first day he'd met her outside the steps of the Cathedral of the Assumption. Nearly four years of marriage had not dampened his love for her, but what quickened his pace up the driveway was something more akin to lust. He'd spent all day at the medical school, splitting time between the smells of the lab and the even worse smells of the dissecting room with Professor Philpot. His arrival at home was the moment that fueled him throughout the day.

He hoped the sound of their Model T pulling onto the gravel driveway didn't alert her to his early arrival. It was four o'clock in the afternoon and she wasn't expecting him until five. The professors had let all of the students out early. The toes of his right boot scraped narrow grooves in the rocks as he dragged it along. He wasn't ashamed of it any longer. It was the deformity and the limp that had first drawn Rose's attention years ago. With that limp she'd seen character, a story that needed to be told. He moved with a uniqueness to his hurried gait that Rose had come to call his gallop. So Wolfgang galloped along the driveway, creating tiny dust clouds in his wake. Pink buds had bloomed on the dogwood trees that lined the front of their brick Portland neighborhood house. The azaleas were in bloom, flowering in purple and red alongside the house near the shaded porch.

He hoped she didn't suddenly open the door to find him. It made his day to surprise her. On the other side of the porch was a rose garden. Wolfgang squatted down and perused them all, rows of roses in various stages of growth. He spotted the perfect rose and plucked the stem low to the ground, snapping it carefully, avoiding the thorns. Today's rose. Tomorrow he would choose another. He knew it was childish, but it was a ritual he did not want to get rid of. He snuck in the back door, quietly sliding inside the screen, and spotted her from the laundry room. Rose was in a chair in the kitchen with her back to him, reading. Wolfgang tiptoed across the linoleum floor, where sunlight abounded and purple flowers and green vines bordered yellow wallpaper. Rose's hair had grown out since the first day they'd met. Now it was curly and pulled back in a ponytail that shielded most of her ivory neck. Her dark hair had a red bow in it. He felt sure she'd heard him coming, but her heart was too big to turn around and spoil it for him.

And then suddenly she closed the book and stood in her yellow summer dress that swayed around her knees. She turned toward him.

"A rose for a Rose," said Wolfgang, as he had so many times before.

And she smiled as usual, but her eyes seemed tired. She smiled as if she were happy. So why was she crying?

Wolfgang awoke with a start and sat up in bed. She had seemed so real that the smell of her still lingered inside his cottage. Sleet pinged off his rooftop and tapped against his windows. He faced the right side of his bed. He pictured Rose beside him, the fingers of her hand spread out against the curve of her hip, looking into his eyes as she had on so many nights.

Then he imagined the touch of Susannah's lips on his cheek.

His eyes caught a glimpse of the crucifix hanging on the wall. He turned away and forced his eyes closed.

All night he felt Him watching.

CHAPTER 26

Wolfgang squatted in the frosted grass behind his cottage, perusing the rose garden. The cold January air slid unabated into February, a month when temperatures were often sporadic throughout the Ohio Valley. Slivers of ice hung from the tree branches and glistened under the clear night sky. Sleet and snow turned the blades of grass to silvery daggers, except around the rose garden, where the precipitation had melted under Lincoln's heat lamps.

Wolfgang thought of Herman as he searched for the perfect rose. At first, Herman's addition to the choir had a negative effect on the other singers. The children knew him only as the crazy cake man from the rooftop, but it took them only one rehearsal to warm up to this new Herman, who smiled more, talked less, and combed his hair. The adults, on the other hand, were intimidated by him and didn't sing as loud in his presence, as if they were afraid they'd be inferior. For three days, rehearsals dragged on with Herman the only one fully invested, standing a good ten feet away from the rest of the choir with the fork in his right hand. Wolfgang watched their eyes and how they'd watch Herman sing, wondering if the addition was actually hurting the choir. Herman had yet to utter a word to anyone except Susannah, and the concert was less than two weeks away.

Then, on day four, Herman surprised them all. In the middle of a Vivaldi piece, he held up his arms, waving, his fork nearly scraping the solarium's ceiling. Wolfgang halted the choir and musicians.

Herman faced them with a huge smile on his cleanly shaved face. "You can do this." His eyes darted from person to person. "You can do this. I'm better than all of you, but you can do this. We can do this." He ruffled Abel's hair, which sparked nervous grins from the rest of the kids. He opened his arms to a young woman named Clarice in the second row. She looked ready to turn and run, but he stepped closer and wrapped his arms around her slender figure, nearly squashing her with a bear hug. The children laughed.

"What shit is this?" McVain said under his breath from the piano. Josef lowered his violin and watched as Herman moved to the next lady. He hugged her as well. "You can do this," he said with authority, clutching her by the shoulders.

Wolfgang, amused, but surprisingly not worried, watched Herman hug all thirty members of the choir. He reached two of the men near the end and took them both into his embrace. With each hug the choir's uneasiness seemed to lessen. Their insecurity became less with every embrace. By the end, the children were laughing, Susannah along with them. Herman's strange emergence into the group had galvanized them, and he returned to his spot, stood straight again, gripped the fork, and looked ready to sing.

Remembering this, Wolfgang laughed out loud as he clipped a rose. This one would be perfect.

Footsteps drew Wolfgang's attention back to the cottage. "Who's there?"

Lincoln stepped out of the shadows, breathing heavily, his cheeks red from running. "Wolf—"

"What is it?"

"McVain. He's missing."

Wolfgang, Big Fifteen, and Lincoln took flashlights down the body chute, and the deeper they penetrated the seemingly endless tunnel, the more claustrophobic Wolfgang became, to the point where, near the end of the chute, he was scaling the cold walls in fear of doubling over. He'd been inside the chute many times before, but never in a panic, unless he counted the near run-in with the policeman on horseback on the night they'd snuck the piano into the sanatorium. But that had been exhilarating in comparison.

McVain was not the only patient missing. Josef and Rufus were gone as well.

"McVain said nothing to you?" Wolfgang had asked Lincoln as they rushed from the rose garden up to the main building. "Anything that sounded suspicious?"

Lincoln thought for a second. "I ate lunch with McVain today out by the piano. He talked about the Seelbach Hotel. Said he used to play the piano there before he got sick."

"Oh, Lord."

"Also said he was there with Capone a few times."

"But why go there now?"

"Maybe they wanted a night out on the town before—"

"Before what?"

"Before they die."

These were not the first patients to escape Waverly Hills. It had happened before. Three years earlier, four old ladies had snuck out and walked down Dixie Highway to drink Cokes. They were kicked out upon their return, deemed healthy enough to leave if they were healthy enough to escape. Three of the ladies ended up coming back. The fourth one survived. But Wolfgang knew that none of the three men missing now were healthy enough to leave, especially McVain, who seemed to be growing weaker and thinner by the day.

When Wolfgang hit the fresh air at the bottom of the chute, he let out an enormous gush of breath, not realizing how long he'd been holding it in. His lungs ached. He felt as if he'd just had one of his nightmares.

Big Fifteen placed his hand on Wolfgang's back. "You okay, Boss?"

"I'll be fine." Wolfgang stood straight in the grass, where train tracks crossed their path. Three distinct piles of clothes had been left at the chute's entrance. Josef and McVain had tossed their attire in heaps while Rufus had folded his, neatly placing them next to the beginning of the chute. Three sets of footprints marked the icy grass along the railroad tracks. "What are they wearing now, I wonder."

Lincoln and Big Fifteen shrugged.

They weren't supposed to be leaving the hillside, but if Dr. Barker found out that three of his highly infectious patients had escaped the grounds entirely, he'd have an aneurysm. He'd cancel the concert.

Wolfgang started up the slippery slope toward the tracks, and then Lincoln led the way as they jogged toward Dixie Highway. "My uncle's house is only two blocks away. He's the one I get the booze from. He's got a brand-new Cadillac I'm sure he'll let us borrow."

To Wolfgang's amazement, Lincoln's uncle Frank—a short, stocky man in an expensive three-piece suit, fancy brown shoes, and with a head of dark hair slicked back with what appeared to be an entire can of grease—didn't even hesitate when Lincoln asked to borrow the car.

"Be my guest." He patted Lincoln on the shoulder. "Have yourself a ball. You and your buddies." He suspiciously eyed Wolfgang's cassock and instead took a step toward Big Fifteen and offered his hand. "You're one big son of a bitch."

Big Fifteen shook his hand. "Reckon I am."

"I'm Frank." He lit a cigar and looked Big Fifteen up and down. "I could probably use you sometime. Would you like that? Little extra dough for the pockets, hey? Perhaps some women." He slipped a second cigar into Big Fifteen's breast pocket and then turned quickly toward Lincoln. "Have the car back by morning. Got to drive to Cincinnati." He winked. "Important meeting."

Lincoln turned into a madman behind the wheel of his uncle's expensive car, speeding in and out of traffic despite the snowy roads. Big Fifteen laughed in the backseat. Wolfgang's beef-and-rice dinner was about to come back up and ruin Uncle Frank's interior. Lincoln glanced over toward him. "You okay?"

"Maybe you should slow down a bit." Wolfgang cracked the

window about an inch, and the cool air made him feel better. "You know where you're going?"

"Of course." Lincoln gripped the steering wheel harder as the car fishtailed on a patch of ice. He regained control, eyes peeled. "Been to the Seelbach dozens of times with Uncle Frank."

"What exactly for?"

Lincoln shrugged. "Important stuff, you know. But mostly I'd wait in the car. He'd run in for about a half hour, then come back out." Lincoln bounded over a pothole, and it sounded as if something had come off the right tire. Wolfgang rose up off his seat and his head nearly hit the ceiling. He braced his hands on the dashboard. Lincoln finally decreased his speed when the lights of downtown Louisville loomed just over the horizon. The traffic grew thicker as they neared the famous hotel. Lincoln rolled down his window and a rush of freezing air filled the car. He honked the horn at three women standing alongside Fourth Street. "Hey, dolls!" Wolfgang hunkered down in his seat as the ladies waved.

Big Fifteen leaned enthusiastically forward from the backseat. "Never been here before."

Streetlamps were aglow. Snow flurries danced wildly through the air. The clip-clop of a horse carriage echoed off the walls of the surrounding buildings and storefronts. The road turned to cobblestone as they closed in, and the ride suddenly became much bumpier over the patchwork of stone and ice. Lincoln pointed to an old car parked with one wheel on the curb. "Got us a petting party inside that fliver." Lincoln honked and whooped out the window. "Four of 'em with kissers locked." Wolfgang glanced away. Lincoln focused on the road again, where the hotel loomed. "George Remus spent a lot of time at the Seelbach."

"Who's he?" Big Fifteen asked.

Wolfgang rolled his eyes. "Oh, Lord, here we go."

Lincoln's tone was serious. "Cincinnati mobster. Made a fortune running whiskey. That writer Fitzpatrick? He based the main character from *The Great Catspee* on Remus."

"Fitzgerald," said Wolfgang.

"What?"

"And it's 'Gatsby,' not 'Catspee,' you baboon."

Lincoln slowed the car and coasted past a brand-new Oldsmobile with a sharp-dressed couple inside. He tapped the steering wheel with his thumbs, looking for a place to park. The street was teeming with people standing, walking, talking, most everyone wearing extravagant suits and pretty dresses. Wolfgang's modest clerical robes would hardly fit in, but they weren't coming to socialize. If their three Waverly escapees were here, they'd quickly snatch them and be on their way. Wolfgang planted his palms against the dash again as Lincoln cut off a Desoto and dove into a parking spot vacated by a delivery truck.

"I'll wait in the car," Big Fifteen said.

"You sure?" Wolfgang asked.

Big Fifteen nodded and then pulled out the cigar Uncle Frank had given him. "Got a light, though?"

Lincoln tossed him the keys. "Uncle Frank keeps a Banjo in the glove department. A flip and it's lit, Fifteen. Don't burn the car down."

Wolfgang and Lincoln hurried across the busy street. Lincoln's face lit up as he looked toward the top of the hotel, which stood ten stories tall and dwarfed the buildings around it. "McVain said there's a small alcove off the Oakroom where Capone plays blackjack and poker when he's in town. He had a big mirror brought down from Chicago so he could watch his back."

Wolfgang found himself stepping over the cracks in the sidewalk, limping noticeably. "And check out his opponents' cards, I bet." He folded his arms against the cold wind and moved beside a parked horse-drawn carriage. Long plumes of steam jetted from the horse's nose as it fidgeted in the freezing temperatures. They passed a brick building with a poster attached to the front door—KEEP YOUR BEDROOM WINDOWS OPEN: PREVENT TUBERCULOSIS.

On the corner of Fourth and Walnut, the European-style hotel designed with the French Renaissance in mind was brightly lit and alive with people. It was the first skyscraper in Louisville, one of the grandest hotels in the country, and Wolfgang had heard rumors of women fainting the day it opened. Portions of the façade reminded Wolfgang of the grandeur of Waverly Hills. The Seelbach's exterior was made of stone and dark brick pieced together with charm and elegance. Charles Dickens had been ejected from the hotel for showing poor manners. Presidents Taft and Wilson had stayed in the hotel, apparently without suffering Dickens's fate. Already in its short existence, history seeped from every door and window, and Wolfgang felt a rush of blood to his head as he stepped under the canopied entrance and moved up the stairs. The merry atmosphere was contagious. A glass of wine would have felt appropriate for the moment. He remembered Rose and the nights they'd celebrated much as these people did now, carefree and tipsy from alcohol, despite Prohibition.

Wolfgang was first inside the lobby. Behind him, Lincoln paused to take it all in. The boy was awestruck. European marble everywhere, beautiful carpets, exquisitely carved wood, bronze railings, friezes and frescoes on the walls, brass chandeliers and wall sconces, and a skylight above made of hundreds of panels of glass.

Men in suits stood shoulder to shoulder smoking cigars or cigarettes, drinking and laughing, their faces flushed and happy. The women wore their hair bobbed—just like Rose's, Wolfgang couldn't help notice. They wore makeup and long, cylindrical silhouette dresses, Basque dresses, or the popular one-hour dress that allowed more freedom for dancing. They wore silk, cotton, linen, and wool with colors ranging from bright greens, reds, and blues to pastels. Assertive colors. Aggressive colors. Free-spirited, smart, and sexy. Women out on dates without chaperones.

Wolfgang squeezed his eyes shut. How times had changed. How dearly he missed Rose. Then, amid the chattering in the lobby, Wolfgang heard music. "Oh, my Lord," he said. "Beethoven."

Wolfgang fought his way through the clouds of cigar smoke to a larger crowd in the back corner, listening to a musical trio of piano, flute, and violin. Lincoln tapped Wolfgang's shoulder. "I think we found them."

Wolfgang wormed his way through the crowd, close enough to smell the alcohol and perfume and see the intoxication in their reddened eyes. But they all seemed fascinated with the musicians who had set up shop around the piano on the right side of the ornate stairs—a black man on the flute, a violinist with a chalkboard on his chest, and a piano player who dazzled despite missing three fingers on his left hand.

Their music soared high off the lobby's tall ceiling. On the floor next to Josef's feet sat an upside-down bowler hat, the same one McVain had worn the day he arrived at Waverly. It wasn't large enough to hold the bills and coins that had already been dropped at their feet. Where had they gotten the nice suits? How long had they planned this? Wolfgang wondered.

Despite the fact that they needed to urgently remove these three from the hotel, ensuring that no one here got sick and that Barker was none the wiser, it was a beautiful scene to watch. If only Susannah had been there. Maybe one night they'd sneak out and have a harmless night on the town, away from the sanatorium, away from the patients, away from the hillside, and away from the death. There was a world moving on outside the woods in which they roamed daily, and he imagined Susannah's hand in his grip again as he slithered through the crowd. And then he forced the thought from his mind. What was he thinking? And then he remembered McVain's words to him the other night: "You can't have it both ways…"

Wolfgang stopped abruptly. The row of men in front of him wouldn't budge. "Get lost," said a tall man with a pencil neck, evidently not seeing Wolfgang's cassock—or just not caring.

A woman in an orange silhouette dress pointed toward the piano. "Darling, that man only has two fingers on his left hand."

"He's fantastic."

They deserved every bit of this recognition, thought Wolfgang, but he had to get them out all the same. He thought of Mr. Weaver when a fat man with heavy jowls shouted, "Play some jazz! Jazz!"

"Ragtime!" a woman yelled. Ragtime? Jazz? Wolfgang's trio didn't play ragtime or jazz. But during a short pause, McVain, Josef, and Rufus huddled together. The crowd hushed.

McVain looked excited and utterly exhausted at the same time. His skin was so pale. Sweat beaded along his red hairline. Suddenly the three broke from their huddle and readied their instruments. Wolfgang couldn't help but smile with pride, although it soon melted away with a horrific thought: what these crowds didn't know could kill them.

Josef started playing a jazzy sound and McVain chimed in. Rufus joined them a few seconds later, to the delight of the crowd, many of whom began dancing in the packed lobby. Wolfgang felt his legs moving to the beat. When he turned around he saw that Lincoln was having a ball—he'd even found a girl to dance with him.

And then a tall, slender man with jet-black hair and a finely trimmed mustache barged his way into the crowd with an exquisitely dressed woman on his arm. Wolfgang hated him before he even opened his mouth. "Those musicians!" he shouted. Everyone looked at him. "They're diseased!" The crowd hushed. "They all have TB! They escaped from Waverly Hills!"

Rufus dropped to his knees and stuffed money into the hat. Josef grabbed his coat. McVain quickly stood from the piano. They looked around for an escape route. Wolfgang and Lincoln used the moment of stunned silence to skitter past the crowd and join their musicians.

The man was still yelling arrogantly: "They threatened me on the trolley tonight. They let the nigger sit with the decent folks!" The crowd quickly backed away from the trio, gasping. A woman fainted in a red heap to the floor.

The front doors were now blocked, some people still coming in to see the excitement, others now fleeing. Around them, the crowd's fear soon turned to anger. "Up the stairs," Wolfgang said. Lincoln was the first, leading them up the curved stairs. Wolfgang hurried past McVain, who smiled. "Hey, Father."

"Come on." Wolfgang grabbed him by the elbow and urged him along.

The crowd cursed and shouted below them. Wolfgang was afraid McVain would collapse, but adrenaline must have spurred him along. He matched Wolfgang step for hobbled step. Wolfgang yelled to McVain over the chaos. "I'm glad you're having so much fun. You'll probably be dead in the morning."

McVain laughed. "Lincoln...to the Oakroom."

From ahead, Lincoln waved them on. "This way!" He led them directly into the Oakroom, past elegant diners and stunned waiters carrying plates of lobster and pasta and steak. Wolfgang tripped over someone's foot, stumbling into a bullish bodyguard, who then lost his balance and toppled a table of shrimp. The mob was gaining. While the guard was down on the floor, struggling to unwrap himself from a stained tablecloth, McVain moved toward a door in the back of the room. He knocked—three quick taps, a hesitation, followed by one more tap. He closed his eyes, as if willing it open, and then it did. The five of them rushed inside a small, cramped room swimming with cigar smoke. A spring-loaded door slammed behind them, locking them inside just before the guard grabbed for Josef's shirt. Pistols cocked. Five gun barrels materialized through the haze and were pointed their way, one for each of them.

A man's clipped Chicago accent penetrated the smoke. "Don't move a fuckin' muscle."

Wolfgang stared across a poker table at five men in white button-downs and suspenders, sitting around a card table drinking bourbon and playing blackjack—or at least that's what they *had* been doing before this unfortunate arrival. Now they pointed pistols. One of the men held an automatic weapon so big it required two hands. His nose had been broken so many times it no longer resembled any nose Wolfgang had ever seen before. "Butch let you in?"

"Who's Butch?" asked Wolfgang.

"The man supposedly guarding the door," the broken-nosed man said.

McVain discreetly touched Wolfgang's arm. "Yes, Butch let us in."

"Now, why would he do that?" The man who sat in the middle, bald with coal for eyes, yanked the wet stub of a cigar from his mouth and eyed Wolfgang. "Never killed a priest before."

Maybe this was why I wanted the priesthood, Wolfgang thought. For the exact moment in life when he'd stumble upon a table of gangsters and his life would be spared because of his clothing. "I hope you won't start now," he managed to say.

A knock sounded outside the door, the same knock McVain had made. One of the gangsters started to get up, but the middle man said, "Leave him out there."

The mob outside the door was growing louder. They began to

pound on the walls. Lincoln stood beside Wolfgang, grinning like a fool. Wolfgang watched him from the corner of his eye.

"Wipe that smile off your face, you fuckin' cake-eater." The middle man chewed on his cigar. He locked eyes with Josef. "What's with the violin, paleface?"

"He's a musician," Wolfgang said. "We're all musicians."

"I didn't ask you, Father." He pointed his gun at Josef. "Can't you talk?"

Josef wrote on his chalkboard. NO.

"He's got—" Lincoln started.

"Got what?"

"He's a mute, sir," Wolfgang said.

"This some kind of traveling circus?" The middle man gave Rufus a good once-over. Then McVain next. "This clown's missing fingers. What instrument do you play, carrot top?"

McVain was sweating profusely. He straightened himself against the back wall. "Piano."

Middle man laughed. On his front tooth rested a speck of brown from his cigar. "How'd you lose them fingers?"

"The war." McVain buffed the nails of his five right fingers against his lapel. "Not that it's any of your goddamn business."

Only Wolfgang's stifled groan broke the frozen silence.

Then, from outside—sirens.

"Police," one of the men said.

"Fuckin' bulls," said another. They heard screaming outside the doors.

Something clanked and a whoosh of air sucked smoke from the room. The middle man was gone in a flash. A wood-paneled door opened behind the table, and he quickly disappeared down a dark staircase. One by one his men, each of them pointing their weapons at them one last time, followed him down the secret passageway until they were left alone in the smoky room staring at their reflection in the mirrored wall.

Lincoln nudged Wolfgang. "Told you."

McVain labored around the table toward the secret passage. "Those men didn't recognize me."

"I assume that's a good thing?" asked Wolfgang.

"Understatement of the year," said McVain.

"How did you know the knock?"

"Educated guess," said McVain. "Come on. Let's get out of here."

McVain pushed the secret doorway open. The door behind them nearly rattled off its hinges. "You guys gonna wait around for them?"

They funneled in behind McVain. Lincoln could barely contain his excitement. Rufus patted Wolfgang on the back and winked. "You saved us, Father." Wolfgang didn't feel like a hero. His outfit had only bought them time until the police arrived, which Wolfgang thought ironic. Most likely the police had been called to detain his trio of TB-infected musicians, not the hidden gangsters. Wolfgang waited for Josef to pass and then took up the rear as they all headed into the secret passage. The scent of bourbon and cigars led them down the dark staircase and into an even darker kitchen, where McVain doubled over into a coughing fit. Rufus helped McVain along.

Lincoln grabbed a biscuit from a food tray. "They went that way." He pointed to another set of downward stairs. At the foot of the stairs was a basement full of wooden crates, old furniture, broken sinks, brooms and mops, slop buckets, and bottles of bourbon. "Real bootleggers," Lincoln cried out to no one in particular. "This is the best." His voice echoed off the cold, curved walls. He led them into a drainage tunnel that smelled of dirty water, mildew, and cigar smoke. Moisture had collected on the ceiling and dripped to the floor from one central spot. Lincoln inhaled the dank, coppery air. "This is probably how they make the bourbon." He put a finger to his lips. Up ahead, the boots of the final gangster climbed up an iron ladder attached to the grimy walls of the tunnel. The Waverly group waited for a few minutes and then hurried to catch up, the manhole cover in the street still tossed aside. A faint light shone into the tunnel and snow flurries spit downward. Wolfgang was the last up the ladder, and just as he poked his head up into the fresh, cool air of some unknown street, he heard the squealing of two cars. Just like that, the men from the smoky room were gone.

McVain staggered out into the middle of the street. The lights from an oncoming car grew brighter. The car squealed and slid to a stop on the icy street and honked at them. McVain collapsed in the middle of the road.

They all crammed into Uncle Frank's Cadillac, and Lincoln drove straight to the sanatorium with McVain barely breathing in the backseat, his head resting on Big Fifteen's lap. "Don't die on us... don't die," Big Fifteen said repeatedly, stroking McVain's red hair. As soon as Lincoln skidded to a halt on the packed ice and gravel before the entrance, Big Fifteen pulled McVain from the car, cradled him in his arms, and ran into the sanatorium while Wolfgang and Lincoln held the doors.

"Take him to the operating room," Wolfgang said. "First floor!"

"Should I get Dr. Barker?" asked Lincoln, his face near panic, his night of fun a distant memory.

Wolfgang hesitated. "Yes. Go get him." Dr. Barker was a better surgeon, and they couldn't risk McVain's life to conceal the night's events. "Go. Hurry." Lincoln sprinted out across the road while Wolfgang led the way to the operating room.

Dr. Barker was ready within ten minutes. He didn't ask any questions, just ordered a quick x-ray and got down to business. He said nothing of their pulling him from his slumber in the middle of the night. There was a man's life to be saved, or at least prolonged. Dr. Barker first tried the pneumothorax procedure, inserting a needle in between the ribs that encaged McVain's left lung. He attempted to push air through the needle and into the pleural cavity that surrounded the left lung, which in McVain's case was the one with the largest lesions. His right lung was diseased as well, but according to the x-rays they'd taken since his arrival, the small lesion on the right lung had not grown. By introducing the air they would be able to collapse the left lung and allow it to rest.

"It's not working," said Dr. Barker. "His lung is sticking to the chest wall." The doctor reached out his right hand. "We're gonna have to open him up."

Dr. Barker opened McVain's chest with swift tugs of his scalpel and immediately got to work on the thoracoplasty procedure, which required the removal of some of McVain's ribs. Wolfgang assisted the surgery and monitored McVain's doses of ether to keep him sedated. He watched Dr. Barker work. The doctor's face was red, his eyes intense and focused, but still he asked no questions about what had happened earlier, and for this Wolfgang was grateful. There was no need to fight over the man's body in the middle of surgery. That would most assuredly come later.

Dr. Barker's jaw never unclenched in ninety minutes of surgery. When he pulled his hands from the wall of McVain's open chest, his gloves and wrists covered with blood, he shuffled away from the table in silence. Wolfgang began to stitch McVain's chest while Dr. Barker washed his hands and then left the operating room without a word.

McVain's breathing was shallow, but he was alive. Five ribs on the left side of his chest had been removed. The lung was now collapsed.

Wolfgang looked at the x-ray they'd taken of McVain's chest before they'd operated. The lesion on McVain's right lung had grown as well. And now there appeared to be two of them.

CHAPTER 27

D r. Barker stopped Wolfgang outside the chapel first thing in the morning. He slapped a folded newspaper against his open palm and then unfolded it to the front page when Wolfgang turned his way. "'TB Patients on the Loose. Three Patients Have a Night on the Town.' Real headlines, Dr. Pike!"

Wolfgang could hardly look at it, but then again he knew it wasn't totally his fault. "Do you think I encouraged this, Dr. Barker?"

Barker forced the newspaper into Wolfgang's chest. Jesse Jacobs emerged from the chapel to see what the commotion was about. When Wolfgang told him everything was okay, Jesse moved slowly down the hall. Dr. Barker waited until it was clear to continue. "Bad press. Your trio nearly started a riot."

"A night on the town."

"The city is already panicked. They didn't need this. Now they think we have no discipline," he said, eyeballs bulging. "They were highly contagious patients. You may not have known, but you've encouraged them by your actions. Careless actions."

"Are you more worried about the people or your reputation?"

Dr. Barker's nostrils flared. "How dare you."

Wolfgang backed off. "Thank you for last night. McVain's stabilized somewhat."

"What else was I to do? Let him die because of the foolishness?"

Wolfgang had nothing to say.

Dr. Barker wasn't finished. "Rehearsals are canceled until further notice."

Wolfgang started to disagree, but stopped. It was a good idea. McVain would not be capable of playing for several weeks, if ever again. He needed rest. He didn't need a crowd around him. Wolfgang lowered his head and started down the hallway.

"And Dr. Pike."

Wolfgang turned toward Dr. Barker again. "Yes."

"I've written a letter to the diocese."

"Why?"

"I'm going to have them force the issue with you. Either you return to the seminary, or I'll have you transferred."

"Transferred?"

"To another abbey perhaps," said Dr. Barker. "One far away from whatever distraction is keeping you here."

For the rest of the day, Wolfgang could think of nothing else. Transferred? It was only a threat, he told himself. The diocese certainly wouldn't listen. They only transferred priests. They couldn't transfer seminary students. And after so many years of stagnancy with his studies, Wolfgang wondered, was he even a student anymore? Barker could technically fire him as a doctor, but Wolfgang knew he wouldn't. He couldn't afford to lose another staff member.

"Father?" Wolfgang looked down at the top of Miss Schultz's head as he wheeled her to her room. She continued to grow stronger every day, and after her new hairdo today her face was full of life and color. "Something bothering you?"

"I'm fine. Thank you, Miss Schultz."

She looked up at him. "You were right. Our new barber does nice work."

Wolfgang wheeled her across the solarium porch, eyeing several of the patients as he passed. So many of them were new. He wondered if his attackers had passed away, as well. He hadn't heard from them in a while.

"Where do you put all of them, Father?"

Wolfgang put on a fake smile to disguise his true thoughts of possibly having to leave Waverly. "They go straight to heaven, Miss Schultz."

She waved her hand through the air, as if swatting his answer to the wind. "Always quick with your answers." She held up her crooked index finger. "But I figured it out."

"You have, have you?"

"You sneak them out somehow," she said. "So we don't see the hearse pulling up here so many times a day. That would be bad for our morale, wouldn't it?"

"Far be it for me to contradict you, Miss Schultz."

She looked over her shoulder. "Don't give me that. I know I'm right."

Susannah held baby Fred in the lobby while Wolfgang stepped outside with Mary Sue. Mary Sue took a deep, healthy breath of the cool air and then nodded toward Wolfgang. "I'm ready."

They started down the winding road that cut through the wooded hillside. Mary Sue took it slow at first, but then she gained momentum on the steep downhill.

"Not too fast," Wolfgang said.

She didn't listen.

At the bottom of the hill Mary Sue took a few seconds to catch her breath. She was doing great, smiling, and then she broke down crying in Wolfgang's arms.

Frederick had taken a turn for the worse ever since he'd learned that Mary Sue was being released. He'd been unresponsive even to her, and he'd still been unable to hold his son. Mary Sue kissed his forehead, held his cold hands, and promised him they would visit as often as they were allowed. She left Frederick's room with tears in her eyes.

A Model T sat idling outside the sanatorium's entrance, a relative waiting to pick up Mary Sue and the baby and take them home. Mary Sue went down the line, hugging the nurses and orderlies who'd assembled to watch her departure.

Wolfgang hugged her and then gripped her shoulders at arm's length. "Susannah and I will keep special watch over him, Mary Sue. I'll do my best to bring him out of this."

She hugged Wolfgang again and backed away toward the car. Susannah took a picture of Mary Sue and baby Fred.

"Tell Frederick I will visit," she said. "We will both visit."

"I will," said Wolfgang.

She grinned. "Until then, Dr. Pike."

"Until then, Mary Sue."

After sundown the temperature dropped drastically, the wind chill putting the mercury in single digits and in danger of plummeting further. Wolfgang worked with his requiem on his lap, watching McVain sleep. He hoped the freeze would finally waken McVain from his surgery. It had been nearly twenty-four hours.

McVain's hand moved involuntarily against his bed sheets. Wolfgang scooted up in his chair, praying he would open his eyes, hoping he would live to play the piano again. *Please, God, don't let it end like this.* They'd come so far. The concert was only twelve days away.

A neighboring patient down the solarium opened an envelope, pulled out a letter, and smiled as he began to read. In all his time at Waverly Hills, Wolfgang hadn't seen McVain receive one piece of mail from anyone. Not a wife, a sibling, or even a friend. Had he burned that many bridges? Was he really so alone? Yet on the hillside he seemed magnetic at times, a leader of sorts.

McVain's eyelids fluttered. His hands moved again. Wolfgang

scooted closer and felt McVain's forehead. It was warm. Perhaps the cold temperature would help to lower his fever. McVain's eyes opened, blinked, and opened again. Wolfgang gripped his mangled left hand. McVain's green eyes moved left, right, and then left again before settling on Wolfgang. He smiled, which was rare. His voice was low.

"They loved us," McVain hissed.

Wolfgang nodded. "Yes, they did. Until they learned the truth."

McVain looked past Wolfgang toward Mr. Weaver's bed. It no longer housed Mr. Weaver. Now an older man with white hair called it home. "Where's Weaver?"

"He died this morning."

McVain stared at the man in Weaver's bed. "Then the jazz we played was for him." He made a move to sit up, but then winced deeply and settled back down. "I feel dizzy."

"Your temperature is nearly a hundred and four," Wolfgang said. "You were in surgery last night. Dr. Barker collapsed your left lung. Removed five ribs. I'm surprised you're even lucid."

McVain blinked slowly. "I don't have much longer, do I?"

Wolfgang couldn't lie. McVain was one patient who could handle nothing less than the blunt truth. "The lesions are growing on your right lung, as well." Wolfgang paused to let his words sink in. "What you did last night was dangerous."

"Barker?"

"Rehearsals are canceled for the foreseeable future," Wolfgang said. "But don't worry. He hasn't canceled the concert. I think he's afraid to let the patients down."

McVain shook his head. His pale face showed little gratification at the news, as if his flesh wouldn't allow it. "My father was…a bartender at the…Seelbach's basement. The Rathskeller. Then we moved to Chicago. I liked it there…until Prohibition started. Moved back home to get away from it up there. Had it in my head that I'd start a speakeasy…downtown somewhere." He closed his eyes as if focusing on the memories. In its day, the hotel bar was the premier watering hole in the city, one of the first air-conditioned rooms ever built, with ornate columns and terra cotta ceiling.

McVain's eyes fluttered open again. "I wanted…to go back there… one more time…"

Wolfgang could see the truth festering behind those stark green Irish eyes. "Tell me about your father, McVain."

"Like yours…mine wanted me to be a famous…musician."

"But you became one."

McVain readjusted his bed sheets and pulled them up higher, wincing noticeably. "He died when I was in Europe. Went crazy… shot himself."

McVain's anger had probably turned further inward after his father's suicide, thought Wolfgang. Tragedy in layers. "Barker sometimes reminds me of my father," Wolfgang said. "This is why I have a natural inclination to disobey him."

A brief smile from McVain again.

"You guys were responsible for a riot."

"They loved us. They tossed money. Did Rufus get it all?"

"He still has it." Wolfgang sighed. He couldn't be mad at them. "Who was the man with the mustache?"

McVain tried to laugh. "We took a trolley downtown. That flat tire and his wife were sitting…near the front when…we came in." McVain closed his eyes and took a few painful breaths. "We sat down and the guy…he said no niggers were allowed up front."

"Poor Rufus."

"I threatened to…bump him off, you know." McVain licked his lips, and even that task seemed difficult. He swallowed, wincing. "'Niggers,' I said to him…'how dare you call…Rufus a name like that.'" McVain sniffed. His eyes grew heavy. "The wife went hysterical. Then Josef started…writing on that…damn chalkboard." McVain wheezed another laugh, and tears pooled in his eyes from the pain.

Wolfgang touched McVain's shoulder. "What did he write?"

"'We all have TB.'" McVain coughed so violently his reddened eyes bulged. "I waved my mangled hand…in the man's face. He cringed back so hard he fell…off his seat."

Wolfgang wanted to look stern, but he was enjoying this story too much.

"They jumped up...ran to the back of the trolley...so fast it nearly...tipped over." McVain's eyes wandered toward the piano at the foot of the bed. "How'd I get back?"

"Lincoln drove like mad. Fifteen carried you in all by himself."

McVain nodded, took it in. "And the Oakroom? Was that neat or what?"

Wolfgang tried his hardest not to smile. McVain, Rufus, and Josef had all lived the horrors of war and were now dying of an incurable disease, but for Wolfgang and his deformed foot, staring into the eyes of a drunk gangster and his gun was the most danger he'd ever experienced. It was as if he were going against his mother's wishes all over again.

McVain grinned. "He nearly shot us all...but he didn't count on you. You and your buddies." He pointed his left pinkie heavenward. They both burst out laughing.

Wolfgang paced the length of the small center aisle in Waverly's chapel. It was the second night Susannah had left early in the past week and a half, and he didn't have to wonder about where she was going. No, he knew. He paced in the dark, his footfalls clicking against the floor. In his hand was a wine bottle. He tipped it to his mouth, drank, then wiped the warm taste from his lips. He envisioned Susannah and Dr. Barker together. His hands touching her bare flesh. Wolfgang tilted the bottle back again, then raised it in the air. "Sacramental wine, Dr. Barker."

Susannah had asked, *How am I supposed to find anyone to marry on this hillside?* And Dr. Barker was having problems with his marriage—at least that was the rumor. Had Susannah filled the void?

Wolfgang breathed deeply, starting to feel the alcohol. It hit him like a tsunami wave. It was wrong of him to spy on Susannah, but he had to know. He placed the open wine on the altar, cracking the bottle with the force of the movement. His head was swimming. The top of the altar had been a foot higher than he thought. Glass sprinkled to the floor of the chapel, and the remaining wine dripped down the glass like blood. He left it to pool and spread.

Wearing only a thin lab coat over his cassock, he felt his skin turn to ice in the temperature outside. His feet were numb by the time he'd entered the woods and found the footpath on the far side of the main road, which was covered with frozen patches of snow. It was eleven o'clock, and the wind chill had dropped to near zero. He buried his hands in the folds of his coat, hunkered down, and plowed his way over fallen limbs and ice-smothered leaves. His nose was beginning to run. The hair inside his nostrils felt like daggers. Up ahead was Dr. Barker's cottage. Smoke puffed up from a stone chimney. He dragged his numb right leg down the footpath and spotted the glow of a light coming from the side window of Barker's one-floor home, which, unlike Wolfgang's, had a narrow veranda with posts that wrapped around three walls of the structure.

Wolfgang didn't hesitate up the side steps. He knelt down on the wood-planked porch, wetting the knees of his pants, and peered into a frost-smeared window. A fire burned on the other side of the room. In the center was a yellow couch. Behind it was a desk with a lamp. Susannah sat at the desk with two stacks of papers in front of her, and Dr. Barker stood behind her with a glass of something in his hand. Something golden brown on ice, like whiskey?

Then Dr. Barker placed his hand on Susannah's left shoulder. Susannah looked up at the man, but Wolfgang couldn't tell if she was smiling or unnerved. Wolfgang lowered his head. He heard Dr. Barker's voice.

"Can I get you anything?" he asked.

"No, thank you," said Susannah.

"Are you sure? Not a drink? I've got bourbon."

There was a hesitation before Susannah answered. "I need to be getting home anyway."

Wolfgang agreed. She needed to be getting home. His vision swirled; his ears were so numb they hurt. He felt foolish sitting here but didn't want to venture back out into the cold. His head was already starting to throb. He peered in through the window again. Dr. Barker stood by a closet next to the desk.

"Let me show you something." Barker waved her over toward the couch. "Come, sit for a moment."

Susannah clutched her manuscript against her chest. She walked reluctantly to the couch and sat on the edge. Wolfgang could tell Dr. Barker's cottage made her a bit uncomfortable, which he found to be a bit of a relief. Perhaps she *was* there only on business. The doctor returned to the closet beside the desk and opened the door. Wolfgang nearly fell over and rolled down the steps as Barker pulled out a massive instrument: a double bass that nearly stretched his own height. He carried it over to the couch and sat beside Susannah.

Her eyes grew large. "Dr. Barker..."

He plucked a few strings and grabbed a bow from beside the couch. A low hum resonated throughout the cottage and seeped through the windows. "I can play music too, Susannah." He gave the strings another strike. "I've played for most of my life."

"I don't understand," said Susannah.

Dr. Barker put the double bass aside and scooted closer to her. "We work long days here. Nonstop work. And misery. We all need release." He put his left hand on her knee. She didn't move it away.

Wolfgang held his breath.

Susannah clutched the manuscript against her chest, holding it with both arms folded. "Dr. Barker, you're married."

"Call me Evan," he said. "Anne won't touch me anymore, Susannah. She fears it."

"We all do."

Dr. Barker leaned in and kissed her neck.

Wolfgang wanted to crash through the window, but Susannah jumped up from her seat on the couch.

"How dare you?" She held her manuscript tighter.

"You're making a fool of yourself, Susannah." Dr. Barker stood, red-faced and seething. He pointed to the door. "You're in love with a man you can't have."

Susannah paused and then hurried to the door. Wolfgang didn't have time to leave now or he'd be seen. He stayed in his spot on the side porch of the cottage as Susannah burst out the front door. He watched her hurry toward the footpath. She stopped as if she had forgotten something and then looked up into the dark sky. Wolfgang looked up as well. Past the main sanatorium, thick, heavy clouds of billowing smoke hovered over the horizon. It hung over the colored hospital down the hillside.

Susannah turned and shouted. "Dr. Barker!"

A few seconds later, Dr. Barker stood on the front porch, hands on the railing, his eyes focused on the same smoke Susannah had seen. "Jesus."

"I think the colored hospital is on fire."

Susannah and Dr. Barker took off into the woods.

Wolfgang gave them a few seconds' head start before heading off in the same direction. He quickly fell behind, feeling himself sober up, planning to tell them he saw the smoke too from the sanatorium. He limped quickly over the main road and hurried across the frozen mud and sloping grounds. He saw Abel standing next to the entrance portico on the south side of the sanatorium, dazed.

"Abel, what are you doing up?"

Abel didn't answer. He stared into the woods, shivering. Wolfgang hugged the frightened boy and rubbed his back to warm him. "You need to go inside right now. Do you hear me, Abel? Go inside and warm yourself."

Abel nodded. The wind ripped into Wolfgang's face as he moved downhill, brushing aside tree branches in a rickety, ominous song. After another twenty yards Wolfgang heard footsteps. Branches moved and cracked. Lincoln emerged from another cluster of trees, huffing his way down the hill toward the smoke below. Wolfgang did a double take—the right side of Lincoln's face was swollen, and a cut had scabbed beneath his right eye. "What happened to you?"

"I was attacked in the chute," he said as they continued down the hill. "Someone knocked me out. I just came to and found the coffin empty."

"What? They took a body?"

"No, Wolf. I was on my way up with another batch," said Lincoln. "They broke the bottles. Must'a known when I get my stuff."

When they finally burst into the clearing around the colored hospital, the wind blew a thick haze of smoke into Wolfgang's face. Lincoln stormed ahead. Susannah was bent over in the grass, coughing. Wolfgang helped her up.

She looked at him. "I stopped by your cottage."

"I was at the sanatorium." Wolfgang crouched and shielded his eyes. Smoke swirled low as they stood on a slope overlooking the hospital. Nearly a hundred patients huddled in groups along the tree line as three men from the maintenance staff shot water from hoses toward the front of the hospital. The flames had been put out. Thick, dark, billowing smoke stretched up past the tips of the trees. The fire hadn't been as bad as the smoke had made it appear, touching only the front entrance of the hospital. He searched the crowd for Smokey and found him sitting on the ground next to the tree line, his baseball bat resting on his thighs, staring at the smoke.

Dr. Barker stood about ten yards from the building, ushering an old black woman up the hill toward the others. Susannah watched. Soot and smoke darkened Susannah's wet cheeks. She coughed again into her hand, still clutching the manuscript to her chest. When she saw Wolfgang looking at her pages, she started to offer an explanation of why she'd run through the woods with her prized book but then lowered her head and said nothing. Her chest rose and fell with deep gasps. This air was stifling.

Wolfgang touched her shoulder. "Susannah, go back up the hill. Check the sanatorium. Every bed. Every room. If anyone's missing, we'll know the reason why." She nodded and ran back into the woods. "Start with the fourth floor," Wolfgang shouted, watching as she disappeared into the darkness. Then he caught up with Lincoln, who was consoling a young boy who couldn't find his mother. Only then did he realize that he'd just sent Susannah into the woods alone.

"Wolfgang?"

It was Rufus, hobbling up the incline, his boots crunching.

"Rufus, was anyone hurt?"

"No." His breathing was labored. "We were lucky." He held the flute in his left hand. Behind him, Wolfgang could see the damage to the charred front of the building was extensive. Water dripped from the eaves. The wooden posts had splinted and snapped in half. The roof had separated from the main building and drooped toward the ground. It would all have to be repaired quickly. "Dr. Barker was down here in a flash."

Another question hit Wolfgang suddenly. "Where's Fifteen?"

Rufus surveyed the surrounding woods. "Haven't seen him."

Lincoln approached. "Where's Big Fifteen, Wolf? He would have been down here."

"Yes, I know." Wolfgang turned toward the woods up the hillside. "He would have…"

"What?" Lincoln asked.

Wolfgang's eyes lit up. "They've stolen alcohol. Fifteen is missing. I think the fire was a diversion."

Wolfgang hurried up the hillside. The alcohol in his body had worn off. He moved in fits and starts around the trees, unsure where to go but following Susannah's general direction. A pungent odor emanated from somewhere in the woods, a nauseating but familiar stench. "You smell that, Lincoln?"

Lincoln wiggled his nose. "Smoke."

"No, something more." They continued on. They checked Big Fifteen's dormitory but found it empty, everyone apparently down with the fire. Wolfgang moved farther up the hill, bouncing from tree to tree, he and Lincoln calling Big Fifteen's name into the wind. Wolfgang sniffed, the sweet odor becoming more noticeable. "Ether. Lincoln, it's ether."

"I can smell it now. A whole truckload of it. And bourbon." Lincoln grabbed Wolfgang's arm. They stopped and listened. Someone was crying. Wolfgang followed the sound. It was a child.

Lincoln found him first, sitting with his back against a tree trunk, and called out to him. "Abel?" The boy's face was muddy. Tears streaked the grime on his cheeks. His teeth chattered.

Wolfgang knelt beside the terrified boy and clutched his small shoulders. "What happened? Abel, what are you doing out here?"

Abel pointed to his left.

Lincoln darted off toward the trees to their right. "Oh my god."

Big Fifteen's massive bulk hung from the strained limb of a white oak. Fingers of light bled down from the moon above, spotlighting his body with light and shadow, darkness and blood. The ether and bourbon permeated Big Fifteen's entire body as it rotated slightly from the tree limb. His red eyes bulged and his wet body trembled beneath the noose as empty bottles of bourbon littered the grass below.

Wolfgang felt nauseous. An ether-soaked towel rested on the grass next to the base of the tree, where another bottle leaned, half empty. Knocking him out with ether would have been the only way to move Big Fifteen's body to such a position. But still, the strength it must have taken to get him up into the tree. How many men were responsible for this?

Lincoln ran to Big Fifteen, grabbed his swaying right foot, and tried to support his weight. Abel leapt from Wolfgang's arms, ran to Big Fifteen, jumped up, and caught the swaying left foot. The tree limb cracked, then broke. Big Fifteen collapsed in a heap to the forest floor.

Wolfgang remembered cutting Rita down weeks ago, but this was no suicide. Wolfgang squatted beside Big Fifteen's body, which reeked of ether, bourbon, and urine, and felt for a pulse—and found one! His neck was a bloody mess, and wadded socks had been stuffed inside his mouth. Wolfgang pulled them out and draped his lab coat over the man's waist. Big Fifteen moaned, his breathing shallow.

Lincoln knelt beside them. "They were gonna light 'im on fire, Wolf."

Wolfgang remembered Big Fifteen carrying McVain's lifeless body into the sanatorium the other night. Had that been the final straw? Was that his crime?

Big Fifteen's eyes focused on Dr. Wolfgang Pike. "Boss?"

Wolfgang grinned. "Yes, Fifteen, it's me. Boss."

Big Fifteen smiled. His face and chest had been lacerated with slashes as if by whips or chains. How long had they tortured him?

"Boss…"

Wolfgang gripped both of his hands now. "Don't talk. Lincoln, run for a stretcher and a couple of men—four men—to carry it. Find Jesse. Look in the chapel." Lincoln ran off.

Just then Susannah emerged from the trees. Abel ran to her and hugged her. Susannah saw Big Fifteen's body and dropped to the ground, crying.

Wolfgang checked Big Fifteen's pulse again but felt almost nothing. He'd stopped fighting, stopped moving. His eyelids blinked. "My...my papa called *me* Boss... I...I respected my papa..." He choked, his chest rose from the frozen ground, and then his body settled. His eyes no longer moved.

Wolfgang, out of desperation, rolled Big Fifteen onto his stomach and positioned his friend's head to the side, resting on the palms of both hands. He applied upward pressure at Big Fifteen's elbows, slightly raising his upper body, hoping that the pressure on the back would force air into his lungs. But the attempt at resuscitation proved futile. Fifteen's body was too big, the dead weight too heavy, the heart beat long gone. Wolfgang pounded the hard ground with his fist, closed Big Fifteen's eyes and prayed over his body. Then he stood, weak-kneed and stiff, and hobbled over toward Susannah and Abel. His right foot was numb. He embraced them, and Susannah cried into his chest.

Moments later Lincoln arrived with Jesse and three men from the maintenance staff. Jesse peered from the shadows. "Dr. Pike. Is he dead?"

Wolfgang looked up from Big Fifteen's body. "Yes, Jesse. He's gone."

Only then did Jesse move out of the darkness, stretcher in hand.

CHAPTER 28

Wolfgang stood at the private cemetery at the bottom of the hillside, where a dozen headstones stuck up from the ground, chipped and cracked, protruding like uneven teeth from the grassy gums of the earth. Every ambulatory patient from the colored hospital was there, as were many of the staff and a few of the white patients from the top of the hill. The sunlight shone brightly for Big Fifteen's funeral. He would not go down Lincoln's Death Tunnel.

Wolfgang said a prayer. Susannah knelt down and placed a handful of flowers over the grave, then slid her hand inside the bend of Wolfgang's arm. Wolfgang watched her stare at Big Fifteen's grave, crying quietly. He held her close, knowing that Dr. Barker stood watching them in the crowd.

"We will remember Big Fifteen wheeling his supply cart up and down the hillside three times a day, in the heat, in the cold, in the snow. We will remember his kind smile. His generosity. His big feet for which he was so appropriately named." This drew laughter from the crowd. "Yet he had an even bigger heart." Nodding from the onlookers. "His last moments will not be what we remember of him. Instead, they will be replaced by the memory of him running down Fourth Street toward Uncle Frank's new Cadillac with Tad McVain draped over his shoulder."

More laughter. Susannah squeezed his hand. They all stood silent, and then Wolfgang started the procession back up the hillside.

Susannah said, "When I was a little girl, my mother was robbed by a black man. It scared me. For years I had nightmares." She glanced at Wolfgang before going on. "I loved Fifteen as you did. Just was afraid to show it."

"I know," said Wolfgang. "And Fifteen knew as well."

Susannah smiled as they all walked up the hill.

Abel had seen nothing in the woods last night, and Susannah had no luck searching the sanatorium for missing patients. Because of the smoke and the noise down the hillside, most of the patients had been out of their beds gawking from the solarium porches. So either the murderers had been fast to get back or Wolfgang's theory about their being patients was shaky. They'd found no white Klan robes, no whips or chains, only broken booze bottles up and down the steps of the chute. No guilty faces anywhere. The police came briefly to investigate the fire and Big Fifteen's death, but they left the grounds quickly. "No dying patient could have done this," they'd said.

"Not everyone here is dying," Wolfgang had told them.

"Even so," said the lead cop, a burly, yellow-haired man with a toothpick between his lips. He couldn't stop glancing at the sanatorium's façade the entire time.

They'd turned to leave, but Wolfgang wasn't finished with them. "If Big Fifteen had been white, would you have tried harder?"

"Don't push us, Father."

Wolfgang walked back up the hillside, kicking various twigs from the footpath. The grass in the clearing was wet, soaking his black shoes. He opened the sanatorium's front doors and entered the Grand Lobby, which was busy with nurses pushing new patients in wheelchairs, visitors talking, and a red-haired, middle-aged woman in a long beige coat standing with her hands clutching a blue purse. The woman looked up, noting Wolfgang with interest.

"Wolfgang."

He stopped. She stepped forward hesitantly. He didn't move. The woman reached out and grabbed his right hand.

"Wolfgang, it's good to see you."

Wolfgang slid his hand from her grip. "Mother, what are you doing here?"

"Is there somewhere we can talk?"

He studied her hands. They'd aged slightly in ten years. Her red hair was longer, curlier, and streaked with gray. Her eyes were marked with crow's feet. She was still a pretty woman, though, and part of him wanted to embrace her, hug her as tightly as she used to hug him. Instead he motioned toward the front doors. "There's a bench outside…in the sunshine, where it's warmer."

Outside, a black Model T was idling near the main road, with a dark-haired man in the driver's seat. The man waved to Wolfgang, but Wolfgang ignored him. He assumed the man had come with his mother. Her driver? He didn't want to know. Wolfgang led her to a wooden bench near the tree line. They sat together, with space between them. She squinted as she unbuttoned a few of her coat buttons. "The sun feels nice."

Wolfgang nodded.

"You look good, Wolfgang." He watched her from the corner of his eye but didn't face her. "I like the beard. It's very becoming."

"What do you want, Mother?"

She folded her hands on her lap. "You used to call me Mom."

He shot her a glance and then faced the sanatorium again. Her idling car puffed clouds of smoke from an annoyingly loud muffler. The sun glistened off the windshield, smearing the man's face in a prism of blinding light. "Rose died years ago."

"I know, Wolfgang…"

"You didn't come to the funeral."

"I…" She sighed, flicked the handle of her purse with her thumbs, and turned toward Wolfgang on the bench. "Why did you turn against me, Wolfgang? I needed you after your father passed away."

Wolfgang finally looked at her. His eyes were moist. "I know what you did."

Doris Pike's face sagged. Her wrinkles became more pronounced.

"Are you going to deny it, Mother?"

"Wolfgang…"

"I saw you lock the door. I saw his feet, Mother. You stood on your tiptoes for more leverage."

Doris wiped tears from her eyes. "How—" she started.

"I used to watch your bedroom," said Wolfgang. "There was a hole in the wall. I saw him hit you with his inkwell."

"Your father was a troubled man, Wolfgang."

"Was that the only time he ever hit you?"

"Yes…"

"Is that why you did it?"

Doris folded her arms and bit her lip. "Wolfgang, I didn't murder your father." She scooted closer on the bench.

Wolfgang had nowhere to go except to stand up. He remained still.

"How could you wait twenty years to bring this up?" she said.

"I had nightmares for years. You came to my bed and smothered me with a pillow."

Doris's hand covered her mouth.

"Every night, when I was unable to move because of the polio."

"He asked me to, Wolfgang." Her hands trembled. The gold bracelets around her wrists clanked together like wind chimes. She clutched her purse to keep her hands from shaking. "He begged me to do it."

Wolfgang stared at her.

"Of course, I resisted, and we prayed together. Finally, God told us it was time, Wolfgang. He told—"

"God would never—"

"He had cancer," she said. "It started in his stomach and ended up in his liver. He was in so much pain. You saw him. You heard how much pain he was in. When it became too painful to even hold a pen…he didn't want to live anymore. He begged me for days. He didn't want you to see him like that. He wanted you to remember him as a strong man." She paused. "So I got myself drunk enough to do it and…I did."

Wolfgang remembered her tears. It made sense. And Charles had held the Bible in his hand as if in preparation. He let out a breath. Euthanasia, the "good" death. Several patients had asked Wolfgang to do the same over the years, but he'd refused.

Wolfgang placed his hand on his mother's. He looked at the idling black car. The sun had moved on the windshield and the man's face was visible again.

"I don't regret it," she said. "God did not want him to rot from the inside out. He was losing his mind. That was not the man..." she trailed off.

"Why are you here?" he asked again, more gently. He moved his hand back to his lap.

"I'm moving to Minnesota, Wolfgang. I'm married again—to Bruce over there. He's a minister." She waved, and from the car Bruce waved back. Wolfgang nodded at him this time. "We're going to Minnesota to start a church. That's where he's from. Would you like to meet him?"

"No," Wolfgang said. "I don't think so." He looked at her again. "You came to tell me you were leaving, that's it?"

"I came for Charles's violin," she said. "You took all of his instruments. I'd like to have one to keep."

"Which one?"

"You know the one."

Wolfgang braced his hands on his knees and stood. He walked a few paces and stopped to face his mother again. "Wait here."

Wolfgang limped past the Model T. He moved as quickly as he could down the footpath to his cottage. Inside, seven of his father's violins rested against the wall, the eighth being used by Josef. He grabbed the P violin and started for the door, but then he grew suspicious of his mother's sudden arrival and even more so about why she'd requested the violin. Did she really want it for sentimental reasons? He ran his fingers over the small F-holes and then slid them beneath the strings. He shook the violin and heard nothing moving inside. He turned it over and saw a circular groove about the size of a baseball in the back of the violin. And a tiny metal latch. Out of curiosity he'd opened it before, seeing nothing. But he'd never felt inside. He unlatched it, removed the round wooden plate, and felt around until his long middle finger brushed up against something. He flattened his hand as far as he could and reached inside until the skin between his thumb and index finger felt as if it would split against the carved wood. Finally it came loose in his fingers, and he pulled out a stack of bills. One hundred dollars.

"I see," he said aloud.

The front door blew lazily open. Wind rustled leaves across his porch. His mother was still out there, up the hill, waiting. So that was why she'd come, for the money? She could have it. It felt like poison in his hand. He fixed the back of the violin and carried it by the neck out the door.

Doris Pike waited patiently on the bench. She stood when Wolfgang approached. Wolfgang handed her the stack of bills but held on to his father's favorite violin. "You can go now."

"Wolfgang…" Doris grabbed Wolfgang's hand, placed the money inside of it, and closed his fingers over it. "I want the violin. Not the money."

He lowered his fist and offered her the violin. He hadn't seen her smile so widely in twenty years. Relief showered over her face, a smile that instantly made her look young again. He'd taken every one of his father's instruments ten years ago without a thought that he'd be taking one of the only parts of his father that Doris cherished most—his music. He'd left her nothing.

Doris took the violin from him and clutched it to her chest. "Thank you." She kissed his cheek and he didn't pull away. "Your father trusted no one, Wolfgang. Not even the banks. Do something good with the money." Then she grinned as she walked around the hood of her husband's Model T and stopped before opening the passenger-side door. "Good-bye, Wolfgang."

"There's a concert." Wolfgang stepped closer to the car. "Valentine's Day. On the rooftop. You can come."

Doris didn't answer. He could feel her peering at his cassock, hiding her distaste. She lowered her head into the car and closed the door. She waved as Bruce pulled away, leaving Wolfgang standing in a pocket of car fumes and rock dust.

That afternoon, Wolfgang attempted to coax Frederick into talk-ing but couldn't tell if the man was too weak or just refused to do so. Wolfgang feared that more than anything else, depression could kill Frederick now. For the rest of the day he moved slowly from patient to patient, gave a homily at Mass that lacked passion, and started the afternoon's rehearsal with uncharacteristic flatness. Both Susannah and Lincoln had seen Wolfgang outside with his mother, but they didn't pry. He would tell them eventually.

The cold wind whistled through the porch screens. McVain watched from his bed, still unable to sit up, let alone play the piano. Five minutes into rehearsal, which had quickly taken on the emo-tionless mood of their choirmaster, Dr. Barker entered the solarium. "Wolfgang, shut it down."

Wolfgang's shoulders dropped. "We just started."

Dr. Barker shouted, "All of you, back to your rooms…please." He shot Susannah an angry glance and she looked away.

"The concert is almost here, Dr. Barker."

"There will be no concert!" He stormed off. "It's finished."

Herman watched Dr. Barker until he was gone. Then Susannah took the big man by the arm and walked him up to the rooftop.

Wolfgang stood alone as the choir departed. Dr. Barker blamed him for what had happened to Big Fifteen, that much was clear. He blamed Lincoln for what had happened in the chute.

Later, when Wolfgang dropped Susannah off at her dormitory, there was no hand-holding and no kiss on the cheek. He watched her until the door was closed and then walked home, craving his sacramental wine.

He took off his lab coat and dropped it on the floor next to the bed. He unbuttoned a few buttons near the neckline of his cassock, took a bottle of wine from the kitchen, and stared for a moment at the theology books stacked against the wall, covered in dust.

In his pocket he found the money from the violin.

Do something good with the money…

He grabbed one of the violins and turned it over. It too had a secret compartment on the back. After some fiddling inside, his hand came out with a stack of bills. Two hundred dollars. He dropped the violin on the floor and reached for another one. More cash—three hundred dollars. That violin he hammered to the ground, snapping the instrument at the neck and sending tiny slivers of wood across the floor. He chuckled and drank from the bottle again. He checked the violins, one by one, and compiled a stack of cash worth nearly a thousand dollars. *He asked me to do it… He asked me to kill him, Wolfgang.* He stood with a grunt and hobbled across the room. He pulled out his father's cello, viola, and bass from the closet. Five hundred more dollars.

He pictured Dr. Barker playing the bass the other night, trying to impress Susannah. Turning the bottle up again, he staggered toward the bed, where he sat on Rose's side. He pictured Susannah standing naked in the middle of his floor with a shower of water soaking her hair and body. He got up too fast and nearly fell over. Before he knew it, he was outside, bundled in his heavy winter coat. He stumbled up the hillside, bracing himself on every tree in his path, a grown man acting like a child. *Dear God, what am I doing?*

His body was warm from his thick coat and the alcohol. He stumbled past the front porch of the nurses' dormitory, his back against the side wall like some thief. A voyeuristic mock-priest, drunk from an entire bottle of wine and searching desperately for a peephole, which—come to think of it—might have just been another one of Lincoln's stories. Wolfgang's vision cleared momentarily, just long enough to spot the log in the grass about ten feet away. Lincoln's log. Wolfgang lifted it up with both hands. He carried it, hunched over, closer to the ground next to the building's concrete foundation, his vision swimming, searching the wall. He looked up—was that it? He stepped up onto the log and balanced himself.

The log shifted beneath him.

By the time he hit the ground, Wolfgang blacked out.

Everything happened for a reason. *It was God's will, Wolfgang*—the words his mother had told him weeks after his father died in his sleep.

So now was it Rose's time to go? Was it that simple?

Rose looked up at him from her bed inside the small sanatorium room as Wolfgang raked his hands through her hair. Waverly Hills was just a mere fleck of the size it would be in the coming years. For now, it was overcrowded and badly in need of expansion. Wolfgang left his hand in Rose's hair, never wanting to let go. He was her doctor and he refused to let the tuberculosis take her. The day after he'd graduated from medical school, he'd volunteered to help the sick at Waverly, arriving weeks after Rose had been admitted.

This was not God's will, Wolfgang said to himself. *This was God's cruel punishment.* His mother would believe the same thing had she and Wolfgang still been speaking. Rose had been sent to him on the steps of the cathedral as a test. A devilish vixen, a temptress luring him away from the righteous church.

His Rose.

They had attempted to start the family they'd always talked about. "He'll send us children when the time is right, Wolf." That was what Rose had told him. But it was as if God hadn't wanted their children to grow up without a mother, because none came, and now here was Rose, at Waverly.

A new nurse walked in with a cart of food. She had blond hair and kind eyes that smiled. "Hello, Rose. Are you hungry?"

"Hardly, dear."

The nurse began to unload a plate of mashed potatoes and gravy and roast beef. "Dr. Barker's orders. You must eat."

Wolfgang stepped forward. "Rose, this is our new nurse. Susannah, is it?"

"Yes, Dr. Pike." Susannah stood beside her cart. "My second day, actually."

Rose sat up in bed. "Well, God bless you, then."

"Thank you." Susannah started to push the cart out to the porch. "Anything that you need, Doctor?"

Wolfgang looked up. "No, not right now. Thank you, Susannah."

After Susannah left, Wolfgang gripped Rose's hand and sat beside her bed again.

"Tell me your thoughts, Wolf?"

Coughing sounded up and down the small, crowded porch out-side Rose's room. Wolfgang had little hope for her, but he couldn't say that. "I think only of your recovery, Rose." Wolfgang prayed silently to God and demanded that He listen.

Rose rubbed his hand. "I will wait for you in heaven, Wolf."

"Don't say such things, Rose."

She laughed. "I'll answer your questions if there's a way." She coughed. "I'll speak to you from the other side. You'll know I'm there. You'll never be alone."

Wolfgang's eyes peeled open. A raccoon sniffed his left boot and something was crawling across his forehead. He jerked, frightened the raccoon into the woods, and wiped his face. His ears were fro-zen, his nose like ice. His head ached. How long had he been out?

The stars were still out. An owl hooted.

He felt sick to his stomach when he remembered where he was lying. Moments later, he was up on his feet, leaning against the brick wall. He headed back up the hillside to the sanatorium, blowing into his hands repeatedly. A long hot bath would be nice, he thought, but the piano on the fourth floor was calling to him more loudly.

Inside, he walked quietly beside McVain's bed and started to remove the requiem from the box underneath.

McVain's voice startled him. "I'm freezing." His breath came out in clouds.

Wolfgang held out his hands. "My fingers are numb."

"You look like shit," said McVain, eyeing Wolfgang's clothing, which was matted with frozen leaves and sticky burrs. "Fall asleep in the woods?"

"Yes."

McVain watched him suspiciously.

Wolfgang handed McVain an extra blanket. "How are you feeling?"

"I think that bastard Barker stitched me up with barbed wire."

"I stitched you."

"Well, I feel like I'm dying."

"Not until the concert."

"My curtain call, huh?"

"Or the great awakening."

"You think he'll come around on the concert?" McVain asked.

"He has to."

"We'll figure out something." McVain's two left fingers gripped the blanket. He sighed. "I'm not going to make that walk, Doctor."

Wolfgang sat stunned for a moment. He looked away, but only momentarily. "We can't ever know—"

"Spare me the platitudes," McVain said. "I can—"

"Trust me, McVain, I've seen it. Patients on death's door, and then Waverly somehow helps them to make that walk. I need go no further than Rose, if you want examples."

McVain's head settled on his frozen pillow as he listened.

"We were married for five years," Wolfgang said, "all through medical school. I was set to go to the priesthood. I believed that was my calling."

"And you met her?"

Wolfgang smiled. "I was home from Saint Meinrad with four years of high school and two years of college under my belt. I saw her on the steps of the cathedral. She had beautiful eyes and dark hair. I waited for dozens of people to enter the church just so I could hold the door for her. An innocent gesture, right?"

"Sounds like a man who knows what he wants."

"She was a weekly churchgoer. But I soon learned her other side as well."

"Was she trouble?"

"No, she was stylish and brash and unpredictable. Just what I needed. She was a walking example of what I'd never had in my life."

"A flapper, huh?"

"Short skirts, makeup, everything. And I trusted her. I knew my parents wouldn't have approved, but that was part of the allure."

"She saw a naïve, shy stick-in-the-mud."

"I'd devoted my life to the Lord." Wolfgang laughed, but it hurt his head. "Rose turned my life upside down." He rubbed his eyes and blinked the pain away.

"Are you drunk, Doctor?"

"Possibly," Wolfgang said. "The ladies of the church used to question my decision to join the seminary. 'You're too handsome,' they said."

"Please."

"'You should get married,' they'd say. 'I am,' I'd tell them, 'to the church.' But I knew the moment I saw her that the priesthood wasn't for me. Not then, at least."

"And now it is?"

"Things have changed."

"Have they?"

Wolfgang fidgeted with the zipper on his coat and spotted the rose and vase atop the piano. "We had a rose garden. I would pick one for her every day. 'A rose for a Rose,' I'd say." He took a deep breath. "One morning, we were nearing our fifth anniversary, and I approached her in the kitchen with a rose. She was crying, and she kissed me on the cheek. Not on the lips, you see."

McVain listened.

"She told me she had been to the doctor, which surprised me, because she hadn't mentioned anything to me. She had TB." Wolfgang sighed. "My heart sank."

"That's when you moved here?"

Wolfgang nodded. "I became a doctor here. She was a patient just before this building was built. The sanatorium was much smaller then." He pulled McVain's blanket back up where it had fallen from his arm. "I took care of her every day. Rose was strong."

"But TB took her anyway."

"No." Wolfgang shook his head slowly. "She was one of the few whom our rest and fresh air cured."

McVain furrowed his brow. "I don't get it."

Wolfgang wiped his mouth and sat straight. "She left this place free of disease eleven months after we'd arrived. She'd lost a lot of weight, but she was in the clear. She Made the Walk with little trouble."

Rose promised she was healthy enough to go out, and perhaps Wolfgang, as her doctor, should have forced her to take her recovery slowly. But Rose was Rose, and as her husband he couldn't deny her the pleasure of going out to celebrate. She'd beaten tuberculosis in eleven months, and they were both young and eager to continue on with their lives.

"Besides, Wolfgang." She giggled, kissing his neck. "We lost so much time at Waverly."

He held her at arm's length. "What, you didn't enjoy spending our five-year anniversary on the hillside with the other patients?"

"Of course I did," said Rose. "Dining on stale cupcakes and milk was a delight." She wore the yellow summer dress he liked so much. A red rose bloomed from her hair, a rose he'd given her earlier in the day. "Come on, Wolf. It's warm outside. We'll eat, have a few drinks. We won't stay out too late."

Wolfgang took her hand and followed. "Well, it *is* Valentine's Day."

They dined at Abe's White Doorknob on Preston Street. It was either there or Cunningham's at Fifth and Breckinridge; both were known for their supplies of illegal liquor. Cunningham's was owned by a police captain, and Rose had joked that she didn't want to celebrate their late anniversary within view of the police, so they'd taken a horse carriage to the Doorknob. They both ordered steak and potatoes and laughed in the dim light. They stole kisses in the shadows of their private corner table and sipped on illegal bourbon. Rose leaned over the table and whispered, "Let's go home, Wolf."

They walked hand in hand out on the sidewalk, both tipsy from the bourbon. Rose showed no signs of the disease, and despite her loss of weight, her energy had fully returned. Wolfgang thanked God for her recovery as they walked along. The sun set behind the downtown buildings in smears of red and orange. A block down, a man in a top hat gave a hot dog to a little girl in a green dress. A horse-and-buggy hurried down the street, the carriage wheels bouncing noisily over the potted road. Wolfgang felt the breeze of the carriage as it sped by.

Then the heel of Rose's left shoe stuck in a crack in the sidewalk and her foot came right out of it. She laughed as she stumbled forward. Wolfgang stopped to get her shoe. It was red. She'd worn the shoes because they matched the rose in her hair. Her favorite colors were red and yellow. Wolfgang heard the car before he saw it. Kneeling on the sidewalk, he looked up to find Rose a few feet out into the street, her back turned to the oncoming car. She stood on one foot, tipsy, trying to remove her other shoe.

"Rose!" Wolfgang screamed.

She looked over her shoulder, a smile still etched on her face.

Rose's body folded. She hit the windshield, and when the car finally stopped, her body flew through the air and landed in the middle of the street.

Wolfgang hurried with her red shoe still in his grip. He knelt beside her. Her eyes followed his. Blood pooled on the street behind her head. A crowd gathered around, and the driver jumped from his still running car, left his door open, and ran toward them. Wolfgang's outstretched hand kept him at a distance.

"Rose…" Wolfgang ran his hands across her hair and face.

She found his eyes again and smiled. Only Rose would smile. Blood stained her dress, bright red on yellow. Wolfgang spotted the rose from her hair a few yards away, propped against the dirty curb.

"Wolf…"

He touched a finger to her lips and stretched to examine the wound in the back of her head, shocked that she was still alive at all. He kissed her forehead, inhaling the scent of her. He pressed his hand against the wound, but the blood continued to pump through his grip.

Rose stared upward. "Wolf…where do we go?"

Then the life vanished from Rose's eyes. He closed them for her and looked up toward the sky, and he blamed God.

Fourth Movement

Allegro con brio

CHAPTER 29

God continued to deliver. A new patient, a fifty-year-old man named Cecil, arrived three days after Big Fifteen's death. He'd played the clarinet for forty years and agreed to join the ensemble if and when Dr. Barker reinstated the concert and allowed the rehearsals to go on. Two days later a new nurse arrived at Waverly. Beverly was a twenty-five-year-old brunette with a deep southern drawl and a budding violin hobby, and was spotted taking tips from Josef after hours on her first night on the job. Four new patients volunteered for the chorus, three men and a woman— not professionals, but willing and eager to sing—and their ranges included two tenors, one contralto, and one soprano.

Wolfgang stopped Dr. Barker in the hall one afternoon. "God continues to send musicians. I truly believe we all have a purpose here." Barker moved on without comment.

The new arrivals fueled Wolfgang. He continued to work with the choir members individually and in small groups, by their bedsides, as often as he could. He encouraged them to not give up hope, leaving the door open for Barker to have a change of heart. He visited Frederick several times a day and played for him beside his bed. On one of his visits, Wolfgang left him with the picture Susannah had taken of his wife and son. Frederick placed it beside his pillow.

Valentine's Day was rapidly approaching, only a few days away. Despite the spotty security in the woods, or maybe because of it, Wolfgang continued to walk Susannah home every night and then returned to the piano and the fourth-floor solarium to work on the requiem. It was progressing quite well. He was three-fourths of the way through and moving quickly, even more so now that rehearsals had been canceled. But underfoot he was beginning to feel the quagmire of doubts that had bogged him down before McVain's arrival. He was still in need of the perfect ending.

Herman was ranting again, shouting Dr. Barker's name from the rooftop, as loud as his tubercular lungs would allow. Wolfgang endured it for a few minutes before slamming his pen down, standing from the piano and marching down to Barker's office, where he found his boss at his desk, massaging his temples.

"What does that lunatic want?" Barker asked Wolfgang.

"I don't know." Wolfgang leaned against the doorway. "But he won't stop until you pay him a visit."

Dr. Barker stood so fast that his chair toppled over.

When they reached the nurses' station on the rooftop, they found Susannah standing at Room 502. Apparently Herman wouldn't even allow her inside. He was still chanting, "Dr. Barker… Dr. Barker…Dr. Barker…"

Barker ignored Susannah and hammered on the door. "Herman, open up, it's me. Stop screaming…HERMAN!"

Maverly Simms showed herself in the doorway to her darkened room. "Maverly at Waverly…Maverly at Waverly…"

Dr. Barker turned toward Wolfgang and hissed. "Shut her up."

Maverly started to whimper. The doctor pounded on Herman's door again, and finally Herman stopped. The door opened a crack and Herman's face was visible, his wandering eyes looking Barker up and down.

"What is it, Herman?" asked Dr. Barker.

The door opened wide and Herman took up most of the doorway. "You stopped the concert."

Dr. Barker closed his eyes and sighed, as if trying with every fiber of his being not to strangle Herman.

Herman stepped closer. "You stopped my concert." Wolfgang saw the overhead light glisten off the polished tines, but he couldn't shout in time as Herman brought the fork down into the meat of Dr. Barker's left shoulder.

Barker allowed Wolfgang to stitch him up, but he remained silent.

And when he left for the night, he stalked past Wolfgang and Susannah through the Grand Lobby, still in a silent fury, a hump underneath his coat by his left shoulder, where he was heavily bandaged.

The door to the entrance opened before Dr. Barker reached it. He froze. His wife, Anne, walked into the lobby with a gray satchel in each hand. She stood in her black shoes and ivory coat, staring at her husband. Her hair was brown but beginning to gray beneath a rounded ivory hat.

Wolfgang stopped and watched the estranged couple. Anne was normally quite friendly to Wolfgang, but this night she didn't smile. Her green eyes were tired and focused on her husband, the surprise on her aged face as apparent as the shock on Dr. Barker's.

Then Anne coughed into her fist.

Dr. Barker's head lowered, and Wolfgang understood.

The newest patient had arrived at Waverly.

CHAPTER 30

The next day Dr. Barker surprised Wolfgang with an appearance in the chapel near the end of Mass, where seven choir members had volunteered to sing. Wolfgang's slight choir viewed him cautiously from afar, never slowing their song as the doctor leaned against the column in the back of the chapel and waited for Mass to finish. After everyone cleared out, he accosted Wolfgang in the center aisle. "Are you behind this?"

"Behind what?" Wolfgang asked.

"The choir members. And others. A hundred others. They're refusing to take any medication. They're refusing to eat. They're refusing treatment unless I reinstate the concert."

"I knew nothing about it," said Wolfgang.

Dr. Barker's mouth closed. He held up his index finger. "Have your damn concert. But only by my rules. We're being reckless as it is. Rehearsals are limited to thirty minutes. I've seen your program; the concert itself must be shortened." He stopped before the last row of chairs. "And any work with Rufus will be done down the hillside."

"Is that all?"

"And no more secret practices after I leave at night." He smirked. "Did you think I couldn't hear you?"

"What if I need to work at the piano at night?"

"I have no problem with that." He pointed to his ear. "But give me some credit. I can tell the difference between you and McVain on the piano."

"How?"

"I know the difference between a genius and a dabbler."

Wolfgang couldn't flex his fingers enough. No matter how much he moved or blew into them, they remained numb. Tiny white cracks in the skin scarred his knuckles and the webbing between his fingers. He stared at the rose atop the piano. It needed to be changed.

McVain coughed behind him on the bed. Wolfgang turned around on the piano bench and faced him. "How are you feeling?"

McVain cleared his throat. "Hollow."

"It must be torture to watch us practice."

"What's torture is listening to you play." He winked. "Concert back on? Told you I'd think of something."

"Blackmail? Cute. Almost as sneaky as making women appear on the fourth floor overnight. It was Lincoln, yes? He helped wheel the ladies up here for you?"

"You got me," said McVain. "How could I keep the truth from a fake priest?"

"McVain…"

McVain simply smiled.

"It troubles me to know how much pull you have here." Wolfgang faced the piano again. "He would have reinstated the concert anyway."

McVain was silent. When Wolfgang turned to him again, McVain was staring at the wedding band on Wolfgang's right hand. "Ever think of marrying again?"

Wolfgang folded his arms, hiding his right hand. "You never quit, do you?"

McVain chuckled. "Good thing the seminary-from-afar makes it easier for you."

"Tell me about *your* wife, McVain."

"I'm divorced." Wolfgang waited. "We were happy before the war. When I came back…" He stopped.

"How long has it been since you've spoken with her?"

"Not as long as you went without seeing your mother," McVain said. "Six years if you need to know."

"What happened during the war?" Wolfgang asked.

McVain sniffled and then wiped his runny nose. "I wasn't a violent man. I'd never fired a gun in my life. But I got pretty damn good at killing."

Wolfgang leaned forward. "Tell me about it, McVain."

"Don't act like my psychologist."

"Go on..."

"Trench warfare." McVain's eyes looked at the piano, but his real vision was probably somewhere much darker. "Mud and rain. Bombs everywhere. Mustard gas. I started smoking to calm my nerves. Couldn't sleep."

Wolfgang thought about the man's restless sleep. "Do you dream about it?"

McVain looked at Wolfgang sharply. "I chased a Kraut out of a trench one time. He got stuck in the barbed wire without a gun. I couldn't understand what he was yelling at me, but with his tone I could tell he was pleading for his life. I shot him. First in the face. Then in the heart. It was like I was standing there outside myself, watching from a different person, a different place." McVain coughed heavily, leaned to his side, and spit into the bucket.

Wolfgang leaned closer. "Go on."

McVain sighed. "Another night. I'm tired."

"Rest then, my friend." Wolfgang stood.

"You said you believe in fate." McVain stared blankly toward the ceiling. "A man makes a choice to avoid danger only to then walk right into it. Choice A or B. I made a choice at Chateau-Thierry that determined my fate." He wiggled the nubs of his mangled hand. "I chose B."

"Everything happens for a reason, McVain. Perhaps A would have killed you."

"Might have been better."

CHAPTER 31

A snowstorm blew in unexpectedly from the southeast, dumping seven inches of pristine white fluff atop the hillside overnight. The morning walk up to the sanatorium was like walking through a painting of beauty. The air seemed fresher than normal, untainted by the wet leaves. A trio of deer watched from thirty yards away, the lower halves of their skinny legs hidden under the accumulation. Squirrels danced overtop the snow, sprinting to avoid sinking. Susannah stepped on a patch of snow-covered bramble and her foot sunk to the knee. Instead of helping her up, Wolfgang made a tightly packed snowball and hurled it toward her, hitting her on the rump.

When they reached the sanatorium, Susannah bent to tie her shoes. Then as Wolfgang walked up the stairs, an explosion of white fluff hit the center of his back.

Upstairs, patients too close to the end of the solarium's screen windows had been rolled to the middle to avoid direct contact with the snow. Someone had thrown a blue tarp over McVain's piano. When Wolfgang asked about it, McVain shrugged, claiming he'd first seen it when he'd opened his eyes in the morning.

Mid-morning Wolfgang lifted Frederick up and placed him in a wheelchair.

"Gonna remove another rib?"

"You're speaking now?"

"Where are you taking me?"

"For a walk," said Wolfgang. "And no, we're not taking out another rib. Your lesion has not grown in weeks."

He wheeled Frederick out to the fourth-floor solarium and parked him right next to the screen. "Enjoy the scenery. And bundle up with those blankets. It's cold out here." Wolfgang pointed out over the treetops toward the road leading up the hillside. "You see that road? That's where Mary Sue Made the Walk. She wept when we got to the bottom. You are not dead yet, Frederick. You want to hold your son?"

"Of course I do."

"Then start breathing," said Wolfgang.

Wolfgang sat beside Anne Barker's bed and played his piccolo for her. She'd requested his music and he'd played nervously, stopping after several miscues before continuing, afraid at any moment that Dr. Barker would hound him for disturbing his wife. He lowered the piccolo and Anne thanked him with her magnetic smile.

"It isn't the music that he dislikes, Wolfgang." Anne said. Her smile had faded. "Give him time. He's just confused."

Wolfgang almost laughed out loud. "Aren't we all?"

Wolfgang opened the door to the chapel's small freezer and removed a bag of frozen communion bread, hoping it would not be as hard as the last batch, which had caused most of the crowd to chew for several minutes after they'd returned to their seats. The bread would not be changed into Christ's body and the wine would not be changed into his blood, but the Catholics who attended his service asked for communion anyway. A Baptist in the chapel mumbled, "as it should be," as all the Baptists believed that the bread and wine merely represented the body and blood of Christ and could not be changed into the real thing anyway. And that was a process Wolfgang refused to emulate until he was ordained to do so. As he carried the bread to the altar to thaw, he spotted Susannah and Abel entering the chapel. Abel appeared a little distraught, his face blotchy. Wolfgang knelt down and touched the boy's skinny shoulders. "You've been crying."

Abel stood stiff with his hands to his sides. Susannah squatted beside Abel and put her right arm around his back. "He didn't sleep all night."

"I have a confession, Dr. Pike," Abel said. "I'm a liar."

Wolfgang gave him a warm smile. "How so?"

"I did see somebody." Abel looked up toward Susannah, who kissed his forehead and nodded encouragement. "The night we found Fifteen in the tree." He wiped his nose with a fist. "A big man. Dressed in white. With a hood. I ran into him when I was going through the woods."

"Then what happened?" asked Susannah.

"He knocked me down in the mud. Said he'd kill me if I told anybody."

Wolfgang sighed heavily. "I see. Did you recognize him?"

"No, but I seen 'em coming out of the maintenance shed."

"The shed?"

He nodded. "He was watching me last night."

"Watching you?"

"From the woods." Abel became more courageous. "I was in bed on my porch. He watched from the woods, staring at me with his white hood on. Like a ghost. He put his finger to his face like this." Abel put his right index finger to his lips.

Susannah squeezed Abel's shoulders. "They're trying to scare him, Wolf."

"You're sure it wasn't just the snow and shadows?"

Abel shook his head adamantly. "No, he was there to remind me—not to tell."

Wolfgang pulled Abel forward and embraced him.

That afternoon, two white robes with hoods were found behind an old tractor in the back of the maintenance shed, concealed under

a wooden crate that still carried the smell of ether. The maintenance staff had been questioned thoroughly, but none of the three
men seemed strong enough to pull Big Fifteen up into a tree, and
their answers had all checked out. They'd been too busy fighting the
fire at the colored hospital to hunt down Big Fifteen in the woods
and hang him.

Dr. Barker demanded that the police bring in more security to
stand guard at the children's pavilion. Susannah wanted Abel to
stay with her, but he'd insisted on sleeping with the other children.
He claimed it was his job to keep *them* calm.

After Wolfgang and Susannah dropped off Abel and met with
the three new police officers, Susannah felt more comforted. The
men were dressed warmly for the night shift, and they seemed to
take their jobs seriously. They all had children at home. Wolfgang
believed Abel and the children would be safe.

Before Wolfgang and Susannah left the officers to their duty,
one of them startled Wolfgang with a question. He had a handlebar
mustache and big brown eyes. "Father, we've gotten a few letters
from someone at Waverly recently."

"Oh, about what?"

The man chuckled and scratched his mustache. "About some
bootlegging activity into the sanatorium. Booze, Father."

Wolfgang laughed right along with him, as if the notion itself
were preposterous. "Bootlegging, huh? Demon rum…into a hospital?
Not a bad idea, though. We could serve the patients shots of whiskey right after they down their nightly milk."

The officer chuckled again. "Thought I'd ask about it, at least.
Don't mean to bother."

Wolfgang smiled. "No bother. Was there, by chance, a name
attached to the letters?"

"No. No name."

"Anonymous," said Wolfgang. "Of course." The officer turned
away and headed toward the children's pavilion. Wolfgang watched
him until he disappeared into the tree shadows. The KKK was a
major supporter of the Anti-Saloon League. They took pride in root-
ing out bootleggers, breaking up speakeasies, burning saloons across

the South, and apparently foiling the plans of a sanatorium's orderly who sneaked the demon rum up the hill through empty coffins.

"Fame and attention." Wolfgang stared into the shadows. "That is what most villains crave, Susannah. Advancement. To be promoted inside an organization built on hate. Which means he has plans on Making the Walk soon."

"Come on, Wolf. Let's go." Susannah took Wolfgang by the arm and started him down the hill. She followed Wolfgang home and they lit a fire. They shared a bottle of wine and Wolfgang told her about his mother's visit. In the silence that ensued, Susannah stood from the couch and lifted one of the violins on the floor. She laughed as she tried to play. Wolfgang joined her back on the couch, where the heat of the fire had warmed the cushions. She giggled, gripped Wolfgang's shirt, and pulled him close, so close he could smell the sweet wine on her breath. "I feel safe right now," she whispered.

It was snowing outside again. The doors were locked. The fire snapped beside them. Shadows caressed the angles of her cheekbones, the curve of her lips, the rounded turn of her chin...and no one was watching. Wolfgang bent down, closed his eyes, and softly pressed his lips against her mouth. He felt as if a bolt of electricity had struck him. Her mouth eased open.

She ran her fingers across the back of his head and through his hair. And then suddenly she pushed him away. Wolfgang dropped to his knees beside the couch, staring at her, mortified. How could he have done it?

"I'm sorry," he whispered.

"Don't be. I can't...I just can't. I'm sorry." She turned away and closed her eyes.

He stood up, hobbled because his right food had gone numb, and backed away. He blew out all the candles. He couldn't get the cottage dark enough, not with the fire licking the stones of the fireplace. He wanted to crawl into bed and never come out.

Eventually he drifted off to sleep, but not until he heard her snoring.

Susannah was still asleep on the couch when Wolfgang shot up in bed.

The porch steps creaked under the weight of an intruder.

The clock on the wall read four in the morning. A loud thump sounded against the door. Susannah shifted on the couch but her eyes remained closed. Wolfgang moved around the foot of his bed, grabbed the iron poker from beside the fireplace, and walked quietly toward the front door. The knob rattled. Something slid down the outside, calling to Wolfgang. "Doctor…" It was more of a groan than a threat.

Wolfgang kept the poker in his hand, opening the door. A male patient knelt on the porch, shivering. Blood dripped down his chin. Wolfgang recognized the thin young man from the east wing of the fourth floor, Ray Lot. He couldn't have been far from death. What was he doing here?

"Doctor…I have a confession."

Wolfgang knelt. Ray's eyelids fluttered. He coughed up blood. "What is it, my son?" Wolfgang glanced over his shoulder; Susannah still slept. He returned his attention to Ray.

"I was with him…when he tossed the brick." Ray unfolded his legs and rested back on the porch, his head in a pile of hardened snow. "I helped…that night, in the woods."

Ray's hands shook violently. Wolfgang grabbed them and it seemed to calm him somewhat. "Go on," he said.

Ray had attended many of his Catholic Masses over the duration of his stay at Waverly. Now tears dripped from his eyes. "I told him not to hang that nigger. He only wanted to…to…to scare him. I promise." His teeth chattered. "It was always *his* idea."

"Who?"

"We hid our Klan robes in the shed." His eyes widened. "He scared that boy last night."

"Who did this?"

"This is a confession, right, Father?" Ray gulped and breathed heavily. Loose fluid gargled in his weak lungs. "Just between you and me, right?" Wolfgang nodded. "Promise me you won't go after him." Ray coughed up blood. "Promise me you'll just let him die like me. Let the white wind take 'em."

Wolfgang gritted his teeth and lifted Ray's head from the porch. "I promise. Tell me and the good Lord shall judge you."

"Will I go to heaven?"

"If it's God's will."

Ray stared for a second. "Jesse."

A huge ball of rage suddenly arose in Wolfgang's throat. Jesse—Ray's roommate, whom Wolfgang had taken under his wings, the young man who had eagerly claimed to be interested in the priesthood. Weeks ago, Wolfgang had entered the chapel and Jesse had given him a note, claiming it had been left on the altar. Or had Wolfgang nearly caught Jesse in the act of writing it? He'd claimed to be illiterate, but it dawned on him that Jesse had probably written those anonymous letters to the police. He was the reason they'd been snooping around the train tracks weeks ago. And Jesse had the size, thought Wolfgang. He was getting stronger, closer to Making the Walk. Jesse must have only pretended to be simple-minded, and he'd gotten close to Wolfgang, conning his way into the chapel, so as not to be expected of the crimes he'd committed.

"We got the ether from the hospital…to knock him out. The rope from the shed. It was Jesse's idea…" Then Ray closed his eyes. "Our secret."

Wolfgang waited until Ray was silent before checking his pulse. Finding none, he stood and retreated inside to wash the infected blood from his hands.

CHAPTER 32

Wolfgang stood at the foot of Jesse's bed the next morning and watched the doughy farm boy stare at Ray's vacant bed. Wolfgang had checked Jesse's records before starting his rounds or playing the first song on his request list. Jesse was twenty-five years old. One of five brothers. Born in Louisville but currently living just north of the river in southern Indiana. Wolfgang knew that the Klan was heavily entrenched in Indiana; one in every four men supposedly wore the white robes.

"He died on my doorstep," Wolfgang told him.

Jesse's eyebrows furrowed. "He was a good kid, Father. I prayed for him last night."

He's mocking me, thought Wolfgang. Wolfgang cleared a divot of snow from the footboard of Jesse's bed with his fingers and flicked it to the floor. He hoped Jesse's tuberculosis spread painfully and quickly. *What an odd feeling for a man of medicine and God*, he mused. Unfortunately, Jesse appeared stronger than the day he'd arrived. The fresh air was helping.

Wolfgang just smiled. "Rest up," he said and walked away.

Determined to take advantage of the sunny weather, Wolfgang scheduled another rehearsal that day. He wheeled Frederick out to the fourth-floor solarium so he could get some air and be closer to the music.

The musicians' sense of ensemble reflected their growing cama-raderie, and with the addition of Cecil on the clarinet and Beverly on a second violin, they played like five functioning chambers of the same heart. The choir's quality had increased tenfold just by the addition of Herman's booming voice, which gave the others the confidence to sing even louder. Herman—without his fork—was allowed out of his room for the first time in several days and stood in his typical spot away from the rest of the choir.

"Herman, why do you insist on standing away from the group?" Wolfgang asked him before rehearsal had started.

"I don't want to catch their TB," Herman said.

Wolfgang stared up at him, wondering if he'd crack a smile. He did not.

Anne Barker arrived ten minutes into rehearsal. "Room for another?" she asked.

"Of course." Wolfgang walked her over toward the women's section beside Susannah. Anne Barker apparently knew her music. Her voice was soft, overshadowed by the rest of the women, but she already knew most of the pieces. Her smile was a pleasant addition to the chorus, and her arrival at Waverly had made her husband less belligerent. He was by her bedside every day, and often Wolfgang had seen them laughing.

They were barely over their allotted time when the choir suddenly stopped.

Wolfgang turned, his arms still in midair. Dr. Barker stood behind him. He was staring at his wife in the crowd. "Shut it down, Dr. Pike."

"But—"

"Shut it down." His voice was somber, his eyes sad. For once Wolfgang didn't argue. Dr. Barker held out an envelope. "This came today from the diocese."

Wolfgang took the envelope and waited until everyone had left before opening it.

February 1st, 1929

Dear Dr. Wolfgang Pike,

The diocese has learned of certain activities on your part deemed deceitful and unethical as pertaining to the Catholic Church. We have received word that you have been performing the Sacrament of Penance and saying Mass in the name of Christ without the authority to do so, and, on occasion and with witnesses, given communion to fellow Catholics under the impression that you are a Catholic priest. We have been in contact with the abbot and monks at the abbey at Saint Meinrad in regard to your status as a student, and although they explain your importance as a doctor at the Waverly Hills Tuberculosis Sanatorium and admit that they allowed you access to their books and vestments during this horrible epidemic, they couldn't deny the fact that you have not been to the abbey in years, nor could they, with any confidence, say that you would ever return. Although we don't like to deny anyone what they consider to be their calling, we feel it is within our rights to remove you from any further positions within the Catholic Church should we learn that your behavior continues and you have not enrolled "officially" at the abbey by the end of the month.

Yours in Christ,
Father Reinhart, assistant to Bishop Floersh
Diocese of Louisville

Wolfgang's hands shook as he lowered the letter. The concert was only a couple days away. It was mid-February. He had only two weeks on the hillside.

The pressure to finish his requiem was now magnified, bearing down on him that night. Every so often Wolfgang glanced over his shoulder at McVain, who appeared asleep. Occasionally McVain's eyes opened, watching Wolfgang or staring out toward the woods.

Wolfgang's couch had remained empty ever since the kiss, and Susannah had only spoken to him in fits and starts, mostly about work, nothing meaningful. He contemplated telling her about the letter but dreaded the actual conversation. He'd decided to wait to tell anyone, just in case he found a way out of it. How could Dr. Barker do this to him? A fellow doctor? He was trying to deceive no one. He was simply filling a void, hearing confessions, and helping to ease peoples' souls before they passed away.

McVain startled him by calling out from his bed.

"Where is she?"

Wolfgang touched the pen to the paper. "Who?"

"Who do you think? Susannah."

"She went home early. She felt tired." Wolfgang returned to his work. He began to play again, stopping every so often to jot down notes. Ten minutes later, when he looked over his shoulder, McVain sat with his knees propped up below the sheets as if hiding something in his lap. Wolfgang quietly lifted off the piano bench and hurried to McVain's bedside. McVain was slow in shoving an envelope under the sheets.

"What do you have there?"

McVain scowled. "Nothing."

"Looks like a letter."

"Speaking of letters, what did yours say?"

"Church business, McVain, which means none of yours." Wolfgang sat down on the chair beside the bed. "You've been here for how many weeks without getting one piece of mail? Who's it from?"

McVain pulled the letter out from under the sheets. The envelope looked as if it had been through hell getting into his hands. The penmanship on the front was curvy and elegant. McVain held up his left hand, showing Wolfgang the nubs. "You wanted to know how I lost my fingers?"

"It has something to do with that letter?"

"Long story."

"I've got all night."

In May 1918, just before Wolfgang came home from the seminary for the summer and met Rose, Tad McVain was dodging bullets in Europe and praying to God every night to keep him safe. He had a wife at home in the States. He had a bright career; before the Selective Service Act had taken him, he'd been making his name as a pianist and composer. He'd begun to garner acclaim, not only in his country, but also from other countries around the world. He prayed every night for the Lord to keep his hands safe.

The Germans were closing in on Paris, breaking the French line to pieces. McVain was in the Third American Division, sent to defend the Marne, up to Chateau-Thierry to fight under French command. Chateau-Thierry was a nice river town thirty-five miles northeast of Paris. When McVain's division arrived, most of the citizens had fled. But by the time McVain stepped onto the abandoned streets of the small town that would endure forty-one days of continuous fighting, he had already mentally checked out. Months of killing and trying not to be killed had all but locked him up. He moved around stone-faced and answered no one. He smoked constantly. His hands trembled so violently that he struggled to even aim his gun. Twice he'd frozen during combat, tempting fate as the Krauts closed in, only to be saved by his fellow soldiers.

"McVain…" They called out to him. "McVain…"

A buck-toothed soldier from Iowa they called Jaw Scratcher dove and knocked him out of the way of enemy fire on day five of the fighting. Jaw Scratcher lay on top of him in a ditch. "McVain? You froze out there, man. Gonna get yourself kilt."

"But I'm a pianist."

"Not no more, piano man." Jaw Scratcher helped McVain up and handed him his gun. "Now snap out of it and start killin' some Krauts."

McVain did kill another Kraut that day and he killed him good. The poor boy had red hair like McVain's and was probably only eighteen or nineteen years old. Younger version of himself, thought

McVain. They both drew their weapons, but McVain shot him first. When he got close, he saw blood gurgling from the boy's neck. But he was still alive and choking up blood. McVain looked down on the boy, hoping he would hurry up and stop breathing. God damn it, he was looking right at him and trying to talk, but he couldn't on account of the gurgle. It was a sound McVain would never forget, and he had to end it as soon as possible. He pulled the German boy by his arms over toward a wall of rubble. He knelt beside the boy and took out his knife. He entertained the notion that he was killing his German twin. Before the idea grew legs, he slit the boy's throat, and the boy didn't try to talk anymore. Bullets whizzed by and bombs exploded. Blood spread from the boy's body, but his arms and legs still moved. McVain sat next to the German boy and gripped the kid's hand. He held it until the boy had completely stopped moving.

"McVain," someone called out. "The fuck you doing?"

Another called out, "Holding that Kraut's hand. McVain..."

McVain dropped his gun on the slain boy's chest and walked back through the fighting, oblivious to the passing bullets, ignoring the men around him calling his name. He took his helmet off and concealed his hands inside it as he instinctively ducked and moved back toward base.

He never fell asleep that night. Just smoked one cigarette after the next, and half of them were wet and tasted like trash. But he smoked them to help calm the trembling in his hands. Every day he fought cautiously when everyone else around him was brave. Then the Germans were threatening their position and McVain's division was called to the west bridge to make a stand. But McVain had seen too many limbs blown off. He'd had too many friends come back with massive head injuries. He didn't want to fight anymore. So he ran.

They'd been fighting on the outskirts of Chateau-Thierry, so he hurried back to the abandoned town and ducked inside a small stone house. He cowered in the dark corner of a back bedroom that smelled musty. He listened to the fighting in the distance and flinched every time a shell exploded. Light flashed against the walls, flashing and fading, flashing and fading...

Eventually the fighting died down, like rumbling thunder moving away. The room was pitch-black. He dropped on the bed against the wall. The sheets were tousled, as if the former occupant had left in a hurry. Somehow he dozed off—with his pistol on his lap. He awoke a few hours later with a fuzzy glow inside the room. He aimed his pistol at it, and the tremble immediately started again with his hands. He doubted he could have even hit his target if he'd tried. Standing right there in the middle of the room was a woman holding a candle. A French woman with short dark hair and dirt on her face. She was pretty, probably in her twenties, and she wore a blue dress and no shoes. The candle shook in her grip as she stared at McVain's gun. Tears rolled down her cheeks.

McVain lowered the pistol and waved her closer. She hurried to the bed, buried her head in McVain's chest, and started crying. He rubbed her back and rested his chin on her head, and for some reason wondered if Jaw Scratcher was dead.

He moved his lips next to her ear. "Shhhhh. It's gonna be okay." He wondered if she'd lost her husband, or parents, or siblings. Or possibly even her children? She appeared old enough to have had them. McVain leaned back against the headboard and accepted her weight against his. She nestled her head beneath his shoulder and then fell asleep while he stroked her back and hair. He looked at his hands, which were still stained from the German boy's blood. So much dirt and grime under his fingernails. He blew out her candle on the floor and closed his eyes. He fell asleep again to the imagined sound of a piano.

McVain loved his wife, but that life seemed so out of touch with his current reality that he'd convinced himself he would never see her again. The Unites States might as well have been on another planet. That night he cheated on his wife. Being close to the French woman was the only thing that made sense to him. Part of him wondered if what they'd done during the night had been a dream. Visions of her moving on top of him swarmed into focus. Her hair tickling his cheeks. Her breasts pressing against his chest. And when the sun shone through the window, he noticed that she was naked under the sheets and his shirt was off. She kissed McVain on the cheek and then hurried from the room. Cabinets opened and closed in the other room, and moments later she returned with a bottle of wine, a block of moldy cheese, and some stale bread. She slipped back into her dress and they ate like they were starved.

She couldn't speak English and he couldn't speak French. They communicated with their eyes and with their hands, and when they finished eating they continued what had been started in the middle of the night. They made love to block out the sound of warfare in the distance, and he discovered every inch of her body. Under her left breast she had a small birthmark that looked like an apple. She giggled silently when he acted like he was playing the piano on her bare back.

The second night she pulled him from the bedroom and led him out into the street, where a mangy dog hurried by, chasing a squirrel. She took his hand and ran him across the street and into a stone church with heavy wood doors. It smelled of incense and candles even though it hadn't been occupied for weeks. Their laughter echoed. She took him to the back of the church and lit a candle next to the altar. There in the shadows was a piano. She sat on the bench and played for him.

She wasn't very good, but McVain could tell it helped to quell her fears, and the sound of the piano nearly brought tears to his eyes. She was an angel who had stolen him from the worst hell he could have imagined. He never knew why she'd stayed in town. He knew nothing about her, yet he knew enough to trust her. She patted the bench beside her and scooted over to give him room. He believed that God had answered his prayers.

At first his fingers were stiff against the keys, but they soon loosened and became familiar with the feel of them again. She was shocked at his talent, looking upon him as if he were some kind of guardian angel himself. She looked up to the arched ceiling and motioned the sign of the cross. They took breaks a few times to make love on the floor of the church as the mice watched from the corners. They drank more wine and ate until the bread was gone. He played for her much of the night and then they slept on the floor.

The next morning, the muted sunrays bled through a cracked

stained-glass window. McVain awoke on the floor, slow-brained from the wine the night before. She was on the piano bench, half dressed and dabbling. No bombs sounded in the distance.

From the silence, he sensed trouble right away. He heard footsteps outside the church, and then the doors creaked open. In walked an American soldier named Cotton Meeks. Crazy son of a bitch from Mississippi. He walked up the center aisle with his eyes on McVain's French girl. McVain watched from the floor, groggy.

Their division had been successful holding the bridge without McVain, and Meeks had returned to check out the town. He looked like a rabid scavenger. Must have heard the piano. Meeks spoke in his southern drawl, "So what do we have here? Some French cunny?"

She jumped from the bench and hurried to McVain on the floor. McVain had no idea where his gun was. He didn't even have his pants on. Just his undershorts. Meeks pointed his gun right at McVain. "Well, if it ain't the piano man. Missed you at the bridge."

McVain's hands shook as he raised them, pleading; Meeks was crazy enough to kill them both. Meeks liked to pick on McVain anyway, saying that he liked music more than bullets and that McVain had been drafted while Meeks had volunteered.

Meeks pulled the trigger, and McVain's left hand exploded in a cloud of mist and bone.

Later, McVain opened his eyes to find Meeks's buttocks in clear view. He'd bent the French girl over the altar and was pounding away at her with his pants around his ankles. McVain found his pistol on the floor. He stood quietly, his left hand a clotted mass of skin and bone. He approached Meeks from behind and pulled the trigger.

"We hid Meeks's body in an alley behind the church," McVain said. "Left him for the dogs. I got a medal for being wounded." He held up his left hand. "The battle at Chateau-Thierry."

"What happened to the girl?"

McVain wiped his nose. "Never saw her again."

Wolfgang eyed the letter in McVain's right hand. "That's from her, isn't it?"

McVain opened the envelope and pulled out a folded letter. "She's been looking for me for years. But she didn't even know my name. And I didn't know hers." He unfolded the letter to reveal a picture. "Amelie. She learned English."

"Where is she now?"

"Here. In Louisville. She hunted me down. Wants to visit me." McVain handed Wolfgang the picture. "It's a few years old."

Wolfgang took the black-and-white picture from McVain and stared at the dark-haired woman named Amelie. She was pretty, with shiny hair and sympathetic eyes. Standing in a light-colored dress that ended at the knees, her eyes dark, her face friendly, her stance one of shyness and insecurity. In the background was a small house, and behind it was a winding river spotted with trees and edged with farmland. Beside Amelie was a little boy, probably seven or eight years old. Wolfgang focused on the boy's eyes. He wondered if his hair was red. In the face he looked like a young McVain.

McVain took the picture back and looked at it. "She thinks he's mine."

Or Meeks's? No, thought Wolfgang, the resemblance was too uncanny. The boy had to be McVain's. "Will you see her?" Wolfgang asked.

"If she comes. I don't think I have many days left."

Wolfgang stood slowly from the chair, his knees stiff.

"I made a choice at Chateau-Thierry," McVain said. "I ran from the violence to avoid injuring my hands. If I'd gone to defend that bridge—"

"You could have been killed."

"Or come back whole." McVain studied Wolfgang. "Try living with that. Was that fate or coincidence, Doctor? Or was it a result of my actions? A punishment?"

"God doesn't work that way."

"You don't really believe that, do you?"

Wolfgang looked down. "What do you believe?"

"At first I believed it was a punishment."

"But now?"

"Now that I've ended up here—and met you—maybe I believe in fate."

On Wolfgang's way out he stopped by Jesse's bed, where the boy snored annoyingly loud in the cool air. Wolfgang grabbed a spare pillow from a chair beside the bed and took a few steps toward Jesse. There were no others around. *How easy it would be*, Wolfgang thought. He gripped the pillow with both hands, squeezing and releasing repeatedly. Was this how his mother had felt?

Just let him die, like me, Ray had said.

"Let God play God," Wolfgang muttered. He dropped the pillow and left the solarium.

That night, in his cottage, Wolfgang lit a fire. A letter from Saint Meinrad had arrived during the day. It was a short note from Friar Christian—all his notes had seemed to grow shorter over the years. Wolfgang sat next to the fireplace and read it.

February 7th, 1929

Dear Wolfgang,

As always it is a pleasure to hear from you, and I pray daily for the White Death to subside. I understand your intentions at the sanatorium as they relate to the Catholic Church, and I sympathize with your delicate situation, but what I initially hoped would be months of off-campus training has turned into over three years of absence. I fear that you have lost sight of your goals, and, I'm sorry to say, some of reality. I worry that the patients who call you Father truly mean it, and you can't continue to allow that deceit, albeit unintentional, on your conscious.

The abbot has been contacted by the diocese and questioned, and I have been questioned as well. Please know that I have nothing but positive things to say about you. It has been several years since you left to be with Rose, but you continue to be one of my favorite students. Rest assured that I believe you to be doing God's work as a doctor at Waverly, but a decision on the priesthood is long overdue. I pray for you now as I write this, and I will pray for the decision you have ahead of you.

Yours in Christ,
Friar Christian
Saint Meinrad, Abbey

Wolfgang folded the letter from Friar Christian and slid it back into the envelope. He picked up the letter Dr. Barker had given him from the diocese and tossed it into the flames, where the edges quickly curled in the heat. He knelt beside his bed and folded his hands to heaven. "Bless me, Lord, for I, your humble servant and unworthy student, have sinned."

CHAPTER 33

Wolfgang woke up shivering. His pillow was cold, his nose even colder, and his ears felt like ice. Susannah would not arrive for over an hour, but he could not fall back asleep, for the frigid air had slivered beneath the sheets and found his toes.

The windowpanes had frosted over during the night. He spotted the brown leather sack he'd left beneath the window. In it was all the cash he'd found inside his father's instruments. He now knew exactly what he was going to do with the money.

He dressed quickly, grabbed his black bag of instruments, and sat on his couch like a statue. He waited for Susannah.

Forty minutes later he paced across the floor, the arch in his right foot throbbing. It was after seven. Susannah was never late. He hurried up the hill alone, his shoulders tucked into the headwind.

When he knocked on the door to the nurses' dormitory, Nurse Marlene greeted him with a kind smile. "No hot water either, Father?"

Wolfgang noticed she was looking at his hair. He touched the top of his head with his hand and found several strands of hair sticking up. "Is Susannah in, Marlene?"

Nurse Marlene shook her head. "She left in the middle of the night."

"Where did she go?"

"I assumed she went to…" She hesitated.

"Where?"

Marlene blushed. "Your house, Doctor."

Wolfgang covered his embarrassment with anger. "Don't be ridiculous."

"Maybe she was working."

Wolfgang left Nurse Marlene in the open doorway as he turned, fuming, up the hill to the sanatorium. Susannah never worked in the middle of the night. Perhaps she'd gone to visit Dr. Barker again? Wolfgang opened the door to the sanatorium lobby and dashed inside.

Dr. Barker stood there, as if waiting for his arrival, and then grabbed his arm. "Slow down." He rubbed his forehead, as if lost for words. "I'm sorry, Doctor."

"About what?"

"Third floor," Dr. Barker said. "Room three-oh-seven. I admitted her in the middle of the night."

Wolfgang's face went slack. It couldn't be. He sprinted up the stairwell, nearly knocking over several nurses and a new young doctor he'd yet to meet. He kept a hand on the brick wall to brace himself, hurdling the steps two and three at a time. Admitted last night? Patients he passed spoke out to him, but he didn't stop to listen. None of them mattered now. Outside Room 307 was one bed. The woman on it was middle-aged with short blond hair and curious eyes.

"Doctor?" she said.

Wolfgang stepped past her bed and into Room 307, and there she was, resting beneath a thin sheet, on her back, her fingers laced together on her stomach, staring at the ceiling. Susannah leaned up from her pillow. "Wolf?"

Wolfgang hurried to her bedside, collapsed onto a wooden chair, and gripped her right hand. She didn't look sick like the others. She looked tired, but no more than usual.

Her smile was kind, not frightened. "You had to have seen it coming."

Wolfgang could only squeeze her hand.

"I've been coughing now for weeks. My temperature comes and goes." Susannah moved her hand from his grip. Her fingers slithered away, weightless, like tethered ribbons. "I'll still sing with the choir."

"We've caught it early, then."

"Much earlier than the rest of my family." She spoke confidently, much like she would to another patient. "Barker met me here last night, Wolf. We ran tests. Both lungs are infected." She stared at him for a moment, her eyes unwavering.

"Both?"

"Yes."

"Dear God."

"Abel doesn't know." This news would crush the boy. "Can you bring him here?" she asked. "I'd like to tell him myself."

"Of course." Wolfgang patted her hand. "Fresh air and rest. That's what we prescribe here at Waverly Hills." He pushed her bed out onto the solarium porch and parked her as close to the screen as possible, beside the blond woman he'd ignored on his way in. The patients were turning over too quickly. He couldn't keep up. "How's this?"

"Perfect."

The longer he stared at her, the more frustrated he became.

"Wolf, remember that Rose was cured."

"And look what happened." Wolf looked away and started to walk off.

"The other night." Susannah spoke softly so that no one could hear. Wolfgang froze, his back to Susannah. "It was wonderful. I pushed you away because I knew I was sick. That was the *only* reason, Wolf."

Wolfgang nodded. Then another patient farther down the porch leaned forward, gasping and coughing, and he hurried away from Susannah.

Later, Wolfgang found a spot on the porch where shadow and wind kept patients away. He needed a small break. Suddenly he was furious. He cleared his eyes and walked up the stairs to the fourth-floor solarium, determined to confront Jesse Jacobs.

To Wolfgang's surprise, Lincoln was standing next to Jesse's bed with a gurney.

Lincoln looked at Wolfgang sadly. "I'm sorry, Wolf. I heard about Susannah."

Wolfgang ignored him. Jesse's face was pale, his lips parted but unmoving. His eyes were closed. His meaty right arm lay lifelessly off the table. Lincoln heaved Jesse onto the gurney. "He's dead?" Wolfgang asked.

"Dr. Barker noticed him early this morning. Must have passed during the night."

"How?"

Lincoln, his face still bruised from the attack in the chute, gave a slight chuckle and then quickly masked it. "Wolf, he had tuberculosis."

"He wasn't that sick." Wolfgang paced beside the gurney, focusing on Jesse's bloodless face. "He was due to Make the Walk soon."

Lincoln started to push the gurney away.

"There'll be an autopsy?"

"Not unless you do it," Lincoln said. "No time, too many bodies, and we know how they died." He eyed Wolfgang suspiciously. "I know you got to know him pretty well, Wolf, but what's going on?"

Wolfgang pointed at Jesse's body. "He killed Big Fifteen."

Lincoln's mouth opened. "How do you know?"

"I also know he wasn't deathly ill last night."

"Swift justice then." Lincoln pushed the gurney past Wolfgang. "The Lord works in mysterious ways?"

Wolfgang stood in the darkened chapel. He knelt before the altar and stared at the crucifix on the wall—the stake pinning Christ's feet to the wood, the stakes at his wrists and the crown of thorns upon his head. He spoke softly. "Last night I prayed for Jesse's passing, and now he's gone. My wish granted." The candle flames flickered in the quiet chapel. "Something is granted, and then something is taken away. Is that how it works, Lord? Susannah is sick now."

Nonsense, his mind cried. *Mere coincidence*. Just like when Rose was cured and then tragically died weeks after leaving Waverly Hills. Fate.

Or was this some kind of punishment?

Footsteps broke his concentration. He could tell by the footfalls that it wasn't a woman. The nurses' shoes had a different sound. These were hard shoes. Dr. Barker's. He couldn't turn to face him now.

The doctor sat a few rows behind Wolfgang. It was silent for a moment before Barker spoke in a hushed tone. "Will you hear my confession?"

Wolfgang didn't turn around. "Yes."

He could hear Dr. Barker's nerves, the trembling in his voice. The rubbing of his dry hands sounded like sandpaper. "Jealousy has blackened my heart."

Wolfgang took a deep breath. His posture straightened as he continued to kneel. "Go on."

More rubbing of the hands. A sniffle and a large exhale. "For months now...I've had improper thoughts...about another woman." Dr. Barker exhaled again. "I love my wife. I love her more than anything."

Wolfgang nodded, still gazing at the crucifix on the wall. "You're forgiven. Go and sin no more, Doctor."

He heard Dr. Barker stand. "The music has brightened Anne's spirits..."

Wolfgang didn't turn around until Dr. Barker's footsteps faded.

Wolfgang left the sanatorium; he needed to be alone. Totally alone.

Inside his cottage, he slid to the floor, crying with his head in his hands. He'd been lied to his entire life and spent his infecting others with the same lies. Faith...what was faith? His faith was lying in a hospital bed a few hundred yards away, dying because she insisted on helping others live.

Daylight lit the floor where the piano used to stand, a rectangle striped with the grid of the window frame. Against the wall was a bottle of wine left from…he couldn't remember. He popped the cork with his thumb, tilted, and swallowed three gulps.

He'd finished the bottle within minutes. He tossed it into the fireplace, where it shattered against the stones, and then made his way over to the closet and opened the doors. He yanked his vestments from their hangers and threw them to the floor. He kicked his Edison phonograph off the table and sent his cylinder records spinning across the floor like giant bubbles of quicksilver.

He reached inside the dark closet and pulled out a framed picture, a canvas painting that had hung over the fireplace in his home with Rose. He remembered how Rose had approached the artist to strike up a friendship. He'd asked to paint her and she'd agreed. In the painting Rose wore a yellow dress, the same one she'd had on the day she was killed. In her black hair was a rose. Wolfgang studied the curve of her full lips and the slenderness of her neck, her profile with her head turned slightly, facing the artist, curious and dignified. He loved this painting.

He leaned it against the wall and sat beside the bed on the floor, staring at Rose's portrait until he fell asleep.

CHAPTER 34

Rose had seen him first, sitting alone in the back of the cathedral. She nudged Wolfgang and nodded in the boy's direction. He appeared to be about sixteen years old. Wolfgang returned his focus to the pulpit and the reading. Rose had only been out of Waverly for less than a week, and Wolfgang was intent on thanking the Lord for her recovery. She was thinner than she had been before she'd gotten sick, and the other people in church had stared at her. Once a Waverly patient, always a Waverly patient.

She nudged him again. "Wolf, look at him."

"I did," he whispered, knowing that he'd seen the boy before but not certain as to where.

The boy had brown hair with curls that covered his ears and most of his neck. His chin was awkwardly narrow, disproportionate to his eyes and cheekbones. He was tall too, well over six feet, his legs folded inside the pew. His arms were thin, but his wrists were even thinner.

"Look at his fingers," Rose whispered. Certainly she wasn't making fun. It was just Rose's nature to find the differences in people and migrate toward them.

They were the longest fingers Wolfgang had ever seen. They watched the boy return to his seat from communion with a slight limp, as if his feet hurt. His lanky arms swayed, his fingers reaching past his knees. His index fingers had abnormally long nails and they were pointed like daggers. The rest of his nails appeared clipped. His fingertips were stained with color, some fingers marked by one distinct color and others smudged with mixtures of all.

Rose wasted no time confronting him after church. "Excuse me…"

He turned toward her voice, his eyes to the ground.

"I think you've got beautiful hands," Rose told him.

He lifted his chin and met her eyes. He felt comfortable with her. Rose had that gift of making anyone feel special. She lifted his hands. "What is your name?"

"Jonah." His voice was low and distorted. The boy had a speech impediment, probably caused by the deformation of his palate, Wolfgang realized. Then it hit him. He remembered where he'd seen the boy before. Inside the Baroque, where Charles Pike used to go drinking. On Wolfgang's post-polio walks he'd peeked inside the Baroque on many occasions. The boy had been painting at a table next to the window one evening.

"What do you do with these hands?" Rose asked.

Jonah smiled. "P-p-paint."

"With your fingers?"

Jonah nodded.

Rose touched the sharp index fingernails. "And these?"

"F-f-f-for detail." Jonah looked at Wolfgang as if for permission before reaching for Rose's right hand. He turned it over so her palm faced upward. With his right index finger he began to trace letters onto her open palm, softly. Those letters formed words, and when he lifted his hand Rose was blushing.

"What did he spell?" Wolfgang asked.

Rose touched her cheek. "He wants to paint me."

A few days later, Rose and Wolfgang were in the loft of Jonah's barn, which was tall enough to allow a glimpse of the cornfields along West Market Street and the downtown Louisville buildings over the horizon. The boy's long fingers dipped into the paint and touched the canvas with a technique Wolfgang had never seen before, while Rose sat patiently and with ease on a stool, her face partially bathed in the sunlight that bled into the muggy loft. Jonah worked in a brown cloak and sandals. His fingers maneuvered effortlessly on the canvas. He was particular in the way Rose sat on the stool. He'd lift her chin one way, tuck the rose in her hair that way, and turn her face ever so slightly away from the light. He slouched, he knelt, he squinted, and he stepped back and viewed from his wooden chair, where he would sit loosely with one leg tucked beneath the seat and the other stretched out in front in the style of Caesar. He paced periodically with a Louisville Slugger baseball bat, a Babe Ruth bat he'd given Wolfgang along with the painting when they'd left.

Jonah had often been at the Baroque because his father played the piano there, but before playing, he'd spun wood making bats at the bat factory. Jonah claimed that their house was full of bats. But it had been the portraits on the wall of the Baroque that had inspired him to paint.

He carved detail and grooves in the paint with his fingernails, scraping and lining like a sculptor, a master. Wolfgang would never forget watching him work and how fulfilled Rose appeared posing for him. Such a unique and special talent—a boy stricken with the worst Marfan syndrome Wolfgang had ever seen, a connective tissue disorder that affected the skeletal system, cardiovascular system, the skin, and the eyes. The gene defect caused too much growth in the bones and resulted in abnormally long arms and legs. Wolfgang watched him paint with his fingers and was convinced that God touched everyone in some way.

Lincoln was moving around inside the cottage when Wolfgang awoke. He was in bed, naked, covered with a blanket.

Lincoln stared at him. He was gathering up the broken pieces of the records Wolfgang had thrown across the room. "We thought you'd died, Wolf."

Wolfgang sat up.

"How long have I been in here?"

"Too long," Lincoln said. "Valentine's Day is tomorrow."

"Our concert."

Lincoln helped Wolfgang to his feet and walked him over to the couch. He returned a few minutes later with a glass of water and a wet rag. "McVain has been asking for you."

Wolfgang looked over toward the front door. The knob was broken.

Lincoln shrugged. "I'll get it fixed. McVain said to do whatever it took to get you out of here."

"Why, how's his health?"

"He said he has a confession to make."

Wolfgang took a bath, shaved, and trimmed his beard while the aroma of coffee wafted in from the kitchen. By the time he dressed, Lincoln had already cleaned out the wine bottles and wiped up Wolfgang's mess. The busted front door moved in the breeze, allowing sunny glimpses of the cottage floor. Lincoln had left, his job done.

Wolfgang hurried up the hillside alone. It wasn't the same without Susannah. All that day, the cassock he wore felt like a badge of deceit, but he still heard confessions, calmed the patients' fears, and listened to their stories. He played songs for several patients, ate lunch alone, and kept busy during the afternoon. In his mind, he rehearsed tomorrow night's performance. He ran through the pieces they would play, making last-minute adjustments to the choir. He'd already decided Herman would have a solo, as would each of the original instrumental musicians. He met briefly with Dr. Barker, and without going into the details of Ray's confession itself, he was able to convince him the KKK threat was over and the culprits had been escorted by Lincoln down the Death Tunnel. It would be safe for Rufus to return up the hillside for the concert.

Thoughts of the program fueled Wolfgang through the day. At every sneeze and cough, he thought of the performance. When a patient spat on the floor or screamed of a high fever, he thought of Herman's voice or Josef's violin. He thought of how far the music would carry from the rooftop. It was the only way to get his mind off of Susannah resting on the solarium porch; in fact, he managed to avoid her floor all day until after dinner, when he finally went upstairs, catching sight of her bed several rooms down.

He stood in the shadows so she wouldn't spot him right away. Abel sat in a chair beside Susannah's bed, reading a book. They seemed to be happy together. He badly wanted to join them, but he didn't. He couldn't. Of all things, he realized, he was mad at her. She'd enticed emotions out of him that he'd thought he'd had under control ever since he'd recommitted his life to serving the Lord. And he was mad at her, because under the laws and oaths to which he would ultimately be sworn upon entering the priesthood, he simply could not have her.

Wolfgang was furious.

Maybe going away *was* the best solution—to find himself at the abbey at Saint Meinrad and devote all of his thoughts to being a servant of the Lord, a true servant, as he had planned after Rose's death.

His fury began to subside. He closed his eyes and envisioned the peaceful trees and grassy hills of the abbey. He could hear the monks chanting and birds singing from the church transepts.

Wolfgang tended to a few other patients nearby. Then he ducked back into the stairwell and sought out McVain.

The days had grown progressively longer, the sun hovering a few extra minutes at dusk each day into February, and the sunset now was orange over the treetops. Tiny buds of green dotted many of the branches.

McVain seemed not to see Wolfgang until he was right next to his bed. "You're smiling."

McVain looked up. "That a crime?"

"No, not a crime," said Wolfgang. "Just odd, for you."

Three members of the choir had arrived early for evening rehearsal. They stood in a cluster next to the porch screen, staring toward the woods, leaving McVain and Wolfgang to talk.

"I wrote back," McVain said. "To Amelie. Told her about the concert."

"Think she'll come?"

He shrugged and then looked out toward the trees. "I'm sorry about Susannah."

"Thank you."

"Thought you might have killed yourself."

"I think I may have tried," said Wolfgang. "It's all kind of fuzzy still."

Wolfgang looked up past McVain's bed and saw Frederick—Frederick!—in a wheelchair, slowly spinning himself toward the gathering choir. Wolfgang's smile was instant, warming his body, which still felt badly sick. "Frederick?"

"Hi, Doctor." Frederick was pale, hunched inside the chair. His white shirt couldn't hide that the left side of his chest was still sunken from the invasive procedures. But in his eyes Wolfgang saw the first sign of fight since Mary Sue had been released. "Can I sit in on the rehearsal?"

"Of course, Frederick." Wolfgang touched Frederick's shoulder. "Join in if you feel the strength to do so."

Frederick rested his head back and watched as the choir arrived to take their positions.

McVain's skin looked paler than ever. His eyes were swimming in dark pockets. Wolfgang leaned close. "Lincoln said you had a confession."

"Tonight. When we're alone."

Wolfgang started toward the piano. McVain caught Wolfgang's sleeve. "Still believe in heaven?"

"I believe there is a God, and for now that's enough."

"Do you have to be a believer to repent?"

"Not on my hillside," said Wolfgang. "Just a conscience and a heart."

"Will you listen to my sins so that I can die?"

Wolfgang patted his arm. "No, McVain. I'll listen to your sins so that you can live."

During rehearsal, Wolfgang caught Susannah watching him. His eyes quickly moved away each time, as if nothing had bothered him. She appeared tired, and he felt guilty for keeping the secret of his departure from her. He couldn't stop his eyes from straying to McVain's bed, though, where he was still beneath the covers. He had to make it through tomorrow night. He'd be too sick to play the piano, but Wolfgang wanted him alive to witness it. Wolfgang would have to play the piano and conduct from the bench. Somehow he'd work it out. They were ready.

He hoped the weather the next evening would be as pleasant as tonight—mid-fifties and clear. Dr. Barker had publicized the event. A local church had donated five hundred chairs for the front lawn. It was all coming together. Wolfgang finally dismissed rehearsal, his confidence brewing beneath the surface. He slapped several choir members on the back as they said good night and returned to their floors. He watched them go and pretended not to see Susannah several feet away, waiting with her arms folded.

"Wolfgang?"

Wolfgang spun toward her, acting surprised. "Oh, yes?"

"Why are you ignoring me?"

Wolfgang stood silent, heart racing.

"Is it because of the disease?"

"You know that's not it."

"Then why don't you talk to me?"

Wolfgang looked down. "I don't know." He looked back up only when he heard her departing footsteps.

McVain's voice called to him. "You know we'll have to move it up there."

"What?"

"The piano," McVain said. "How are we going to get it to the rooftop without Big Fifteen?"

Wolfgang turned toward McVain. "Lincoln and a few others are on their way now. One more floor shouldn't kill us." And it didn't, not with the six helpers Lincoln had gathered—three cooks and three men from the maintenance staff—knowing from experience they'd need them. Wolfgang spent an hour positioning the chairs for the choir along the rooftop, close enough to the edge to be seen when they stood, but not so close to be in danger of falling.

Afterwards, Wolfgang stood alone, taking in the cool air, welcoming the stiff wind on his face. Eventually he made his way back to the fourth-floor solarium, where his chair awaited beside McVain's bed. The requiem rested in his lap.

"Put that away, McVain." Wolfgang lifted the music from McVain's grip and slid it under the bed. "You need rest."

McVain stared. "I'll know soon enough."

"Know what?"

"Where we go when we die," McVain said. "Isn't that what you've always wanted to know?"

Wolfgang gave him a warm smile. "We've got more music to play."

McVain wiped his runny nose on the back of his hand. "I'm a murderer."

"War," Wolfgang told him. "Kill or be killed. It's not the same as murder."

"Are you going to hear my confession or not?"

"Sorry. Of course. Tell me."

"Fate." McVain played with the sheets while he spoke. "I told you I didn't believe in fate until I met you."

"Fate brought *all* of us together," Wolfgang said.

"More than the music."

"What then?"

"I was a different man after I returned home from the war," said McVain. "I was full of hate. I blamed God for…" He looked at his fingers and then closed his eyes. "Before the war, I never had violent notions. But my wife noticed the change right away. Said she noticed it the moment I walked off that train in downtown Chicago. She left me four months later.

"I moved back to Louisville when Chicago was starting to get the squeeze," said McVain. "Started bootlegging here. I lost all my money betting on bangtails at Churchill Downs. I was in debt. Then I started getting sick."

"You were brought to Waverly, McVain," said Wolfgang, "to begin all of this."

"The music is only part of it," McVain said. "That's the good part. But there's always a bad, right?"

Wolfgang didn't answer. There was always a trade.

"I know how you think, Wolfgang." McVain sat up straighter in bed, the movement causing obvious pain. "I know that Jesse killed Big Fifteen."

"How—"

"Susannah was on your couch," he said. "She heard. And she knew that—"

"Knew what?"

"That even though you aren't a priest yet, she knew you would be devoted to your vows. And that you wouldn't talk."

"The patients here confide in me, McVain. What are you saying?"

McVain shifted in the bed with a grimace. "I was brought here for a reason, and on the day Big Fifteen was killed, Waverly needed me. Otherwise Jesse would have Made the Walk and gone free."

Wolfgang's hands began to tremble.

"You would have left it up to *God* to decide." McVain exhaled.

"You're too sick to even get out of bed, McVain. How could you even do it?"

"I had Lincoln wheel Jesse's bed away from the others. Somewhere off in the shadows. He never asked me why, but I wasn't going to tell him. I didn't want him to be part of my plan, none of them. They would have helped me anyway. Everyone loved Big Fifteen."

McVain coughed. Wolfgang held his breath, waiting.

"You know, Doctor, there's only one man on this hillside bigger than Jesse. And crazy enough."

It finally dawned on Wolfgang. "Herman…"

McVain nodded. "I told Nurse Cleary I needed to meet with Herman about the concert. She agreed."

"Of course." Wolfgang clenched his jaw. "Anything for McVain."

"I told Herman that he wouldn't be allowed to sing," said McVain, "unless he did something for me. But not just for me. For Waverly. I told Herman what Jesse had done. Everything. Told him not to leave any marks." McVain grinned. "He knew what do to. He came back to my bed ten minutes later and handed me a pillow."

Wolfgang's eyes perused McVain's bed.

"It's gone," said McVain. "I told Lincoln it smelled funny. Told him to wash it."

"Where is Herman now?"

"Up in his room, where he should be." McVain reached his good hand toward Wolfgang. "I'm sorry, Wolf, but it had to be done."

Wolfgang knocked McVain's hand away. "You had no right, McVain. God would have judged him."

"Where was God when Jesse poured bourbon all over Fifteen's body? He would have lit him on fire—"

"But then I showed up."

"You are not God."

Wolfgang stood up quickly. "And I don't claim to be."

McVain shifted again on the bed, wincing. "I saw you the other night."

"What are you talking about?"

"You held a pillow too. You wanted him dead. What kept you from doing it?"

"You know damn well…" Wolfgang turned away.

"Exactly. So I had it done."

CHAPTER 35

Sleep didn't come that night.

Wolfgang sat on the floor by the fireplace, the warmth of the flames against his back. Firelight cast shadows across the room while he dabbled with the violin. Shadowy figures danced along the far wall, wavering, floating, ducking in and out of the light. He sipped sacramental wine from a glass. Glimpses of Rose flashed across his mind's eye. Every Valentine's Day was the same. Her blood ran through his fingers onto the street, but he was helpless to stop it. He rocked her in his arms, but the blood continued to flow. The street had turned to chaos. *What if I had not stopped to get her shoe? What if I had never let go of her hand? What if…*

He sipped more wine and pushed back the memories. He grabbed the envelope that enclosed the latest letter from Friar Christian and contemplated reading it, but he put it down without opening it. He knew what it said. The concert was less than twenty-four hours away. All his thoughts then funneled toward McVain. Could God forgive him?

Wolfgang had prayed for Jesse's death after Ray's confession. He'd actually prayed for the Lord to take another man's life. What McVain did…was Wolfgang any better? Had the Lord worked through McVain, the answer to Wolfgang's own prayers?

Wolfgang grabbed his coat and made his way up the hillside. He needed to see McVain's face, though he had no notion of what to say. The woods were quiet except for his footsteps and heavy breathing, but by the time he'd entered the sanatorium he'd composed himself.

On fourth-floor solarium Wolfgang was shocked to find McVain's bed empty.

"Doctor?" It was a woman's voice. Nurse Cleary approached. "He's gone."

Wolfgang pointed toward the empty bed. "Is he in the morgue?"

"Not dead," Nurse Cleary said. "Gone. Disappeared."

"How—"

"I've been searching the floor for him."

"Father?" A man's voice.

Wolfgang ignored it. "How can a dying man just—"

"Father?"

Wolfgang's eyes moved from the empty bed to the man. He didn't know him. He was a new patient, brought in sometime during the night, and like most, he assumed Wolfgang was a priest. He had brown hair and a short beard. "The man who was in that bed—"

"McVain," Wolfgang said. "His name is McVain."

"He got up in the middle of the night…"

Wolfgang's heart jumped. "Where did he go?"

"He couldn't walk," the man said. "He had something in his arms. He crawled on his hands and knees across the porch. I offered to help him, but he told me to get lost." The man pointed across the solarium to the stairwell. "Went up them stairs."

Wolfgang sprinted to the stairwell. Spots of blood trailed up the steps. Wolfgang rubbed a spot with the tip of his boot and the blood spot smeared. It was fresh. On the rooftop, he saw nothing in the predawn darkness but the chairs set up. He checked over the wall; nothing lay in the shadows below. He turned around. From this angle, the piano's silhouette looked awkward. McVain was slumped across the keyboard, unmoving.

"No."

And then McVain blinked. Wolfgang let out his breath. Nurse Cleary rushed over. McVain lifted his head slightly from the keys. He clutched at some sheets of music on the piano's rack. "Wolfgang.…"

Wolfgang pursed his lips. He turned to Nurse Cleary. "See that he makes it back to bed."

CHAPTER 36

Wolfgang's fingers were shaking before he touched his feet to the floor. Instead of his vestments he dressed in a black suit and tie. His fingers settled slightly as he downed his morning coffee, pacing as he sipped, but the tremble resurfaced as he eyed Rose's portrait leaning against the wall next to the fireplace.

The couch was empty. He pictured his sick father stretched out on their couch so many years ago, pleading for Wolfgang to play. Wolfgang remembered fighting back tears and staring at the crucifix on the wall as he clumsily struck the keys.

Someone knocked on his door. He immediately thought of Susannah and rushed to open it.

Lincoln stood on the porch. "The volunteers are here with the chairs, Wolf. They're beginning to set up."

"Thank you, Lincoln. I'll be up in a few minutes." He closed the door and inhaled deeply. He turned toward the middle of the floor and began moving his arms as if conducting. Only then did he realize the number of people who would be attending the performance—patients, family visitors, and staff—it would number in the hundreds. He took another deep breath and his focus returned to the empty couch again.

He gathered all of his father's string instruments and lined them up vertically on the couch, just as Charles Pike used to do, and then he headed up the hillside.

Wolfgang found that if he kept himself busy, it helped calm his hands, so early on he'd insisted on helping with the hundreds of chairs. Lincoln had taken charge of setting up the front lawn. Lincoln wasn't a musician and he couldn't carry a tune, but he was helping the best way he knew how. He pointed toward one row of chairs as he talked to Nurse Beverly and then motioned toward another section and hollered to Nurse Marlene, who immediately responded by altering the rows near the back. Then he approached Wolfgang.

"I've got it covered out here, Wolf." Lincoln smiled proudly. "Go on in with your choir. Leave me to the mindless work."

Wolfgang did his rounds, he checked x-rays, he read charts, and he took temperatures—anything to convince himself that it was just a normal day. But nothing proved to calm his racing heart, which seemed to beat more rapidly as each hour ticked by on the clock.

At one point, he looked out over the grounds from the third-floor solarium and spotted Dr. Barker talking to Lincoln. They spoke at length about something, and then Barker moved up the grassy slope toward the sanatorium. He stopped to straighten a row of chairs before moving on.

In the afternoon he spotted Mary Sue Helman getting out of a black car with little Fred in her arms. She carried Fred in between the rows, rocking him and whispering in his ear. And then Lincoln approached, pushing Mary Sue's husband, Frederick, in a wheelchair. Mary Sue's smile was visible from Wolfgang's spot on the solarium. She hurried to Frederick and kissed him. Frederick opened his arms, and Mary Sue placed Fred in his father's embrace. After a few moments, Mary Sue took the baby back, and the three of them sat in the front row.

A car rumbled nearby, the throttling engine becoming louder and louder. Wolfgang looked through the woods, and in between the trees he spotted the car climbing the road leading to Waverly. The car wasn't alone. At least five more trailed behind it. The crowd was arriving.

The chest pains started when he saw lines of Waverly's ambulatory patients walking—some on their own and others aided by the staff—out to the rows of chairs facing the sanatorium. The sun was going down. The day had passed so quickly. Scattered torch lamps hung from posts around the rows of chairs. The lawn was beginning to glow.

Wolfgang leaned down as another pain shot through his chest. His stomach felt empty. He hadn't eaten a good meal in nearly three days, and his tongue craved the warmth of wine. Charles Pike would have never admitted it to his son, but Doris had told Wolfgang about the panic attacks his father had before auditioning for orchestras. Was this what he'd felt? Like someone was stabbing him in the heart with a dagger?

Wolfgang had spoken to most of the choir members and musicians throughout the day, but only in passing. He had yet to speak to them as a group and suddenly realized he dreaded it. Seeing them early would have made him even more panicked. They were ready, of that Wolfgang felt certain. But was he? It seemed as if the day was progressing no matter what he did or didn't do. What he'd set in motion so many weeks ago had taken on a life of its own. From his spot in the shadows of the fourth-floor solarium porch, he could see all the way down the hillside. He looked toward the colored hospital and noticed a meandering line of black patients making their way upward to sit with the white patients.

He coughed and covered his mouth with a fist.

And then he heard something—the sound of a piano. It traveled from the rooftop, carried by the wind. It slivered through the floor and reverberated off the walls. And then it stopped. Wolfgang began to pace, but he remained in the safe confines of the shadows. Moments later, he heard a violin tuning up. And then the clarinet. The choir was warming up too.

Another chest pain struck him, nearly doubling him over.

He heard Herman…then silence. Was the warm-up over?

Even from one floor below, Wolfgang felt acute pangs of stage fright. Would the concert go well, or would they fail miserably? He closed his eyes and dreaded the worst, wondering how it had come to this, too scared to face a crowd he had assembled.

Wolfgang opened his eyes only after he heard total silence from above. Were they waiting for him? Any minute the piano would start playing Mozart, the first piece on the list. It remained silent. He knew he had to go up, but he felt as if his feet had grown roots.

Down below, all the seats were full.

Wolfgang turned toward the sound of footsteps and looked up to find Dr. Barker wearing a suit and tie with no lab coat. Barker straightened his glasses, pointed toward the stairs in the distance, and grinned. "It's showtime, Dr. Pike."

Wolfgang eyed him suspiciously. Was he only being kind because he'd forced Wolfgang's hand and knew Wolfgang could be leaving Waverly in a matter of weeks? Or had his wife's emergence changed his outlook so suddenly?

Dr. Barker's face grew serious. "You stood in my office weeks ago and told me that we lose one patient an hour here. I know it was an exaggeration, but I did the math. I checked the case files on the musicians. In the length of time you've had this choir, the sanatorium could have had a near turnover in patients. Yet not one"—he held up a finger—"not one patient from our choir has died."

Wolfgang felt numb. Dr. Barker was right.

"It's not a cure, but I believe your music is…helping," Dr. Barker said. "That is not fate or coincidence, Dr. Pike."

Wolfgang stood straight.

Dr. Barker started to turn but then stopped. "Come on. They're waiting."

"Is that an order?"

Dr. Barker didn't smile. "Yes, Dr. Pike. That was an order." And then he moved on.

Wolfgang's heart still raced, but it was at a pace he could handle. He took a few moments, breathing deeply. He heard music from above. But it wasn't Mozart. Nor a piano. At first he might have mistaken it for the rumble of plumbing or even the bowels of the earth opening up. But it was the sound of a double bass. The deep droning of a bow pulled across tight strings shook his bones even through the floor.

What were they playing? It sounded so familiar. Wolfgang's ears perked. It was the opening measures of *The Requiem Rose*. But it wasn't finished yet! It was just as he had imagined it sounding, but better. He could picture Rose's coffin being lowered into the ground, the fog rising around his feet, the grass wet with so much dew, the air thick with moisture.

Wolfgang moved along the fourth-floor solarium toward the stairwell. And then the violin sounded, softly, followed by the clarinet. In his mind, he turned the page of music to the next, following along, his body swaying to the rhythm, his arms beginning to move as if conducting. And then he heard Susannah's voice. She was singing the introit. His pace increased. Her voice, infused with the Latin words, hovered with the wind and trickled below like a pleasant summer rainfall, soporific in its descent. She sang beautifully and with passion. And then her voice led into the sound of Rufus's flute and Josef's violin.

Wolfgang ran, what Rose had referred to as his gallop. He thought of McVain as he reached the stairwell. That was what McVain had been doing last night on the rooftop. He'd crawled on his hands and knees up the stairs and across the terra-cotta to finish the requiem. But how did the musicians know it already? McVain must have met with them, secretly, perhaps individually, or in groups...but that didn't matter now. The deed had been done.

Wolfgang made it to the rooftop and looked down. The audience sat, poised, with smiles on their faces. A crescent moon hung like a glowing cat's eye in the middle of the darkness. The sky was black and full of stars. The music would carry for miles. The lawn was packed with rows of patients on either side of a wide center aisle that cut down the knoll like a grassy road that would be trampled and worn by the end of the night.

Wolfgang spun around the railing. A woman and a young boy sat ten feet away from the stairwell. She was young, with dark hair and piercing brown eyes. She wore a long red coat, a red bonnet, and black shoes. Beside her, in a suit and tie, a boy with fiery red hair turned to look at Wolfgang with eyes as green and ornery as McVain's.

For the first time Wolfgang faced the musicians. They had gathered about thirty feet away. The men were dressed in suits and ties and the women wore pink dresses. He didn't know where the clothing had come from, only that they all looked stunning. He spotted Susannah in the middle of the choir, her solo completed. Now she was singing with the others. She looked beautiful in her pink dress with white lace. Her curly hair was gathered behind in a flowing plait.

The musicians never broke stride as Wolfgang approached the podium. He picked up the baton beside his requiem's score. McVain sat slumped over the piano keys, barely clinging to life, but yet clear, precise notes still rang out. He didn't look at Wolfgang, but Rufus winked and Josef nodded as he played, the bow dancing with authority on his violin strings. And the double bass? It soared through the treetops. Dr. Barker stood behind Josef and Beverly with the weight of the instrument leaning against him. He drew his bow across the strings again, and a sound emerged from the instrument so deep that Wolfgang's heart vibrated. Anne Barker stood with the choir, singing proudly.

Wolfgang straightened his posture as if his father had been standing behind him and knocking his knees with a violin bow. He flipped through the score to catch up, clutched his baton, and began conducting them through the music of his orchestral Mass. Herman's voice boomed over the soft ebb and flow of the violins. The big man stood ramrod straight, sweating, his hands clenched into fists although without the security of his fork.

Near the end of the requiem, Wolfgang turned the page with a snap. It was time. This was the end. It began with a short passage of solo piano. McVain played it with passion and soul, pouring out his heart while his body, so recently put back together with stitches, continued to slouch lower and lower toward the keys. His forehead nearly rested on the music rack above the keys. Four hundred patients listened below. Torch flames lit their faces.

As Wolfgang's arms moved, he drifted back to the day of Rose's burial again, her coffin resting in the wispy fog.

He shook the thoughts away, checked the score on the podium, and nodded toward Josef. Josef delicately drew his bow over the violin strings and then held one high note for eternity, it seemed, before Rufus eased in with a smooth, relaxed whistle from his flute, the soft sounds of the two instruments intertwining, coiling like water meandering downstream, a trickle and a pull. Moments later, Dr. Barker lifted his bow to the double bass for a long passage that reverberated with its deep, rumbling tone. McVain reclaimed the lead next with a piano interlude. Then the choir—the children and women first, followed by the deeper voices of the men, and finally Herman. Their voices carried far over the trees, hovering on unseen wings.

And then the ending—a duo by McVain and Josef that left Wolfgang's jaws trembling by the time the final cadence sounded. Wolfgang held on to that final chord, not wanting it to end but knowing it had to, his hands shaking by the time the requiem melted into silence. The crowd hushed. Wind rippled their clothing. McVain eased his hands from the piano keys. He looked at Wolfgang with his tired, reddened eyes.

Wolfgang nodded.

McVain nodded back.

The crowd rose as one in a standing ovation. Wolfgang took a bow, his eyes panning the patients below, taking in the smiles, the warmth, the healing. He gripped the final pages tightly. He knew this handwriting. It *had* been McVain.

"Perfect," Wolfgang whispered. On the last page. At the bottom, McVain had written: *For Rose.*

Rufus stepped forward and patted Wolfgang's shoulder. "Welcome, maestro."

The musicians and choir all appeared eager to move on, to now tackle the concert Wolfgang had planned. The crowd below listened, and after each piece their applause invigorated the musicians and choir even more. McVain sweated profusely. His skin looked a waxy, pale shade of green in the moonlight. But he refused to stop playing. After Tchaikovsky, they played Mozart, Beethoven, and the final movement of Vivaldi's *Four Seasons*. They took a brief intermission, where Wolfgang panned the crowd again in search of his mother, and after not finding her through several passes, they continued on with the concert with selections by Bach, Haydn, and Brahms.

The patients applauded, but they weren't the only members of the audience. Down Dixie Highway, hundreds of citizens had gathered along the street, their curiosity aroused by the music coming from the cursed castle atop the hillside. The Waverly wind, ushered in with beautiful harmony, moved their bangs and clipped their noses, but still they stood and listened.

The applause grew after every piece, silenced only by a new burst of music at the start of the next piece. In the finale, Herman enthralled with his solo, "Ol' Man River" from *Show Boat*. Their resident madman was a king tonight. Barker leaned comfortably against his double bass, listening to Herman and stealing glances at his wife in the choir. Under his suit coat a bandage still covered the fork wound in his shoulder.

At the very end the ensemble and chorus joined together as one force, and had the harmony not been so perfect, Wolfgang's eardrums might have burst from the sheer volume. He raised his arms high and slowly brought them together just above his head and then stopped abruptly. The concert was over.

The singers were silent. The music stopped on Wolfgang's cue.

The applause then came with a roar and finished minutes later, long after the musicians and choir had taken their bows.

Wolfgang looked at Rufus and Josef, who wore smiles nearly as wide as their faces. And then he saw McVain. McVain looked at

Wolfgang and then stared over toward Amelie and his son. "He plays the piano," McVain said quietly.

"He looks just like you." Wolfgang knelt beside the piano bench and lifted McVain's chin. "Does he know?"

McVain braced his right hand on Wolfgang's shoulder. "She didn't tell him who I was."

Wolfgang understood. He thought of Abel. How would that little boy feel, meeting his father for the first time, only to have him die?

"His name is Ryan." McVain's shoulders slumped. "From the Irish name meaning Red."

Wolfgang nodded. "His Irish eyes are smiling now."

McVain coughed up blood. "Get 'em out of here."

Wolfgang stood slightly under McVain's bulk and waved Amelie down the steps. She didn't hesitate in taking her son's hand and turning him away from the piano.

McVain coughed again. Something snapped inside his chest. Phlegm and blood rocketed up and onto his chin. He collapsed on the piano bench and then rolled to the rooftop floor with a thud.

Wolfgang and Lincoln carried McVain down to the fourth-floor solarium and put him on the bed, but McVain resisted.

"Wheelchair." McVain conjured the strength to lean on an elbow. "Ain't gonna die lying down."

Lincoln hurried down the solarium and came back moments later with a wheelchair. They helped McVain into it and wheeled him next to the screen window. Down below, several orderlies stacked chairs from the concert.

Lincoln patted McVain on the shoulder and moved on, lower lip quivering.

Wolfgang grabbed a chair and placed it next to McVain. He sat down and looked out over the woods, both men staring as the wind whistled through the screen.

"Thank you, McVain."

"I've got a request, Doctor."

"Yes."

"I've got a lot of thoughts going through my head." McVain slumped in the wheelchair. "I'm not gonna make it through 'em all if you talk all night."

Wolfgang chuckled. "Going out the way you came in, huh?"

McVain closed his eyes and took in a deep breath.

Wolfgang touched McVain's leg. "Very well, but I'm not leaving."

McVain sighed. "Suit yourself."

They sat that way for an hour, staring into the woods as the torch flames died out on the lawn, each to his own thoughts. But every time he glanced over to the wheelchair it seemed McVain's breathing had become more labored. Two times Wolfgang thought McVain had stopped breathing, but when he'd made a move to check for a pulse, McVain's eyelids fluttered.

The third time McVain didn't move. His open eyes remained fixed on the woods, and there was no reaction when Wolfgang reached over to close them.

Wolfgang sought out Dr. Barker after they'd taken McVain's body to the morgue. He was in his office, still dressed in his suit and tie.

"Thank you," Wolfgang said. "For playing." He turned to go.

"I spoke with the diocese," Barker said.

"You must be good friends with them by now."

Dr. Barker let out a push of air, his final combative breath. "I made a mistake sending them the letter, Wolfgang. I never thought they'd act on it." He scratched his gray hair and straightened his glasses. "I convinced them that I need you here. In both capacities. And that everything you have done was with honest intentions."

"Thank you."

Dr. Barker touched the lapels of his coat. "Do you like it? A clothing store downtown donated all of the clothes."

"How's your shoulder?"

"I'll live."

Wolfgang laughed. "How long have you played the bass?"

"Twenty-five years. My father never found out. I kept it at my grandmother's house and practiced there."

Dr. Barker stared down at Wolfgang, waiting, as if he knew Wolfgang had something else he wanted to get off his chest.

"McVain," said Wolfgang. "I'd like to have him buried on the hillside."

"Of course," said Dr. Barker. "I'd have it no other way."

They looked at each other for a moment before Dr. Barker tidied his desk. "Time to go home. Perhaps tonight I'll have a glass of wine myself. Medicinal, of course." They shook hands. "Good night, Wolfgang."

"Good night, Evan."

CHAPTER 37

They buried McVain next to Big Fifteen. Lincoln, wearing the fedora McVain had given him, pounded the dirt with his shovel and stepped back. They stood around the freshly covered grave for a few moments. Susannah wiped tears from her cheeks. Wolfgang draped his arm around her shoulders, hugging her from the side. He kissed the side of her head, which she rested on his shoulder.

Josef's chalkboard sat propped against the trunk of a nearby tree. Wolfgang suddenly laughed.

They all looked at him. Although McVain himself would probably have considered rude laughter a fitting farewell, most of them appeared shocked. Not Josef, though. He attempted to shield his laughter with a closed fist, and then Rufus joined in.

"Before we started playing last night," Rufus said, "McVain asked Josef to give us a pep talk. Except he said to *write* us a pep talk."

The chalkboard faced them all: FUCK OFF, MCVAIN.

Wolfgang walked up the hillside feeling something akin to optimism. For a moment he felt like a celebrity, like Babe Ruth walking through a crowd of fans. Not a response he had hoped for, but thrilling nevertheless.

Dr. Barker stopped him outside the chapel after Mass. "Wolfgang, can I have a minute?"

"Sure."

"I found a leather bag on my porch this morning," Dr. Barker said. "It had a few thousand dollars in it."

"Really?"

"Anonymous donor, it said. You know anything about it?"

Wolfgang shook his head. "Can't say that I do."

"The note said to use it to renovate the colored hospital."

Wolfgang nodded, pursed his lips. "I think that would be a grand idea for it." And then he turned away. Halfway down the hall Barker's voice called out to him.

"You know, Doctor. Is concealing the truth a sin?"

"No, I believe not. Not when one chooses to remain anonymous."

Dr. Barker smiled. "I'll see that the money is used as suggested. And Waverly Hills thanks you."

Wolfgang hurried home that evening and bathed, trimmed his beard, and changed his clothes, which he covered up with his lab coat. In his rose garden he clipped a dozen red roses and bundled them with a length of twine. He hurried back up the hillside, watching the sunset with flowers in hand, a pleasant breeze in his face, and sweaty palms. Inside the lobby of the sanatorium he ran into Miss Schultz, who was wearing a pretty blue dress and carrying a suitcase.

"Miss Schultz." Wolfgang spread his arms out wide. "You will be missed." He gave her a hug and then hid the flowers behind his back. Miss Schultz was on her way out of Waverly as a cured woman. She'd Made the Walk early in the morning.

"You really shouldn't have, Dr. Pike."

"What?"

"I saw the roses," she said.

Wolfgang hesitated before showing the bundle of roses. "What, these?"

She held her hand out and he handed them to her. Before

stepping outside she looked over her shoulder toward Wolfgang. "Now you can tell me where the bodies go."

Wolfgang grinned. "Never."

Wolfgang headed for the stairs with his right hand in his pants pocket and felt the surprise he had planned between his fingers. Miss Schultz could have the flowers. No matter. Lincoln had come through for him. Wolfgang found Susannah asleep on the second-floor solarium. She opened her eyes after Wolfgang pushed her bed a few feet toward the very end of the porch, as close to the screened window as possible.

"Wolf, what are you doing?"

"Privacy." Wolfgang parked her bed a good twenty feet from the other patients. He cleared her bangs from her forehead and felt for a temperature. She was cool, certainly not feverish. "How are you feeling?"

"What are you up to, Wolfgang Pike? You ignore me for days, and then—"

Wolfgang put a finger to her lips. "Just needed time to think, Susannah. I miss walking up the hillside with you every morning."

"I—"

"Shh, let me finish." Wolfgang knelt beside the bed. "The best part of my day, every day, was that moment when your knuckles touched my front door. Because I knew you were safe. The anticipation of opening my door and seeing your face made the sun rise for me. I'm a very ordinary man, Susannah Figgins, but I do love you."

Susannah stared. Wolfgang took her hand. "The church doesn't believe a priest can love a woman and be fully committed to serving God. I disagree." His mouth felt dry. "Your childhood dream was to get married. You doubted you'd ever find anyone on the hillside."

"I didn't."

Wolfgang gazed into her eyes. "Marry me."

"You're to be a priest."

"I'm just a confused seminary student who has fallen in love with an incredible woman." Wolfgang reached into his pocket and pulled out a ring. The diamond in it sparkled under the florescent porch light. "God will have to share me with you. Walk down the aisle with me, Susannah."

She wiped her eyes again. "I want to more than anything, but you can't have both, can you?"

"I'm not asking for both." He scooted closer and squeezed her hand in both of his. "I will love you for the rest of my life."

"In sickness and in health?"

"Especially in sickness."

"And Rose?"

Wolfgang slid the ring onto her left ring finger. It was a little big, but it stayed on. "Rose would want me to be happy."

Susannah stared at her ring finger, moving her fingers and rotating her wrist as if it were the first time she'd ever seen a diamond. "Where did you get this?"

"I have my sources."

"Lincoln's uncle?"

Wolfgang just smiled.

Susannah took her eyes off the ring, but only for a second. "I heard a rumor you were leaving Waverly. I wondered when you would tell me."

"I'm not going anywhere." He leaned down and kissed her closed lips. "We've got a wedding to plan."

Lincoln insisted on taking care of the wedding dress. His uncle Frank knew a guy who could get them cheap, "for next to nothing," he'd said, and they were the finest in town. He'd bring in a few and let her pick her favorite one. Wolfgang knew enough of Uncle Frank to not doubt the authenticity of the dresses, but he made sure Lincoln knew he didn't care to know the details of how the dresses came to be. "Just the bill," he'd told Lincoln the night after he proposed to Susannah, "and hush-hush about it." Lincoln started to hurry off when Wolfgang stopped him. "Go ahead and see if your uncle Frank knows a guy who can get me a tuxedo while you're at it."

A week later Lincoln had them both outfitted and ready to go.

Without a proper minister on the hillside, Wolfgang sought out the most official person he could find to perform the ceremony, and it ended up being Dr. Barker. The doctor was hesitant but agreed to do it after his wife had nudged him in the ribs and said, "Come on, Evan. It'll be romantic."

"Desperate times," said Dr. Barker. "But promise me as soon as Susannah is able, you'll take her to the cathedral and do it right."

"Of course," said Wolfgang. "I would have it no other way."

Butterflies swirled in Wolfgang's stomach. It was a windy evening, one spotlighted by stars and no cloud cover. He paced along the edge of the rooftop. Then he stopped and placed his hands on the concrete-capped wall and stared out toward the trees. He leaned against the wall and sat on the edge with his back to the woods. Across the rooftop, Nurse Cleary and Nurse Marlene fiddled with Susannah's dress and veil. Susannah was beautiful. Her hair was long and curled around her slender neck that rose from her shoulders like a swan. Wolfgang wiped his sweaty hands on his pants and began pacing again.

"Relax, Wolf." Lincoln clapped him on the shoulder and straightened his jacket.

"How do I look?"

"Like a Catholic priest about ready to marry a tuberculosis patient."

"I'm not a priest, Lincoln."

"Yes, I understand that, but after seeing the way you've dressed the past several years, I'm having trouble picturing you as anything other than a priest."

Rufus and Josef walked toward them, smiling. Josef held up his chalkboard: YOU READY?

"Guess so." Wolfgang turned toward the piano. "I only wish McVain were here with us."

"Oh, he is," Rufus said. "I saw the piano keys moving earlier, and there wasn't anybody sitting by it."

Josef wrote. JUST THE WIND.

Rufus looked at him. "Don't you believe in ghosts?"

Lincoln smacked Wolfgang's chest. "Here she comes, Father."

"Lincoln…"

Abel walked before her, dropping rose petals down their imaginary center aisle. Wolfgang sat at the piano and played a quick bridal processional. Josef and Rufus accompanied with their instruments. It was a small crowd: Susannah, Abel, Nurse Cleary and Nurse Marlene, Dr. Barker and his wife, and the four men.

Wolfgang stopped playing when Susannah took her position beside the piano. His knees shook as he stood from the bench. He stared into her eyes and took both of her hands. Reading from the notes Wolfgang had given him, Dr. Barker married the two of them right there on the rooftop with Herman singing in the background from Room 502 and Maverly from Waverly chanting. The small group of friends formed a protective circle around them.

The bell chimed from the tower. They all looked upward but remained silent as the reverberation hummed out toward the woods. Wolfgang felt as if he'd been transported back in time to the foggy morning calls to prayer at the seminary. He squeezed Susannah's hands, stepped closer, and kissed her.

Wolfgang returned to Waverly in the middle of the night, when most of the patients were asleep. He tiptoed past her neighbors on the third-floor solarium and knelt beside Susannah's bed. He tapped her arm.

Susannah opened her eyes. "Wolf? What—"

Wolfgang silenced her by placing his hand over her mouth. Beneath her sheets she still wore the wedding dress. He slid his arms under her slight weight and lifted her from the bed. He carried her to the closest stairwell with a smooth rhythm to his limp, and they laughed like teenagers until Susannah insisted that she walk on her own.

"Susannah, I have something to tell you."

She took his hand. "What?"

"I was tested for tuberculosis at the same time Rose was here," Wolfgang said. "I was infected as well."

Susannah paused. "Wolf—"

"I don't know if I gave it to her or she gave it to me," he said. "But it doesn't matter. She was cured. Mine never became active."

"So then you are probably in the clear."

"It has remained dormant for as long as I've had it. Yes."

"Why did you never tell me?"

"I don't know. Maybe because I was never contagious."

He led her out of the sanatorium, and no one saw them leave. They hurried hand in hand down the hillside to his cottage.

She squeezed his hand as they neared the front porch. "I've something to tell you as well, Wolfgang Pike."

He noticed her broad smile. "And what would that be, Susannah Pike?"

"In our shower room at the dormitory…there's a hole someone has burrowed into our wall."

"Yes?"

She giggled. "I must confess I used to imagine you watching me…"

Wolfgang scooped her up in his arms and carried her over the threshold, both of them laughing. He kicked the door closed and set her on her feet again. His cottage was lit with candles. A fire crackled in the fireplace. He gripped Susannah's hand and walked her to the bed.

"Wolfgang," she whispered. "What are you doing?"

He pulled back the covers that had enshrined Rose's memory for so long.

"Wolf?"

He gently lifted her onto the bed. She leaned back and rested her head on the pillow. He knelt above her, his knees locked against her slender waist. "You're beautiful, Susannah."

She reached up and traced her fingers across his beard, his chin, and then down the side of his face. She loosened his tie and unbuttoned his shirt. He leaned down and kissed her forehead. She was breathing heavily. "We can't," she whispered. "It's too risky."

"We can." Wolfgang kissed her neck. Her breasts heaved against the lining of her dress. She pulled his face to hers. Their mouths opened instinctively. Wolfgang pressed his lips against hers, but she pulled away and kissed his cheek, carefully avoiding his parted lips. Her lips touched his nose, his neck, and danced around his mouth. She kissed every part of his face *but* his lips, as if afraid to infect him. They paused, panting, petting, stroking each other's hair and face, and then Susannah ripped Wolfgang's shirt free of the buttons that held it together. Buttons flew across the bed. She giggled and bit her lip. She ran her fingers across his chest and then gripped him around the neck again. In the awkward, passionate kissing that ensued, she never touched her mouth directly to his, but he felt her warm breath against his cheeks, his neck, his ears, and his eyes. He pulled her dress down, revealing the strings, laces, and frills of her corset.

"We can't," she whispered, but the words had no life to them.

Wolfgang kissed her bare stomach and then looked up into her eyes.

"We shouldn't," she said. "I'm sick. I might be dying."

Wolfgang kissed her open lips. "Then so will I."

CHAPTER 38

Susannah was back in her bed when Dr. Barker came by for his morning rounds. He'd noticed her smile. She'd told him she was feeling stronger. Wolfgang had the piano moved down to the third floor, where he played for her every evening and held her hand until she fell asleep every night.

Wolfgang's mind hadn't been so peaceful since before Rose died. Susannah understood him in the same way Rose had. No, not in the same way, he thought one morning, but in her own unique way, yet just as deeply.

They listened to the radio a lot to pass the time. Herbert Hoover was inaugurated as the thirty-first president of the United States, succeeding Calvin Coolidge. Susannah and Wolfgang were optimistic about the country's future, about their future. She continued to work on her book, and Wolfgang helped her by typing and writing when she was too tired to do so.

One morning on his way to the sanatorium, Wolfgang took a different route. He walked by the livestock and stumbled across Abel and a couple of his friends, who didn't realize he was watching from the trees. Abel lifted the gate to the pigpen and lured three pigs out with a handful of acorns. The boys laughed and ducked into the woods. That evening Wolfgang had taken Abel up to see Susannah. She surprised him by wrinkling up her nose and snorting like a pig. They'd all laughed over it. His game was up. Susannah made him apologize to Lincoln the next morning.

As the months moved on, Susannah's health declined. The

infection had spread from her lungs to her bones. Wolfgang tried to remain optimistic, and he had reason to be. Josef no longer had to use the chalkboard to talk. He and Rufus would meet several times a week to play music together. Wolfgang was no McVain, and he never pretended to be, but sometimes the three of them would play for Susannah. Their music never failed to bring out her smile.

Spring came, along with the thunderstorms and rain showers, and Susannah seemed to have a constant fever. She improved briefly during the beginning of the summer—just about the same time that Anne Barker checked out of Waverly, cured, with her husband escorting her to their idling car.

For several weeks Susannah's energy level rose, her complexion improved, and her appetite grew. Wolfgang had begun to make plans of possibly finding a house for the two of them, but he never allowed himself to become too engaged with the future. In late August they laughed together at the new *Amos and Andy* radio show. They couldn't wait for it to come on each week. He loved the way Susannah's nose pinched when she laughed.

In November, Susannah took a turn for the worse. Her coughing increased, and after a while, she began to spit up blood. Not enough fresh air. Not enough rest. For the first time, Wolfgang began to truly fear for her life. On the surface he still urged her to fight. By the end of November she'd aged ten years. She lost weight. Flecks of gray began to show in her hair.

They celebrated Christmas on the third-floor solarium—Susannah, Abel, and Wolfgang. Susannah was too weak to see the Christmas tree that Wolfgang had set up at his cottage, so he'd arranged to have it brought to her. Abel had helped decorate it. They opened presents and drank hot chocolate.

The New Year brought with it eight inches of snow. Wolfgang held Susannah's hand all night as she shivered her way into the new decade. Wolfgang wiped snow from her cheeks and covered her with blankets. After midnight, when the party in the cafeteria had died down and most of the patients had gone to sleep, Wolfgang crawled into bed with Susannah. He covered them both with a blanket, scooted behind her like a spoon in a drawer, and draped his left arm over her. He held her tight, as if his closeness could reduce the heat that was making her half delirious.

"Wolf."

"Yes."

"I cried when Rose died." Her breathing was shallow. "I cried when I heard you were planning on becoming a priest." She nestled up closer to him on the bed. "When I heard you were coming back to Waverly, I thought it was unfair."

"We never know what the future holds, Susannah." Wolfgang squeezed her softly. "I would take your pain in an instant if I could." He kissed the back of her neck and smelled her hair. "Maybe we should sneak off to Lover's Lane."

She laughed. "Why are you crying?"

He sniffled. "I miss you."

She coughed. Wolfgang could hear the disease rattling loose inside her frail body. "Take care of Abel."

"I will." Wolfgang gathered her in a warm embrace. His left hand rested on her left breast. He wanted to feel her heartbeat, which was growing weak.

She squeezed his hand. "I think heaven, Wolf, is now." She coughed. "Or maybe in heaven we return to the place in our lives where we were most happy...and comfortable...and safe."

Wolfgang kissed her neck. "And where would that be for you?"

"Here, at Waverly," Susannah said. "Right now. With you."

Wolfgang opened his eyes in the morning to the caress of Susannah's hair against his cheek. He nudged her. Her hand was freezing cold. Her eyebrows had collected a few scant snowflakes.

A look of peace marked her face.

Later he would have to call Lincoln and the nurses. But for a few moments, Wolfgang just lay with Susannah, until the cold and the snow blowing into the solarium forced him back inside.

EPILOGUE

Wolfgang's original ensemble and choir quickly dwindled, but others replaced them. In November of 1930, Josef was given a clean bill of health. He left Waverly Hills a cured man, Making the Walk arm in arm with his wife. Three weeks later, Rufus was released, cured, free to play his music wherever and whenever he wanted. Abel was released two weeks after Rufus, and after hearing the news that Josef and his wife were taking him in to keep him from returning to the orphanage, he ran down the hill in excitement.

Dr. Barker stood beside Wolfgang outside Waverly's entrance, watching Abel descend the road that wrapped around the bend of trees.

"I do believe he's the first person to ever Make the Run," said Wolfgang.

Dr. Barker squinted, trying to spy him through the trees. "I just hope he doesn't fall down."

One day a little boy asked Wolfgang the very question Rose had often teased him about—the afterlife. Without hesitation he told the boy about heaven and clouds and angels and God. His answers calmed the child, however mundane they had been. Yet afterward the question got Wolfgang thinking about Rose and Susannah. Were they together somewhere? Could they hear his thoughts?

One day before Wolfgang was set to open his door and venture up the hillside to the sanatorium, he heard a knocking on the front door. He opened it to find no one there. Just a few rustling leaves.

Wolfgang still played for the patients even though his choir and cluster of musicians hadn't regained the glory it had attained with McVain, Josef, Rufus, Herman—who would probably be at Waverly for eternity—and Susannah. Wolfgang often walked along the rooftop for inspiration. He carried a picture with him at all times, one taken a week before the big concert of McVain, Josef, Rufus, Susannah, and Lincoln. He often looked at it and laughed. Whether it had been fate, coincidence, or God's doing that brought them all together during the winter of 1929, nothing could change the fact that it had indeed happened. Stories of McVain circulated through the staff and patients until his name became legend. The seven-fingered pianist.

One day at lunch, Wolfgang laughed with Dr. Barker about McVain and their run-in with the gangsters at the Seelbach Hotel. They both grew silent as a familiar patient approached their table, walking unaided and quickly. "Doctors."

Wolfgang looked up with a smile. "Ah, Frederick. Is there something we can do for you?"

"Sorry, I'm a little anxious."

Dr. Barker checked his watch. "Is it that time already, young man?"

Frederick smiled from ear to ear. "Yes, sir, it is."

Wolfgang stood, placed his arm around Frederick Helman, and walked him toward a window overlooking the entrance to the sanatorium. Mary Sue stood outside next to a baby stroller. Wolfgang patted him on the shoulder. "Two and a half years. Is that right, Frederick?"

"Yes."

"Come on then," said Wolfgang. "I'll go with you. It's about time you Made the Walk."

Mary Sue and little Fred, who was big enough to take some steps on his own, Made the Walk with Frederick as a family, and Wolfgang accompanied them. He walked behind and allowed them private conversation. Frederick and Mary Sue walked side by side, taking turns pushing Fred in the stroller.

The sun was out, warm against the skin. Wolfgang strolled casually and with a sudden sense of freedom, his mind clear. He walked with his hands in his pockets, occasionally glancing up through the overhanging trees toward a sky that was so blue and clear that only God could have painted it. Wolfgang smiled as a certain harmony consumed him, and he immediately began to compose in his head. He could hear the music. It would be a requiem Mass for Susannah. He could see it all so clearly, even the ending.

That evening, before he started, he sat as his desk and gripped his pen. He had another letter to write.

December 15th, 1930

Dear Friar Christian,

So many months have passed since our last correspondence, but much has happened here at Waverly Hills. We shall discuss it in time, and perhaps by then I will be able to explain it all. Before then, however, please know that I have searched deeply, and I've prayed. Finally, I have come to a decision...

HISTORICAL NOTE

A *White Wind Blew* is a fictional story about a very real place. In 1900, Louisville had the worst tuberculosis rate in the country. Waverly Hills Tuberculosis Sanatorium, built on one of the highest hills in Jefferson County, Kentucky, was considered the most advanced tuberculosis hospital in the country. But antibiotics hadn't yet been developed, treatment was primitive at best, and most came simply to die. According to legend, at the height of the epidemic, patients were dying at Waverly at the rate of one per hour. Because the sight of the hearses pulling up to the sanatorium so often would have broken the morale of the patients, the supply tunnel was used to slide the dead bodies down the hillside to the railroad tracks. It became known as the body chute, and later as the Death Tunnel.

There was a separate hospital down the hillside for the African American patients. There was an African American man in the 1920s who walked the hillside three times a day, carting food and supplies between the two hospitals. They named him Big Fourteen because of his fourteen-inch feet and his enormous hands.

The patients spent most of their time on the solarium porches so they could breathe fresh air. Even in the winter, patients were kept outside in their beds, and because the solarium windows only had screens, it was not uncommon for snow to accumulate inside.

Doctors and nurses risked their lives to care for patients and try to find a cure for tuberculosis. Many contracted the disease and died with their patients. Many relationships formed between patients in tuberculosis sanatoriums because of the long duration of stay and because so many of the stricken were in the prime of their lives. It was not uncommon for patients to eventually marry men and women they'd met while sick or caring for the sick.

Because of the experiments performed at Waverly Hills and hospitals like it, tuberculosis began to decline near the end of the 1930s. It wasn't until the discovery of streptomycin in 1943 that doctors had the first real medicine to fight the disease. By the 1950s, tuberculosis had been mostly eradicated.

In 1961, Waverly Hills Sanatorium was closed. The building was reopened in 1962 as the Woodhaven Geriatrics Sanitorium. The doors were closed for good in 1982 due to horrible conditions, budget cuts, and evidence of patient abuse. From that point, the building went the way of decay and rumor. Tales of unusual experiments, electroshock therapy, and patient mistreatment began to surface. Some have been proven false, but not all. Rumors that it was once an insane asylum came forth. Vagrants moved in. Vandals defaced every inch of the place. Stories were told of satanic rituals held within the walls. It was a place of death and disease, a place of legend, a place where, many believe, the haunted still roamed the halls. According to legend, well over sixty thousand patients died inside Waverly Hills. Some say the number is much less; some believe it could be more.

Waverly Hills has become known as one of the most haunted places in the world, spotlighted on Fox Television's *Scariest Places on Earth* and dubbed the world's mecca of paranormal activity. One of the most popular legends revolves around Room 502, which was rumored to house mentally ill patients. Folklore says that two nurses committed suicide in this room: one hanged herself, and another jumped five stories to her death.

The building's current owners have begun a restoration project and great progress has been made. Tours can be arranged and all proceeds go to renovating the building. I took a tour of the abandoned building several years ago, before any restoration. I've been inside the body chute and Room 502. Of the rolls of film I shot inside the building, all but four pictures came out clearly. Those four blurry pictures were all taken inside Room 502, as if something didn't want the pictures to be seen. In many of the pictures, mysterious orbs are visible, none more prominent than those inside the Death Tunnel, or body chute, where we seemed surrounded by them.

Although it was the intrigue of hauntings that brought me to Waverly, I soon realized that the most riveting stories could come from its former flesh-and-blood inhabitants and from former patients. So I looked down the length of the massive fourth-floor solarium porch and imagined the patients lying in their beds. I imagined the sound of a violin hovering over the swaying trees. I imagined a piano and a choir and Wolfgang Pike conducting at a podium with his deformed leg, and the story came to life.

More than two million people still die from tuberculosis every year, mostly in developing countries. Someone in the world still dies of TB every eighteen seconds. The tragedy is that most of the deaths could be prevented with money and existing treatments.

James Markert
2013

READING GROUP GUIDE

1. At one point in the novel, Herman says, "I'm like you, Father. I have secrets." Discuss the many characters who reveal secrets throughout the story.

2. At the end of the novel, Wolfgang's future is left open for interpretation. Would he be more suited to remain a doctor or become a priest?

3. What do you think about the themes of fate and coincidence in the story, specifically with the musicians, McVain, and Wolfgang?

4. As an alternative to medicine and science, music is portrayed as a healing influence. Are there times in your life in which music may have had a similar impact?

5. It was a common belief that Prohibition caused more problems than it solved, and crime was a major example. What role did Prohibition have in the plot of the novel?

6. What role did racism play in Wolfgang's motivations?

7. What are the influences Rose had on Wolfgang's life, both before and after her death?

8. Many of Wolfgang's decisions, from childhood to adulthood,

stem from his curiosities of the afterlife. What do you think about the question Wolfgang asked his mother soon after his father died: "Where do we go when we die?"

9. What are the influences of faith in the novel, both positive and negative?

10. Because of the dire circumstances on the Waverly hillside, confessions (whether official or not) play a major role in the story. Which character has the biggest sin to confess?

11. Which character changed the most from the beginning of the novel to the end?

12. Wolfgang's father introduced him to music at an early age, but it was Rose who planted the seed of musical healing during their time with the soldiers at Camp Taylor. Reflect on a time in your life when someone influenced you to do good things for others.

13. Who is the main villain in the novel? McVain? Barker? Disease? Racism? Other…

14. What do you think about McVain as a sympathetic character, despite his shortcomings?

15. During the height of the TB epidemic, Waverly Hills was viewed by the rest of the city as something akin to a leper colony. Discuss more modern diseases, illnesses, and epidemics that carry the same stigma that TB had in its time. Was it similar to AIDS? Others?

16. In a sense, Waverly could be viewed as a city within a city. Discuss the pros and cons of its isolation.

17. Wolfgang's father never fulfilled his dreams as a musician. How does this failure influence Wolfgang's musical quest at Waverly?

18. Who was "healed" the most by the rooftop performance at the end of the book?

19. Aspects of our personalities, especially our fears, are oftentimes forged by childhood memories. Wolfgang witnessed the horrific death of his father, only to learn the truth of what he had seen, tragically, years after the fact. Discuss a time in your childhood that you may have seen something you didn't understand.

20. How do hope and redemption play a role in the novel?

21. Two women were pregnant during the story: Mary Sue, who delivers a healthy baby, and nurse Rita, who commits suicide out of fear. What were the fears of the time as they pertained to bringing a new life into a world of incurable disease?

22. McVain and Wolfgang had a strained relationship. How are they similar? How are they different? How did Wolfgang's learning about McVain's tragedy during the battle of Chateau Thierry change these opinions?

23. At one point, McVain jokingly mentions Wolfgang's fear of having two wives in heaven. Discuss Wolfgang's relationships with both Susannah and Rose.

24. If you were a patient inside Waverly's walls, how would you have been involved with the choir and the orchestra?

25. In a movie, what actors would you cast for the various characters?

26. Waverly Hills is widely considered one of the most haunted buildings in the world, even eighty years after the story takes place. If the spirits did still roam the solarium porches, which character in the novel would you most want to meet? Where? What would you discuss?

ACKNOWLEDGMENTS

Many thanks to Butler Books for bringing this story to life in its original form, *The Requiem Rose*. Carol, Billy, Eric...*A White Wind Blew* thanks you! And to the late Bill Butler, our conversations inspired me to keep writing. To my parents, Bob and Patsy Markert, for your continuous support and values...to Dad for all your help with the history of Saint Meinrad. Any mistakes are mine. To my brothers, David and Joseph, your friendship has always inspired me to be creative. To my sister, Michelle—all of those countless hours of practicing the piano...I was listening. The sound of your playing helped inspire this story. To Mickey and Roger Keys for your help with all things musical. To my cousin John for reading through that very first draft. Your advice is always helpful. To Craig, it's always fun to talk stories. To Peter Gelfan and the Editorial Department for teaching me so much about fiction. To all those who read various drafts and let me bounce ideas off of them over the years...so many to name, and I'd be afraid to leave someone out. You know who you are. Thank you! Bobby Hofmann, loyal first reader, always. Thanks to everyone at the Louisville Tennis Club and Blairwood for all of your support. And to my Indiana tennis families, thank you, I've been truly blessed. The Internet sure came in handy while researching, as well as the *Encyclopedia of Louisville*. To Gill Holland for everything you've done for me and my career, giving me the opportunity to juggle books and movies. To Tim Kirkman, the best director I know: working with you made me a better writer and storyteller. To my amazing editor, Shana Drehs, for helping make this story the best it could be, and all of my new friends at Sourcebooks! To my agent at Writers House, Dan Lazar, I can't thank you enough for what you've done for me. I used to think an agent's main job was to reject manuscripts, but no—they know what they want, and they know how to get it, and they make dreams come true. Thank you, Dan, for what you do not only as an agent, but also as an editor! Most importantly, I'd like to thank my wife, Tracy, for working so hard and allowing me the time and freedom to chase a dream.

James Markert
2013

About the Author

James Markert is a novelist, screenwriter, producer, and USPTA tennis pro from Louisville, Kentucky, where he lives with his wife and two children. He has a history degree from the University of Louisville. He won an IPPY Award for *The Requiem Rose*, which later became *A White Wind Blew*. He is the writer and co-producer of the new feature film and tennis comedy *2nd Serve*. He is currently working on another feature film, a drama/comedy about food. He is also working on his next novel, *The Strange Case of Sir Isaac Crawley*, a story that takes place in the late nineteenth century and involves the theater scene, a lunatic asylum, a theatrical version of *Dr. Jekyll and Mr. Hyde*, and possibly a few gaslights, some cobblestones, and an eerie fog.